BURN AFTER READING

www.penguin.co.uk

BURN AFTER READING

Catherine Ryan Howard

bantam

TRANSWORLD PUBLISHERS
Penguin Random House, One Embassy Gardens,
8 Viaduct Gardens, London SW11 7BW
www.penguin.co.uk

Transworld is part of the Penguin Random House group of companies
whose addresses can be found at global.penguinrandomhouse.com

Penguin
Random House
UK

First published in Great Britain in 2025 by Bantam
an imprint of Transworld Publishers

A CIP catalogue record for this book
is available from the British Library.

ISBNs
9781787636620 (hb)
9781787636637 (tpb)

Typeset in 11.5/16pt Sabon LT Pro by Jouve (UK), Milton Keynes
Printed and bound in Great Britain by Clays Ltd, Elcograf S.p.A.

The authorized representative in the EEA is Penguin Random House Ireland,
Morrison Chambers, 32 Nassau Street, Dublin D02 YH68.

For the real Mark

Muffled, furtive footsteps. The creak of a floorboard. A gentle tinkling, metal on metal.

These sounds first reached Emily in her dream, which so far wasn't making any sense. She was at home in Dublin with Mark, but it wasn't their apartment and Mark didn't look like Mark. In the middle of the night, Not Mark had woken her up to show her the first finished copy of his new book, which he said had just arrived. But when she'd turned on the bedside lamp, taken it from him and cracked its spine, she saw her name all over its pages. His book was about *her*. She was about to ask Not Mark what was going on when she heard it.

Footsteps. Floorboards. Tinkling of metal on metal—

Emily opened her eyes.

—and the unmistakable *clink* of a key in a lock.

It took her brain a beat to slip the bonds of sleep and piece together where she was and what was happening. Lying, fully dressed, on a couch that wasn't hers. The couch was in a house in the town of Sanctuary, Florida, where she'd been staying. Working. Helping a man to protest his innocence, to write a book about why he wasn't the murderer of his wife, actually. She'd had half a bottle of wine instead of dinner and that was why she had a dull headache now. The noises were real.

The noises were real.

Had someone broken in?

Was someone else in here with her right now?

Emily jerked upright, into a sitting position. She was in the lock-off, a small studio apartment attached to the main house. From the couch, almost all of the space was within her eyeline and there was just enough light – moonlight? Street light? Security light? – filtering through the thin window blinds to see it.

The light had an odd quality to it, like a sunrise over snow.

Someone could, theoretically, be hiding in the bathroom or behind the breakfast bar, her two blind spots. But how could anyone have got in? Over the last twenty-four hours, she'd become paranoid about safety chains and deadbolts and window latches, checking and double-checking all of them before she went to sleep.

Maybe she'd forgotten to do it earlier.

She hadn't been thinking straight after what had happened.

But this was moot, because Emily saw now what was making the noise. She was the only one in the lock-off, but she wasn't alone: there was a shadow on the other side of the glass in the front door.

A tall figure, bent at the waist, head level with the lock.

Trying to get in.

Emily's heart began to hammer beneath her breastbone. She needed to banish the dark. She jumped up and smacked the light switch on the wall behind her, but nothing happened. She flicked it again, and again, but no light came on. She lurched at the lamp on the end table, knocking it over, catching it just before it fell, feeling its ceramic neck for its switch – but it clicked uselessly too. She jumped up and ran the five steps to the bathroom, hitting the switch on the wall there. Still nothing.

The power was out.

She looked back at the front door: the shadow was gone.

She took a few tentative steps forward to get closer, to get a better view, to double-check.

There was no one out there now.

They must have seen her shadow moving inside and run off. Or maybe there'd been no one out there to begin with. She could've imagined it, confused the twilight zone of her dreams with reality.

Then she smelled the smoke.

And she *saw* the smoke now, too: a thin, lazy haze, hanging in the air. It was what had made the light look odd to her, she realized in hindsight.

Where was it coming from?

Maybe someone had built a bonfire on the beach. Maybe the dry, wiry brush that sat between the house and the sand had caught and now smoke and the smell of it burning was wafting inside. This was her first thought, despite the fact that all the windows were closed and she couldn't see anything like a bonfire through the windows on the beach side.

In fact, the beach looked pitch-black.

Emily picked her phone up off the end table. Only 11:20p.m. She'd been asleep for, at most, a couple of hours.

When she activated the phone's flashlight, the smoke became a grey, ghostly mist in its beam. She turned slowly, sweeping the light across the room, until it landed on the door that connected the lock-off to the main house.

Smoke was drifting lazily in from underneath it.

The door had a mate on its other side, like doors in

adjoining hotel rooms. Ever since she'd arrived in this place, she'd been making sure that the one on her side was securely locked, its bolt slid into place. Now she ran to it to reverse the action and pulled back her door, revealing the other connecting door closed behind it.

She rapped a fist against it, once, twice.

'Hey!' she called out. 'Hey!'

When there was no response, she pressed both palms flat on the door.

The wood felt warm.

A snippet of health and safety training she'd had a few months ago came back to her: *don't open a door if it's warm or hot to the touch.*

And then she thought, *Get out get out get out get out get out.*

That same health and safety seminar had said to leave all valuables behind, but Emily ran to the breakfast bar, to where her backpack was hanging from one of the chairs. She unzipped it and shoved a hand inside to confirm what the weight of it suggested, that her laptop and notebook and voice-recorder were still inside. She slung the backpack over one shoulder and shoved her phone into the pocket of her jeans.

The smoke was getting thicker by the second, feeling gritty in her eyes and hot in her mouth.

It had a solidness now, a physical presence. Its tendrils were reaching into the back of her throat to snatch at her breath. Emily started coughing, which only drew more smoke down deeper into her chest.

But it was OK, everything was going to be OK, because she was at the front door now, sliding the deadbolt back, and in a second she'd be outside, in the fresh air, safe.

Emily pulled on the handle, braced to run—

4

The door didn't budge.

Confused, she pulled harder. Checked the deadbolt. Depressed the handle more. Pulled even harder on it again. Put both hands on the handle and leaned back, putting all her body weight behind her, pulling until her arms burned with the strain.

The door rocked a little on its hinges, but didn't open. It was jammed shut.

Emily didn't know why this was happening but she knew there wasn't time to figure it out. Her chest felt like there was a large weight settling on it and she was starting to feel funny, as if her head were too heavy for her shoulders.

She needed to find another way out, quick.

She thought, *balcony*.

It must be twelve, maybe even fifteen feet off the ground, but she might survive a fall. She definitely wouldn't survive suffocating or being burned alive. She'd land on beach scrub and sand, and there were cushions on the balcony furniture. She could throw them over first.

She just had to make it to the other side of the room.

The distance may as well have been an ocean. Emily feared she'd drown before she made it to the other shore.

Wet a rag and hold it over your nose and mouth.

She felt her way along the kitchen counter to the sink, and to the neatly folded towel she knew she'd left there this morning. She soaked it in cold water from the tap and pressed it to her face. The cold water was glorious against her hot skin, on her parched lips. She wanted to drink some of it too, but there wasn't time.

Stay low – crawl beneath the smoke.

She dropped to her hands and knees.

It had been eerily silent, but now noises were coming from the other side of the connecting door. An occasional *whooshing* sound. Popping and crackling. A dull, loud *boom* as something heavy fell over.

Emily found the balcony door by touch, and then, when she reached up, its handle. It only had one lock, a simple knob that turned easily through ninety degrees. She flipped it clockwise, hoisted herself to her feet, pulled open the door and went to run—

Blooms of white, hot pain exploded across her vision as her forehead instantly met something solid and hard.

Emily fell over backwards, landing on her left side, onto the backpack, the corner of the laptop jabbing painfully between her ribs. When she opened her eyes, she saw yellow-red flames flickering around the edges of the connecting door.

She remembered something else from that health and safety seminar, something one of her colleagues, a twenty-something with a head of thickly gelled hair and a red rash on his chin, had whispered to her during the video part. *Burning alive only hurts at the start.* After the flames burn away your nerve-endings, you don't feel any pain.

Emily was tired, her eyelids heavy. Every breath was a battle. She'd lost the wet towel. She had an overwhelming urge to stay where she was and succumb to sleep. But . . .

She thought of Jack's scars, his melted skin.

No. She had to get out.

She was at the balcony door, inches from being outside, from being almost safe. From being able to breathe again.

All she had to do was go through it.

Move. Come on. Get up.

Slowly, she hoisted herself back up onto her knees. When

she reached out her right hand, it closed around the edge of the door. So she *had* opened it! But when she reached out her left, into what should now be a portal to the outside, she felt something hard and smooth and ... Metal? Plastic? She dragged her hand down the length of it.

She felt evenly spaced horizontal ridges—

And sick to her stomach as she realized what they were.

The hurricane shutters.

She'd found the switch on the evening she'd arrived and pressed it just to see what it did. There'd been a mechanical *whirr* and then off-white aluminium shutters had started to descend over the windows and door at the back of the lock-off, covering up all the glass that faced the beach. The shutters were down now and with the power out, she didn't know how to get them back up again.

And the front door wouldn't open.

Emily was trapped.

She felt for her phone, but her jeans pocket was empty. It must have dropped out as she'd crossed the room, or when she'd fallen. It didn't matter now anyway. Unless help was already right outside, she was out of time. She'd made a mistake. On seeing the smoke, she should have immediately found something heavy enough to smash through the glass of the front door and got out that way. It was too late to do that now. There was so much smoke, and she felt so sleepy . . .

Emily thought about how quickly everything could change. A few minutes ago she'd been asleep on a couch in a house by a beach, and now she was going to die in a fire.

But then, this *hadn't* happened quickly, had it?

This was an ending to a story that had been years in the writing. She'd forever be a character in it now too.

Someone had made sure of that.

The shutters must have made a loud, grinding noise as they descended. She wouldn't have slept through it. And since when had half a bottle of wine knocked her out? There must have been something in it, something to keep her asleep while someone else came in and brought the shutters down.

The shadow hadn't been trying to get inside. It was someone locking the door behind them as they left.

Locking *her* in.

Making sure that, when the fire took hold, she wouldn't be able to get out of here. And that everything that held the truth, the only things that did – her laptop, her notes, the voice-recorder – would be destroyed.

Taking this job was the worst mistake she'd ever made, and that was saying something.

Well, Emily thought, *at least the book will have an ending.*

As she closed her eyes, she wondered who they'd get to write it now.

I

THE GHOST

1

One week ago

I'm in Dublin on Monday. Can we meet?

Emily read the sentence for what was at least the tenth time this hour, hoping that *this* time, the words would reveal what Beth Blake, an editor at Morningstar Books, wanted to talk to her about.

Out of the blue. On short notice. And *in person*.

Now, after all this time.

Because there were only two possibilities, and both of them were bad.

The last time this had happened, it had changed her life. Six years ago, a different editor at Morningstar had messaged to say they wanted to publish her novel and commission her to write a second, in exchange for an amount of money that sounded like a lottery win. Five years ago, *The Witness* had debuted as a number-one bestseller – but ever since, Emily had struggled to write the follow-up. A pandemic happened, buying her time, but she'd failed to take advantage of it. The 'how's it going? Just checking in!' emails started to lose their jaunty exclamation marks, then decreased in frequency. Two years ago, they'd stopped coming altogether. Her agent retired. Her editor at Morningstar moved on. Emily stopped trying to write.

Finally, she stopped pretending to be trying.

Admitting defeat, if even just to herself, lifted a thousand pounds off her shoulders but lodged a permanent brick of dread in the pit of her stomach. After all, she'd signed a contract she hadn't fulfilled. She'd been paid an advance on royalties for a book she'd never delivered, and that money was long gone. Every single morning her first thought upon waking was, *Today could be the day someone at Morningstar remembers me.*

And now, this afternoon, the email.

Emily angled her phone so Alice could read the message for herself. They were standing inside the door of BOOK WITH US, a new bookshop off the quays whose signage contained no upper-case letters, watching people gather for the launch of the inaugural issue of a literary journal. The event was scheduled for six, which in Irish time meant proceedings would reluctantly begin at six-thirty. That was only five minutes from now and yet the crowd was still embarrassingly sparse and mostly made up of contributors and bookshop staff.

Emily hoped there'd be a last-minute influx, for Mark's sake.

She had come because she was duty bound; *Loose Leaf: Vol. I* contained a new poem by her boyfriend. Alice was in attendance because when Emily first saw Beth's email, she'd panicked and begged Alice to meet her here, even though she'd known her best friend for twenty years and ten minutes would've been long enough to know that this wasn't her scene. But she needed someone to talk her off this ledge, and she wanted to let Mark enjoy his night in the limelight.

Or under the harsh fluorescents of this mostly empty bookshop.

'That's it?' Alice said, frowning at the phone's screen. 'That's the whole message?'

Emily nodded. 'What do you think?'

'What do *you* think?'

'I feel sick.'

'That's probably just from this wine.' It was classic book-launch fare, cheap and room-temperature; Emily had met Alice at the door with a glass in each hand. 'What *is* this place, anyway?' Alice asked, looking around. 'I thought I'd got the wrong address. It looks like some kind of wanky pseudo-Scandi design studio from the outside.'

The head of another attendee, a serious twenty-something reverently stroking a hardcover copy of *House of Leaves*, snapped in their direction.

'It's a concept store,' Emily said, lowering her voice in the hope that Alice would too. 'According to Mark.'

'What's the concept? Shut in Six Months?'

Emily shot her friend a warning look, even though she thought Alice had a point.

The tables on the shop floor had nothing on them, but did have chairs tucked underneath: an invitation to sit down and read the book you hadn't yet paid for and mightn't ever need to now. The walls were fitted with narrow picture-ledge shelves that could only display books one or two titles deep, and facing out. There was no BESTSELLERS bay, and despite being in the path of thousands of tourists visiting nearby attractions like the Ha'penny Bridge and Temple Bar, there were no Ireland travel guides, postcards or copies of *Ulysses* either. It was more like a gallery displaying books than a shop offering them for sale. They'd never turn a profit at this rate.

Which makes it the perfect place to launch something like Loose Leaf, Emily thought, and then immediately felt bad for thinking that.

When she'd got here, she'd discovered that the 'literary journal' Mark had been on about for weeks was ten A4 pages printed on someone's home inkjet, inexpertly hole-punched and bound with brass fasteners.

'That's the point,' he'd said when he'd seen her face, and she'd said, 'Oh, right. Clever,' even though she didn't think it was, especially.

His naked need for her not to be unimpressed had cracked her heart a little.

'It's probably just a friendly check-in,' Alice said now. 'Which is why she's being so casual about asking you. I bet she's coming over anyway, for something else. They have an office here now, don't they? Let's be real: this woman is not flying over from London especially for a meeting on Monday morning that she only suggested you have on Friday afternoon. She's got other things happening. She's just hoping to fit you in.'

'A friendly check-in?' Emily repeated. 'After *two years*?' She shook her head. 'Not a chance. This is about the money. They want it back.'

Her headline-making six-figure advance had consisted of an equal amount for each title, which was paid in stages throughout the publication process. One of those had been 'commencement' – they had paid her, literally, to start writing the second book. And she had. She'd drawn up a plan, saved a new Word document, started a fresh notebook and everything. But since it was an advance against royalties and she'd thus far failed to *finish* writing it, Morningstar were well within their rights to recover that sum.

These days, Emily's bank balance typically ran to only three digits and, more often than not, there was a minus sign at the start. The idea of owing that amount of money, of needing to suddenly, somehow, come up with a sum that large . . .

The wine's vinegary afterburn surged up into her throat.

Alice rolled her eyes and said, 'That never actually happens,' which was no consolation because she didn't know anything about publishing outside of what Emily had told her over the years. Alice was a dentist.

'It'd be fair,' Emily said. 'They've given me so much time and I've never given them anything.'

'*Could* you give them something? I mean, what if you went home, mainlined Red Bull and just went hell for leather for forty-eight hours?'

'Maybe,' she said doubtfully.

'I don't see what the problem is. Didn't Donna Tartt take, like, ten years?'

'Yes, but to deliver a book by *Donna Tartt*. This isn't quite the same situation.'

Alice took a slow, deliberate sip of her wine.

The door to the shop swung open, letting a roar of street noise into the space. Everyone in the huddled group Mark was a part of turned hopefully towards the sound, but it was just a man with a suitcase who quickly realized he was in the wrong place and promptly left again.

Mark saw Alice. She waved at him. He waved back, but made no move to come join them.

15

'He doesn't like me,' Alice said.

Emily rolled her eyes. 'Not this again.'

'He doesn't.'

'He's just intimidated by you, that's all. I mean, you *are* qualified to brandish a drill inside people's mouths.'

Emily caught Mark's eye and tried to smile reassuringly.

'I should really hire you to write our website copy,' Alice said, giving her a sidelong glance. 'I presume you haven't said anything to him?'

Emily shook her head.

Honesty wasn't always the best policy in a relationship where both partners' professional situations were so agonizingly opposed. Mark was constantly writing a novel but had never managed to get one published. He scraped together a living mainly by writing book reviews, submitting poems and short stories to the kind of literary journals that paid in free copies, and working in a branch of a well-known bookshop chain, selling other people's realized writing dreams for eight hours a day, three days a week.

Including hers, presumably.

He'd never mentioned it, but the paperback of *The Witness* was still in print and the odds were, in a busy city-centre bookshop, he'd served at least one customer buying a copy of it by now.

Meanwhile Emily, having got her dream, had let it die. She was in a job that had nothing to do with books – a call centre that handled the helpline for a supermarket chain's customer loyalty card – and that was a relief. She still had a publisher waiting for a novel that they'd promised to pay her handsomely for once she delivered the manuscript, but she hadn't managed to write a word of it.

Not a *good* word, anyway.

They were both standing with their feet planted firmly on the other's faraway greener hill. Mark longed for the opportunity she was ostensibly throwing away, and she wished she could go back to where *he* was, full of words and possibility and daydreams, free of the choking pressures of a legal agreement, expectation and a ticking clock.

At least, for now, they were still holding hands across the valley.

Emily wanted to keep it that way.

'You should go,' Alice said. 'I mean, I think you have to go. Call in sick and go find out what it's about. And it's just a meeting with a nice woman who works in publishing. What's the worst that could happen? Either this is about the next book, in which case you say you're still working on it, or they want the money back and you have to go away and figure something out. But it's better to know, isn't it? Your imagination is always worse. And maybe it's not even about what you think. It could be something *good*.'

'Yeah,' Emily said noncommittally.

As a tinkling of pen against glass signalled that proceedings were set to begin and a hush descended, it occurred to her that, actually, there was a third possibility as to why an editor at Morningstar might want to meet with her.

Out of the blue. On short notice. And in person.

Now, after all this time.

And it was much worse than her inability to write a second book, or her having to find twenty-five grand from somewhere.

This thought made her chest freeze up in panic.

They've found out.

2

The weekend passed in a blur of broken sleep, catastrophizing and hiding from Mark the fact that there was a very real chance her life was about to spectacularly implode.

He made that easy to do by waking up on Saturday morning seized by the idea of turning their tiny, windowless storage room into an office. This necessitated redistributing all the crap they'd thrown in there over the past year between the bins, the nearest charity shop and other places in the apartment, of which there were very few; repainting the space with a half-can of Magnolia he'd found in his parents' garage; and trawling through local online adverts looking for free-to-a-good-home desks and chairs. Emily had indulged his hare-brained scheme in part because she recognized this particular brand of self-delusion. *If I just had that pen* ... Or notebook. Software. Coffee machine. New iMac. Standing desk. *Then* the magic lock will click open and the words will flow!

It was a bonus that this activity kept him occupied while she curled up on the couch for forty-eight hours and thought of terrible things. Monday morning approached like a freight train and, up ahead, she was tied to the tracks. If only she knew what the meeting was about. She'd thought she might have got a little more info when she replied to tell Beth yes – because Alice was right, she had to attend – but there wasn't much to glean from *Great! Fitzwilliam Hotel at 11:00a.m. good for you?* She'd gone back with *Perfect. Do you need anything from me in advance?* but hadn't got an answer.

All too soon, it *was* Monday morning and the collision was mere moments away.

Emily entered the Fitzwilliam's lobby dulled by insufficient sleep, hollow from a lack of appetite and thrumming with nerves. There was a dampness at the back of her neck and under her arms, and she was convinced her face was puce. She was scanning for a sign promising toilets when a voice said, 'Emily?'

A thirty-something woman had popped out from a little nook behind the bell stand. Her blonde hair shone in a razor-sharp bob, just like it did in the professional headshot Emily had found on the Morningstar website, and she glowed with the kind of healthy, outdoorsy tan you couldn't fake.

They exchanged smiles and shook hands, Emily acutely aware of her damp palm.

'We're just in here,' Beth said.

The nook was book-lined and narrow, with two couches facing each other over a table; if there'd been a window on the rear wall playing landscapes rushing past, it could've passed for a compartment on a luxurious train carriage.

Emily was still processing the *we* when she saw that another, older woman was already seated there, in a spot that had previously hidden her from view.

'Carolyn,' she said, raising an arm to shake hands but not rising from her seat. She wasn't smiling. 'Hello.'

'Can we get you something to drink before we begin?' Beth asked. 'Coffee? Tea?'

'A coffee would be great,' Emily answered on a delay, distracted by trying to remember where she'd seen Carolyn before. She thought it was on the same page of the Morningstar website where she'd seen Beth's professional bio, only at the top because Carolyn was . . .

Shit.

Carolyn was Morningstar's publishing director. Beth's boss. That couldn't be good.

A waiter was summoned and three coffees were ordered. The women made stilted small talk – about how warm the weather was, how busy Grafton Street was, how lovely the hotel was – until their drinks arrived, along with three glasses of iced water.

Emily immediately picked hers up and gulped a third of it down.

'So,' Beth said, clasping her hands together. 'Are you writing?'

She said she was, nodding vigorously. She explained that the success of *The Witness* had messed with her head a little bit and that it had taken her a while to reset. She mentioned the pandemic, and having to completely go back to the drawing board once or twice, and life being so busy and not being able to see the forest for the trees and Difficult Second Album Syndrome, and then she saw Carolyn pressing her lips together and realized she was babbling, that she'd been babbling from the moment she opened her mouth, so she said, 'But things are going well now,' and abruptly stopped.

'Great,' Beth said. 'Good to hear. So . . . I believe there's a book outstanding on your contract?'

'Um, yeah. Yes. It was a two-book deal.'

'And your agent is . . . ?'

'Lynne Reilly.' Emily shifted in her seat. 'Well, she *was* my agent. She's retired now.'

'So who is . . ?'

'Well, ah, Lynne worked alone and I've just been focusing on finishing the book.' Emily could feel the red on her face crawling down her neck and spreading across her chest, which only made the spread happen faster. 'I don't have an agent, technically. Not at the moment.'

'Of course.' Beth smiled kindly. 'The thing is, Emily, well, it's just been so long. Three years past the original delivery date, by my estimation. Now, we totally understand that this is a creative process and things don't always go as planned, and if you'd needed an extra year or even two, I'm sure my predecessors could've worked with you on that. But we find ourselves in a situation where *so* much time has passed, well, the problem is that Morningstar itself has changed.'

Emily didn't know what that meant.

'We all loved *The Witness*,' Beth continued, 'and we were immensely proud to publish it. But since then, we've really moved our focus onto non-fiction so, you see, if your novel landed on my desk today . . . It wouldn't be a good fit for our list.'

'The new book is very different to *The Witness*,' Emily said.

And indeed it was, in that one existed and the other did not.

'I'll be delighted to take a look when it's ready. And help you, in any way I can, with placing it elsewhere.' Another kind smile. 'But in the meantime, from Morningstar's point of

21

view . . . Unfortunately, we're going to have to draw a line under this.'

A boiling-hot geyser of panic shot up into Emily's chest.

'What does that mean?' she asked weakly.

Beth looked to Carolyn. 'We understand there was an instalment of the advance paid out at some point?'

'Twenty-five thousand,' Carolyn said, nodding.

'Twenty-five thousand,' Beth repeated, turning back to Emily with a grave look on her face. 'I'm afraid that, in this instance, we would be looking to recover that sum.'

Emily said nothing. She feared that if she opened her mouth, a cascade of dry desert sand would come pouring out. Her face was burning. Sweat was pooling in the small of her back. She felt dizzy. In the absence of any other ideas, she picked up her water glass and drained the rest of it.

She didn't have anything like that kind of money to hand.

Yes, once upon a time, she'd been paid what seemed like a lot to write two books. But she'd only written one of them, and there was her agent's commission and tax stuff to deduct, and the rest had been paid piecemeal over a period of years. In the end, she'd been paid less to write books than she was currently making at a normal job – and these days, she had to work for an hour just to *buy* a book. She'd received the last payment – the one Beth wanted to recover – four years ago. If she borrowed that amount now, it would take her forever to pay it back, and that was if she even qualified for a loan in the first place.

Which she really doubted she would.

And then, like a wave rising up behind all these other feelings, came anger, directed entirely at herself.

This was all her fault. No one else's. She'd squandered this opportunity. She'd got in her own way.

All she had to do was make up a story, for God's sake. How hard could it be?

'But,' Beth said brightly, 'there may be another option.' She reached into the large leather bag at her feet and withdrew an unmarked manila envelope. 'Before we continue, can I get you to sign this?' She extracted what looked like a thin contract and slid it across the table, along with a pen, smiling apologetically. 'It's just a standard non-disclosure agreement.'

Emily made a show of scanning the pages, but all she could see was blurry text. On the last one, she scribbled an 'E' followed by a squiggly line as blood rushed in her ears. She was desperate to hear what Beth was proposing. She was biting down hard on the *I'll do it!* already waiting on her tongue.

Beth slipped the signed agreement back into the envelope, then turned to look at Carolyn, who looked at Emily and said, 'What do you know about Jack Smyth?'

The question was like a radio transmission from deep space: alien, incomprehensible and utterly unexpected.

'Jack Smyth?' Emily repeated.

She thought Carolyn couldn't possibly mean Ireland's most famous innocent guilty man until the other woman added, 'It's big news here, right? Have you been following the story?'

'Ah, yeah. Sure. I mean, sort of.'

You had to follow it somewhat, whether you wanted to or not, because it was everywhere. Front pages. TV news headlines. Your auntie's WhatsApp dispatches, the kind the app warned had already been *forwarded many times*.

Jack Smyth, the handsome, well-liked, retired road-racer

whose celebrity had only grown since he'd hung up his cycling shoes, had lost his glamorous TV presenter wife, Kate, in a fire at their home last November. At first, the national heart bled for what seemed like only the latest tragic turn in this talented man's life. He'd already lost his dad in a car accident as a teen, his childhood best friend to suicide just before his first Olympics in Rio, and his promising cycling career to a horror crash on a wet French hillside that had left him with a permanent limp. And yet he'd managed not only to survive, but to thrive. He had a successful athleisure brand called Exis, was patron to several high-profile charities and was a much-in-demand motivational speaker, earning huge fees for his electrifying appearances. For a while, there'd even been talk of him getting back on the bike.

But then, aged just thirty-one, he'd arrived home too late to save his wife of one year from the fire engulfing their house, but just in time to watch her die in his arms.

He'd used that line in a primetime television interview shortly after the tragedy that one in every four people in Ireland had watched go out live.

When it emerged that Kate Smyth had died of a broken neck before the fire had started, prompting the Gardaí to open a murder inquiry, the public mood had turned. In the absence of much fact, rumours swirled and spread like an especially virulent infection. He'd pushed her down the stairs and then set the fire to cover his tracks, for reasons that changed with the day of the week. Money problems. Infidelities. A change in his personality brought on by a head injury sustained in the cycling crash.

Reddit threads grew like knotweed. Self-styled body-language experts studied clips of his TV interview frame-by-frame and

24

posted their conclusions to TikTok. Everyone knew someone who knew somebody who'd heard something from a friend of theirs who knew a Garda. *They know he did it*, people said with authority over pints, across dinner tables and huddled on the steps of the church after Mass. *They just can't prove it – but they will.*

What the hell did *he* have to do with anything?

'We've signed his memoir,' Carolyn said. 'Not his life story, but his side of *this* story.'

'Oh.' Seeing as Emily had absolutely no idea where this could be going or what it had to do with her, it seemed like the safest response.

'You see,' Carolyn continued, 'Jack is trapped in this hellish limbo. Innocent until proven guilty, but precisely *because* he's innocent, he'll never get the chance to prove that he is. No charges have been brought, but there's all this speculation and suspicion . . . It's suffocating. It's ruining his life. What life he has left. So he's decided to take matters into his own hands. He's going to do a book. Tell his story, in his own words. And we're going to publish it.' She paused. 'His share of the royalties is going to go directly to his charitable foundation, so profiting from the proceeds of crime won't be an issue, as far as we're concerned.'

'And anyway, he didn't commit a crime,' Beth added.

'Oh,' Emily said again.

There was an open and active murder inquiry, so the inquest into Kate's death had been adjourned and the coroner's report, aside from a few basic facts, sealed from the public. No one had been brought to trial, which meant there'd been no opportunity for evidence to be heard in open court, and Ireland's draconian libel laws prevented the media from reporting anything other than the most basic, innocuous facts.

On top of that, Jack Smyth had all but disappeared from public life.

This black hole where information should be only increased the demand for it. People were as ravenous for details as horror-movie zombies were for flesh, and the longer they were forced to go without a feed, the more crazed with hunger they became. In her mind's eye, Emily saw Black Friday-style stampedes at bookshops on Jack's book's publication day. She wouldn't be among them, but she'd definitely trawl through all the articles and tweets rushing to give all the major revelations away.

What did any of this have to do with *her*?

'We're handling it from our London office,' Beth said, 'because we know Dublin is a village' – she smiled briefly at this – 'but we and Jack are in agreement that whoever helps him to tell his story should be Irish too. We're trying to move as fast as possible in order to minimize the chances of this getting out, so we have an exceptionally tight schedule and almost no wiggle room. That, combined with the nature of the project . . . Well, this isn't everyone's cup of tea, which we understand. It's been a struggle, to be frank.' She brightened. 'But then, we thought of you.'

Emily wasn't following. She worried that she'd accidentally zoned out and missed something crucial.

'We'd protect your identity,' Beth pushed on, 'so your involvement need never be public. We'd fly you to Florida at the earliest possible opportunity, to spend a week interviewing Jack. Then we think maybe four, possibly six weeks to write the book? But we can talk about that. In exchange, we'd cancel your existing contract with no money owed, there'd be a standard ghostwriting flat fee and we'd of course cover all expenses. A mutually beneficial solution.' She turned up her palms. 'So, what do you say? Is this something you'd consider doing?'

'I'm sorry,' Emily said. 'I'm not quite—'

'Jack Smyth needs a ghostwriter,' Carolyn said. 'And we'd like it to be you.'

Friday, 10 November 2023
Adoran, Co. Clare

Kate sits in the car she parked outside SuperValu ten minutes ago and tells herself to open the driver's door and get out.

Now. Come on. Just do it. Let's go.

But she doesn't move.

It's the same routine every time. Or almost the same, because lately it feels like it's been taking her longer and longer to obey her own instructions.

This, whatever *this* is, started over a year ago, back when she and Jack were still living in Dublin. A gradual, increasing awareness that whenever she was alone in a crowd, there was an electric anxiety thrumming inside her that she didn't feel when she was at work, with others or at home. Walking around the city, she'd always been aware that people were looking at her – and they actually were, either because they'd recognized her from TV or because they were trying to work out where they recognized her from – but at some point, it had started to feel as if they were *watching*.

One night, after too much wine, she'd told a friend too much about it.

'That's burnout,' the friend, a make-up artist who'd worked with her on *Sunrise*, had declared with total confidence. 'What you need is a break.'

Perhaps Kate shouldn't have accepted an official diagnosis from someone who, as she was making it, had swung a wine glass with enough force to send some of the liquid sloshing over the lip and into Kate's lap – and who, besides the obvious disadvantage of not being a qualified mental-health professional, wasn't in possession of all the facts – but it was an explanation, and one which came with the consolation that this was not the first crack in the eventual rupturing of her sanity, but something other people felt too, casually, in their daily lives.

There were even articles about it. Escape fantasies, a few of them said, were often a symptom.

When she'd broached the subject of quitting her presenting gig on *Sunrise*, Jack's reaction had surprised her. She'd never been on as much money as people thought, but it was enough to have to worry about how they'd manage without it. He'd pointed out that he didn't need to physically be in Dublin; Exis, at the time, was in the process of moving its warehouse to an industrial estate near Shannon Airport. If she didn't need to be there either, they could sell their apartment in Ranelagh and move across the country to live in Adoran full time.

So they did.

But here, in the tiny village they were trying to call home, everyone really *was* watching her.

Because in this place, they were the only strangers. The blow-ins from the Big Smoke. The failed athlete and the D-list TV presenter who'd bought the former parochial house, outbidding a local, and then added a modern extension and erected an electronic gate to rub salt in the wound. *An electronic gate? Who do they think they are, eh? Michael D and Sabina?* Jack was rarely home long enough to hang around the village so Kate took the brunt of its spotlight of scrutiny.

Her brain couldn't differentiate between whatever had caused the anxiety she'd felt back in Dublin and this annoying but harmless nosiness. It all got mixed up, and grew, and now something as ridiculously mundane as going to the supermarket is enough to disassemble her of a Monday morning.

Almost.

All she has to do, she tells herself, is get out of the car. Everything will be OK if she can just do that. Once she's out, she'll be fine.

OK, not *fine*, but being outside will mean that she has to pretend to be fine and usually the pretending is enough. She'll be able to do what she needs to get done and then she can get back in her car and head home again, where she feels safe and calm and not like a vibrating bomb of rising panic.

But getting out of the car is the hardest part.

Kate checks her reflection in the rear-view mirror, telling herself *after this, you're going to go.* She's discovered through trial and error that if she goes around in leggings, unwashed hair and a bare face, people openly stare, shocked by the difference between Kate Smyth on morning television and Kate Smyth in reality and, around these parts, not at all bothered to hide it. But if she gets all made up, all dressed up, they'll stare too – and whisper comments to their companions she's convinced are along the lines of *Who does yer wan think she is? Where does she think she is?* So she aims for a middle ground. Make-up, but not much. Jeans, but not sweats. Avoid eye contact, but never wear sunglasses.

Kate picks her bag off the passenger seat. She checks her reflection again. *Get out.* She sees the person who parked beside her moments after she arrived returning to their car with two bulging bags of shopping.

This is ridiculous. You're being ridiculous.

She takes a deep breath, opens the door and gets out.

Finally.

She feels a wind at her back, pushing her towards the entrance. Autopilot grabs a basket as she walks through the automatic doors. She starts her well-trodden route around the aisles.

You're OK, she tells herself silently, over and over – and now that she's out of the car and moving around inside the store, she might be.

It's just the village that makes her feel this way, which is why she tries to avoid it. There is no delivery service prepared to travel all the way out to their house; she checks the apps regularly, in case the situation changes. On Saturday mornings, she and Jack drive to the Dunnes Stores forty-five minutes away, and in preparation she makes lists and plans, and when they're there she buys extra, but still, two or three days later, notes appear on the little white board they have stuck to the fridge. *Bananas. Almond milk. Steak for dinner tonight?* ☺ Jack is working, so it's only fair that day-to-day household stuff is her domain.

And anyway, she needs the wine.

Kate pushes through the swinging barriers at the entrance to the off-licence section and looks around as if she doesn't know exactly what she wants and where it's located. She gets two bottles to put in the fridge and two spares to keep hidden. Plus a half bottle of champagne, for the sake of the woman with the purple rinse who's shuffling past, her gaze crawling all over the contents of Kate's basket, and the girl on the checkouts who'll carefully appraise each item as she beeps it through the till and then go home and give her mother a full report.

Because no one with a drinking problem buys *champagne*, now do they?

Not that Kate has a drinking problem. She really doesn't. She never even gets drunk. She has a *sleeping* problem, and a few glasses of wine of an evening are the easiest antidote. But Jack is so clean, so healthy, so *optimized*, that if he knew, he'd suggest exercise and keeping her phone in another room and meditation, and she won't be able to explain why none of that would help.

So she hides her self-prescribed cure. She sips a couple of glasses while they watch TV in the evenings but, when she goes out to the kitchen to refill from a bottle from the fridge, she refills first from a bottle hidden in the utility room and knocks it back.

Kate knows why she's not sleeping. It's because she also knows that what she's been experiencing isn't burnout. Or social anxiety or agoraphobia or sensory processing disorder or any of the other diagnoses the internet has offered up.

It's because she's afraid.

The latest reason is in her pocket, on her phone. The messages have started up again, and Kate can't tell anyone.

Especially not Jack.

3

Emily stumbled back out onto Stephen's Green feeling dazed.

It was an unusually hot September day; the heat and the glare were an assault on two fronts. The street around her was a blur of moving crowds and a white-noise hum of engines and conversation. She darted in front of a tram already sounding its warning bell, crossed the tracks and entered the park, making a sharp left turn at the first patch of green dotted with pale, languid limbs and plastic picnics, and straight into a cluster of pecking pigeons gathered around a man tearing chunks off a baguette. Several of the birds launched themselves into the air close by her head. While trying to avoid them, she bumped against an Italian family trying to take a selfie.

She didn't know where she was going, only that it was *away*.

She wanted to be somewhere dark and cool where most other people were not. She needed to think. To tell someone what had happened, to say the words out loud, to make it real.

Morningstar want me to do a ghostwriting gig for a man the whole country is sure is a murderer. If I say no, the small fortune I owe them immediately falls due and they'll want payment in full.

And I have no money.

And I'm not a ghostwriter.

Emily left the park through a side gate and found herself walking down Dawson Street, towards the bookshop where Mark was currently on shift. He was on the second floor, in Cookery, muttering complaints to a colleague of his about having to find room for yet another book of air-fryer recipes.

'All it is is a countertop oven,' he was saying as she approached. 'How much longer are we going to let this madness continue?'

'Mark.'

He turned towards her voice and said, 'Hey,' in happy surprise, which immediately switched to confusion, then quickly became concern. 'Everything OK?' He searched her face. 'Why aren't you at work?'

'Do you have a break coming up, by any chance?'

'What's going on?'

She told him everything was fine, that she just needed to talk to him about something, which did nothing to convince him that the first part was true. He told her to go to the coffee shop next door and that he'd join her there as soon as he could. Thinking *wine*, she suggested the Italian restaurant next to that instead.

Mark was frowning. 'Are you sure you're OK?'

'Everything's fine,' she said again.

On the way back down the stairs, she spotted a sign for the Reference section. There were three books about ghostwriting on its shelves, which was two more than she'd been expecting. *Ghostwriting: The Art of Writing Other People's Books*, *The Ultimate Ghostwriting Handbook* and *The Ghost: Everything You Need to Know to Break Into the World of Ghostwriting for Profit – and Break Out!* The first one was twice the price of the other two and she refused to become a person who bought books with exclamation marks in their titles, so she took *The Ultimate Ghostwriting Handbook* to the till.

The woman behind the counter smiled at her pleasantly, then did a double-take.

'Wait,' she said, recognition dawning. 'Aren't you—?'

Being book-famous was a strange and specific thing. At first, only your friends and family knew that you wrote. Then you got a book deal and people in publishing became aware of your existence. As your release day neared, that small flame of fame spread to other writers, to booksellers and to media types, until finally, on publication, it reached members of the general reading public. What had surprised Emily was how, on the other side, it retracted in the exact reverse order. Readers forgot about you first. Then the media no longer had any reason to be interested in you. Booksellers reverted to treating you like any other customer. You lost touch with your writer friends because you were no longer invited to the events and parties and festivals where you might have met them. Ultimately publishing forgot about you too, and finally your friends and family stopped asking about it.

'—Mark's girlfriend?' the girl behind the counter finished. 'Emer?'

'Emily,' she corrected, forcing a smile.

Part of her wanted to be forgotten. What was she supposed to say when someone remembered? *Yes, that's me. Yeah . . . Yes, still writing. Well, no. Not really. Trying to. Drowning in a sea of self-doubt except when I'm writhing in the flames of self-loathing, thanks for asking.* But another, more confusing part of her needed not to be, because it was in those moments of recognition that she was thrown life buoys and fire extin-guishers. People were so impressed, *ridiculously* impressed, with the act of having written a book and got it published. They didn't care about anything that had come after, or what now never might. And so it was nice to play along, to feel like somebody who was better at this, if only for a few minutes.

To feel *better.*

The other woman whispered conspiratorially about giving her the staff discount which, considering the current state of affairs, was probably more meaningful than recognizing her as an author.

The Italian restaurant was practically deserted, still await-ing the start of the lunchtime rush. Emily had her pick of tables and chose the one furthest from the door, tucked into a tight corner. She was hot, thirsty and on edge, so she ordered water, a Coke and a large glass of pinot grigio, and got a strange look from her server just for free.

While she waited for Mark, she took out her phone and Googled Jack Smyth.

There were, as expected, an infinite number of virtual column inches about the case, but very little actual detail. The Irish media had trodden carefully and they continued to. No one wanted to get sued, especially by someone who could demonstrably prove a hitherto good reputation and had the resources to hire the best libel lawyers around to do it for him.

The coverage didn't speculate. By law, it wasn't allowed to. It simply dropped the cold, hard facts on the ground and invited you to pick them up and fit them together.

Jack and Kate had lived in a former parochial house in a village near the River Shannon called Adoran. One Saturday night last November, Jack was at a local pub waiting to meet a friend when a neighbour alerted him to the fire. He'd dashed home, getting there moments before the emergency services. Witnesses said he ran straight into the flames, screaming his wife's name. He said he found her at the bottom of the stairs. The first responders saw him carrying her outside, an act which cost him third-degree burns on his hands and forearms, and permanent lung damage from the smoke. Jack would later tell the media that Kate had died in his arms, but an autopsy showed that she'd died of a traumatic head injury – a skull fracture, 'not inconsistent' with a fall – and that her lungs were clear of carbon monoxide and there were no traces of soot in her nose or mouth.

In other words, she'd stopped breathing before the fire had started.

Photos taken the morning after showed the ground floor of the house mostly intact and untouched, at least on the outside. The upper level was scorched and blackened, its windows gone and its roof tiles completely missing in a large section at one gable end. Blue and white Garda tape stretched across a gravel driveway choked with marked vehicles. Various figures milled about in white coveralls and face masks: members of the Garda Technical Bureau at work.

A murder inquiry was opened. Still recovering from skin-graft surgery, Jack was interviewed by detectives but never formally arrested or charged. No one else had ever been either.

Ten months later, the case remained open and active and unsolved.

And now, for some unfathomable reason, the only suspect there'd ever been was *writing a whole book* about how he didn't do it.

Or *she* was.

Maybe.

An image search suggested that, physically, Jack had had three eras. Back when he was cycling, he'd been a darkly tanned, hollow-cheeked twenty-something with veined legs, skinny arms and hair shorn to the scalp. The pictures from then were all of him in action, sweaty and smiling on podiums and power-posing in liveried Lycra, sometimes so thin that when he smiled, his teeth looked too big for his head. In one of these, he was wearing a silver Olympic medal around his neck.

Post-retirement he'd put on some weight and grown out his hair, and looked all the better for it. That Jack was tall, dark and blandly handsome, stubble covering his newly filled-out cheeks. He seemed relaxed in business casual on various brightly lit stages, in arty headshots taken to illustrate glossy profiles, and looking lovingly at his wife in a photo they'd shared with the press of their wedding day. He seemed like A Nice Guy.

Most recently, he was pale and bearded, haggard, forever frozen mid-stride crossing a road or getting into a car, wearing a baseball cap and with a phone to his ear. Sometimes thick bandages were visible on one or both forearms. All of those pictures had the blur of being zoomed-in, having been snapped at a distance, their subject seemingly unaware – because these were furtive paparazzi shots of a man who had maybe killed his wife.

Or *probably* killed her.

After all, didn't these things always turn out that way?

'Hey.' Mark had arrived. He was leaning over her, bending to kiss the top of her head. She put her phone down. 'I got someone to swap lunch with me, so I have an hour.' As he pulled out the opposite chair, she saw him see the wine. 'What's up?'

'I've had a weird morning,' she said.

Then she told him why.

'Why didn't you tell me?' was his first question when she was done. 'On Friday, when you got the email?'

'I don't know,' she lied.

She'd met Mark nearly two years ago, four years after *The Witness* had been published in paperback. He'd been sitting at a busy bar on a Thursday night, alone, drinking whiskey and reading, and she'd fallen for it hook, line and Ishiguro. It took him less than half an hour to tell her that he was a mostly unpublished writer and her nearly a month to reveal to him that she'd authored a critically acclaimed bestselling book.

He'd been proud.

She'd been practically apologetic.

Alice had told her repeatedly to cop on, to adopt the confidence of a mediocre white man, to override the Irish person's inherent terror of being accused of *having notions*. But it was easier said than done. Ideals were called that for a reason. Real life was messier. Her success was in the distant past and Mark was looking like her immediate future. What was there to gain by going on about it?

She'd given him the bullet points, and he'd dutifully read *The Witness* and said all the right things. Since then, the subject of her having had a successful book was something they were both hyper-aware of but avoided addressing directly, as if they were a second marriage in a crime novel and *The Witness* was the beautiful but dead first wife.

'But *ghostwriting*?' Mark said. 'Do you know how to do that?'

'Funnily enough, that doesn't seem to be relevant. Beth said all that matters is that it's a good book and that she knows I can produce one of those, and there'll be an assistant to help with everything else. She said Jack wants to tell his story and I just have to help him write it down and then polish it up afterwards.'

'Are you going to do it?'

'I don't know,' Emily said. After a beat she added, 'I *do* know I don't have twenty-five grand.'

'But what if he did it? You'd be giving him a platform.'

'*I* wouldn't be giving him anything. I'd just be the hired help. And my saying no isn't going to stop this from happening. If I don't do it, someone else will.'

'You want to do it.'

He made it sound like an accusation.

'What I want is for this to be over,' Emily said.

'There are other ways.'

'Like what?'

'You could write the book.'

I can't write the book, she protested – but silently, because she didn't want to get into a pointless conversation where he told her all the reasons that that fact wasn't true. She said, 'That's not an option anymore. They don't want it. They're

40

focusing more on non-fiction these days. My contract is getting cancelled either way.'

'Then write the book, sell it to someone else and use that advance to pay off this one.'

I can't write the fucking book! 'That's not how it works, Mark.'

Even if she somehow managed to pull a book out of her blocked brain, selling it to a publisher wouldn't be easy. It might not even be possible. The ones big enough to pay an advance that would get her out of trouble only dealt with agents, so she'd have to get one of those first. It would take time. It might take forever. And the moment she said no to this ghostwriting gig, the money she owed Morningstar would fall due.

'I know how it works,' he muttered under his breath.

He didn't, but she let it go.

'They need to know by five,' she said, trying to move the conversation on. 'And if I say yes, I'd leave tomorrow.'

'*What?*'

'In the morning, if they can get me on a flight. My US travel approval is in date, from that time I was supposed to be going to New York.' Hoping to go, until she did the sums and realized she couldn't afford to. 'They want this to get going as soon as possible. I think they've already wasted a lot of time trying to get someone to say yes.'

'What does that tell you?'

'That they're desperate,' Emily said. 'Which is perfect, because so am I.'

A beat passed.

'You know,' Mark said then, 'this could bring a lot of attention.' He paused. 'Unwanted attention.'

'They said my name won't be made public.'

'Anonymity means nothing now. Not with the internet. What if your name does get out? What if everyone knows it was you who helped this guy write his book? It could be very exposing.' Mark shifted in his seat. 'Isn't it weird that we never talk about it?'

'What?'

'Writing the book.'

She looked at him like he was crazy. 'God, why would I *want* to talk about it? That would only make it worse. Imagine it's Sunday night and you haven't done your homework. Imagine you feel like that all the time, every day – and you *can't* do your homework, but you still have to go to school. Then someone comes in and says, "Have you your homework done? No? Let's talk about that for a while." Is that really going to help?'

'I meant *The Witness*,' he said quietly. 'What it was like, writing it. I mean . . . Why was it easy to write that, and impossible to write anything else since?'

She felt his eyes on her, the prickly heat of his attention.

It wasn't easy, she said silently.

'I don't know,' she lied again.

4

In the end, it fell to Alice to be the voice of reason.

Calmed by two lunchtime glasses of wine and a pizza-induced carb coma, Emily had left her a long voice-note debriefing her on the Morningstar meeting. In less time than it took to record it – Alice listened to everything on 1.5 speed – she'd got a text back. *Can't talk right now but Q1: are you comfortable doing something like this? If no, say no. If yes then >>> Q2: If this job was PAYING €25k, would you take it? (Because it IS. Bonus: Florida.) Crucial: totally anon by law so nothing to worry about there. Do it and be free!* This was followed by the infamous picture of Nicole Kidman reportedly leaving her lawyer's office after her divorce from Tom Cruise was finalized, and then another text that said, *I'll call later but only to say the same things out loud.*

There was no need. Emily knew Alice was right.

She rang Beth to say yes just after four o'clock. Half an hour later, there were plane tickets and a detailed travel itinerary in her inbox. Ten minutes after that, there was a contract for her to sign in there too. She emailed her manager at work to say she had a family emergency that required her to go to Cork right away and stay there for maybe as long as a week, and then she started packing a bag.

Mark's reaction to her decision was subdued. He said he understood why she was doing it and agreed it made financial sense, but that he was worried about her.

'Don't be,' she said. 'This isn't a big deal. It's basically a transcription job, with a bit of editing afterwards. It'll barely be a month of my life, all in – a month that will completely neutralize the stress of the last *six years*. And who knows? Maybe afterwards I'll even be able to write again.'

'I hope so,' he said. 'I really do.'

She didn't ask for clarification on which bit he was referring to.

Emily had lain awake all night, staring at the ceiling, waiting for all of this to start feeling real. It was happening so fast, her brain hadn't had a chance to catch up.

By the time her second flight taxied to the terminal building late on Tuesday afternoon, Florida-time, it still hadn't.

There was no distant cityscape out the plane's window, just a treeline on flat land. But when the nose of the plane turned ninety degrees, Emily could see, in the middle distance, a long row of open hangars. Each had one or two planes parked neatly inside, their bodies gunmetal grey and their shape at once both strange and familiar.

No, not planes – fighter jets.

She'd only ever seen them on CNN and in action movies like the one she'd fallen asleep halfway through on her first flight. They made her think of threat and fear and trouble, and she hoped they weren't a portent.

Destin-Fort Walton Beach Airport was tiny. There were only two baggage belts. The journey to them from her seat only took five minutes, and that was with a bathroom break along the way.

While she waited for her suitcase to appear, she saw Tall Blonde Woman by the exit, talking on the phone.

Emily had first seen her back in Dublin Airport, waiting to board the same flight to D.C. She'd noticed her because she looked like Emily wished she could: fit and toned, beautiful barefaced, the kind of short, messy hair that said *I don't waste my one wild and precious life styling this*. She'd seen her again waiting to board this second flight, which was weird, because Emily's itinerary was last-minute, awkward and circuitous: Dublin to Dulles, taxi to Reagan, three hours south in the air to here.

Why would anyone else be on the exact same route?

Unless Morningstar had tapped someone from their Dublin office to be her assistant on this.

Emily didn't want to approach her to ask, just in case the answer was no. She may not have actually read the non-disclosure agreement, but it was a safe bet that chatting to strangers in airports about Jack Smyth's memoir would be a breach.

She wondered if they were going to share a car, but Tony, her driver, said he was only expecting one passenger.

Arrivals was just a few square feet of carpeted hallway; she spotted him right away. When he saw her looking quizzically at the sign pointing to the 'Freedom Lounge' and raising her eyebrows at more American flags than she'd ever seen in one place, he explained that she was on an Air Force base.

'Largest Air Force base in the world,' he said as he led her to the exit. 'The airport is shared: half military, half commercial. That's why you don't see any private jets. Not allowed for security reasons.'

'I see,' Emily said, as if she'd noticed.

Tony's car was parked right outside. The air was a hot, humid soup, solid and heavy. There was nothing much to see except the rest of the airport car park, more distant trees and road signs pointing to NICEVILLE and DESTIN TOLL BRIDGE. The sky was bright blue and cloudless, the sinking sun an intense, primordial glare, as if the layers of pollution that dulled it everywhere else had never gathered here.

Inside the car it was mercifully cool, the air-conditioning cranked to a level that could've safely refrigerated meat. Tony asked if she'd any objections to early nineties power-ballads and offered her a bottle of water from a cooler. He said the drive would be about forty-five minutes if traffic was on their side.

'You been to Sanctuary before?' he asked.

'No, never. This is my first time in Florida.'

Emily had Googled Jack Smyth, but it hadn't occurred to her to look up the place where she was going to spend a week with him. She'd just assumed it was, you know, *Florida*. The non-Disney part. She thought Beth had said something about a hotel – but had she?

Now, she couldn't recall exactly.

'Sanctuary' sounded like a resort overlooking a stretch of sugar-white sand gently kissed by crystal-clear, shimmering water. The kind that had swaying palm trees, a swim-up bar and over-the-top water features, like fountains set to music. Nearby, there might be a city strip composed of high-rise hotels, Art Deco facades the colour of ice-cream flavours, Versace prints and oily, muscular men in tiny—

Miami, Emily realized. She'd been picturing Miami, the only place in Florida she'd seen anything of, and that had been on a TV screen.

But here was definitely not there.

They were on a highway, ramrod-straight and smooth, cutting through a sprawl of strip malls, empty lots and busy intersections. The scenery appeared to be on a loop. There'd be a sign for a Dollar Tree, then a Wendy's, then a Regions Bank. Cue a billboard shouting something like CALL-850-HURT and then bam, it was the Dollar Tree again.

There was no sign of any coastline or anything taller than one storey high.

This went on for about forty minutes or until Michael Bolton was crooning about having said he loved you but lied for the third time. Then Tony took a right turn onto a two-lane road cutting straight through dense woodland. The trees had oddly flat tops, as if someone had taken to them horizontally with a hedge trimmer, and every so often they'd stop to make room for a stretch of swampy marshland or a lake with homes on stilts clustered together on its far shore. Occasional signs warned DANGER! DO NOT FEED OR MOLEST! beneath pictures of annoyed-looking alligators and, perplexingly, NO GOLF CARTS.

'Almost there,' he said.

And then, suddenly, there were houses.

They had appeared abruptly, in a blink: enormous homes, facing the road, that looked like they belonged on the covers of aspirational magazines called things like *Coastal Living* or *Ocean Home*. The kind that had wine fridges and TVs the size of dining tables and sectional sofas bigger than Emily's apartment, and driftwood signs demanding that you LIVE, LAUGH, LOVE or insisting that LIFE IS BETTER AT THE BEACH.

Residential streets stretched away from them with smaller versions of these homes sat in neat rows on either side. They were clad in white clapboard siding, trimmed in sherbet pastels and not far behind a white picket fence. Although no two looked exactly alike, they all looked different in exactly the same way. Cohesion but not conformity. Quirky design features abounded: towers, widow's walks, porthole windows under the point of gabled roofs. The architecture was oddly timeless, somehow both futuristic and old-fashioned, like spaceships in a movie from the sixties. It could pass for a village of dolls' houses blown up to life-size, or something the Disney Imagineers would build in one of the theme parks, or the set of *The Truman Show*.

Emily was thinking there were worse places to spend a week when Tony drove on, out of the town, leaving the dolls' houses behind.

'That was Seaside,' he said. 'Sanctuary is the next town along.'

Town?

'Or it will be,' Tony added, confusing her more.

The roadside became a smattering of single homes and stand-alone businesses – a diner, a surf shop, an estate agent's – until eventually they thinned out and then completely disappeared.

Then it was just trees.

Then it was a long stretch of highway, its tarmac newly resurfaced, with nothing to see but sand dunes to the right and marshland to the left.

Emily spotted two objects in the distance, one on either side of the road. They were gleaming white, tall as houses and shimmering in the rising heat. There were in the shape of – she couldn't think of anything else except – *giant traffic cones?*

'*This* is Sanctuary,' Tony announced.

'What are those?' she asked, pointing.

'They call them the butteries.'

'What's a buttery?'

He shrugged a shoulder. 'Those things, I guess.'

As the car passed between them, Emily saw SANCTUARY etched into each one in letters three-foot high. Beyond them, a group of white stone buildings clustered together on the right-hand side of the road. In the distance was another set of butteries, presumably marking the development's other end.

Tony turned onto a cobbled street whose stones were so clean they might have been freshly laid. The white buildings were homes, she saw now, densely built but neatly arranged in short, stubby blocks. Their architecture seemed vaguely Spanish in style, with smooth masonry and curved lines, but Emily also glimpsed horseshoe arches and a courtyard with a fountain in it that made her think of Marrakech.

As it had been back in Seaside, each house's design seemed unique but with strict limits on the scope of the differences, so in a way they all looked the same.

Although here, *everything* was white.

Not just the walls of the houses, but their doors and window frames too. The roof tiles: white. The footpaths, completely smooth and unblemished: white. The street lights, which had been designed to look like old-fashioned gas lamps: white. The street *signs*, pointing to places with names like BUTTERFLY

LANE and TURTLE DRIVE: white with pale grey lettering which, in the glare of the sun, made them challenging to read.

There was so much white that when you looked up and saw the blue of the sky or glimpsed a patch of lush green grass on a street corner, the colours registered as a shock.

Sanctuary was also completely deserted.

There were no pedestrians. No other cars. No noise. No *anything*. Just rows of stark white buildings, perfect and pristine, silent and waiting.

And then, as Tony took another turn, a massive building site.

Now, there were pristine homes on one side of the car and a messy effort to, presumably, make more of them on the other. Emily could see the sunken holes of foundations and timber frames, skeletons of homes to come. There were diggers and cement mixers and flatbed trucks. Piles of materials were stacked neatly under plastic tarps. The ground was bald and dusty and surrounded by chain-link fence. Numerous signs affixed to it warned in both English and Spanish about safety and shouted to KEEP OUT! Everything on the site was completely still and, like the streets she'd seen so far, entirely devoid of people.

Tony pulled up to the kerb and killed the engine, outside a house that seemed to have no windows on its ground floor. There was just a garage door and a small white marble plaque etched with the words BEACH READ.

'You here on vacation?' he asked, twisting around in his seat. 'I didn't think they were renting out anything yet.'

'I'm, ah, visiting friends.'

'You'll have a bit of noise during the day, but once the crews go home, you'll practically have the place to yourself. Like

50

now. No sleeping-in, though. They start pretty early around here, to try and avoid the heat.'

'But people are already living here?'

'No one lives here,' Tony said. 'These are all third and fourth homes, and investment properties.' He winked at her. 'Your friends must be doing pretty well for themselves.'

When they got out of the car, they were met with an eerie silence. There was no sound at all that they weren't making, not even distant traffic noise.

Tony lifted her suitcase onto the footpath and gave her a small key on a ring alongside a white plastic fob. He pointed at the garage door. When she pressed the fob to its keypad, there was a low mechanical whine and the door began to shudder and rise, revealing a space big enough for two cars, empty and clinically clean.

'It's through there,' he said, gesturing at an archway in the rear. 'Have a good one, OK? I'll see you on Monday.'

She thanked him, waved him off and walked through the opening with her suitcase rumbling loudly on the cement floor.

And into another world.

A lush courtyard, tiled in multicoloured mosaics and over-filled with leafy things planted in clay pots. At its centre was a small plunge pool, shimmering turquoise, with a cascading water feature that was making a soothing tinkling sound. There were armchairs, sun loungers, a hammock strung between two marble columns – and beyond them, huge floor-to-ceiling windows that offered a tease of the luxury waiting inside the house itself.

But the scene had an uncanny quality to it. This wasn't a lived-in oasis that had been designed and built and grown organically over time. It was all too perfect, too clean, too new – literally new; one of the chairs had a price tag hanging from its underside. It felt like a purpose-built set, or an upscale home staged for sale.

And where was everyone? Where was she supposed to go?

'You're in the lock-off,' a voice said from behind her.

Emily turned around to find herself face-to-face with Jack Smyth.

5

Seeing him in the flesh felt like a small electric shock: for one heartbeat every nerve ending flared, but by the very next everything had returned to normal.

He was in jeans and a long-sleeved T-shirt, standing with both hands dug deep into his pockets. This was Post-Retirement Jack – a healthy weight, grown-out hair, stubbled and handsome – but a nervous, diminished version, shoulders hunched and chin down.

Emily searched him for signs that he had taken a life, but of course there weren't any. She'd known there wouldn't be, even if he had.

'I'm in the . . .?'

'The lock-off,' he repeated. 'I'd call it a granny flat, but that's how the property manager referred to it.'

Jack pointed over her shoulder and she turned to look.

Behind her was a dining table and chairs, sitting beneath a pergola strung with greenery. A narrow spiral staircase was tucked into its deepest corner, next to a sign that said

BOOKMARK. An arrow beside the word pointed upwards. When she raised her gaze, she saw a deck with two white Adirondack chairs sitting on either side of a front door with a large pane of glass in it.

She turned back to Jack.

'I'm Emily, by the way,' she said, extending a hand.

He hesitated before doing the same with one of his. She glimpsed tributaries of shiny new skin snaking up his forearm, an angry red river cutting across an otherwise pale landscape. As they shook, she felt an unusually smooth and hard palm, rough fingertips, a weak grip.

'Jack.'

'Nice to meet you,' she said automatically.

He jammed both hands back in his pockets. 'How was your journey?'

'Fine. Long. When did you get here?'

'This morning,' he said. 'I was in New York before, for a couple of days.'

'So at least you were already in this time zone.'

'Nearly. We're one hour behind here.'

'Are we?'

Jack nodded. 'It's Central, this far west.'

If the captain had told his passengers that as Emily's plane had landed at Fort Walton Beach, she'd been too distracted by the war machinery outside the window to hear it.

Now, she did the sums in her head. It must be approaching six in the evening, local time. That meant her body thought it was almost midnight. In five hours, she'd have been up for a full twenty-four.

She swallowed a yawn.

'Is the assistant here?' she asked. 'From Morningstar?'

Jack frowned. 'Assistant?'

'Beth said something about there being one on-site . . .'

'Oh – you mean Grace? No, she's gone to her hotel. She's not staying here. She's down the road a bit, in Watercolor, but she'll be back first thing in the morning.'

'Watercolor?' Emily repeated.

'And Sanctuary.' He made a face. 'Yeah, I know.'

'I saw signs for somewhere called Niceville on the way here.'

'We can't really talk though, can we?' Jack said. 'After all, there's Borris-in-Ossory.'

'And New Twopothouse . . .'

'Nobber.'

'Muff.'

'*Muff?*' Jack blinked at her. 'Where's that?'

'Donegal,' she said. 'And, ah, they have a diving club.'

'You're kidding.'

'I think they are too, to be fair. They have merch. They may not do any actual diving.'

Jack laughed and she saw the lifeless, broken limbs of a woman tumbling down a flight of stairs. What the hell was she doing? This guy was the prime – only – suspect in a murder. He had said things about the night his wife had died that couldn't possibly be true. And not even five minutes in, she was joking with him about *place names*?

But then, what was she supposed to be doing? This was going to be a long week if she didn't build some kind of rapport with him, and she didn't want to be rude.

Because what if he hadn't done it? What if he was innocent? What if this was all some tragic, unjust mistake?

'So what is this place?' she asked.

'Sanctuary? A town, according to the brochure. A new

town, built from scratch.' When he saw her expression, he said, 'I know. It's weird. But it's actually quite common around here. I guess because they've got the space. Think of it like one of those massive housing estates they built back home in the seventies, but instead of space for a corner shop, there's an entire town square and a hotel and a golf course. Or there will be when they finish it. Did you come through Seaside on the way in? That's the same kind of thing.'

'Is the house yours?'

'God, no,' Jack said. 'Not my style. It belongs to a friend of mine. He knew I needed somewhere to hide out and do this, so he offered it to me. There really wasn't anywhere at home we'd have been able to go unnoticed, and going anywhere in Europe would only have been a Ryanair ride away for the vultures, so . . . They only got the furniture in a few days ago. We're the first people to stay here.'

'Nice,' Emily said absently.

She was trying to picture Jack Smyth killing his wife. In her mind's eye, she saw a man standing at the top of a staircase, crazed with rage, moving to push two hands against a woman's back and then rushing to set a fire that would destroy the evidence.

But at best, he was only *this* man's doppelgänger, a physical match but otherwise unrelated and disconnected from the guy standing right in front of her.

She just couldn't marry the two.

Jack cleared his throat. 'Um, by the way, I wanted to say thank you. For stepping in. Neil really let us down, dropping out at the last minute. Thanks for saving the day.'

This was the first Emily had heard of any Neil. She didn't know how to respond because she didn't know what Jack

56

knew. What had Morningstar told him? Had they been up-front about their struggles to get someone to be his ghostwriter, or had they come up with some kind of cover story to smooth everything over? In her experience, no one in publishing ever wanted to come straight out and deliver bad news. Beth's gentle *We need to draw a line under this* was by far the harshest thing she'd ever heard.

She should check with Beth, before she stuck her foot in it.

'No problem,' she said. She stifled another yawn, but less successfully; Jack caught this one. She blushed. 'I'm sorry. I'm just a bit of a zombie after all the travelling. I've missed an entire night's sleep.'

'No, no, of course. I'll let you get settled.' He took hold of her suitcase. 'Let me bring this up for you.'

He was off with it before she could protest, so she had no choice but to follow him under the pergola, up the narrow stairs and onto the deck.

He walked with a slight limp, she noticed.

'There you go,' he said, setting the case outside the front door. He was flushed, winded from the act. She remembered his reported lung damage, the after-effects of smoke inhalation. 'I think Grace said we'd start at ten tomorrow morning, but she was going to text you. If you need anything in the meantime, I'm in there' – he jerked a thumb at the main house – 'so just shout.'

'Great. Thanks.'

'I, ah . . .' Jack shifted his weight from foot to foot. 'I appreciate you treating me like a normal person. When people have prior knowledge of me . . . Well, you can guess how it goes.'

Jack turned around and headed for the stairs before she could respond. She watched him go, itchy with unease.

This was all so confusing.

She didn't know how to act, how to behave, how to treat him. She didn't want to be rude, but nor did she want to be commended for being nice to a murderer. She wanted him to like her enough to get this book done and done well, but not any more than that. She didn't want to like him, but she didn't want to dislike someone because of something they hadn't actually done.

She wished there was a rule book for this. An etiquette guide. *The Ghost: Everything You Need to Know to Help a Man Who Might Have Murdered Someone Write His Story – Including Exactly How to Behave Around Him Without Turning Your Soul Necrotic!*

Emily unlocked the door, dragged her case over the threshold and felt her anxiety dissipate.

Because Bookmark, her home for the next few days, was *adorable.*

It was a studio. Directly opposite the front door was a kitchenette, separated from the living area by a breakfast bar. There was no bed, but Emily suspected that the plush, overstuffed couch pushed against the side wall turned into one. Everything was white or woven, and despite the limited space there seemed to be every possible luxury: a top-of-the-range TV, a complicated coffee machine, even a little drinks fridge with three bottles of rosé inside.

If Jack hadn't told her they were the first people to stay here, she'd still have known. The contents were obviously brand new. The couch cushions didn't have as much as a dimple in them, the glass pot of the coffee machine had a small pamphlet of instructions inside and the TV screen was still protected by a film of clear plastic. The space even *smelled* of newness, which was to say it didn't really smell of anything at all.

There was a small, neatly typed card stuck to the fridge with the wifi network name and password on it. Emily connected and waited while various messages and notifications flooded her phone.

Most of them were pointless noise that she could swipe away without a second thought. Both Mark and Alice had sent messages. She responded to each one, letting them know she'd made it here in one piece.

Then she checked for new emails.

There were three.

One was from Beth, hoping her journey was good and wishing her the best of luck. One was from a time-management app Emily had cancelled her subscription to months ago, trying to convince her to come back at a discounted rate. And one was from *her*.

A message with her own name as the sender and an empty subject line.

Emily blinked at it in confusion.

What the . . . ?

She opened it and saw its body shouting I KNOW WHO YOU ARE in all caps.

Her mouth went dry and her heart began to pound wildly in her chest. She stared at the words until everything else in her line of vision disappeared.

Don't overreact, she told herself. *It's just an email. It's probably spam.*

Yeah – spam. That must be it. Because she'd heard about stuff like this, hadn't she? They wanted you to think someone had hacked into your email account and them emailing you from it was proof, so you'd transfer all your Bitcoin to stop them from sending deep-fake nudes to all your contacts or whatever.

And now, actually, when she inspected it, she saw that the email address itself was a string of random numbers at Hot-mail.com. It *hadn't* come from her account. Someone had just signed up for an email address and put her name on it.

Probably not even a real someone, but a bot.

Spam. It had to be.

Emily's shoulders dropped a little as she exhaled, long and loud.

She tapped to move the message to 'Junk' and listened for the reassuring *whoosh* of it being transferred there.

Then she poured herself a very large glass of wine and took it onto the balcony at the rear of Bookmark, the one on the beach side.

And gasped.

The windows had offered framed swathes of sea, but the balcony provided an endless vista. A stretch of unspoiled white sand dotted with navy-blue parasols stretched away from the house in both directions. The water was turquoise and calm, its waves lapping lazily against the shore, while above it the setting sun had streaked the sky with oranges, pinks and purples. The beach, like Sanctuary itself, was deserted. It was a little distance from the house and on the other side of a sand dune; only this upper level had a Gulf view.

When Emily went inside for a refill, she spotted a set of switches by the door. Presuming they were for the lights, she pressed one – and startled at the sudden loud mechanical *whirr*. Aluminium shutters started to descend over all the glass at the rear of the property, covering the balcony door and the windows on either side of it. Panicked, she jabbed at the button again, sending them back up.

Off the main space was a small nook with two doors. The bathroom was one, and Emily expected a walk-in closet or a utility room to be behind the other, but instead, she found solid wall.

Or what at first glance looked like solid wall, but was actually a closed door.

And then she realized: *lock-off* was literal.

Just like connecting hotel rooms, Bookmark was separate from Beach Read but it didn't have to be. If both these doors were opened, the nook would become a hallway, allowing passage from this self-contained unit into the main house and vice versa.

And on the other side was a man who was maybe a murderer.

Five days before the fire

Kate sees the photographer to the door, murmuring apologies to him as they walk along the hallway.

'He hates having his photo taken,' she says. 'That's all.'

Miles, grizzled in appearance and gruff in nature, is unmoved. 'Well, love, it's like this. I've got a job to do. And I've shot far more important fellas than him. So there's no need to be a prick about it, you know?'

Kate fixes a tight smile to her face.

What she wants to say is, *That's my husband you're talking about.* And, *You have no idea what kind of stress he's under.* And, *It's actually you who's being a fucking prick – personally, I wouldn't trust you to do a passport photo.* But being honest is a luxury she can't afford, so all she actually says is, 'Well, anyway. Thanks again. Safe home.'

Miles raises a hand in farewell and stomps off across the gravel driveway, back to his car. Kate waves him off, shuts the front door, presses her forehead to it and closes her eyes.

She'd known, from the moment she opened them this morning, that today was going to be one of those days.

She made a mistake last night. Didn't eat enough and then

had one glass too many. She fell into bed and went straight to sleep – mission still accomplished – but woke up feeling like her stomach had spent the night on a spin cycle and her head in a vice. Small mercy: Jack was already up and gone. He'd sent her a text saying he was out for a run, time-stamped a half-hour before. She figured she had another half-hour to right herself. She knew the treatment: a breakfast of two paracetamol, ice-cold water, strong coffee and a slice of toast, followed by a long shower with the temperature as hot as she could stand it.

She was watching the steam reveal a pattern of smears in the shower door when a blur of movement on its other side startled her.

Jack, back sooner than expected.

'Don't kill me,' he'd said, looking sheepish.

It had been arranged three days ago. He'd forgotten to tell her, and then forgot today that it was happening at all. A photographer was coming from a national broadsheet to take a portrait. It would illustrate some feature that was going in their weekend glossy magazine about businesses born during lockdown. Miles had interrupted Jack's running playlist with a call to say that he was lost somewhere on the wrong side of the village and needed an Eircode. He'd be here any minute.

She'd stepped out of the shower, dripping on the floor, leaving the water running behind her.

'But it's just you, right?' she'd asked, panic rising. She needed at least forty-five minutes to go from sopping wet to photo-ready.

'Just me.'

Jack was already pulling off his running gear, preparing to get in.

'What do you need? Product?'

One of the bedrooms was filled with boxes of Exis garments. They had a branded display and a rail they could throw some stuff on.

'I don't know,' he said. 'Maybe.'

'Sort yourself as quick as you can,' she'd told him. 'I'll stall.'

Miles had managed to find the house, but couldn't hide his surprise at Kate's appearance. Wet hair scraped back, flat to her head; sweatpants and a T-shirt from a charity run; bare-faced, pink-cheeked and shiny with sweat, from rushing. She admitted immediately that they'd forgotten and Miles had grinned and said, 'I thought that all right,' with a knowing confidence that annoyed her.

She'd steered him into the kitchen for coffee and small talk, and then to the office at the other end of the house so he could get his gear set up.

As they'd passed the bottom of the stairs, she'd heard a hairdryer going.

'*Sunshine*, right?' Miles had asked. 'That's what you're on?'

'*Sunrise*. And I was. I don't do TV anymore.'

'How did you end up all the way out here?'

'This is Jack's office,' she'd said, ignoring him. 'It's the room we normally use for stuff like this.'

'Normally,' Miles had repeated, but quietly, under his breath.

Mocking her, Kate had realized on a delay, which made her clench her fists until the tips of her fingernails threatened to pierce the skin.

Jack's office is the house's original living room. They haven't done much to it yet – replastered and repainted the wall a dark forest-green, installed some black, flatpack bookcases and relocated the tan leather couch they'd had in their Dublin apartment – but it makes for a nice backdrop.

Or it has in the past.

This morning, Miles had looked around, made a face and said, 'There's no cycling stuff in here.'

Cycling stuff.

The rest of the day – the sequence of events that was about to play out – flashed before Kate's eyes.

'He doesn't really keep it out,' she'd said. And then, for good measure: 'Most of it is actually in storage.' Just in case: 'All of it, really.'

'They told me to get cycling stuff.'

'But I thought this was about Exis.'

'Exe-who?'

'My husband's company.'

'I don't know anything about any company, love. I just do as I'm told.'

It was at that point that Miles had dug his phone out and showed her the message from the photo-desk outlining his instructions.

'I understand,' she'd said, 'but there isn't any.'

Jack had appeared then, and she'd tried to flash him a warning look before leaving the two of them alone in the office. She could've listened at the door, but there was no need. She knew exactly what was about to unfold.

Miles, pushing for his 'cycling stuff'.

Jack, politely declining, trying to keep the focus on the business.

Miles, pushing harder.

Jack doubling down, as was his right.

Miles, not understanding, being rude.

Jack's patience wearing thin.

And then, eventually, raised voices. They'd been loud enough for Kate to hear from the extension all the way at the other end of the house. She'd hurried into the hall and met Miles coming out of the office with his equipment, rolling his eyes, about to tell her that he thought her husband was a prick.

Kate turns her back to the front door now and walks down the hall, pausing outside the office door to steel herself.

On the other side, she finds Jack standing by the window, arms folded tightly across his chest, watching Miles drive off.

'What happened?' she asks.

'Every fucking time,' Jack mutters.

'Did he get a shot?'

'I don't care what he got.'

'We should've said no.'

'I did.'

'To the feature, I mean. To the whole thing. From the start.'

'It was *supposed* to be about Exis,' Jack says. 'And I was clear: I didn't want to talk about cycling.' He shakes his head. 'I'm never going to get away from it, am I?'

Kate goes to join him at the window. She stands behind him, wraps her arms around his waist and rests her cheek against his back. She stays like that until she feels his body relax, the tension slowly leaving it.

He can stop having to hold himself together for these few moments.

She'll take over, do it for him.

'People don't understand,' she whispers. 'But they can't unless you tell them. If you told the truth about it all, you wouldn't have to go through things like this. You wouldn't have to pretend.'

She feels his body tense up again, pull away from her.

'Kate, don't,' he says.

'I just think if—'

'*No.*' It isn't angry, but it is firm and final. 'You know as well as I do that I can never say a word.'

II

SANCTUARY

6

E mily wanted a shower and needed to wash her face and brush her teeth, but instead she lay on the couch and idly flipped through what seemed to be hundreds of TV channels until she found one that was showing nothing but the American version of *The Office*. One minute she was watching Michael Scott burn his foot on a George Foreman grill and then the next thing she knew, it was cold, dark and 4:55a.m.

She changed into the old T-shirt she'd intended to sleep in and washed the grime of a full day's travel off her face. She went to the trouble of turning the couch into a bed, which turned out to be hardly any trouble at all; one good pull unfolded it to reveal that it was already neatly made with crisp white linens. She set the thermostat to something less chilly, got back into bed and closed her eyes.

But her body had already had ten hours' sleep and had no interest in any more.

She picked up her phone and, with a held breath, opened her email app.

No new emails.

It *had* been spam. Not something to worry about. She was annoyed at herself for even briefly thinking it might have been.

She opened WhatsApp. Grace, the assistant from Morning-star, had sent a message saying she'd meet Emily in the courtyard at 9:45a.m. Both Alice and Mark had replied over-night. Mark said to give him a call later and Alice demanded pictures. She sent them both thumbs-up emojis.

Next, she opened the browser and searched for *Neil Ireland ghostwriter* and *Neil Ireland writer Morningstar* and then *Neil ghostwriter Ireland Jack Smyth*, but couldn't find any potential candidates for the guy who'd said yes to Morning-star before her, then changed his mind.

When she typed *What is a buttery?* into the search box, the top result was a highlighted line from a Wikipedia page explaining that it was a cellar under a monastery where food was stored, which left her none the wiser. She sent Mark another message. *BTW do you know what a buttery is???*

Emily got out of bed, took a long shower and got dressed. After a couple of non-starts and a YouTube video, she man-aged to make a cup of coffee in the fancy machine. By then the sky was lightening so she took it outside, onto the balcony.

The view of the beach at sunset the evening before had been beautiful, but at sunrise it took her breath away. Miles and miles of unspoiled white sand stretched in both directions. The angle of the sun, still low in the sky behind the house, made the water a steely grey and illuminated a mist hanging low over the surf. She took a video, panning from left to right, and sent it to Alice, who immediately replied with a *How absolutely AWFUL for you.* She sipped her coffee and watched the view slowly change as the sun ascended.

Then, come 7:30a.m., noise.

The chugging engines of large, heavy vehicles. The hissing of their brakes. The *beep-beep-beep* warning of their manoeuvrings. Drilling. Banging. Hammering. The nasal roar of a chainsaw. The disembodied voices of hyper-early-morning talk-radio hosts, blaring from someone's car stereo. Men, shouting instructions to each other.

It didn't happen in stages but seemed to come suddenly and all at once, as if the construction crews were an orchestra who'd been poised over their instruments, eyes on the conductor, waiting for the signal to start.

Rolling her eyes, Emily went back inside.

There were still two hours to kill until she had to meet Grace. She'd been toying with the idea of going for an early-morning walk around what town there was, but the building-site soundtrack had turned her off it.

Instead, she dug out *The Ultimate Ghostwriting Handbook* and flipped through it.

It was weird that no one else in this process seemed at all concerned that she had no idea what she was doing. When she'd pointed out her total lack of ghostwriting experience to Beth and Carolyn, Beth had assured her it wasn't a problem and Carolyn had waved a hand like it wasn't even worth mentioning. Yes, Beth said, there were experienced ghostwriters who wrote other people's books for a living, but many ghostwriting projects enlisted writers who'd never ghosted before. They were chosen because the subject liked the writer's style, or they happened to know them personally, or the publisher played matchmaker, thinking they'd be a good fit personality-wise.

Or the writer owed the publisher twenty-five grand.

She'd been advised not to overthink it. 'Listen to Jack tell his story,' Beth had said back in the little nook at the Fitzwilliam. 'Consider what questions you'd want answered if you were the reader, what details you'd want to know. Probe him for more if you feel he's created any bald spots or left holes. This week is primarily about collecting raw material.'

She'd made it sound quite simple and straightforward, and it felt that way when Emily thought about it in those terms. But when she started thinking about how she was in some weird, half-built town in Florida helping Jack Smyth tell the world that he didn't kill his wife, it looked more like a terrifying fever-dream and felt like drowning in water tens of feet deeper than Emily was tall.

Five minutes before she was due to meet Grace, Emily left Bookmark with her backpack slung over her shoulder. A wall of heat met her outside the door, despite the early hour. The courtyard's design completely blocked all views of the outside world but could do nothing to dampen the noise from the construction site.

A woman was standing by the edge of the pool with her arms folded.

'You must be Emily,' she said.

The woman had an American accent, which was as precise a classification as Emily was able to make. She could fairly reliably identify New York, Boston and *Fargo*, but that was about it.

'Grace?'

The other woman nodded.

She was not Tall Blonde Woman from the plane. Grace was much younger, twenty-one or twenty-two. She had dark, curly hair, and had swamped her small frame in the kind of shapeless cotton jumpsuit that, on her, whispered *I might work in fashion* but, on Emily, would shout *All I'm missing is my high-vis and hard hat*. Her make-up was the kind that men mistook for natural beauty and she appeared to be wholly unaffected by the already oppressive heat.

Emily absently tugged on the hem of her T-shirt, feeling frumpy and undone by comparison.

'Good to meet you,' she said. 'Finally.'

'Finally?' Grace lifted a wrist to peer at a tiny gold watch with concern. 'Am I late?'

'Oh no. No, I just meant, you know – I've been looking forward to getting started and I'm glad the time is finally here. That's all.'

'I heard you met Jack?'

'Just briefly.'

Grace met Emily's gaze and held it for a beat longer than was comfortable, and Emily thought that this was it, that now they were going to have the inevitable conversation.

What do you think of him? This is all a bit weird, isn't it? Two women spending a week alone in a place like this with a man who could've killed his wife . . .

What will we do if we start to feel afraid?

Are we safe?

Are we terrible people for being a part of this?

But Grace said, 'Everything's good for you?' and the moment passed.

'Yeah, great. The beach is beautiful. And this house . . . Gorgeous. The town, though' – Emily made a face – 'not so much.'

She was expecting a conspiratorial *I know, right? We're staying on a building site! And what's up with those traffic cone things?* but instead, one perfectly manicured eyebrow slowly rose in question.

'What do you mean?' Grace asked.

'Well, it's just not what I was expecting. And yesterday evening, when I arrived, it was kinda eerie. No one at all around and—'

'I don't think you'll have much, if any, free time, so—'

'No, I know. I was just—'

'—it doesn't really matter and—'

'No, sure, yeah,' Emily said quickly.

'—you know you can't talk to anyone about why you're here, right? Do you understand that?'

Grace seemed to be picking up every single thing that came out of her mouth completely wrong, so Emily just nodded in response, afraid to say any more.

'That's actually why I wanted us to meet a little early,' Grace said. 'To go over the arrangements for the week. And the rules.' Her gaze flicked to Emily's backpack. 'Let's head on up.'

Emily wordlessly trailed her into the main house, down a long corridor and across a large foyer. The noise from the building site disappeared. By the time they'd walked through a pair of barn-style sliding doors, she'd lost her sense of direction and was surprised to find herself facing a wall of windows. Through them, two banners of stunning blue: higher up, cloudless sky, and below that, shimmering water, chromatic and calm. It was the rear wall of the living room, which was filled with light and furnished in a palette of whites and beiges, seemingly chosen not to distract from the view or perhaps in resigned acknowledgement that nothing could possibly compete with it.

Through an archway was a kitchen and beside it a narrow

staircase tucked in an alcove. Grace started up it and Emily followed.

'These are the back stairs,' she explained. 'They're the quickest way.'

The first floor of the house was a swathe of rattan carpet and a collection of closed white doors.

They made Emily think of her connecting door back in Bookmark and wonder where the corresponding door on this side might be. Logically, it would be in a hallway or a nook, like hers was. If an opportunity arose, she'd have a snoop around for it.

'You're in here,' Grace said. She'd stopped at an open door-way and was motioning for Emily to enter first.

She obeyed.

It was a huge room that shared a view with the living room below – they must be directly above it. On the right was a king-sized bed, dressed as if for a photoshoot, the decorative cushions karate-chopped and the sheets completely crease-free. On the left, an L-shaped couch faced a large oak-coloured desk with a dark grey MacBook, a small, silver device that looked like a vape and an unopened box of ballpoints sitting atop a stack of legal pads. A nearby dressing table had been commandeered as a snack bar, replete with cans of seltzer, a capsule coffee machine, and a half-dozen of those tall, cylindrical water bottles that look like something geologists in disaster movies would store core samples in.

In keeping with the rest of the property, everything looked and smelled like it was fresh out of the box.

'You and Jack will meet in here every morning at 10:00a.m.,' Grace said. 'Each day's interviewing will last for a minimum of four hours and a maximum of five, with a half-hour break after the first two for lunch. Lunch will be brought in. Afterwards, you can use this room to listen back, make notes, prep for the following day – but you need to be out of the main house no later than five so Jack can have his evenings to himself.'

'Sounds good,' Emily said. 'But, ah, I could just leave right after we finish each day's interview? Do anything I need next door, in my place?'

That was her plan.

On the balcony, watching the sunset, with wine.

'No,' Grace said firmly. 'We have provided a computer, voice-recorder and thumb-drive for you to use, and they cannot leave this room or be connected to any network. Any related materials, such as handwritten notes, have to stay in here too. You cannot use your personal devices. In future, I'm going to ask you not to bring anything in here with you, including your phone. I'll secure it and your bag for today, and you'll know not to bring them with you in future. Also, if there's to be any communication with Morningstar, it needs to go through me. I'll call Beth from my phone. No emails, no messages, no direct calls from you from now on. Everything about this project has to be kept as secure as possible. Do you understand?' She pressed her lips together and stared at Emily, as if braced for a challenge.

'Of course,' Emily said. 'I understand.'

And she did, but she also felt condescended to.

Grace clearly wasn't so much an assistant here but Morningstar's representative on the ground. She was in charge.

Emily really *was* the hired help.

Dinner, Grace was explaining now, would be delivered each

day at a time of Emily's choosing, to Bookmark. Otherwise she should make a grocery list, and Grace would go shopping for her.

'Can I not just come with you?'

Grace pressed her lips together again. 'We'd rather you stay here, in Sanctuary, for the duration. Same goes for Jack.' She started towards the door. 'Is there anything else you need at this point?'

'Ah, actually, just so I don't say the wrong thing . . . Does Jack know?'

'Know what?'

'About, you know, *me*.'

Grace looked at her blankly.

'About why I'm doing this,' Emily clarified. 'The contract, and owing Morningstar for the second book. Just because he said something about a guy called Neil pulling out, and I didn't know what to say because—'

'Morning,' a new voice said.

Jack was standing in the doorway, his hands dug in his pockets.

'Morning,' Emily said, too brightly, too obviously trying to pretend that she wasn't worried that Jack had just heard what she'd said.

'All good?'

'Great.'

He glanced at Grace, but said nothing to her.

'Right, well.' Grace reached out a hand. 'I'll just take that bag and your phone, and leave you to it.'

Emily took a quick mental inventory of the contents of her backpack. There was her battered laptop, which was password-protected, and her phone was too. A notebook, but it was

79

brand new, completely blank. Mark's Olympus digital voice-recorder, which she'd taken without asking.

She hadn't checked to see if there was anything on it but if there was, it was him practising spoken-word performances. If Grace was nosy enough to listen, that'd be her own bad luck.

She handed it all over.

'I'll be downstairs if you need me,' Grace said. 'Lunch will be here at noon. I've ordered sandwiches for today but I'll take orders for tomorrow. So I guess, all that's left to say is . . . Good luck.'

Emily smiled and said thanks.

Jack nodded silently.

Grace turned and walked out of the room holding Emily's backpack by its hook, pinched in her fingers, like it was contaminated. She had to pass Jack, who was still standing just inside the door, and when she did, she looked up at him for longer than a glance, as if waiting to catch his eye and communicate something without speaking.

But he didn't look at her at all.

Then Grace left and closed the door behind her, and they were alone.

Jack crossed the room to sit on the couch with his hands buried together between his knees. It seemed that no matter what position he was in, he hid his injuries.

Emily pulled out the chair beneath the desk. 'OK,' she began. 'So—'

'I didn't kill Kate,' Jack said. 'Can we start there?'

7

Emily kept her expression neutral. She didn't want to look sceptical, didn't want Jack to think that she thought he was guilty. She didn't want to appear shocked either, in case he *was* guilty and had said that to get a reaction out of her. She shouldn't give him the satisfaction. Or was neutrality the wrong call? It could seem cold, as if she didn't care about what had happened to him, but was only here to do a job. Which she was. But if he felt that, that job would probably become a lot harder to do. Then she began to worry that several seconds had passed and she still hadn't responded, and that that was worse, so she said, 'You and I can start wherever you want, but I probably wouldn't start the book there.'

He looked surprised. 'No?'

She was surprised too, at her newfound, confident insight into the structure of true-crime memoirs. (If that was even what this was? She couldn't think of a better label, even though that one was far from a perfect fit.) But wasn't it just common sense? No one would be parting with their hard-earned cash to read seventy thousand words that proved Jack Smyth *didn't* kill his wife, actually.

Readers would go through this book forensically, hoping to find a killer's confession between the lines. She knew this because that's what she'd do, were she one of them. Put a declaration of innocence in the very first paragraph and they wouldn't even bother taking the book out of the shop.

'I think what's important,' she said, 'is to get the reader on your side from page one.'

Jack scoffed. 'Good luck with that.'

'No one can be certain of your guilt except you.' His face fell slack in shock and Emily was reminded that she didn't know what she was doing and should tread carefully. 'There's no member of the public who can say, "I know he did it."' OK, even *more* carefully. 'What I'm saying is,' she pushed on, 'everyone has to admit to themselves that, despite what they may believe, they don't *know*. So we have to get in there, at the start, and widen that crack. Say, yeah, OK, but what if he *didn't* do this? What if an innocent man has lost his wife in tragic circumstances and then, compounding his pain, people think he was responsible? How would you feel if this happened to you?'

'I'm not following,' Jack said evenly.

Emily didn't blame him. She took a deep breath, tried again.

'What I'm suggesting is that we start with your lowest ebb,' she said. 'A moment when you'd been brought to your knees, when you truly thought you couldn't take one more thing, and then something even worse happened. When you were asking yourself, when will this nightmare end? Why is this happening to me? How did I even get here? Then we go back to the beginning and answer that question. Because starting with "I

82

didn't kill my wife" will just make people think, *Well, that's exactly what someone who'd killed his wife would say.*'

Jack was silent for what felt like a long time, and Emily worried that she'd completely fucked this up before she'd even got a chance to hit RECORD.

What if she *did* fuck it up? What if he fired her? She'd be back to square one.

No, she'd be worse off than that, because she'd have had a second chance and totally squandered it.

And she'd have to get that money from somewhere.

Just thinking about it made the coffee she'd drunk earlier slosh around her otherwise empty stomach.

'OK,' he said then. 'But how do we actually *do* this?'

'Well,' she said, trying to hide her relief, 'we only have a few days here. Afterwards, when we're both back home, we can hop on a call if we need to clarify something or add something in. It's not like we'll never speak again. But this is probably the only time we have to sit in a room together and talk uninterrupted. So I just want you to tell me your story. I might interrupt to ask a question or because I want you to go a little deeper into some specific thing, but I'm primarily here to listen and record, and to make sure we get everything we need. When I get back home, I'll type up what you said, editing as I go—'

'Editing?' Jack said in alarm.

'Polishing,' she corrected. 'Moving things around. Adding some connective tissue, for context. So it reads like a book. But don't worry, because the next step will be you reading it to check that you're happy. Nothing will go to print without your approval. Remember, this is *your* book.'

But Jack still looked worried.

'So why a book?' Emily opened the laptop, booted it up. 'Why not a print interview or a podcast or whatever?'

The question was mostly to distract him from the idea that she'd twist his words, and to give her a chance to get her bearings before she blurted out another phrase like *someone who'd killed his wife*.

'A podcast?' Jack made a face. 'No bloody way. And I've had enough of print interviews. They record exactly what you say, then they go back to the office and write something that twists it all around, and the headline will be by far the most stupid thing you said that has nothing to do with anything *else* you said, taken completely out of context – and that's all most people bother to read these days. Television gets edited too. Even if it's live, you're still at the mercy of the interviewer, and they don't care about you. They just want clicks and views. No. All that stuff, it's about someone else using me to get what *they* want, what *they* need. And I know there's an element of that here. I know Morningstar aren't publishing this book as a public service. But at least this way, I get what *I* want too.'

'And what is it you want?'

'To tell my side of the story. To have my voice heard in all this. For people to know I had nothing to do with Kate's death.' He paused. 'There's a guy I used to ride with, Anthony Baume – do you know him?'

Emily shook her head. 'Now might be the time to confess that I know nothing about professional cycling. The Tour de France is a thing, the winner wears a yellow jersey and Lance Armstrong cheated. That's the extent of my knowledge.'

'The *leader* wears a yellow jersey.'

'See?'

'Well, I don't think you have to worry. They told me to keep cycling out of this book as much as possible and that's fine by me.' He paused. 'I don't like talking about it.'

Emily knew that by *they* he meant Beth and Carolyn, because they'd said pretty much the same thing to her.

'So – your teammate?' she prompted.

'Ant,' he said. 'Yeah. He had a bad accident. Was in a lot of pain. Liked the pills they gave him for it a bit too much. One thing led to another . . . He ended up writing a book about it, about the addiction and the recovery, and then his comeback. It was amazing. I mean, I'm not a big reader, but I felt like I was listening to him. I could hear his voice. I met him later at some charity thing, and I was gushing about it, and that's when he tells me he didn't write a single word. He used a ghostwriter.'

'Was he happy with the result?'

'Completely, yeah,' Jack said, nodding. 'He'd tell the ghost-writer about, say, going to rehab, and then the guy would go away and write it up, jazz it up – Ant isn't exactly a word-smith, watch any of his post-race interviews and you'll see what I mean – and then Ant would read it and give it a go/no-go. There wasn't a single line in that book that wasn't exactly what he'd wanted to say, and there was enough space for him to say everything.'

'So when *you* had something to say . . .'

'I thought, *book*. Well, I thought *ghostwriter*.' He paused. '*The Witness*, right? That was your book?'

'Yeah,' Emily said after a beat.

'What's it about?'

'Well, ah . . .' She shifted in her seat. 'It's about a twelve-year-old girl. Roxie. And how she . . . It's, like, a coming-of-age sort of thing.'

Jack frowned. 'I thought Beth said you'd written a crime novel.'

Emily wondered what else Beth had said during a conversation clearly designed to convince Jack that the only writer they'd managed to get wasn't the worst possible choice.

'There *is* a subplot about two local teenage girls who've gone missing,' she said. 'Roxie's following all the news reports obsessively, oblivious to the fact that her father might be the culprit. The reader realizes it could be him halfway through, but she stays oblivious. So I don't know if I'd call it a *crime novel*, but there is a crime in it, I suppose.'

'How does it end?'

'With a flash-forward,' Emily said. 'Roxie's in her twenties, standing outside a Garda station, trying to decide whether or not to go in.'

'To tell them about her father?'

'Maybe,' she said. 'Maybe not. It ends there.'

'But *you* must know. It's your story.'

'And as far as I'm concerned, it stopped when I stopped typing it. There's nothing *to* know.'

'Is he guilty?'

'That's for the reader to decide.'

Her stock phrase, deployed for the first time in a long time.

Jack nodded slowly, gazing at something in the middle distance, and she wondered if he was thinking about the eventual readers of *this* book and what they might conclude from his story. He'd stopped hiding his hands at some point, and her gaze dropped now to the red, angry scars, the gloves of melted skin.

She looked back up at his face and saw that he had noticed.

'Does it hurt?'

'Not right now,' he said. 'But my doctors tell me I have more surgeries in my future. It's OK, though. I'm used to pain. Cycling is suffering, after all.'

'What do you mean by that?' She picked up the voice-recorder. 'Mind if I . . . ?'

'We're starting now?'

'If that's OK?'

He nodded.

She pressed the RECORD button, set the device on the desk and turned it until the microphone was pointing at Jack.

He stared at it, unblinking, like it was a grenade she'd just pulled the pin out of.

'Cycling is suffering,' she prompted.

He cleared his throat. 'Ah, yeah. So . . . If you're good at road-racing, what you're really good at is pushing through pain. There's this guy, Tyler Hamilton. Used to race for US Postal. Famously tough. He once broke his shoulder during the Giro, but kept going. Finished second with a cracked shoulder blade. Afterwards he had to have, like, a dozen teeth replaced. He'd ground them down to stumps during the race.'

Emily winced.

'A few weeks later, he shows up to the Tour with a twisted spine and a broken collarbone, and *wins a stage*. One of the other team directors wouldn't even believe it. Accused him of a PR stunt. They had to show him the X-rays. That's the level of suffering we're talking about.'

'That sounds horrific.'

'I'm not saying you ride out with broken bones every time, but on a tough climb, those stretches when you're up in the mountains day after day – it can feel as bad as that. And I could take it. Always. In a weird way, I kind of *liked* it.'

'Why?'

'If you break your leg,' Jack said, 'all you can think about is how much your leg hurts, right? But if every single part of you is in pain, you can't think about anything. Your mind is blank. You're just a body, pushing on the pedals, going as fast as you can. The outside is on fire, but you're inside, totally safe.' He looked her right in the eye. 'Does that make sense?'

Emily opened her mouth to respond, but didn't quite know what to say.

Jack's face changed as realization dawned.

'Sorry,' he said, swallowing hard. 'Bad choice of words. Hey – don't put that bit in, OK?'

Four days before the fire

In the dark, Jack wakes her to kiss her goodbye.

He's driving to Dublin this morning to meet with some potential investors, three guys over from Monaco for a day and night. They have a bigger sports brand and might buy Exis out. There's going to be a formal presentation, followed by the requisite wining and dining. He won't be back until tomorrow lunchtime at the earliest.

'You could come with me,' he whispers, his breath on her bare shoulder. 'Come out with us, tonight. They'd love you.'

She knows this is an apology for yesterday and for last night. The incident with the photographer had soured his mood, but the phone call from the features editor a couple of hours after that was what had really done the damage. They needed art, she'd told him, and Miles hadn't been able to get anything useful. They were going to have to drop him from the line-up. She'd made vague promises about doing something in-depth about Exis in a couple of months' time to make up for it while Kate, watching Jack listen to this, said a silent prayer that the call would end before his well of politeness did. After that, he'd barely spoken two words for the rest of the evening.

She rolls over now, into him, nuzzles her face against his chest – her acceptance of his apology, her silent acknowledgement that he was justified in his upset, her assuring him that she knows it wasn't personally directed at her.

'I can't,' she says. 'I have plans. Big ones. I'm going to light a fire, lie on the couch and read a book.'

'Exciting times.'

'It will be, for me.'

'I'm jealous of your sleeping abilities,' he says, sighing.

She tenses. 'What do you mean?'

'I was tossing and turning all night, but you slept like the dead. Not as much as a stir.'

'Were you?'

'You know, when I get back, everything might be different.'

She lifts her head to meet his eye. 'It *will* be.'

'Yeah,' he says. 'It will be.'

Kate wishes him luck. He gets out of bed and she drifts back into a lighter sleep that's occasionally infiltrated by the sounds of her husband leaving the house. The squeak of the shower knob being turned to OFF. Clattering crockery in the kitchen. His footsteps crunching on gravel as he walks to his car. When she wakes again, it's an hour later and the bedroom is lit by a weak winter sun, because – she sees now – Jack opened the curtains before he left.

She groans and throws an arm across her face, to block out the light.

He probably did it automatically, without a conscious thought. He may not compete anymore, but some of the neural pathways years of training built in his brain are too strong to

90

break. One lingering side-effect is that he is physically incapable of sleeping in. Once he wakes, he has to get out of bed. Early in their relationship, Kate took this personally, hurt by all the mornings she woke up alone. During the *Sunrise* years, it had made them a perfect match; she had a 4:00a.m. alarm during the week which would feel like torture if she risked any later than 7:00a.m. over the weekend. These days, she wishes he'd take things a little easier.

But she probably *should* get up.

She checks her phone, but there's nothing new.

Downstairs, she discovers that Jack forgot to turn off the TV too. It's on mute and tuned to *Sunrise*.

She's pointing the remote at it with her finger on the power button when she's met with her own face, twice as big as it is in reality, creased by hysterical laughing.

She turns on the sound and soon establishes that Peter, the weather guy, is leaving, and this is a clip package they've put together to send him off. She never got a goodbye – the downside of deciding to leave during the summer break.

No one knew her last show was her last show, including her.

Kate switches it off, replacing the glossy Technicolor of the *Sunrise* set with the reflection of their clinical kitchen in the black mirror of the TV screen.

The day stretches ahead of her, long and quiet and shapeless and empty.

When they decided to leave Dublin, she couldn't wait to get away from the sirens and the crowds and the *go, go, go*. She didn't consider what she'd be leaving behind, which was everyone who filled her days: her colleagues, her friends, her family. Now, whenever Jack isn't at home – which is a lot, especially since Exis started floundering – she feels at a loose end.

91

Sometimes she wonders how she got here.

But blue skies and freezing is her favourite weather. Perfect for getting outdoors, especially as it's too cold for most people. She should go for walk on White Point Strand, she thinks. She decides she will.

She dresses in layers, digs out a hat and gloves, and makes herself a flask of coffee. Then she locks up the house and drives an hour west, to the coast.

Jack calls her en route.

'Where are you now?' she asks him.

'Almost on the M50.'

'Already? That was quick.'

'Well, I did leave two hours ago. Where are you?'

'On my way to White Point Strand.'

'For what?'

'To go for a walk.'

'Are you mad? It's like one degree.'

'I like this weather.'

For a beat, the only sound is the rush of each car echoing in the other one.

'One of the guys had to cancel,' Jack says then. 'There's only two coming now.'

He sounds defeated already and her stomach sinks.

'Maybe it's a good thing,' she suggests. 'You can focus now more on the other two.'

'I have to go,' he says abruptly. 'I'll call you later, OK?'

'OK,' she says. 'Love you.'

But a *click* from the speaker comes too soon for him to have heard that.

She makes a mental note to take the champagne out of the

fridge before he comes home, just in case. It's not there because she thinks he'll return with news worth celebrating, but he doesn't know that, and if he *doesn't*, it'll just remind him that he's failed and that he's failed in front of her.

She knows, because it's happened before.

When Kate gets to White Point she finds it exactly as she wanted it: deserted, almost, and sitting under the same blue sky. The wind is high, sending pulses of shifting sand skittering across the beach like snakes, and making her eyes water the moment she steps outside. There are only two other vehicles, a VW camper van and an SUV, and she's parked as far away from them as she can. She's reversed in, so she can sit in her open boot and drink her coffee with a view of the ocean.

She decides to have a cup before her walk as well as after.

While she's pouring still-steaming liquid into the lid of her flask, another car arrives, a Mini Cooper, and parks closer.

Kate sips her coffee and watches the crashing waves and hopes that Jack comes home tomorrow with some good news.

For both their sakes.

'Excuse me,' a voice says. 'Did you drop this?'

Kate only glances at the woman a few feet to her right, collecting a vague impression of short blonde hair and a red puffer-jacket. But she looks directly at her outstretched hand and the small, velvet purse it's holding. It's the colour of English mustard and has the name of a clothing brand printed on a label stitched to its front, the kind of thing you might use to protect jewellery. The way it's bulging suggests that it's been repurposed as a purse.

'No, sorry,' Kate says. 'Not mine.'

She smiles briefly and turns back to the view.

'It's Kate, isn't it? Kate Smyth?'

There's a tiny dot in the water not far from the shore, which if Kate had better eyesight could be a surfer, and a man walking behind his dog on the sand. She can't see any other people. That's how deserted this place is, this morning, in this weather. And yet she's had the bad luck to meet someone who not only recognizes her, but wants to let her know that they have.

Forced now into raising her gaze, Kate finds a woman her own age looking down at her.

'Yes,' she says, deploying a warmer smile. 'Nice to meet you.'

'We've met before, actually.'

Kate searches the other woman's face, waiting for some ping of recognition, but nothing comes.

'I'm so sorry, but I don't . . . ?'

'Jean,' she says, pressing the hand that isn't holding the purse to her own chest. 'Jean Whelan. I worked for Sync. When Jack was there.'

'Oh, no way?'

But as Kate expresses this pleasant surprise, her brain is calculating the odds of there being just the surfer, the dog-walker and a woman who used for work for Jack's former cycling team on this beach this morning.

A team he spent one season with, four years ago.

And this woman has just got out of a car that arrived soon after Kate did.

'You and I only met once or twice,' Jean is saying now, 'and I looked very different then, so . . .'

'Do you live around here?'

'No.' Jean meets Kate's eye, holds her gaze steady. 'I was a

94

soigneur. And the only other Irish team member, after Jack and Ben.'

Ben.

Kate hates hearing his name, but Jean saying it is confirmation that whatever this is, it isn't a coincidence.

She looks again at the little purse in Jean's hand and wonders what would happen if she said, 'Actually, you know something? That *is* mine,' and held out her hand for it, because she's starting to think that she'd find this woman's own cards and cash inside.

'How is Jack these days?' Jean asks.

'I'm so sorry.' Kate stands up, steps aside and reaches up to close the lid of the boot. 'I have to be going.'

'Kate, wait.'

She looks down in surprise at the hand gripping her arm, then back up at Jean's face.

'I need your help,' Jean says. 'Please.'

'I don't know what you mean.' Kate yanks her arm free and starts around the side of the car, heading for the driver's door. 'I don't know anything.'

Jean follows her, right behind.

'You wouldn't say that if it was true,' she says. 'You wouldn't know there was anything *to* know.'

Kate opens the door, gets inside, reaches to pull the door closed – but Jean is holding it open.

They both freeze in motion and hold their positions for a beat, each woman looking pleading into the eyes of the other, but desperately wanting different things.

'I don't know anything,' Kate repeats. 'I can't help you. I'm sorry.'

'He still sends me messages, you know. He doesn't sign them but I know they're from him.'

Kate freezes.

'*How* do you know, then?' she asks. 'How do you know it's him?'

'Because of what else I know,' Jean says. 'He knows I have enough to destroy him. The messages are threats.'

8

At a quarter to twelve, there was a sharp rap of knuckles on the door and then, abruptly, Grace was in the room with them. The suddenness of her entrance and the way her eyes were now darting around gave her the air of a school-teacher who'd smelled cigarette smoke in the hall and then kicked open a cubicle, confident she'd catch a student red-handed.

But it was just a ghostwriter and her subject, surprised by the interruption and looking to her for an explanation.

'Lunch,' she said. 'It arrived early.'

Jack excused himself to make a call. Grace mumbled something about emails and didn't immediately follow Emily downstairs. It seemed obvious that she was hanging back so she could speak to Jack alone, probably to get a report out of him as to how the morning had gone that she could send back to London.

Emily wondered if he'd ask Grace about what he'd almost certainly overheard just before he'd entered the room, and what she'd tell him in response. She really needed to find out what he'd been told, so she could stick to the same story.

But that aside, after a somewhat shaky start, she was feeling cautiously optimistic.

Jack had spent the last hour talking about cycling: how he'd got into it, why he'd got into it, what being into it was like. Most of it wouldn't make it into the book – readers would just skip ahead, scanning for Kate's name – but she thought the pain and suffering stuff might prove useful, and it gave Jack an opportunity to warm up on neutral territory. After lunch, she planned on broaching the subject of his and Kate's first meeting. She wondered if he'd get emotional about it.

But then, what was the 'right' response?

If he was stoic about his dead wife, people would say he didn't care that she was dead. If he sobbed uncontrollably, the widower doth protest too much. If he started one way and ended up another, people could accuse him of being a psychopath who was able to turn his feelings on and off like a tap.

He couldn't win.

It didn't really matter to the book – it was Jack's story, written in the first person – but on a personal level, Emily was curious to see how he'd react. So far, she was finding it almost impossible to imagine him doing what he was accused of. Already, for increasingly long stretches, she found herself forgetting to try.

There were two plastic trays on the kitchen table, jammed with enough pinwheel-sandwiches to feed a family of ten, plus a large salad bowl, bags of crisps and pretzels, and a handwritten note saying cold drinks were in the fridge. It seemed to Emily like this spread could've survived until they were actually due to break for lunch in fifteen minutes' time, but she wasn't complaining. She was famished.

She piled a plate high, grabbed a bottle of water and took her lunch outside, to the courtyard.

It was a beautiful day. Clear blue skies, bright sunshine, hot but not unpleasantly so in the shade. The courtyard blazed with colour and life, the gemstone pool shimmering at its centre. The noise of engines and shouts was still coming from the building site but, mercifully, the drilling, hammering and boom of talk-radio had stopped.

She chose a seat close to the edge of the pool, and started on a sandwich. She wanted her phone and wondered where Grace had put her bag.

And then she wondered where Grace was.

And, come to think of it, Jack.

Were they going to join her? Had they opted to stay in the kitchen? Did they think her rude for staying outside?

Emily strained to listen for voices coming from inside the house, but couldn't hear any.

She had several large windows in front of her and to the left, but the angle of the sun had rendered them dark mirrors. They all presumably offered a clear view of her from inside the house, but all she could see in them was a woman sitting on a chair in a courtyard, balancing a plate on her knees, wondering where everyone else was.

And now, getting the distinct feeling that she was being watched.

Emily's skin prickled.

She told herself to cop on, but the sensation refused to go away. So she did what any normal, confident, stable, thirty-something woman would do. For the benefit of any would-be audience, she animated her face to suggest she'd suddenly remembered something she'd forgotten, in the style of a bad soap-opera actor. Then she stood and hurriedly carried her lunch across the courtyard, under the pergola and up the steps to Bookmark.

Realization was just dawning that her key was in her bag and that her bag was God knows where Grace had put it when she reached the deck and saw that there was a key already sitting in the lock. She assumed that maybe a house-keeper was inside – hadn't Jack mentioned a property manager? – but when she opened the door, she immediately spotted her backpack sitting on the couch and then her phone on the breakfast bar.

She stuck her hand into the backpack's side pocket to feel for her key, but it wasn't there. Which meant that not only had Grace let herself in, she'd dug around in Emily's bag in order to do it.

Was this a rude violation or a thoughtful favour? Emily genuinely couldn't decide. But she supposed it was too hot to leave a bag containing a laptop and a phone sitting outside for two hours in direct sunlight, and if Grace had left the bag any-where else, she'd have to go looking for it now.

She took another bite of chicken-salad sandwich and unlocked her phone – and stopped chewing when she saw that she had a new email. *It's probably nothing*, she told herself as she moved to tap the icon.

Sitting at the top of her inbox was another message from 'Emily Joyce'.

At the sight of it, the food in her mouth instantly adopted the texture of soggy paper.

Emily didn't have time to try to convince herself that it was the same message again, that this was merely spam on a repeat offence, that the only problem here was that her email app's automated filters weren't as good as they could be. She could already see this one's threat, shouting at her from the preview pane.

I KNOW WHAT YOU DID.

She sucked in a breath, pulling a piece of half-chewed something back into her throat, sending her into a fit of coughing and spluttering.

As she recovered, she stared at the words, blurred now by her watery eyes.

Then she called Alice and told her about it.

'*I know what you did*,' Alice echoed.

'And *I know who you are*, before that.'

Silence.

'Do you think—?' Emily started.

'No,' Alice said firmly. 'Not at all.'

Her confidence made Emily feel better, until she began to wonder if Alice was just trying to *sound* confident so she would.

'You know, when I got that first email from Beth, the editor at Morningstar, I thought maybe they'd found out.'

'But they didn't,' Alice said.

'Did *you*?'

'What?'

'Think that that might be a possibility? When I told you they wanted to meet with me? Just because . . .' Emily bit her lip. 'We haven't talked about it at all. Even after I found out what this was about.'

A rush of air on the line as Alice sighed deeply.

'What's there to talk about?'

'I don't know,' Emily said. 'Didn't it cross your mind that there are, you know, *parallels*?'

'No.'

'Not at all?'

'What I thought,' Alice said, 'and still think, is that this was a solution to a problem that you really needed to solve. Your involvement is anonymous and all you have to do is write down what he says. So *this* is nothing like *that*. And the reason I didn't bring it up is because I know what you're like and I didn't even want to put the thought in your head.'

'Well, it's in there anyway.'

'Well, get it out.'

'You know, Mark said something weird to me before I left. He asked me why it was so easy to write *The Witness* and then impossible to write another book. And he was all, "If you take this job, it could be very exposing." That was the word he used. *Exposing*.'

'I think you're reading way too much into that. And that those emails are just uninspired spam.'

'But what if—?'

'Emily, darling, this is going to sound harsh, but I say it with love, to reassure you: you're not that important.'

Alice's delivery made her snort. 'Gee, thanks.'

'What I mean is, no one is sitting at home obsessing over how they can mess with your head via an anonymous Hotmail address and a blatant disregard for the lower case. It's just spam. You know I'm right.'

'Yeah,' Emily said. 'Probably.'

But she wasn't sure Alice was, on this occasion.

'*Anyway* . . . How's it going? Tell me all.'

'It's going OK and there's not that much to tell yet.'

'Does he seem—' But Alice stopped, interrupted by someone in the background saying something Emily couldn't make out. 'Shit, sorry. I have to go. My root canal is here. Talk later?'

'My later will be your already-asleep-in bed, but I'll leave a voice-note if anything exciting happens.'

'I want a full podcast this week. New episode every morning.'

'I'll do my best.'

'And don't worry.'

'I'll try not to.'

But she mustn't be trying very hard, because she could already feel dread swirling in her stomach.

After Alice ended the call, Emily read the email one more time before banishing it, like its predecessor, to Junk.

It's just spam.

She repeated it silently several times, like a mantra, as if it had the power to push her feelings of dread away.

When it didn't, she went on Amazon to look up Anthony Baume's memoir in a bid to distract herself.

The cover of *The Crash: Cycling to Hell and Back* featured an extreme close-up of Anthony's bruised and muddied face. The only physical editions available were second-hand, a sure sign it was out of print, but a digital one was still on sale. She tapped the Read a Sample button and navigated to the title page. It was only a hunch but . . .

The Crash: Cycling to Hell and Back

Anthony Baume

with Neil Wallace

Neil.

She allowed herself one moment of extreme smugness, then Googled him.

The top result was his website. On it, she found a bio that mentioned several ghostwriting projects, and a contact form.

She could contact him. But should she? What was it she wanted to say, exactly? *Hey, you don't know me and I think this message is in violation of a legal agreement we both signed, but (a) were you at some point Jack Smyth's ghost-writer and (b) if so, why aren't you anymore, because (c) I'm just curious in case an experienced ghostwriter would have a reason not to touch this gig with a bargepole.*

The phone began to ring in her hand – MARK.

'Oh,' he said, sounding surprised. 'I wasn't sure you'd be able to answer. What time is it there?'

'I'm on a break. Lunch.'

'Well? How's it going?'

'Fine, I think.'

'What's he like?'

'He's . . . You know, normal. Nice.'

'Aren't they all?'

'Who?'

'Husbands who kill their wives,' Mark said.

'We don't actually know he killed her.'

'There's no smoke without fire. Pardon the pun.'

That's not a pun, Emily said silently.

She walked to the window, one that looked out over the beach. The sun was overhead now, turning the surface of the Gulf into dancing tiles of light.

There was someone on the sand, she saw, directly in front of the house: a man, standing at the water's edge.

But with his back to it, facing her.

She thought it must be Jack, just as she registered that it couldn't be. This man seemed to be taller and thinner, and had what looked like much lighter hair.

He was motionless, as still as a statue.

Staring at her staring at him.

Emily felt a chill, an icy finger tracing a line down her back. She bolted backwards, ducking out of sight, but caught her foot on the edge of the rug and then banged her shin against the sharp corner of the coffee table.

She swore at the sudden, sharp bloom of pain.

'Em?' Mark said. 'You all right?'

'There's a—' But she stopped before she could say *strange man outside watching me.*

Because with the downslope of the dune and the breadth of the sand, you could probably fit two tennis courts between Bookmark's balcony railing and the shoreline. No one could possibly see into her windows from that distance; she could barely make out the man's features as it was.

And why would anyone be looking? Who even knew she was here?

It was just a guy walking on a beach who'd stopped to admire the architecture or something.

It's just spam.

'I'm fine,' she said, sitting down on the couch. She rubbed her throbbing leg. 'What were you saying?'

'I was asking if you're getting, you know, bad vibes or whatever.'

'He's not Hannibal Lecter, Mark.'

'Has he cried for you yet? If he turns on the waterworks, then he definitely did it.'

'You learned that from all that true crime you've been watching, did you?'

'*And* reading,' he said with a smile in his voice. 'It's all I've been doing since you left.'

They both knew Mark had never knowingly consumed anything that might be labelled *true crime* in his life.

'Anyway, the reason I'm ringing . . .' His tone was different now, gentle and serious. 'An envelope came for you this morning, by registered post. The return address is Roche and O'Reilly Associates on Mount Street. I looked them up, thinking they might be a literary agency or something, but they're, ah . . .'

'You *looked them up*?'

'Just out of interest,' he said quickly, dismissively. 'But Em, they're a firm of solicitors. And it's a really thick envelope. That I had to sign for.'

She closed her eyes, feeling the swirl of dread in her stomach turn into a wave of it gathering offshore, barrelling towards her, about to crest and break and wash her and everything she had clean away.

The timing of this couldn't be a coincidence.

'Will I open it?' Mark asked.

'No,' she said, too quickly, too loud. She'd practically shouted it. She took a deep breath and said in a more normal voice, 'No, it's fine. I'll deal with whatever it is when I get home. Put it away somewhere safe, OK?'

'Are you sure?'

'Yeah.'

A beat of silence.

'Do you know what it is?'

'No.' She truly didn't – and that was the problem. She

couldn't risk Mark seeing something that he shouldn't. *Couldn't.* 'Listen, sorry, but I've got to go. My break is over.'

'But what—'

'Talk tomorrow, OK?'

Emily ended the call before he could say anything else and threw the phone into the couch cushions.

She gave the remains of her lunch a dirty look. She'd lost her appetite.

When she went to the window, the beach was empty.

Her would-be watcher was gone.

9

Emily crossed the courtyard, stopped in the kitchen and walked up the back stairs, all without seeing another person. She found the makeshift interview room empty. Around her, the house was still and quiet, its air dead.

There wasn't much to do while she waited for someone to appear. She'd left her phone behind this time, as instructed, and the laptop wasn't connected to any network. She didn't want to sit in silence, because that only invited thoughts of emails and thick envelopes sent by solicitors, and what they all might mean. She briefly considered a search for the other connecting door, but didn't want to get risk getting caught snooping around the house on day one. She went to the window overlooking the beach and scanned for more mysterious figures, but there was nobody out there. She crossed the room to the window facing into the courtyard just in time to see Jack and Grace emerging from the archway.

They were arguing.

She couldn't hear them – Beach Read's glass was thick

enough to block out the noise of the building site across the street *and* voices from immediately below – but even on mute, the tension was obvious. Grace had her arms folded and Jack was walking a little ahead, both of their faces set tight with annoyance, trading snipes with one another. Emily stepped back, into the folds of the curtain, so she could watch without being seen.

The dynamic was puzzling.

This was, after all, Grace at work, for the publisher of Jack's book – a major acquisition for Morningstar, maybe their most important one in recent memory. But this behaviour was hardly professional and, worse, it suggested a disquieting familiarity. Grace had only arrived yesterday too. She hadn't had the time to get to know Jack well enough to justify talking to him like this.

Emily was also seeing a new side of her – up until now – pleasant, friendly, easy-going subject.

As she watched, Grace stopped and grabbed Jack by his upper arm, stopping him too. He swung around to face her, his back to Emily now, and put his hands on his hips. The stance seemed to telegraph some kind of demand, a *what's the problem?* or a *what do you expect me to do?* Grace spoke quickly, jabbing a finger in the air. Jack's shoulders rose and fell with what looked like a sigh of exasperation.

Then Grace pointed up at Bookmark and Jack shook his head and, with a sinking feeling, Emily realized they were talking about her.

That morning's interview must have gone so badly, Morningstar were firing her but Jack was objecting. Or Jack wanted to fire her and Grace was having to tell him that he couldn't. Or the two of them had been watching her in the courtyard, waiting, until they could convene in the garage to privately discuss their shared dissatisfaction and plot how to deliver the bad news. Or they were talking about something else, a secret they were actively keeping from her, and although it was strange and juvenile and more than a little ridiculous given the circumstances, that possibility inflicted the sting of being left out.

Jack walked off, disappearing from sight, and Grace followed. A moment later, Emily heard a door open downstairs. She flung herself quickly into the chair behind the desk. Footsteps on a hardwood floor. She tapped the laptop to life and tried to settle into the position of someone who'd been sitting there for longer. A creak on the stairs. The laptop screen was showing a virtually empty desktop, but she stared at it with her brow furrowed in concentration. Jack entered the room. She waited a beat, then looked up at him in pretend surprise and saw an apology on his face.

'Sorry,' he said. 'Went for a walk to stretch my legs and lost track of time. You weren't waiting too long, were you?'

'No, no,' Emily said quickly. 'It's fine.'

'Have you had a chance to go explore yet?' He walked past her to retake his seat on the couch.

'I didn't think there was that much to see?'

'It's really weird,' he said, 'but they've already built the town square. They started with it. Nothing's open yet, but it's all there, ready to go. And then there's the art. Sculptures and stuff, dotted all around the place.'

Emily typed some gobbledegook and asked as casually as she could, 'Did Grace go with you? I didn't see her around during lunch.'

110

'No, I needed some time to think.' He paused. 'About what you said.'

'What did I say?'

'My lowest ebb. I think I know what it was.' He nodded at the voice-recorder. 'Do you want to . . . ?'

'Oh. Yeah. Sure.' If she was getting fired, it wasn't happening just yet. She dutifully pressed the RECORD button and checked for the red light. 'Ready when you are.'

'Well,' Jack started, 'this isn't the first bad thing to happen to me – as I'm sure you know. As everyone knows because the Irish media bloody loves a sob story. The biggest mistake I ever made was after I won my first national championship. Some guy comes up to me and sticks his phone in my face and starts asking how I'm feeling, are my parents proud, that kind of thing, and I said, "My dad passed away in a car accident when I was thirteen, so . . ."'

The biggest mistake I ever made, Emily noted.

'And the guy is all apologies,' Jack continued, 'but the very next day, in one of the tabloids, the sports section has a full page about my win being a "triumph after tragedy". From then on, every *single* interview, I'm being asked about the accident and how it affected me and what I thought my dad would be saying about my success if he was still around.'

Emily only knew what Jack's Wikipedia page had to say about what had happened, which was that his father had had a fatal heart attack while driving and crashed their car into a tree. Jack was with him, but emerged relatively unscathed – except, presumably, for the trauma of seeing his father's broken and bloody body in the seat next to him.

'And then,' Jack said, 'just before Rio, one of my best friends

111

died by suicide. Charlie. I'd known him since we'd both been racing as Juniors. His career wasn't going the way he hoped and I guess . . . Well, we don't really know. But it was a shock. I was on autopilot for those Games, just trying to get through it. And I did, but it all sort of built up inside. It had nowhere to go because I wasn't thinking about it, let alone processing anything. I was like a pressure cooker by the time I got back home. So I blew up.'

'What did that look like?'

Emily had asked because she thought he might be talking about a violent episode, but Jack said, 'I suppose you'd call it a nervous breakdown. I crawled into bed and I didn't really get out for, like, six weeks.'

'Have you ever talked about that publicly?'

She didn't think she'd come across that detail before.

Jack shook his head. 'And I don't know if I want to. I'm pretty sure Charlie's family wouldn't want it included and there's no way I'd even risk upsetting them, so . . . Yeah. And then, there was the crash.'

When it didn't seem like he was going to elaborate, Emily said, 'Can you tell me a bit about that? I don't really know the details.'

He shrugged. 'It was the 2019 Tour. My first. I'm on track for a top-ten, maybe even a top-five finish. In my first Tour, which is incredible. I'm feeling good, but the heat has been the problem. Two stages earlier, it was forty degrees. Now, we're coming down the Col de l'Iseran and along comes a freak hailstorm. These things are so huge, it looks like snow on the ground and it feels like ice. In July. There's talk on the radio of landslides further down.' He was saying all this in a flat monotone, as if it were something he was painfully bored of having

112

to recite. 'They decide to neutralize the stage and direct us to take shelter in a tunnel. The team cars will pick us up there. But before I can get to it, I lose it in a corner, go flying off the bike and tumble down the side of a mountain.'

'Jesus,' Emily breathed. 'What happened?'

'Don't know. I don't remember it. Lost grip on the ice, I suppose. My teammate went down too, but at least he managed to stay on the road. He ended up with only scrapes and bruises.'

'What happened to you?'

'Two fractures in my thigh bone, broken right wrist, fractured eye-socket, collarbone, hip.' Jack pointed to each location as he named them. 'And lots of bruises and scrapes, and a concussion. I was completely knocked out.' He paused. 'I still think I could've made a full recovery if it wasn't for the hip. That's what did me in, in the end. There's only so much physio can do. I could've taken the pain, but I just didn't have the strength anymore, after that. So, that was the end. Not just of my Tour, but my career.'

'That must have been devastating.'

'The team kept me around for a while, to trot me out for events and dinners. Sponsor things. I think my official title was' – Jack rolled his eyes at this – '*Team Ambassador*. I wasn't happy about it, but I was trying to stay in the good books, to keep the door open. I was still thinking I had a chance to come back. It was at one of those events that I met Kate.'

'When was this?'

'November 2019. She wasn't on TV back then. Not yet. She was still doing MC-ing, corporate events, in-house marketing . . . That night she was working for Sabin, one of the sponsors.'

'How do you spell that?'

'S-A-B-I-N.'

He'd pronounced it *sabah*, as if it were French.

'What do they do?'

'I've no idea,' Jack said. 'One of those companies that has ads with, like, children running through a field and then a time-lapse of a green shoot coming up out of the ground and then the Earth from space. They could be doing anything, but whatever it is, it's probably ruining the planet.'

'I can look them up. What did Kate do for them?'

'Different things, bits and pieces – but that night she had a crew with her and they were filming something for a shareholders' presentation, I think.'

'Where was this?'

'In Èze,' Jack said. 'It's this crazy rabbit-warren of a town perched on the very top of a hill just outside Nice. Incredible views. But it was absolutely freezing.'

'Do you remember seeing Kate for the first time?'

Jack nodded. 'She was sticking a microphone in my face, asking me how it felt to be part of the Sync-AIC family' – another eye-roll – 'and I wasn't in the mood, and she told me to stop being a grumpy prick and do my job so she could do hers.'

Emily raised her eyebrows in surprise. 'And that's when you thought, *I'm going to marry that woman*?'

'Not at that exact moment, no,' he said with a weak grin. 'But I was definitely intrigued. I mean, at the time, everyone else was treating me like I had a terminal illness. She was having absolutely none of my moping. I saw her a couple more times, at other events, and we'd always end up sort of drifting towards each other, but I didn't want to mortify myself. And I heard she might have a boyfriend. Another rider, actually. Eventually, though, I worked up the courage – or drank enough beers – to ask her out for a drink, and she said no. But she did agree to meet me for a walk on the Prom. Her suggestion.'

'What's the Prom?' Emily asked.

'The Promenade des Anglais, in Nice. The walk along the seafront.'

'Were you living there?'

'I was,' Jack said. 'Kate was living in Newbridge, but she'd tacked a few personal days onto her work trip.'

'So how did that go, the walk?'

'Terrible,' Jack said, 'because it was more of a hobble. You see, the better your body is at cycling, the worse it is at everything else. You're optimized for the bike but you can barely walk a mile. You have weak arms, bad posture, your spine is constantly complaining . . . Not to mention the highly attractive tan lines. And I was all that plus recovering from injury. I was like some hundred-year-old man shuffling along next to my very attractive nurse. I managed for about twenty minutes and then I suggested we get a coffee instead. We went to one of the beach restaurants and we ended up staying there the whole day. Lunch, more coffee, drinks, dinner. Talking about everything and anything, until the sun set. We had to pay the bill at intervals, because our waiters kept finishing their shift. And that was . . .' His voice trailed off as his face fell, a curtain of devastation falling over the happy memory. 'That was it.'

Emily let a beat pass.

'What happened to the other guy?' she asked then. 'The boyfriend?'

'He was dispatched pretty quick,' Jack said. 'And boyfriend was probably a strong word. Are you married?'

'Me? No. *God,* no.'

'Why do you say it like that?'

'Just because, you know, major life events are for grown-ups. I'm not one of them yet. Neither is Mark.'

'What does he do?' Jack asked.

'He's a writer too.'

'Really?'

'Not books but poetry, short stories, essays . . . That kind of thing.'

'What's that like?'

'The poetry?'

'You both being writers.'

'It's fine.'

Jack looked at her, waiting for more.

'We're supposed to be talking about you,' she said, straightening up.

'Right. Yeah . . . Well, my point is, if I hadn't had the accident that ended my cycling career, I wouldn't have met Kate. So, OK, all these bad things happened. But I also got to realize my dream of cycling professionally. I was a national champion, I won an Olympic medal and I got to ride in the Tour de France. I built a successful business. I met Kate. I got to do incredible things and have amazing experiences and see the world and have, on balance, a wonderful life. I've had tragedy and terrible luck and pain and grief, but I've also had incredible fortune.'

Emily's eyes flicked to the voice-recorder, checking for the reassurance of the blinking red light.

'I always thought,' Jack continued, 'that there's a kind of cosmic compensation. In my life, the highs have been incredibly high and the lows unbelievably low. But there's a *balance.*

116

I didn't consider myself any more unlucky than a guy sat behind a desk for forty years who never has anything bad happen to him – because he has to sit behind that desk.'

'Do you still believe that?'

Emily needed the answer to be no, because if there really was such a thing as cosmic balance, then what of the people who *did* the bad things? Wouldn't bad things have to happen to them, for balance? Wouldn't the universe punish them for what they'd done?

I know who you are. I know what you did.

Jack shook his head, once, firmly. 'I stopped believing it the night of the fire. I wasn't able to believe it after that. Because how could that be fair? On top of everything else? How much is a person supposed to be able to take? And then . . . Then, it got worse. Although *worse* doesn't even begin to describe . . . I don't have the word. I don't know if there is one. But there was a knock on the door and it was two Garda detectives and they were coming to tell me that they thought I'd *killed* my *wife*. And that – that was my lowest ebb.'

He wiped at his eyes, bit down hard on his bottom lip.

Jack was crying.

10

As the clock on the wall ticked towards three in the afternoon, 90 per cent of Emily's energy was going into not yawning in Jack's face and the remaining 10 was working to keep her eyes open. He seemed tired too, and more than happy to call it a day when she suggested it.

'It's exhausting,' he said. 'Talking about yourself this much.'

She refrained from pointing out that he had another four days of it to get through and all the bad stuff – the fire, Kate's death, him as a suspect in it – yet to come.

'I think tomorrow we should aim to finish at two,' she said. 'This was probably too long a day for you.'

'But was it OK? I mean, am I doing this right?'

Emily reassured him that it was and he was, although she had no frame of reference. But if that *wasn't* a good day in ghostwriting, what did one look like? Jack had been very forthcoming and they were getting on well. There were over four hours of recorded conversation in the bag and there was some interesting stuff in there.

She already had a few ideas about threading together the things he'd said about cosmic compensation and cycling being suffering, and using that as the opening of the book. A prologue, maybe, with Kate dying in the fire, or him thinking she had. The penultimate paragraph would be one short line: *Then there was a knock on the door.* That would be the Garda detectives telling him about what the autopsy had revealed, and the prologue's final line would be something like, *I wasn't just a widower anymore. I was a suspect.* Or was that too cheesy? Then, Chapter One: a brief history of Jack Smyth's cycling days. Very brief. By the end of it, he'd already be on his honeymoon with Kate. Chapter Two could then skip swiftly on to their relationship in the months leading up to the fire.

In fact, if Emily forgot about the threatening emails, the unopened solicitor's letter waiting for her at home and whatever Jack and Grace had been arguing about in the courtyard earlier, she'd have to say that things were going pretty well, actually.

After Jack left her alone in the room, she got up and stretched, and made herself a double espresso in the machine. But it was only a temporary fix. She stayed at the desk long enough to back up the audio recording to the laptop and write a few notes to herself regarding questions to ask tomorrow, but that was all she could manage. She feared that if she stayed any longer, Grace would find her drooling on the keyboard.

Emily shut down the computer, tidied everything together in a neat pile on the desk and went downstairs. She heard Jack – on the phone, it sounded like – in the kitchen, but there was no sign of the elusive Grace. Maybe she'd gone to get groceries. If she had, that was a bit annoying, because she hadn't given Emily a chance to give her a list yet, or even to make one in the first place.

Entering Bookmark, she refused to even look in the direction of the couch because she knew what would happen: it would pull her into its cushions like a tractor beam and she'd fall into them and then asleep. She'd be awake all night and end up feeling even worse tomorrow than she did today. It was imperative that she keep herself awake.

The only thing for it was a walk around the town.

When Emily stepped out onto the street, it occurred to her that she'd been within Beach Read's walls for almost twenty-four hours, ever since Tony had dropped her off in the exact same spot. It was nice to get out of the house. The construction crews had finished for the day; the only movement in the building site opposite was the lazy rippling of plastic tarps and one lone man in what appeared to be a security guard's uniform, walking away from the chain-link fence. There was no one else but her on the street. Patting her pockets for one final check for her phone and keys, Emily turned left and then left again around the corner of the house, heading for the beach.

She was expecting to find a sandy path cutting through the wiry scrub, or weather-beaten wooden stairs that would carry her up and over the dunes, but instead there was what looked, at first glance, like it must be a mirage: a set of majestic marble steps, about twenty feet wide and blindingly white under the glare of the afternoon sun. Two huge matching planters, as big as bathtubs, sat at the foot of them. They were empty and wrapped in blue protective plastic. The beach was blocked from view, so the steps appeared to lead up into the sky. They looked for all the world like some kind of stairway to heaven.

And all Emily could do was look, through the gate in the

middle of a six-foot-high wooden fence that had been erected in front of them. The gate was locked, the light on its numerical keypad glowing red. Signs warned PRIVATE BEACH: GUESTS AND RESIDENTS ONLY – NO PUBLIC ACCESS and PLEASE RESPECT OUR RESIDENTS' PRIVACY – NO PRIVATE PHOTOGRAPHY PERMITTED IN THIS AREA in red lettering. Emily wondered what incident had led to *that* being erected. Another, smaller sign attached to the fence read TEMPORARY STRUCTURE – PARDON OUR DUST AS WE MAKE SANCTUARY A SANCTUARY FOR YOU.

She pressed her plastic fob against the keypad, but the indicator light stayed red. Whatever you needed to access the beach, she didn't have it.

It occurred to her that whoever the man on the beach had been, he *had* had access. Which meant that he must be staying here, too. She didn't know if that made her feel better or worse – but better, she supposed, on balance. It meant that people other than her, Jack and Grace were staying in town.

Although if they were, they must be in hiding.

Sanctuary's completed streets were empty, its buildings silent. Emily retraced her steps back to the house and then kept going, moving in a straight line until she met the highway and the first pair of butteries. From there, she could see that Sanctuary, so far, consisted of twelve rows of houses along six streets. Everything between the last one and the other set of giant traffic cones in the distance appeared to be a building site or a cleared plot of land, patiently awaiting its turn to transform.

Each existing street looked eerily similar to the others: two rows of homes made of white masonry, with no gardens or driveways. The footpaths ended at the homes' exterior walls

121

and the only place to park a car, presumably, was out of sight, in your garage. The road system was a grid, paved and wide going north–south, narrow and cobbled going east–west. There was only one vehicle parked in plain view: a Barbie-pink vintage convertible with a chrome trim, whitewall tyres and a white leather interior, parked outside a house two streets over from Beach Read, looking like it might have teleported in moments ago via a glitch in the space–time continuum.

Near the highway, she caught the engine of an occasional passing car as it neared, zoomed past and then faded away again. Near the beach, there was the distant roar of the waves. But otherwise, the only sounds were the occasional bubbling water fountain or tinkle of wind chimes in the breeze, and the steady smack of Emily's own shoes on the ground.

The more she walked, the more the streetscapes began to reveal little surprises.

She'd round a corner and meet a sudden expanse of lush, green lawn, or a line of swaying palm trees, or a laneway inviting her to a courtyard with a tiered fountain surrounded by chairs in which she could sit and admire it. At one point, a path of white decking carried her over what must have been a manmade pond, crowded with water lilies. And there was, as Jack had teased, art.

A Romanesque bust, sitting unassumingly on a corner. A two-foot-high silver ballerina twirling on the roof of a house. Three unicorns, fashioned from twists of driftwood, sitting in a patch of long grass. An abstract something sculpted from white marble but splashed with a shock of Yves Klein blue. A cast-iron fish the size of a small car. A river of blue mosaic tiles creeping up a white wall.

Beautiful, but weird.

She couldn't put her finger on exactly why, or even say that weird was the right word. But something just felt off. Perhaps it was Sanctuary's completeness. Even though only part of the town had been built, that part was clean and perfect and *finished*. It was like walking around a showhouse, only in a development that had decided to make twelve rows of them before they got to work on the other houses.

Jack had mentioned they'd also, oddly, already built a town square, but Emily ran out of streets before she saw anything like that. She'd cut a zig-zagging path through the town, and thought that perhaps she'd just missed it.

She turned on her heel and started back towards Beach Read on the pedestrian path that ran parallel to the highway.

And heard footsteps. Quick and purposeful, following close behind.

Her first reaction was relief. *Another beating heart!* She longed to see another human being in this ghostly place.

But when she glanced behind her, there was no one there.

She stopped and turned around, scanning to be sure. She was completely alone on the path and, without any traffic passing at this particular moment, Sanctuary's late-afternoon soundtrack of near-silence had resumed all around her. Who-ever had been behind her must have turned down into one of the streets.

She thought, *weird*, turned back around and kept walking.

Within a few strides, the footsteps came again – and now, so did the icy finger, running a cold unease up the length of her spine.

Emily made a show of pulling her phone out of her pocket and stopped to pretend to check her email.

The footsteps stopped too.

She spun around—

There was no one there. But as she turned, she caught a blur of movement: a tall figure maybe fifteen, twenty feet behind her, ducking out of sight.

Someone *was* following her.

Someone who didn't want to be seen.

It could be Jack or Grace, out for a stroll like she was – but neither of them would have any reason to hide. A security guard? A Sanctuary resident? A wandering day-tripper? But none of them would have any reason to hide either. Maybe it was a journalist who had somehow already found out about Jack's book, flown across the Atlantic and found their way to Sanctuary – but wouldn't a journalist be trying to *make* contact rather than avoid it?

Emily had a sudden, overwhelming urge to go home. Not back to Bookmark, but all the way to Dublin.

She didn't want to be here. She should never have come.

Behind her thoughts, the electric buzz of a gathering panic was threatening to push through. Yes, it was broad daylight, in the middle of the afternoon, in a town – or part of one – secure enough to leave expensive works of art sitting out. But there was no one around, and she was still a few streets away from Beach Read, and if Emily screamed right now, who would come running?

Would anyone even hear her?

She felt for the reassuring hardness of her phone in her pocket, and set off at pace. Where to go? If she stayed beside the highway, she had a much better chance of being seen or meeting a passing motorist. But if she cut through Sanctuary and walked in something resembling a diagonal line, utilizing laneways and cut-throughs, she'd get to Beach Read quicker.

She couldn't hear any footsteps, but it was possible they were just drowned out by the hammering beat of her own heart.

Emily made a sudden left turn, down a narrow lane running behind two rows of houses. Halfway down it she came to another lane, criss-crossing it, and she followed that one to the right, crossed a street, went under an archway—

And emerged into the town square.

It was paved and empty and smaller than she'd been expecting, but more elaborate too; it was enclosed, like a plaza in a Spanish city, with what must be apartment balconies on the upper level and vaulted arcades on the one below. Hidden in their shadows were shop fronts which, like Sanctuary itself, were finished and ready, but also empty and waiting. Some already had signage in place. Emily could see what looked destined to be a restaurant, an estate agent's, a café, a shop selling beachwear and something called THE SANCTUARY SHOPPE. There was a tiered fountain in the centre with water in its basin, but it wasn't turned on.

Emily went to the café and cupped her hands to the window to look inside. There were some fixtures and fittings in place – a counter, a fridge, a glass display case – but no tables or chairs, and no coffee machine.

When she pulled back, she saw him reflected in the glass.

He was tall and lean, with light-coloured hair long enough to flop down over his ears. Dressed casually in shorts and a T-shirt. Standing maybe thirty feet behind her, under the archway that had brought her here. Hiding in its shadows, watching her, waiting to see where she would go.

It was the same man she'd seen on the beach.

She strained to listen for traffic, for other footsteps, for a voice, for any evidence that there was someone else near here who could help her. Nothing. Without turning her head, she glanced right and left, scoping a route out of the square.

Diagonally across it was another archway.

She braced herself, tensed to run.

You can't run, a voice in her head said. *You'll look ridiculous. And crazy. It's just a guy walking around town!* She should confront him. Swing round and go, 'Hi. Can I help you?' But a louder voice in her head said, *He's hiding, waiting to see where you go, and this is the second time you've caught him looking. There's no one around. Don't engage, run. What's worse, getting attacked or looking silly? We don't want to get hurt just because we didn't want to be embarrassed.*

Emily took off, running.

Across the square, under the archway, out onto another street, left around the far corner of the nearest one, onto a wider street—

And straight into the path of an SUV.

Its horn blared and its tyres screeched as it came to a shuddering stop, just as she managed to take a step back and get out of its way. She looked behind her, but there was no sign of the man from the square. When she turned back around, she was looking at Jack.

He was behind the wheel of the SUV, his face full of concern. He slowly pulled the vehicle forward a little, put his window down and called out to her, his eyes wide.

'Jesus, Emily. Are you OK?'

'Yeah. Sorry, I'm . . .' She gulped down a breath, her chest burning. 'Sorry.'

'No, *I'm* sorry,' he said. 'I was fiddling with the air-con, I didn't see you until you were right in front of me.'

So perhaps he hadn't seen her dart out onto the street like a madwoman, so she wouldn't have to explain to him why she'd done that.

Which was good, because now that he was there, now that she wasn't alone and the other mysterious guy was gone, the volume of the voices in her head had switched and it was the louder one saying, *Drama queen, much? You just completely overreacted. Not everything is a threat. Maybe stop watching those goddamn documentaries on Netflix, eh?*

It's just spam.

'I'm heading into Seaside,' Jack said. 'I might grab something to eat.' He hesitated. 'Do you want to come? Or is that, like, against the ghostwriter code or something?'

Emily considered her options. Be alone again, still a ways away from Beach Read, in an eerie, empty town where the only other beating heart was a strange man following her around, or get into a car and go somewhere with Jack Smyth.

Better the devil you know. Wasn't that what people said?

'Actually, yeah. If you don't mind? Seaside sounds great.'

'This feels strange, talking to you like this. But it's time. I want to tell my story. You'll be the first person in the world to hear it in full. Here goes.

Most guys say they were born to be cyclists, that it was in their blood. I became one by chance. I was thirteen when I got my first serious bike, for my birthday. The first birthday without my dad in the house. My mother was, understandably, struggling to cope. The atmosphere in our house became unbearable, like the building, painful pressure of a long-held breath. I think the idea of the bike was that it would get me outside and keep me there. One less child to have to deal with.

I'd climb on it, go as fast as I could, and the faster I went the more my mind would clear. The speed, the wind whipping past, the smooth pumping of the pedals – it was like a force-field. It blocked all the noise out. The faster I went, the better I felt. And I felt even better when I was in pain, when I was pushing, when I kept pushing long after my body started screaming at me to stop. I found I could ignore it, that I had a talent for pushing through it. Because I wanted to feel it. I *liked* it.

In some weird way, hurting made everything easier.

If your body feels like it's on fire, you don't really have the headspace to think about anything else. You can only think about the pain, and physical pain is simple. I knew its cause, and I knew that once I stopped, that pain would stop too. It was a pain I had a control over. The only one I did.

At that age, I didn't even understand how you could cycle for a job. Who paid you, and why? Where did the money come from? I didn't get it, but I knew it was possible. I'd say by the time my next birthday rolled around, cycling was pretty much the only thing in the world I cared about. I marked out the days in training rides, the months in races, the years in how many more I'd have to wait before I'd qualify to be a Junior member of Cycling Ireland and leave the Youth tier – which included the kids – behind.

When I was seventeen, I stopped going to school. I'd presented a plan to my mother: leave school now and get a job, any job, that I could fit around cycling.

She knew where my heart was. She didn't put up a fight.

The aim was to get a pro contract – get paid to race – by the time I was twenty-one. I fixated on that goal. I started doing shift-work, first on a production line in a sweet factory, then as a cleaner in an office block, and soon I was collecting glasses in a pub over the weekend too. I cycled every day and competed as much as I could. I also became very boring. My diet consisted mostly of unseasoned fish and chicken, steamed vegetables and rice. On race days, I shovelled overcooked pasta tossed in olive oil into my mouth without even pausing to taste it. I never drank alcohol. At night, I was probably dreaming about cycling, too.

Not to skip ahead – I'm really trying my best to do this for you in chronological order – but for a while there, I did a bit of motivational speaking, and this period in my life, the time when I was desperate to turn pro but hadn't yet, was always the time I'd talk about the most. Because it was so pure. I wasn't getting paid. I'd no guarantee I'd ever make it to where I wanted to go.

And yet, I was giving it my all.

When I talk to people who . . . I don't know how to put this without sounding judgemental, sorry. But people who don't strive for excellence, who don't have a goal or dream whose achievement becomes their singular focus. Normal people, I guess? When I talk to them about this, I sometimes get the sense that they feel sorry for me. They think I sacrificed too much, that I rejected the idea of having a normal life before I'd even had a chance to find out what normal life was like. They see a boy making uninformed decisions for a man who won't be able to go back in time and make different ones if and when he knows better.

But I was happy. I felt lucky. I still think, even today, that getting to chase your dreams is a privilege.

I know at this point you're probably wondering why I'm telling you all this stuff. But I need you to know how much I wanted this, how much I sacrificed for it, how hard I worked to get to where I wanted to go.

So that you ask yourself, "Why the hell would he have thrown it all away?"'

III

A HOUSE ON FIRE

11

'I feel like we've travelled to another planet,' Emily said. 'Or finally returned to Earth.'

Just twenty minutes' drive back along Scenic Highway 30A, Seaside was teeming with people. They were queuing along the line of Airstream trailers transformed into food trucks. Pushing in and out the doors of its upscale shops and boutiques. Taking selfies outside the picture-perfect post office. Children squealed and ran on the central square's lawn while adults watched from chairs dotted around the palm-tree perimeter, plastic cups of mixed drinks in their hands.

It had only been twenty-four hours, but Emily had never been so glad to see crowds of people, even if it meant they'd had to wait fifteen minutes for a table at Bud and Alley's, a beachfront bar and restaurant bursting at the seams with happy patrons. It was worth the wait. They'd been seated at a high-top on the restaurant's roof-deck and were now enjoying panoramic views of Seaside's beach. What had happened to her back in Sanctuary was already feeling like a vivid dream, one whose details she'd started forgetting the moment she woke. The first sip of cold rosé pushed all thoughts of it from her mind.

They studied the menu, murmuring comments about things looking good and not being sure what to pick. He went for the crab cakes. She went for the hamburger. Their waiter brought water, took their food orders and disappeared again. They sat in silence for a little bit, letting the conversations around them fill the void. Then, simultaneously, they turned to look at each other and laughed awkwardly.

'I actually love this,' Jack said, which made Emily wonder what he thought she'd been going to say.

'It's beautiful,' she agreed.

'It is, but I meant no one having a clue who I am.' He took a swig of his non-alcoholic beer. 'I thought I'd have that in New York, but of course there was an Irish couple checking into the hotel at the same time. I didn't even get up to the room before I was recognized.'

'Did they talk to you?'

'They talked *about* me, loud enough for me to hear.'

'That must be hard.'

Jack shrugged one shoulder.

'What about your flight over?' Emily asked.

'We used the private terminal, but because Dublin has US pre-clearance, they can't drive you directly to the plane for US flights. You have to go through with everybody else. That took ages, and then the flight was delayed so we ended up spending two hours in the main lounge. By the time we boarded, people were openly taking photos of me with their phones.'

Emily was stuck on the revelation that rich people could

134

avail themselves of a service where – surely she hadn't heard this right – you were driven *directly to the plane*?

And then she thought, *Who was the* we?

'I almost wish people *would* say something,' Jack went on. 'The whispering and staring and the pointing-their-phones-at-me is somehow worse. They've no shame *and* no balls.' He lifted his beer bottle, pointed its neck at the beach. 'This is rare for me. To be outside, in a crowd of people, and not feel like I'm being stared at it. It's a safe bet no one here knows who I am. Or gives a shit.'

'Did it ever feel good?' Emily asked. 'Being famous?'

'I don't know if I'd call it being famous.'

'Being in the public eye, then. Strangers knowing who you are.'

'It was funny, mostly,' he said. 'Because, Ireland. Either people know exactly who you are but don't want to give you the satisfaction of letting on, or they think they know you but don't know from where and they assume it's their real life. That you're, like, their friend's friend, or someone they used to work with, or a guy from their gym. And they'll greet you with a big friendly smile and go, "Hi, how are you? How are things?" before the penny drops. Sometimes it never does and they walk off, having had a whole exchange with you, going, "Where do I know that guy from?"'

The group at the table next to them suddenly roared with laughter.

'And look,' Jack said, 'it makes things easier in lots of ways. I acknowledge that. People want to do things for you and give you free stuff and make sure you don't have to wait or queue. So it was never all that bad.' He paused. 'It's what's happening now that's really horrible.'

'You mean . . .' Emily didn't know how to say it except plainly. 'People suspecting you of having something to do with Kate's death?'

'That, and the fact that I'm more famous now than I've ever been. Never mind the Olympics. Never mind competing in the Tour. Never mind my charity work or my successful business or my wife's achievements. No. Fuck all that. All that matters now is that I might have killed someone – and it matters more than anything else ever has.' He twisted his beer with two fingers. 'That's . . . That's what's tough to take.'

'How did Kate feel about it?'

'About being famous?' He shook his head. 'She didn't like it. All she wanted to do was work in TV, in front of the camera. But when things started taking off for her – when she went from weekends to weekdays – in real life, there was a high price to pay.'

'Sorry,' Emily said. 'Weekends to weekdays?'

'On *Sunrise*.'

Emily's face must have betrayed that she didn't know what he was talking about.

'The TV show Kate was on,' he said. 'She used to just do the weekends, but then she got promoted to the main presenting team, the ones who do it weekday mornings.'

'Oh. Right.'

'Didn't you, like, research us?'

'Ah, not really, no. There wasn't time and, well . . . I'm helping you write the story you want to tell. I'm not writing *about* you.'

'I guess we weren't as famous as we thought,' Jack said, bemused.

'It's more that it's been years since I watched live TV.' Emily waited a beat and then said, 'What price did she have to pay?'

'Just, you know, getting recognized more. She was in the changing rooms in some clothes shop on Grafton Street once, and someone, like, pulled back the curtain and started telling her how much they loved the show while she was stood there in a bra and jeans. They even tried to take a selfie with her. Absolutely no boundaries. And those were the *nice* people.'

'And the not-so-nice?'

'Comments about her appearance,' Jack said. 'The way she wore her hair. What she wore. Her accent, even. And I don't just mean online – people would *write in*. They'd sit down and handwrite letters and go to the post office to get a stamp for them. To tell a woman they didn't know what they thought of her. Fucking dickheads.' He exhaled. 'She always denied it, but I think that's the real reason she quit.'

Emily didn't know that she had. 'When did she do that?'

'A year before,' Jack said. There was no need to ask before what. 'She said it was feeling like a grind and that she wanted to take a break and think about doing other things, but I don't know. I mean, I believed her, I just don't think it was the whole story. I didn't need to be in Dublin, so we sold our apartment and moved to Adoran full time.' Then he said, so quietly she barely caught it, 'I watch clips of her on the show, every night before I go to sleep.'

A sudden scream drew their attention to the beach, but it was just a couple of children happily fleeing a parent chasing after them with a water gun.

'How come you bought a house there in the first place?' Emily asked. 'In Adoran?'

'I just wanted somewhere quiet I could hide away.'

'What will happen to it now?'

'I don't know,' he said. 'That's the question. All this, it's taken away my ability to earn a living. I've had to step away from Exis, no one wants me for speaking gigs, and brands aren't exactly beating down my door. I spent what little I had left repairing the damage so I could move back in. I don't want to sell it, but . . .' He sighed. 'It may come to that. And soon.'

'You moved back *in*?' Emily couldn't hide her surprise.

Jack nodded. 'About six weeks ago.'

'Is it not difficult for you?' She didn't think she could live in a house where *anyone* had died, let alone someone she'd known and loved.

Kate had been found at the bottom of the stairs. He must cross that spot a dozen or more times a day.

What did he think when he did?

What did he feel?

'It was difficult,' he said. 'It *is*, sometimes. But that was Kate's home. *Our* home. And yeah, one terrible, horrific thing happened there one night, but before that there were so many perfect days and weeks and months. She wouldn't want me to leave it.' He took another swig of his beer and then said, 'I've been meaning to ask – are you OK?'

Emily blinked at him.

Here they were, talking about his dead wife and him living in the home they used to share, and he was asking if *she* was all right?

'Just because you seemed a bit preoccupied earlier,' he added.

'Did I?'

'Yeah.'

'When?'

A slight grin. 'Are you going to answer me or just keep asking questions?'

'Everything's fine.' She smiled at him with an expression that she hoped communicated the same lie as her words. 'I'm tired, that's all. I went to bed too early last night and woke up way too early this morning.'

'We could get the food to go, if you like?'

'Oh, no, no.' She waved a hand. 'No, I'm grand. Really. This is perfect, actually. It'll help me stay awake until a reasonable hour.' She nodded towards the beach. 'And it looks like we're in a great spot for the sunset.'

'That's their thing, you know,' Jack said. 'This is *the* place to watch the sunset in Seaside, allegedly. It's a local tradition. The restaurant has been here since the beginning, when there were only, like, a dozen houses built. Rumour has it, they ring a bell.'

'A *bell*?'

'Yep. And the very first thing here, before there were any houses, was a farmer's market.' He grinned. 'Aren't you impressed with my useless Seaside knowledge? And there's plenty more where that came from. I fell down a hole on Wikipedia last night.' His face turned serious again. 'The reason I asked if you were OK is because I was worried that maybe you were regretting this. Taking the job, I mean.'

Emily shook her head. 'No, not at all.'

That much was true. What she regretted was getting herself into a situation where she'd had no choice but to take it.

'You didn't know about Neil though, did you? That was just me totally sticking my foot in it and you being too polite to say so.'

'I didn't know about him specifically,' she said, choosing her words carefully. 'But given how quickly everything happened, I assumed it was something like that.'

Not true.

Emily took a sip of her wine and was surprised to see that the glass was already half empty. She shouldn't have been, because she was already feeling the effects. Between the heat, the fact that it had been hours since she'd had lunch and not much of it, the lack of sleep, how quickly she was drinking this . . . Her edges were already losing their shape, getting warm and blurry.

But she was also emboldened. She opened her mouth to ask Jack what *had* happened with Neil—

'Excuse me?' a new voice said. A woman who had been sitting at the next table was now standing between their seats, smiling apologetically. 'I'm *so* sorry, but would you mind taking our picture?' She pointed behind her to a table of equally smiling and apologetic faces.

'Sure,' Emily said, sliding off her stool.

At the same moment, Jack's phone began to ring. Before he plucked it off the tabletop, she saw GRACE flash up on screen.

'I'll just . . .' he said to her, getting up and pointing to the quieter part of the restaurant. He put the phone to his ear and said, 'Yeah?' as he walked away.

'Oh, you're *so* kind, thank you *so* much.' The woman handed over an iPhone. 'Can you try to get the pavilion in the background?'

Emily assumed by *pavilion* the woman meant the only thing visible that wasn't sand, sea or sky: a gleaming white wooden tower, obelisk in shape, through which the beach was accessed.

The group lined up with it behind them, linked arms and

smiled wide. Emily took a few shots, handed the phone back and tried not to look offended when the woman immediately started scrolling through them to check they were up to scratch.

'They're great, honey, thank you.' She looked over Emily's shoulder to where Jack must be standing. 'Want me to take yours?'

'No, we're OK.' *We don't need to remember this moment. We're not actually on vacation, you see. He's suspected of a high-profile murder and I'm helping him write a book about it.* 'Thank you, though.'

The woman returned to her seat.

Emily felt conspicuous now, sitting alone. All of the surrounding tables were filled with boisterous groups and, when she looked over her shoulder, she saw that, up at the bar, every pair of stools was taken by a couple facing each other. Even on the level below, where high chairs were pulled up to the fence that separated the restaurant's ground-floor deck from the sand dunes, there was only one person sitting alone.

And Emily recognized her.

Tall Blonde Woman, from the plane. From *both* planes.

She was half-turned in her chair, her right side facing the beach and her left facing Emily's vantage point. There was a Coke and a nearly empty basket of fries sitting in front of her, and she had a phone to her ear again. Her brow furrowed at whatever the person on the other end of the line was saying and then, with her free hand, she dug out a pair of sunglasses from the bag hanging off the back of her chair and slipped them on.

The airport was about an hour's drive away. Was it weird that, of all the places within its radius – and this whole area was packed with beach resorts and seaside towns – another passenger who'd been on both of Emily's flights was also *here*, in the closest town to Sanctuary?

Or was she just totally overthinking this?

'We have to go.' Jack was back, standing at her elbow. 'Now. That was Grace on the phone. She says someone broke into the house.'

12

Jack must have had a remote fob in the car, because when they turned onto Beach Read's street, its garage door was already rising. He swung the car inside too fast and at too sharp an angle, braking hard just a couple of feet before the headlights would've met solid wall.

'She's all right,' Emily said, trying to calm him.

They'd kept Grace on speakerphone all the way back from Seaside. She hadn't said much and when she did, she'd whispered it – she'd locked herself into a room and didn't want to draw any attention in case the intruder was still inside the house – but a few moments ago, when Emily had told her they were almost there, Grace had sighed with relief and hung up.

'I know,' Jack said, killing the engine. 'But she's scared.'

He got out, slamming his door behind him, and hurried under the archway and into the courtyard.

Emily followed.

The sun had only started to sink in the sky but every last light in Beach Read was ablaze, inside and out. The courtyard was empty except for them, and looked the same as it had when Emily had left it. Jack called out Grace's name just as footsteps came running out of the house and she appeared in front of them, flushed and breathing hard.

'I think he's gone,' she said.

Jack went to her and touched a gentle hand to her back, and asked in a low voice if she was all right. She looked up at him with wide eyes and nodded, her lips pressed together, and then they held each other's gaze while something silent was communicated, after which Jack let his hand drop and they stepped apart.

The exchange left Emily uncomfortable, as if she'd witnessed something she shouldn't have.

For the second time today.

'Tell us exactly what happened,' Jack said.

'I was upstairs, putting the laptop into the safe. I heard a crash. I thought it might have been glass breaking. I assumed it was one of you, but when I looked out the window there was a man down here.' Grace pointed a few feet away, to a spot near the pool. 'Standing right there.'

'Doing what?'

'Nothing. Looking around. I don't know.'

'What did you do?'

'I banged on the window.' She mimed striking invisible glass with two closed fists. 'He looked up and saw me, and then he ran off, into the garage. I locked myself in the room, called you and stayed there until I saw *you* walk out of the garage. I presume you didn't see him in there? Or outside?'

After Jack shook his head, Grace took a deep breath and said, 'Where the hell *were* you guys?'

'What did he look like?' Jack asked, ignoring the question.

A flash of light caught Emily's attention. There was something small and reflective on the ground near the foot of one of the chairs.

She walked to it to get a closer look.

'Tall,' Grace said. 'White. Skinny. I didn't really see his face.'

'He knocked a lantern over,' Emily said, pointing. A number of Moroccan-style lanterns were dotted around the courtyard, and now one of their number was lying on its side just under one of the chairs. Its glass was cracked. 'That must have been the crash you heard.'

'What was he wearing?' Jack asked.

'A white shirt,' Grace said. 'A baseball cap. Shorts, maybe. What does it matter? He shouldn't have been here. We need to call security. Or maybe even the police. Someone *broke in*, Jack. This house isn't secure.'

'This house has staff,' he said calmly. 'Housekeeping, maintenance, pool cleaner – and there's the property manager who let us in. They're supposed to stay away this week but maybe there was a miscommunication. It must have been one of them. How else would he have got in? There's no lock broken or door kicked in.'

'Yeah, well, maybe you didn't close it properly when you left.'

'I think I saw him,' Emily said.

They both turned to look at her questioningly.

'Earlier,' she continued. 'On the beach. Looking up at the house. And then again when I was walking around the town – just before I ran into you, Jack.' She hesitated. 'I think he was following me.'

Silence.

Blank faces.

Then Grace spat, '*What?*'

'What do you mean, following you?' Jack demanded.

She briefly recapped what had happened, after which Grace and Jack exchanged glances.

'Let's not jump to any conclusions,' Jack said to Grace, although it wasn't at all obvious to Emily what conclusion Grace was jumping to. 'A white guy in shorts and a T-shirt pretty much describes everyone around here.'

'But there's been *no one* around here,' Emily said. 'Not after the construction crews go home. I think that's more the point.'

'If he was staff,' Grace said, 'why didn't he ring the buzzer? And why would someone who works here be following *her*' – she jerked a thumb in Emily's direction – 'around town?'

'OK, look,' Jack said, 'I'll call the owner.' He took his phone out of a pocket. 'Find out if that sounds like someone who works here. And if it doesn't, I'll ask him what we should do. Let's try that first before we declare an international incident, all right?' He turned and headed for the house, handing his car keys to Grace as he passed her.

Grace waited for him to get all the way inside before she turned to Emily, folded her arms across her chest and said, 'Where *were* you?'

'We went to Seaside.'

'Was I not clear? You're supposed to stay *here*, in Sanctuary, at all times.'

'Grace . . .' Emily hesitated. On one hand, she abhorred confrontation. She just wasn't built for it. If people were rude, her response was to kill them with kindness or, failing that, find the quickest way to exit stage left. But she was tired. More than tired, she was jetlagged. Her body didn't know what day

146

of the week it was and her brain had been fed more new information today than it had had to deal with in the whole of the last month. A single glass of wine had skipped off her near-empty stomach and shot into her veins. She felt warm and loose and a little tipsy and she had just about *had it* with Grace. So she said, 'With all due respect, I'm not a prisoner and you're not the warden.'

Grace's mouth fell open. '*Excuse* me?'

'If my subject wants to share some of his story in a social setting, I will facilitate that. I didn't take any of your electronic devices out of the house, so there was no security risk. And we're in Florida. Jack said himself, no one has any clue who he is and frankly no one cares. But if you want to talk about if we're all doing what we're supposed to be doing, if we're abiding by the rules and doing our jobs and being professional, then sure. By all means. But maybe we should begin with you. For starters, I'm wondering what you're even still doing here? You told me that Jack needs his own time in the evenings and you're supposed to be staying in a hotel down the highway . . .'

Grace's glare was so cold that Emily felt its chill.

'Members of the public,' she said, pronouncing every word with a disquieting distinctiveness, 'took pictures of Jack at Dublin Airport, and again in JFK. They're all over social media if you know where to look. Everyone knows that he's in the US, so it's only a matter of time before they trace him to here. And then they'll start digging for *why* he's here, and who is here with him. If the Irish media find out about the book, *there will be no book*. But it won't be my fault, because I told you the rules. I *told you* to stay in Sanctuary. I made that perfectly clear. And the reason I'm still here is because I had work to do, for *you*, and Jack had the rental car. Not that that's any of your concern.' Grace moved to go. 'Oh – and Jack isn't your subject. He's your *client*. I know you don't have a clue what you're doing, but at least get *that* right.'

She spun on her heel and stormed off, into the house.

Emily stared after her, dumbstruck. It was a mystery how Grace had got this gig when she had the professional demeanour of a sulking teenager. Whose insane idea was it to put someone that volatile on a project this important? Was she someone's daughter or niece or lovechild? Or had she just done a really good job of pretending to be better back in London?

Emily decided that she'd email Beth about it – *which will be breaking another one of Grace's rules*, she thought with an eye-roll.

And then she thought, *What a day.*

She crossed the courtyard and wearily climbed the stairs to Bookmark.

As she stood on its threshold and felt for the light switch, it occurred to her that they'd just had an intruder in the house, potentially. This gave her pause. But while the front door to the main house, opening into the courtyard, was typically left open all day, Bookmark's front door locked automatically on closing. She'd had to open it just now with her key.

But still . . .

Emily flipped on the lights and scanned the space. Everything looked just as she'd left it. The balcony door was still locked, but she went out there anyway. All good. She went into the bathroom and yanked the shower curtain all the way back. All clear. She pulled on the connecting door, but it didn't budge. Everything was fine.

She drew the curtains, locked the front door from the inside

148

and turned off most of the lights. Another glass of wine seemed like a nice idea, but not a good one. She dug a can of Coke out of the fridge instead.

As she pulled on its tab, Grace's words echoed in her head.

If the Irish media find out about the book, there will be no book.

Numerous other morally dubious memoirs had gone directly from printer to shredder, sunk by tsunamis of public outrage before they got anywhere near the bookshop shelves. Like the film director's career retrospective that conveniently ignored the numerous abuse allegations against him. The political memoir which claimed that the pandemic was caused by mobile phones. The latest pop-sci title by that guy who'd lied about his college degrees and whose work had been discredited on numerous occasions by people who didn't have to lie about theirs. People had got wind of these projects, clutched their pearls – or taken to social media, to Goodreads, to Medium – and, as a result, the books had got pulped.

And rightly so, Emily had thought at the time.

But what if that happened to *this* book?

She wondered if, in that scenario, she'd still get paid – and then immediately hated herself for thinking that. Her problems were only financial. What about Kate's family and friends, forced to relive the worst thing that had ever happened to them, but with Kate replaced by Jack in the role of victim? If any of them believed Jack was guilty, they'd have to stomach her killer getting a chance to plead his innocence, not just with the privilege of his very own book, but in all the publicity that would come with its publication.

And if Jack *was* innocent, he'd be robbed of this opportunity to say so.

149

But the fact remained that Emily didn't have twenty-five grand. She didn't have *a* grand. If this all went to shit, someone would surely find out her name and make it public, and then her boss would find out the true nature of her 'family emergency' and she wouldn't have a job.

She went to her backpack and took out the notebook she'd bought before she'd left Dublin: a large, black Moleskine whose pages were blank. It was the kind of expense she hadn't been able to justify for a long time, but on the way home after the meeting with Beth and Carolyn, she'd slipped into a stationery shop and purchased it, a little giddy with having, suddenly, what looked like a tangible excuse.

It was still in its plastic wrap – thanks to Grace's rules, she'd had no need for it. Now, Emily ripped the plastic with a fingernail and slipped it off. She stroked the newly exposed smoothness of the cover, feeling the universe of possibility underneath. Then she cracked the spine, opened the notebook to the first blank page and laid it flat on the breakfast bar.

This week was an opportunity, but in more ways than one. She had her evenings free and this place to herself. She was afraid that Jack's book wouldn't make it to the shelves; she should use that fear as motivation to start writing something else. To start writing again. To do the only kind of writing she'd wanted to do in the first place.

And in this new place, all these new experiences, people . . .

The restaurant back in Seaside, for instance, that rang the bell every time the sun set. Could there be something in that? Emily imagined a woman, sitting out life on the sidelines, promising herself 'Someday', every day, shaken out of her stupor by the sound that signalled she'd wasted yet another twenty-four hours of her life. She even had a title: *The Sunset*

Bell. Or what about Sanctuary, in all its sterile, silent strangeness? What if, when it was finished, it still felt the same way? Who would build a town like this? Who would live in it? What might happen here? An update of *The Stepford Wives*, mashing together the horrors of AI with the even more horrific #tradwife trend. And Tall Blonde Woman. Don't you always wonder where the other people on your plane are going to, and why? What if you became so unhealthily obsessed with your seatmate that you followed them to their destination, and then stayed there so you could follow them around it as well?

There was, potentially, so much material. A shower of sparks. She should take advantage of it.

She should, at least, *try.*

When Plan A was helping a man who might have committed a murder write a memoir, it seemed wise to have a Plan B.

Emily picked up a pen and started to write.

Three days before the fire

Kate is upstairs, in their bedroom, when she hears the front door open and Jack come in.

She knows it's him because no one else would be letting themselves into their house, but also because she knows the sounds of him. How he always turns the key with much more force than required, as if he's anticipating the lock putting up a fight. How the clatter of the keys in the ceramic tray on the hall table always comes *before* he closes the door behind him. The shuffling as he takes off his coat and hangs it up, followed by the brief silence while he checks his reflection in the mirror on the wall. What's next is usually her name, called out, so she can call back which room she's in, and he can come and find her and kiss her hello again, but he doesn't do that part today – but that's OK. She's just glad he's home.

Her shoulders drop in relief.

She hasn't heard a word from Jack since yesterday afternoon and, outside, it's already getting dark.

There was no call, no text, no call back when she tried him, finally, this morning.

Just now, when she heard the car come up the lane, she

152

hadn't been certain it was his. The footsteps that then trudged across the gravel could have belonged to someone else. Kate had been frozen in place, sitting on their bed surrounded by a mess of old photographs, holding her breath, waiting for the doorbell to ring. To commence the walk down the stairs that would be the last part of Before and the start of After. For the sight of a uniformed Garda waiting solemnly on her stoop with his hat in his hands.

Do they still do that? Do they even wear hats these days?

She consciously sets aside her anger at him for making her worry, because the radio silence can only mean that the meeting didn't go as well as he'd needed it to.

He stays downstairs long enough for her to consider going to him, but then she hears his tread on the stairs.

The man who comes through the door looks nothing like the one she said goodbye to yesterday. Jack hasn't shaved, his hair is wild and he has the grey pallor of someone who never got to sleep the night before. He looks completely deflated.

'I'm sorry,' he says immediately.

'It's OK.'

'I just didn't want to talk about it. I don't.'

'Can you give me a summary?'

'No.'

'Jack, come—'

'No, I mean, that's it. That's the summary. They said no.' He kicks off his shoes and sits down on the other side of the bed. He frowns at the photographs. 'What's going on here?'

'I was looking through my Polaroids.'

'For what?'

'Nothing in particular,' she lies.

She's already gone through all the digital photos she could

find on her laptop, some old thumb-drives and a Facebook account she's long abandoned, as well as running image-searches online, checking news archives and even scrolling through the team websites. The Polaroids are the only other place she can think to look for a face from back then that looks anything like the woman who introduced herself as Jean Whelan does now.

On the drive back from White Point, she'd made a vow: unless she found tangible evidence that they'd actually known this woman – that Jack had – she wasn't going to tell him about her.

He has enough on his plate as it is.

'The box fell out of the wardrobe when I was getting something else down,' she says. 'I started putting them back in and got distracted. Look.' She picks up one that was taken on a winter break to Croatia. It shows them sitting across from one another in a dim restaurant's narrow booth, holding hands over the remnants of a pizza. 'We got that weird waiter to take this for us, remember? The one who kept telling us about his DJ-ing school?'

Jack takes the picture and studies it.

'Hmm,' he says. 'Vaguely.' He hands it back to her. 'And come back again in twelve months' time.'

It takes her a second to understand that he's back to talking about the meeting.

'That sounds promising?'

He shakes his head. 'In twelve months' time, there'll be nothing left.' Jack lies down, on his back, and stares up at the ceiling. 'Ruth thinks we should close the stores. Retract the expansion. Go back to what was working. One small ware-house, online sales only.'

154

'Would that work?'

'I don't know. But we can't keep going like this.'

Kate pushes the photos to the end of the bed, puts the box on the floor and lies down next to Jack.

'Can I suggest something crazy?' she says.

'You've never asked before.'

'Oh, you're funny.' She slaps his arm playfully. 'We cut all our losses. Sell up and go. Escape. Sell Exis or sell the stock off or whatever it is you need to do to kill it. Sell the house. We've added value with the extension so we should have a little left over after the mortgage, and we take it and feck off to France. Or Spain. Or Italy. Somewhere sunny and quiet, by the beach.'

He rolls onto his side to face her, props his head on his hand. 'And do what?'

She rolls onto her side, mirrors him. 'Whatever we want.'

'You just want to go back,' he says with a sad smile.

He means back in time, and he's not entirely wrong. To that first year. After Jack admitted defeat in the face of his injuries from the crash at the Tour, but before she was hired to cover weekends at *Sunrise*, when by chance they'd both found themselves standing on the edge of a summer with no plans, no commitments and nowhere to be. They'd found a cheap, crappy rental up in the hills above Nice – if you ignored everything but the view, it was paradise – and, for almost three months, drank wine on the balcony and lay in the sun on the beach and fell in love.

You always imagine you were happier in hindsight, but Kate actually *was* happy then. Blissfully so. Her memories from that time are all sun-drenched and warm, and feel light. Sometimes she wonders what she thought about all day, that summer.

What the voice in her head was like when there wasn't anything to worry her.

'Why can't we?' she asks gently.

He exhales. 'All our money, everything we had—'

'It's already gone. And so what? It wasn't like we were millionaires. We took a risk, it hasn't worked out, no big deal. We're young enough to start again.'

But Jack looks dubious.

'Ruth and the others,' she says. 'They'll understand.'

A brief grin. 'Tell me you're an only child without telling me you're an only child.'

'She's going to lose her job anyway. They all will, down the line. Isn't it better to sort it out now, before things get really bad?'

Jack reaches out and strokes her cheek softly.

'I can't do this anymore,' he whispers.

'So don't. Stop.'

After a beat, he rolls onto his back again. 'Let me think about it, OK?'

'OK.'

His hand finds hers. 'Is everything else OK?'

She tries not to tense. Does he know about the messages? Could he be getting them too?

'What do you mean?' she asks.

'What I said.'

'Everything's fine. Everything else is.' She sits up. 'In the meantime, let's light a fire and eat pizza and watch something stupid tonight.'

'Is that you asking me to go get a pizza?'

'No,' she says, climbing off the bed. 'That's me telling you.'

'If we do move, let's get somewhere covered by Deliveroo.'

He goes into their bathroom, promising to go on a pizza run as soon as he's had a shower.

Kate shovels the Polaroids back into the box and puts the box back in the wardrobe. She moves to go downstairs, to clear the charred debris of last night's fire out of the grate, when she looks out the front window and sees the car.

Outside, the view is of a thick, solid dark, except for two headlights glowing bright and steady, and pointing directly at the house. Their house is the only thing at the end of a narrow country lane. No one has any business being parked halfway down it.

The lights make it impossible to see if anyone is behind the wheel but the engine is running; Kate can see a mist of warm air illuminated by the rear lamps.

'Jack?'

'Yeah?'

'Come here a sec.'

He reappears, shirtless now, and obeys her silent instruction to look out the window. But just as he steps up to the glass beside her, they both hear the sudden roar of an engine and the car starts reversing at high speed, away.

13

Ten minutes later, Emily realized she was checking her emails.

She hadn't decided to do it. She had no recollection, even, of picking up her phone. But she must have – after putting down her pen, closing the notebook and pushing them both to the side, where they were sitting now.

Because *The Sunset Bell* felt like a short story and Emily didn't know how to write those well. *AI Tradwives* sounded like a *Black Mirror* episode she would totally watch, but writing science-fiction wasn't really her thing. And while she thought a story about following Tall Blonde Woman around like a stalker could be great if, at the midpoint twist, it turned out that Tall Blonde Woman was stalking *her*, she had no idea what would happen for the other 89,950 words of that book.

So her brain, knowing that the giving-up was coming before she did, had run a little ahead of her conscious thought and conveniently put the device into her hand.

Emily sighed resignedly, but didn't put the phone away.

No new emails; at least that. She opened a new message, entered Beth's address and started typing. *Hi Beth. Sorry to bother you, but could we speak? We break here between 12 and 12.30p.m., which I think in GMT is* but she stopped there. She wasn't completely sober and things might look different in the light of day, after she'd got some sleep. It was probably wiser to wait until tomorrow and see if she still wanted to complain to Beth about Grace then. It was starting, already, to feel like an overreaction. She deleted the draft.

She'd thought she might try to find a picture of Jack at the airport, out of morbid curiosity more than anything else, but since Twitter had stopped being Twitter you couldn't search on it without an account anymore, and she no longer had one.

Instead, she went on YouTube and searched for videos of Kate Smyth.

There were hundreds. In most of them, Kate was dressed in blocks of daring colour, wearing shiny lip-gloss and brightly lit, a *Sunrise* logo on screen just below her right elbow. She wasn't one of the two presenters who got to relax on the couch throughout the show, but a roving reporter, sent out into the real world to pre-tape segments about – in the videos Emily watched – getting beach-body ready, the Men's Shed Association and the turning-on of Dublin city's Christmas lights on a soggy November night.

There were also lots of videos of her vox-popping members of the general public, soliciting their views on the news near the top of the escalators in some dreary shopping centre. 'News' in the *Sunrise* universe wasn't what you'd recognize from the headlines, but stories that began with phrases like *A new study suggests*, or *A recent survey of Irish men has revealed*. Kate's interviewees often seemed distracted, better at answering the yes-or-no questions she posed than generating their own complete sentences. A few of them couldn't even seem to manage that. They spent their time gazing at her in naked awe.

Because she was beautiful.

So beautiful she was out of place – movie-star looks inexplicably holding a microphone by the trollies outside a tatty Tesco. But she also seemed to be genuinely interested in the people she was talking to, and she was kind to them, encouraging them and joking with them and putting them at ease, and she had a mischievousness about her that seemed to say to the viewer, *Yes, I know we're trying to get five minutes out of this nonsense but sure look we're having a laugh here, aren't we?*

Emily couldn't imagine anyone sitting down to write a list of insults to this woman, or that woman taking any of them to heart.

She pictured Jack, lying in the dark with the glow of his phone on his face, watching his dead wife interview strangers about how often they changed their bed sheets, and she felt sorry for him.

And now, finally, Emily admitted to herself that she *had* been feeling sorry for him all bloody day.

'Fuck,' she said out loud.

And then she thought *fuck it*, slid off the stool and went to the fridge to pour herself a glass of wine.

She wasn't stupid. She knew that no matter how Jack seemed, no matter how nice or thoughtful or caring, he still could've killed his wife. It could've been an accident, or a moment of madness. People were complicated and good people did bad things.

She knew that better than most.

There was also the possibility that Jack Smyth was a full-blown psychopath wearing a human suit who knew charm was his superpower, and that was why it had taken him less than twenty-four hours to suck her right in.

But it was just so hard for her to *believe*.

If he had accidentally killed Kate, wouldn't he be suffering more, from the guilt? (But how much suffering was enough? What did it look like?) Wouldn't he be wrecked by it all, broken by keeping the secret, stressed by maintaining the lies? (Unless he hadn't done it, in which case none of those afflictions applied.) Why would a person commit murder, proclaim innocence, thus far avoid criminal charges and then decide to write a book about it? (Because if he'd got away with the killing, maybe he felt confident that he'd get away with this too.)

She took her wine to the couch and scanned the headlines on ThePaper.ie. There was nothing there about Jack, but then idle chatter online did not actual news make.

She returned to Neil Wallace's website to digest his ABOUT page for a second time. Not only was he an experienced ghost-writer, but a decorated journalist too. He'd won several awards and published two non-fiction titles under his own name.

Emily tapped CONTACT and stared into the void of the form.

She couldn't turn off her curiosity about why Neil had quit this job. It didn't make any difference to her – *she* was still going to have to do it – and it could be something as boring and innocuous as a schedule conflict.

But she didn't think it was.

There was just *something*, snagging on her insides, like a tiny bit of loose grit in your shoe that you can feel but can't find.

Maybe it was because Neil was a journalist. He'd know

what his colleagues on the crime beat might have unearthed, but couldn't report for legal reasons. Had he said yes, and then found out something that made taking this job too morally repugnant? Did he know something that made him think Jack was guilty beyond a shadow of a doubt? If the answers to both those questions were no and he just didn't like the Florida heat or something, then at least she could stop worrying about it.

She started typing a message. *Hi Neil. Hope you don't mind me reaching out.* She immediately deleted the last two words in a fit of self-loathing and typed *sending you this random message* instead. *I think we might have a mutual ghostwriting client.* Grace would be pleased. *I suspect he was yours before he was mine and I would love to know why the job became available. Am in Florida with him now and it's a LOT – and we're only on day one!* No, she couldn't possibly say that. *Am in Florida with him now and after 24 hours I have more questions than answers.* There was no need to tell him about the location. She changed it to *am with him now* but then thought that sounded like she was sitting next to him, so she changed it again to *am away with him now working on it and would appreciate if we could chat.* She typed out her phone number and then, because it was coded into her very DNA, signed off with *No worries if not!* She pressed SEND before she could change her mind.

Then she went looking for Kate Smyth's Instagram.

Her account had nearly four hundred thousand followers, a huge number for someone whose fame was down to Irish TV. Her last grid post was dated 17 November 2023, the day before she died. Kate's final post was a view of an empty beach under wintry grey skies, with a headland in the distance and what looked like a mile of sand exposed by low tide. There was no caption and tens of thousands of comments, which could easily be identified as being from before and after Kate's death, and before and after Jack became a suspect in it.

The first lot were all some variation of *love that spot* and *STUNNING*. Then came the kind that made Emily's stomach churn with second-hand cringe: OTT social media condolences from people who were almost certainly complete strangers. *RIP gorgeous girl. God needed an angel. Hope you're at peace now*. Finally, there was the *prison too good for him* and *obvious he did it* and *let him burn*. They made up the vast majority. The newest one had been posted just three days ago.

She scrolled down, into the last few months of Kate's life.

In this period at least, she hadn't been a regular user and seemed to post mostly views of beaches and woodland, restaurant meals she'd eaten and, for a stretch during her last summer, close-ups of flowers blooming in what was presumably her own garden. Emily had to rewind to six months before Kate's death before she found a photo of the woman herself, sunkissed and sunglassed, posing on a bluff overlooking a breathtaking stretch of cerulean sea with her arms outstretched.

Looking at the photo made Emily suddenly hot with shame.

This woman had lost her life at just twenty-nine, three years younger than Emily was now, and, in death, been demoted to a supporting character in it.

The story had become all about Jack. This book would be all about Jack.

How *he'd* suffered. How the accusations had made *him* feel. What *he* was doing the night she died.

And Emily was helping him write it.

She scrolled on, looking for another photo of Kate – and when she found one, it made her do a double-take.

It was a group shot, Kate plus five other women, all in evening wear and holding slim champagne flutes, a ballroom behind them.

But there were *two* familiar faces in it.

Grace was in the picture, standing right next to Kate.

Emily put down her wine glass and sat straight up. She zoomed in, to confirm that it definitely was her – and it *was*. Moreover, Grace was tagged, although when Emily clicked on the username, she found the account set to private. But it gave her something new: Grace's last name.

When she put *Grace Park* into Google, LinkedIn offered her some perplexing information.

Grace didn't work for Morningstar.

Grace *worked for Exis*, Jack's athleisure brand. Her current position was listed as personal assistant to the managing director and she'd been in that role for eighteen months.

What the . . . ?

Emily was trying to puzzle this out when she heard a soft knock on the connecting door and then Jack's muffled voice saying, 'Emily? Emily, are you there?'

14

The following morning, Emily woke up already wanting to go back to sleep. She felt heavy and headachy, and her back hurt from a second night spent on the thin, hard mattress of the sofa-bed. She'd slept fitfully, dreaming about the weirdest things – being trapped, at home, in the office-wardrobe that Mark had fashioned for himself while someone hammered on a typewriter right outside; following Kate Smyth around the shopping centre near her parents' house in Cork; Jack breaking through the connecting doors like Jack Torrance in *The Shining*.

She hadn't responded to him last night, when he'd tried to speak to her through them, and if he brought it up today she was going to act dumb and say she'd been watching something with her headphones on and hadn't heard. It had creeped her out and she didn't want to encourage it, didn't want to acknowledge the thinness of the walls between their spaces.

If he needed to speak to her, he could call her phone or come to the *front* door, thanks very much.

While her first cup of coffee brewed noisily, Emily lifted the blinds and saw that the weather was a perfect match for her mood. Overnight, a thick blanket of gunmetal-grey cloud had settled itself over the Gulf, changing the landscape completely, and a strong wind was churning up the surf. She watched for a few minutes as waves crashed furiously up onto the shore, sending spray flying, and saw a new, dark line of seaweed drawn across the sand.

It looked like a different country.

This morning, it felt like one she didn't want to be in.

It was still only a little after eight, so Emily climbed back into bed with the coffee and picked up her phone. She'd had it on silent while she slept, seeing as everyone in her life was in a different time zone and therefore at risk of waking her up in the middle of the night. She saw now that she'd missed a call from an Irish number, a Dublin area code, and the message telling her about the voicemail that presumably went with it.

She only got as far as '*Ah, hi. This is Neil Wallace. I got—*' before she cut the message off and called him back.

'Emily, hello.' He sounded older and very RTÉ news anchor: smooth tone, good enunciation and no detectable regional accent.

'Neil, hi. Thanks for calling me.'

'Thanks for your intriguing message.'

'Ah, yeah. I can't really say too much.'

'Is this about Jack Smyth?'

She hesitated. 'They made me sign something. But if you're wrong, I'll tell you.'

'Well, I've only ever had two ghostwriting clients, and I know Anthony Baume isn't away anywhere because he was on with Oliver Callan about three hours ago, live and in

166

studio, so . . . Hang on one second, I'm going to go somewhere a little quieter.' There were a lot of buzzy voices in the background of wherever Neil was – it sounded like some kind of open-plan office – and then, after a rustling sound, the firm closing of a door and no noise at all. 'Now. That's better. So, yes. Jack Smyth. Gosh.'

Emily didn't think she'd ever heard anyone use the word *gosh* in real life.

'I understand,' she said, 'if you can't tell me anything. But I'm just wondering what happened before I came on the scene.'

'Not at all. I'm happy to chat. It's more that it was all such a long time ago. Must be, what? Two years ago now, at least?'

Two years?

'What was?' she asked, confused.

'My meeting with him. About doing a book.'

Kate wasn't even dead a year, so that book couldn't be this one.

'Sorry,' Emily said. 'I thought you'd been hired for *this* job, that I'm doing now. And that you'd had it up until very recently. I thought I might be your replacement, and I was wondering why you'd dropped out. But it sounds like I'm wrong.' She paused. 'The, ah, the thing I'm helping him write about hadn't happened two years ago.'

There was a long beat of silence before Neil said, 'Bloody hell. Why on earth is he doing *that*?'

'I don't know,' Emily said. 'I didn't know when I came out here and I feel like I know even less now. But he gave me the impression that you'd had this job first. He didn't actually say your full name, but he did mention you in another conversation, about Anthony Baume's book.'

'I met with him about doing a business thing,' Neil said.

167

'One of those, you know, ten life lessons I learned in the saddle or some such. Something for unimaginative people to buy their equally unimaginative fathers and brothers and husbands for Christmas, and then pile high in the airport bookshops afterwards.'

She must have the wrong Neil, then. But this was the Neil that had written Anthony Baume's book, that Jack had mentioned specifically in his reasoning for doing *this* book, and he had met with Jack about another publishing project.

How many ghostwriting, cycling-adjacent Neils could there be?

'Why didn't it happen? If you don't mind me asking.'

'Oh, it was nothing dramatic,' Neil said. 'They just never got their act together. That happens a lot – you have a meeting, everyone appears to be chomping at the bit, and then you never hear a word about it again. So I really can't help you there, but . . .' A pause. 'I do spend three days a week in a newsroom, if that's any use to you? Just on, you know, deep background.'

It took Emily a beat to join the dots.

'What have you heard?' she asked.

'We can't report any of it, you know. You can't.'

'I can't even have *this* conversation. And this is his story. I won't be adding to it. This is . . . This is just out of personal curiosity, really.'

'I see,' Neil said. 'Well, for starters, they found her blood upstairs. A handprint, on the wall. Her hand. Which would mean that she was injured before she fell down the stairs. There must have been an altercation or some kind of attack, before the fall.'

Or push, Emily said silently.

168

'What about, like, forensics? Physical evidence? Do they have any?'

'I do know that there was an issue with his clothing. Jack was injured, of course, and treated at the scene. I don't know if his clothes were damaged, contaminated or lost. Whatever happened, they didn't have anything to test. And, you see, he held her. For a considerable time and tightly, to his chest. Outside the house. Wouldn't let her go. The paramedics had to physically break his grip. Now, you could say that's the desperate act of a devastated husband – or a very clever move from a forensics point of view. He was covered in her blood, but it was meaningless from an evidentiary standpoint.'

Emily swallowed back the sudden taste of bitter coffee.

'How much blood was there?' she asked.

Whenever she'd pictured the scene inside the house, she'd imagined Kate's unconscious body or blackened debris, but never blood.

'Tell me,' Neil said. 'Are you squeamish?'

Yes, very, she answered silently. 'Not particularly, no.'

'All that's been made officially public is the cause of death: skull fracture. It sounds clean, doesn't it? Neat. Bloodless, even. But, you see, for Kate, it wasn't like that at all. She also had a broken collarbone, a broken leg and a shattered pelvis – and there were *multiple* skull fractures, concentrated on the front of the head.'

'You mean on her . . . ?'

'The poor woman's face was destroyed,' Neil said quietly. 'One eye was out of its socket' – Emily winced at this – 'and there was a sort of, ah . . . A *caving-in* effect, for want of a better phrase. When I was a child, there was a terrible accident on the grounds of my school. It had snowed, and one of the

169

older boys was dared to go down the steepest hill in the grounds on a dustbin lid they'd been using as a sled. Straight into a tree, he went. Doing some speed. My father was a GP and one of the first on the scene, and I heard him later telling my mother that the boy's face was in the back of his head.' He paused. 'The guards had to persuade her parents not to view the body.'

'Jesus,' Emily breathed.

'Kate's injuries simply don't add up. You don't get that from a fall down the stairs. And something like 56 per cent of women murdered in Ireland last year were killed by their partners or former partners so, if we go by the odds . . . Are you still there?'

'Yeah. Yes.'

'Are you all right?'

'I'm fine,' Emily said, unsure if that were true. 'It's just that, you know, I'm here with him. I have to go into a room with him this morning and talk to him about this, one-on-one. And it just . . .' She didn't want to say, *It just doesn't* seem *like he did it*, because that was, officially, the absolute dumbest shit she could utter, even if it felt true. 'In a weird way, those details make me move towards him *not* doing it. Like, a push down the stairs could be a split-second thing, a blown fuse, a moment in time. But to inflict those kinds of injuries, and on someone you supposedly love . . . Wouldn't you have to be, I don't know, some kind of monster?'

'How old are you?' Neil asked.

'Thirty-two,' she answered, confused as to why he needed to know.

'Probably too young for *Jagged Edge,* then, am I right?'

'I must be, because I don't know what it is.'

'Glenn Close? Jeff Bridges? The typewriter with the tell-tale "T"?'

'It's not ringing any bells.'

Where the hell was this conversation going?

'Bridges stands accused of killing his wife,' Neil says. 'She's been brutally murdered. Really bloody, violent stuff. "Bitch" in blood on the wall and all that. Her blood, needless to say. Later, the prosecutors are sitting around, discussing her injuries, and one of them goes, "But do you really think a guy could do that to his own wife?" And another says, "Maybe that's the point. Maybe that's what he wanted. For us to look at the photos and go, geez, do you really think a guy could do that to *his own wife*?"' Neil paused. 'You should watch it. Great film.'

'Yeah,' Emily said, feeling like she might throw up.

'And then, of course, there's the issue of the burns. Or lack thereof. Jack's story is that he went in the front door, saw her, grabbed her and dragged her out. But Kate's body didn't have a single burn on it. Which makes sense. She got downstairs before the fire did. It never did, actually. Smoke yes, flames no. The damage to the ground floor was mostly from water, from the hoses. So where and how and why did she get—' On Neil's end, there was a knocking sound and then a new voice saying something about a meeting. 'Ah, sorry, I have to go here.'

'Just before you do – did he do it?'

'Who, Jack?'

'The guy in the movie.'

Neil snorted. 'What do you think? And before *you* go – are you the same Emily Joyce who wrote *The Witness*?'

'Ah . . . Yeah. That's me.'

171

Neil was interrupted again by the other voice on his end, so if there was a reason he'd wanted to know that, he didn't get to tell her.

He apologized for having to go. She thanked him again and ended the call.

Emily fell back against the pillows and wished she'd never contacted Neil Wallace at all.

15

'On the bright side,' Alice said, 'you didn't get any more weird emails from yourself.'

Emily was lying flat on the couch with her earbuds in, showered and mostly dressed, but with no make-up on and her hair soaking a halo of damp into the pillow behind her head. Ever since she'd hung up on Neil, she'd been feeling sick and headachy and generally shite, not from any physiological malady but because her brain wouldn't stop dwelling on the details of Kate's death. They were continuously playing on a loop in her head, like headlines on a cable news channel. *Blood everywhere . . . Eye out of its socket . . . Face caved in . . .* It didn't help that, over on the building site, it sounded like a dozen people were trying to tunnel their way to the Earth's core using only jackhammers. She'd closed every window and door but she could still hear their constant, rhythmic whine.

The only thing for it, Emily had decided fifteen minutes

ago, was to take two paracetamol, be horizontal and call Alice to tell her everything that Neil had told her.

'I did get a solicitor's letter, though.'

'*What?* When? Who from?'

'It arrived yesterday. And I have no idea because I told Mark not to open it, because I don't know if I want him to know who it's from either.'

'What are you thinking?'

'Exclusively bad things.'

Silence.

'You think it's from her,' Alice said then.

'What else would it be?'

'She can't sue you, Em. That's not how it works.'

'Alice, darling, *this* is going to sound harsh, but *I* say it with love: you really do have a remarkable confidence level when it comes to industries you don't actually work in.'

'Stop stealing my lines.'

'It could be, I don't know, damages. Or demanding my notes. Or libel.'

'But none of that makes any sense, Em.'

'To *us*. It might to her. We don't really know what she wants.'

Alice sighed. 'I think we can guess.'

'Regardless,' Emily said, 'it's too much of a coincidence. Isn't it? The emails and now this?'

'OK, look. I don't want to stoke the flames in the paranoia fire, but I've been thinking about the messages and, even if they're not spam, there might be a logical explanation. A not-awful one. This is all top-secret, right? This book?'

'They're worried if it's made public, there'll be an outcry and the book will have to be cancelled.'

'Won't there be one anyway?'

'An outcry after publication equals sales,' Emily said wryly.

'Well, what if those messages are from someone who's found out about it and is threatening to go public? *I know who you are* – Jack Smyth's ghostwriter. *I know what you did* – signed on to work on this book. The next one could say, *So tell Morningstar to pay me a fuck ton of hush money or I go to the papers.*'

It was tempting to believe, but for Emily, it didn't quite fit.

'Maybe,' she said. 'But where does the solicitor's letter fit in?'

'Have you any very elderly, very distant relatives, by any chance?'

'I doubt I've just unexpectedly inherited a fortune, if that's what you're suggesting.'

'You're sure Mark won't open it anyway?'

'He won't. He wouldn't.'

'What if *I* did? I have your spare key. You tell him I need a book back that you borrowed off me or something. I go round, I get the letter, I tell you what's inside.'

Emily liked that idea but . . . 'What if he's at home?'

'I'll make something up. I could go after work today.'

'I don't know,' she said. 'Is it a bit, like, dramatic?'

'"*Dramatic*"?' She could practically hear Alice's eyes roll. 'You're on some haunted movie set five thousand miles from home, interviewing a murderer and worried that you're getting sued. *I'll* be picking up your post.'

She had a point.

'OK, yeah,' Emily said. 'If you don't mind.'

'It's done.'

'Thank you.'

'Are you OK?'

175

'I'm fine.'

'How much of a lie is that, percentage-wise?'

'I'm grand. Really.'

'But . . . ?'

'But, well, what if he did it?'

'Are we back to talking about Jack?'

After a beat, Emily said, 'Yes.'

'You ask that like everything was different yesterday, when it was exactly the same.'

'Is that a riddle?'

'You know what I mean, Em.'

Emily hoisted herself up onto her elbows, then into a sitting position. 'It's first thing in the morning here after a really bad night's sleep, I've only had a half a coffee and I'm getting a headache. So, sorry, but you're going to have to spell it out for me.'

'He *did* do it.'

'We don't actually—'

'Yeah, yeah, yeah,' Alice said. 'I know. Innocent until proven guilty. Whatevs, as the kids say.'

'I don't think they do anymore, actually.'

'But he *probably* did it, didn't he? Statistically and logically. Because what man whose wife was murdered by someone else would write a book about being accused of it, not even a year after her death? I mean, is this really the best use of his time? If *I* had his money and his profile, I might be, you know, offering a reward for information that leads to the arrest of her killer or something. But no, he's over there with you, telling his side of her story. Does that sound like something a normal person would do? Or has he got away with murder and now he wants to get away with the barefaced cheek of writing a book about it? And Em, you *know* the answer. You knew it before you left. Is it that he was nice to you yesterday? That he seems nice? And genuinely sad? Because you and I know better than most that men who do bad things can seem like men who wouldn't do them.' A pause. 'Is the real issue here not what Niall told you but that, before you heard the gory details, you'd started to believe that Jack was innocent?'

Yes, Emily said silently. *That's exactly it.*

'Neil,' she corrected absently.

'Think of the money, Em. Of not owing that money any-more. Of being able to move on. And look, it's only a few days. Jobs are called jobs for a reason. Speaking of which, I must go and spend an hour in a mouth that I'm pretty sure has never even had a one-night stand with a toothbrush.'

'Want to swap?'

'You wouldn't want to, trust me. I'll let you know how it goes with the letter. Let me know if you get any more emails, OK?'

'I will. Thanks.'

'Call if you need me. Call anyway.'

'OK.'

Alice hung up.

Emily was reaching to take out her earbuds when there was a loud, sudden bang that made her jump.

Not from the construction site, but close by.

Inside, even though nothing in Bookmark had moved or fallen and she could see nearly the whole space.

She frowned, confused – until, on a delay, her brain decoded the noise: it was the sound of something hitting the connecting door on its other side.

Living in an apartment block, Emily had already spent too

177

many hours of her life playing a game of What the Hell Are My Neighbours Even *Doing* in There Anyway? Her guess in this instance would be bouncing a football or basketball hard off the door, but it could just as easily have been a foot kicking, or the punch of a fist.

And it hadn't sounded like it had had to travel through *two* doors.

Had someone opened the one on the other side? Why would they do that? Had someone been standing there, trying to listen in on her phone call? Had she been speaking loud enough for them to succeed?

What had they heard?

What had *Jack or Grace* heard, since it had to be one of them?

There wasn't time to dwell on it, because the clock on the wall in the kitchenette informed her it was five minutes past ten.

Shit.

She was late. Emily hopped off the sofa-bed and did a speedy circuit of Bookmark, turning things off, pulling on her shoes, dabbing some powder on her face because something was better than nothing, grabbing her keys and dashing to the door.

Outside, she was met by a wall of noise. It was all the same sounds as yesterday – hammering, drilling, banging – but louder; she wondered if they were working closer to Beach Read today. She understood now why they were the only people staying here. Anyone in their right mind would wait until all the work was finished, or at least had moved off to the other side of town.

She hurried down the steps, into the courtyard.

Someone had removed the damaged lantern and collected the broken glass left by the pool. The door to the main house was closed but not locked, presumably as a defence against the noise. She made sure to close it behind her again.

She didn't bother to check if Grace was in the kitchen.

She ran up the back stairs.

Jack was already in the room, sitting on the couch, looking at his phone.

He seemed completely relaxed and not like someone who, less than five minutes ago, had been pressed up against the other side of a door listening to his ghostwriter talk about how, on balance, he'd probably killed his wife.

'Oh, hey,' he said, looking up. 'Good morning.'

Blood everywhere ... Eye out of its socket ... Face caved in ...

'Sorry I'm late,' Emily said.

'I didn't even notice you were. Don't worry about it.'

She went straight to the coffee machine, which thankfully gave her a reason to turn her back to Jack.

She couldn't remember the last time she'd drunk something that wasn't wine, coffee or Coke. She *really* needed to make an effort to drink some water today.

After this coffee.

'What happened to you last night?' Jack said. 'When I came back out, you'd disappeared.'

It was only then that Emily remembered what she'd said to Grace on the warm buzz of a mild wine inebriation.

Oh God.

Hadn't she basically accused Grace of behaving inappropriately around Jack? And unprofessionally in general? Grace wouldn't say that to Jack though, would she?

What would *she* say if Grace did, and Jack asked her about it?

New rule: no more wine.

'I was just tired,' she said. 'I went to bed early.'

The coffee machine whirred to life.

'Is everything OK?'

'Yeah.' She still hadn't turned around to face him. She was watching the machine's nozzle spit steaming brown liquid into her cup like her life depended on it.

'Are you sure?'

'Did you get through to your friend? The owner? About the guy who broke in?'

'No. Not yet. He's in France. That's where he lives. So with time zones ... I'm waiting for him to call me back. I don't want to do anything until I talk to him. I wouldn't want to get anyone in trouble if there's no need.'

The coffee machine beeped, signalling that it was finished. Emily picked up the cup, steeled herself and turned around.

'Don't let Grace catch with you that,' Jack said, pointing at her jeans pocket.

When she put her hand there, she felt the solid outline of her phone.

'Shit.'

In the rush to get out, she'd forgotten to leave it behind.

'It's not a big deal. Just turn it off and stick it in one of the desk drawers. She'll be none the wiser.' Jack grinned. 'I won't tell.'

She sat down at the desk, set down the coffee and did as Jack suggested.

'Are you *sure* you're OK?' he asked.

The laptop and voice-recorder were there, neatly lined up with the desk's edge. Grace had mentioned something about

180

locking them away, so she'd already been in here this morning.

Emily pressed the space bar, waking up the computer, and saw that overnight a new folder had appeared right in the middle of the desktop.

It was labelled TRANSCRIPTS.

'Yeah,' she said absently.

She double-clicked, and found a single Word document saved with yesterday's date as its file name. When she opened that—

EJ: Cycling is suffering.

JS: Yeah so if you're good at road-racing what you're really good at is pushing through pain. There's this guy Tyler Hamilton. Used to race for US Postal. Famously tough. He once broke his shoulder during the Giro . . .

The document was over a hundred pages long.

Someone – Grace, it had to be – had listened to the recording of yesterday's interview and typed the whole thing up. That's what she must have meant when she told Emily she'd stayed late working.

Which was great news, because it meant that *she* didn't have to do it, and everything would be recorded twice over as they went along. But it also added a new ingredient to her general uneasiness, because it meant that Grace had heard every single thing that both of them had said yesterday.

And Emily had since discovered that Grace worked for Jack, who'd pretended to Emily that Grace worked for Morningstar.

'Because it doesn't seem like it,' Jack said.

She looked up at him. 'What?'

'Emily, what's wrong? Has something happened? You seem—'

'Does Grace work for you?'

He said nothing for a long moment, then, 'Yeeahhh?', dragging out the 'ah' sound to add an undercurrent of *obviously*. 'She's my PA.'

'She's your PA,' Emily repeated.

'Yeah.'

'She works for you.'

'Yeah. Why? Is there a problem?'

'It's just that, when I arrived, I asked you if the assistant from Morningstar was here and you said, "Yes, Grace, she's gone back to her hotel."'

Jack frowned. 'I'm not sure I—'

'You told me Grace worked for Morningstar.'

'No,' he said patiently. 'I told you that Grace, *my* assistant, had gone back to her hotel. You must have misunderstood me, or I misheard you.' Jack laughed a little awkwardly. 'What difference does it make?'

So Grace *hadn't* been hiding the fact that she worked for Jack, actually, and since she did, she had a perfectly good reason to be in a photo with his wife at some event. And no wonder she'd looked so blank when Emily had asked her if Jack knew about the situation with the advance owing and the undelivered book.

'Never mind.' Emily rubbed at her temples. 'It's just that I thought she worked for Morningstar, that's all. That she was on the same side. But obviously I picked that up wrong. I was just off the plane, so . . .' She saw Jack's facial expression. 'I didn't mean *sides*, I just—'

'Then what did you mean?'

Something new was swirling in the air between them, something unfamiliar and cold and uncomfortable.

'I just thought she was working for me,' Emily said. '*With* me. That I could, you know, ask her to do things.'

Jack's head suddenly turned towards the door.

She heard it now too: voices, coming from downstairs.

Multiple voices. Arguing.

'Who's that?'

Jack was already on his feet, moving towards the door. 'I don't know.'

He left the room and she followed him out.

The voices were coming from the living room. When Emily got to its door, she stopped just behind Jack and saw Grace standing with two people she'd never seen before: a brunette wearing a crumpled linen shirt dress, lots of gold jewellery and a designer bag, and a grey-haired, older man in a short-sleeved button-down shirt and chinos with a crisp line ironed into the leg.

'... *not* going to interrupt them,' Grace was saying when Jack said, 'What's going on?'

Three heads turned slowly towards him, synchronized like actors performing a scene they'd rehearsed.

'Jack—' Grace started.

'What are you all doing here?' he asked, cutting her off. 'If you've come to stop this, you've wasted a trip.' Jack turned to Emily. 'Meet my sister, Ruth,' he said, pointing, 'and my solicitor, Joe Roche.'

The solicitor cleared his throat. 'Perhaps we could talk in private, Jack?' he asked, giving Emily a sidelong glance.

'You can speak freely, Joe. She's signed an NDA.'

'I know, I drafted it. But it won't cover this.'

'It's OK,' Emily said, moving to go. 'I'll leave you guys to talk privately.'

'Stay,' Jack commanded. Then he asked Grace, 'What's going on?'

Grace looked to Ruth, who looked to Joe, who looked to Jack.

'I'm afraid your situation has changed,' Joe said, his expression grim. 'We didn't come here to try to stop you writing this book. We came here to tell you that you no longer have the option of writing it. You need to get home as soon as possible. I'm sorry to be the one to tell you this, Jack, but a warrant has been issued for your arrest.'

'The move from amateur to professional was like relocating from the Earth to the moon. Euro-GBA wasn't a top team, and I was only a neo-pro – a rookie, barely trusted to drop back and get the water bottles – but still, there were suddenly people around me whose job it was to help me do *my* job better. A mechanic. A doctor. Drivers. Coaches. Comms. And most importantly, the soigneurs, who took care of everything from food to kit to massages. The hotels were the same standard as the ones we'd previously booked and paid for ourselves – identikit chain hotels off major roads, the kind likely to have their own large car parks and not care when one of the soigneurs barged into the kitchen to boil us up a vat of pasta – but everything else seemed to change.

Turning pro does not mean you've "made it", or even that you get to race in every event. Your *team* might not even get to race in it, so the competition starts there. Our boss, the directeur sportif, along with the coach and other support staff, decides who gets the sacred spots based on our performance – but not just on the bike. Everything from our mood at breakfast to how we take our teammates' successes to how early we get to bed is watched, recorded, considered and weighed.

Everything matters.

Everything has a consequence.

You might think that in a cycling team everyone is just trying to go as fast as they can. But that would be kind of pointless. Wouldn't it be better if, say, the team worked together to get their strongest, fastest man across the line first? If they worked inside the peloton to protect him, to conserve his energy, to keep him safe from attacks, and then, when the time is right, help him break away for a win?

That is what we do.

You're not all going for individual glory.

This may sound strange at first, but I always say: how is it different from a football team? You have different roles there, too, based on what suits their strengths best. Striker, defender, goalkeeper – how often does a goalkeeper score a goal? And what if everyone who knew they couldn't be a striker just didn't bother playing professional football at all? You may not get the individual glory, but you still get to have your dream job. You still get to play football. And when the striker gets the ball in the back of the net, it's the team that wins.

I learned pretty quickly that I made an excellent domestique.

I know this sounds like it might have been a crushing realization. Growing up dreaming of the Grand Tour, of being the rider in the yellow jersey leading the pack down the Champs-Élysées, only to join your first professional team, look around at your competition and realize that you're probably never going to be that guy. But actually, it was freeing. It was a load off. Sometimes I look at athletes who spend their entire careers chasing this one thing – a win at Wimbledon, an F1 world championship, an Olympic gold medal – and I wonder, what happens when it doesn't happen? How can you point everything in your life towards one goal, only to never make it? How can a person recover from that level of disappointment?

I was getting to do what I'd always wanted to do without that kind of pressure. Every day I got on my bike, I felt like I'd already won. I know, that sounds cheesy. But it was true. I was happy. I had made it, even if "it" was different to how I'd imagined.

But I had no idea what was just around the corner.'

IV

CONFESSIONS

16

A warrant has been issued for your arrest.

The words seemed to suck all the air out of the room.

Blood rushed in Emily's ears. Jack half-walked, half-staggered to the nearest chair and collapsed into it. Joe asked the women if they'd mind if he spoke to Jack alone in a way that suggested he wasn't asking, and the three of them murmured their consent and duly filed out into the hall.

Ruth muttered something about needing a smoke before taking off towards the courtyard. Grace turned back to slide the living-room doors shut behind them. Just as they closed, Emily glimpsed Jack, pale and shellshocked, staring straight at her. She only had time to panic about what her face should be doing in this moment – communicating disdain, mouthing *it'll be all right*, nothing at all because she should be neutral? – before the doors shut and Jack was gone, and she was alone with Grace in the hallway.

'I can't believe this,' Grace whispered. 'It's been ten months. We're here *three days* and they decide to arrest him?'

Emily doubted it was a coincidence.

'Has he left Ireland before now?' she asked. 'Maybe the guards thought he was, I don't know, fleeing the jurisdiction or whatever they call it.'

'*Fleeing?*' Grace spat. '*Fleeing what?*'

Blood everywhere . . . Eye out of its socket . . . Face caved in . . .

'I need to get my phone,' Emily said. 'I left it upstairs.'

It was perhaps a sign of how distracted Grace was by the news of Jack's arrest that she didn't react to this egregious breach of regulations.

Or maybe her lack of reaction was because she knew it didn't matter now.

Jack getting arrested didn't necessarily mean he was going to be charged, but it was what had to happen before he could be. It changed nothing and everything. The book would surely be cancelled. Emily presumed that, legally, it would have to be. If he continued with it, he'd risk harming his own defence and profiting from the proceeds of crime, which was a crime in itself.

She wasn't sure how to feel about the fact that this madness was almost certainly over. On one hand, the sick, acidic dread of owing a huge sum of money was working its way back into her chest. But on the other, was having to sit alone in a room with Jack, after this development, the more attractive prospect? It had been one thing when he was a man the general public had convinced themselves had killed his wife. Now that the authorities had formally announced that they felt the same way, things were different. After all, the Gardaí were the ones with all the facts, the evidence, the expertise.

They would *know*.

192

Upstairs, back in the interview room, she retrieved her phone from the drawer. Out the window on the courtyard side, she could see Ruth pacing up and down parallel to the long edge of the pool, smoking. Emily turned away and sat on the couch, consciously choosing the end of it Jack never sat in.

She tensed as she unlocked her phone's screen, but relaxed when she saw that there were no new emails.

Mark had sent a text fifteen minutes ago. *Did you by any chance take my Olympus? Can't find it.*

She glared at the words, acutely annoyed and mentally formulating a response that would adequately explain to him how long down her list of priorities the location of his digital voice-recorder was right now.

But she *had* taken it, actually. It was in her backpack, over in Bookmark. She'd thought she'd need it; it hadn't occurred to her that everything would be provided. She hadn't bothered to ask and then she'd forgotten to tell him.

I have it, sorry, she typed in response and hit SEND.

Then she remembered that Alice was going to call around, so she sent a follow-up. *Alice is going to drop in later to collect something. She'll probably text first.*

Next, Emily opened her banking app and stared at the balance of her current account. The digits were purple, indicating that she was overdrawn. Her salary was due in on Friday and then the same dance could begin again.

It hadn't really bothered her before now, this living month to month. She had a roof over her head, the things she needed and, occasionally, a few of the things she wanted. Every now and then she'd be gripped by the fear that something terrible was about to happen and there'd be a panicked spurt of applying for better jobs – jobs that would pay more, that offered career progression, the kind that people with mortgages and private health insurance and pensions had – but she rarely got as far as an interview and never beyond it.

If she mentioned *The Witness*, they'd start asking questions about writing and publishing that she knew translated to concerns that she only cared about having a proper job temporarily, or that she'd never really care about it at all. If she didn't mention it, it was hard to explain why she'd only ever worked entry-level jobs for little money and why there were so many gaps in her employment.

She didn't know what to do. She didn't know what she *should* do. But regardless of what happened with Jack, she knew that, when she got back home, she was going to have do *something*.

She closed the banking app and saw—

One new email.

And knew with a sickening certainty who it was going to be from.

TELL HIM OR I WILL.

Emily tried to swallow back the stale taste that had suddenly filled her mouth.

I know who you are. I know what you did. Tell him or I will.

Three messages, now. And this last one hadn't come in while she was sleeping, or getting ready to leave Bookmark this morning, or sitting in this room interviewing Jack. It hadn't been on her phone a couple of minutes ago, when she'd first sat down on the couch and unlocked the device. It had just come in now, while she was sitting here alone, holding it in her hand.

Was the sender *here*, in Sanctuary?

Were they watching her right now?

She tapped on her own name and stared at the email address that appeared in its place, willing it to reveal some information. *W9780099282914@hotmail.com*. Something about those numbers . . .

Emily had a strange feeling she'd seen them somewhere before.

But where? No phone number she'd be dialling would start with 978. It was too many digits to be a bank account and too few for a credit card, but what was it? She copied and pasted it into the search box on her browser. When she hit Go, the screen filled with links to places where you could buy a used hardback copy of *The Witness* online.

978-0099282914 was her ISBN.

Every book published was assigned a unique numerical identifier, an International Standard Book Number. Whoever was sending these emails had taken the ISBN for the hardcover edition of *The Witness* and stuck a 'W' at the start to make their email address. If her own name as the sender wasn't, in itself, evidence enough that this was indeed about her and not some random spam shot, then this left no doubt about it at all.

Who the hell was sending these messages?

And *why*?

She typed a search-friendly version of that question – *how can I identify the sender of an anonymous email?* – into the search box and hit Go.

The top suggestion was to contact the host of the email address and ask them for the information, which was about as useful to her as a chocolate teapot when the host in question was Hotmail. The next tip she found was to type the email address into Facebook's search box; if someone had used it to sign up for an account, their profile should appear. But none did, so no one had, unsurprisingly. Clearly, this email had been set up for one purpose and one purpose only. She kept scrolling until she found advice to use the 'show original' option in Gmail's menu to find the sender's IP address, which would give her the sender's general location.

That would at least be *something*.

But when she did it, the email transformed into a huge mass of messy, incomprehensible code. Despite scouring it three times, she couldn't see anything that looked to her like it might be an IP address, or identified itself as one. If it was in there, it was well buried, or as good as hidden from someone who had no idea what they were looking at. And she thought that you probably had to pay to look up IP addresses, anyway.

Tell him or I will.

Who was 'him'? Jack? That would rule out Alice's theory about this being someone who wanted to expose the existence of this book. And how much time was this phantom giving the real Emily to complete the task? And how did they know that she'd even seen these messages? They could be going straight to her spam folder.

Which gave her an idea: she could just ignore them. Pretend she *hadn't* seen them. Set up a filter so all further messages from that address ended up in Junk, where they belonged, so from now on she wouldn't have to pretend. But while that sounded like the easiest option, it made her feel itchy and hot – because *they* wouldn't know that she wasn't reading them and might consider her disobedience a choice.

Unless she played dumb. Like, *really* dumb.

She hit REPLY and typed, *Just FYI I think you may have the wrong person/email address. You've sent this to a person with the same name as you and the message doesn't make any sense to me. Sorry!* She went to press SEND, then thought about her own IP address. She was on Beach Read's wifi. If the sender was more tech savvy than she was, they might be able to find *her* location from this message. And if the 'him' they were referring to was Jack and they knew that she was with him . . .

Replying might just lead this person straight here.

'Does that fucking noise go on *all* day?'

Emily startled at the voice.

Ruth, Jack's sister, was standing in front of her. She hadn't heard anyone come up the stairs.

'They, ah, they stop early in the afternoon,' Emily said, putting her phone face-down on the couch beside her. 'Or at least, they did yesterday.'

'It's such a *racket*. It's going to give me a fucking migraine.' Ruth surveyed the room before choosing Emily's usual seat behind the desk. 'So. You're the ghost.'

Emily nodded even though it hadn't been a question.

'Since when?'

'You mean, when did I get the job? Monday.'

'*Monday?* As in, Monday just gone?'

'I met with Beth and Carolyn that morning and—'

'Who are they?'

'They're with Morningstar, the publisher,' Emily said. 'Beth is the editor and Carolyn is the publishing director. I met them on Monday morning and by Tuesday evening I was here.'

'And they told you up front what the project was?'

The question felt soaked in judgement, which was interesting considering that it was Ruth's own brother who was writing this book.

'Well, yeah.'

'No offence, but why you?'

Emily shifted in her seat. 'Well, I'd worked with them before.'

'As a ghostwriter?'

'No. This is my first time doing that.'

'But you'd written about cycling?'

'No . . .'

'Sport?'

'I wrote a novel.'

'A novel? Would I have heard of it?'

The world's *most* ridiculous question. It was like asking another person 'Am I hungry?' How the hell were *they* supposed to know the answer to *that*?

She wanted to say as much to Ruth, but this was both the sister of her high-profile client *and* a woman who'd recently found out that her brother was being arrested in connection with a murder – and the victim was her sister-in-law – so Emily elected to give her a pass.

'Probably not,' she said. 'It was a few years back.'

Ruth was peering at her like she was an exhibit in a museum. 'Sorry,' she said, 'I'm not trying to be rude. I'm just trying to figure this out. You see, my brother never leaves anything to chance. Every decision, big or small, is considered and researched and weighed up and planned. Whenever he's getting a new phone, I actually tell him: please don't talk to me about it. Because he will drive you mad reading reviews, making comparisons, talking to the guys in the shop, talking to us about ours – and that's his choice of *phone*. You're the person who was going to help him write the most important story he'll ever tell. So I'm wondering, why you?'

'I don't know.'

'But there must be *something*.'

'I'm not sure if he got to pick me.' Emily tried to think back to exactly what Beth and Carolyn had said. Wasn't it something like *we're all in agreement*? 'My guess would be that the publishers suggested me and then he had a yay or nay. I think it would always be the publisher who finds the ghostwriter, as far as I know. Unless there's an existing relationship, which there wasn't.'

Ruth made a *hmm* noise.

'I think they were having trouble finding someone,' Emily added.

An eye-roll. 'Oh, I bet.'

'I guess it's all moot now, anyway.'

'Yeah,' Ruth said with a sigh. 'I tried to tell him it was a bad idea. We all did. But he went and did it anyway. Secretly. We thought he was in New York, taking business meetings. Grace thought that too. Then when they land, he springs this on her.'

So Grace must be the other part of the *we* who had flown with Jack from Dublin Airport.

'How did you find out he was here?' Emily asked.

'Grace called me, freaking out.'

'She doesn't want him to do this?'

Ruth met her eye. 'No one who cares about Jack even a little bit would *let* him do this, let alone encourage it.' She stood up. 'Look, the silver lining to the arrest is that this can't happen now. Although I honestly don't know how he ever thought it could. Or why the publisher agreed to it. I mean, seriously. A confession, but not really? How it happened if he did it but he definitely didn't, because he's innocent, but if he wasn't, here's how it went down? How the hell was *that* ever going to work?'

It took Emily a beat to grasp what Ruth was saying.

Then she thought, *Wait, what?*

Her face must have been saying the same thing, because Ruth said, 'Shit. You don't know, do you? Didn't they tell you? Didn't *he* tell you? God, trust my brother . . .' She shook her head. 'This book – it was going to be Jack's confession. That's what he promised the publisher. That's the only reason they offered him a contract. He was going to tell you how and why he killed Kate, and you were going to help him tell the world.'

17

Jack had initially wanted to do a straightforward book, Ruth explained while Emily tried to ignore the insistent buzzing in her ears. The one he had described to her, his side of the story. But no publisher was interested. *No one wants to read that*, they told him. *No one cares*. So he came up with a different pitch. A fictional confession. A hypothetical one, because it had to be, because Jack was innocent. He didn't kill Kate or start the fire in their home, but if he had, this was how he would've done it. But he didn't.

The doublethink made Emily's head hurt.

'I don't understand,' she said.

'Join the club.' Ruth rolled her eyes. 'The way he explained it to me was that he was going to tell his story, his true story, the one he'd wanted to share, up until the night of the fire. But then, in the penultimate chapter, he'd *confess*' – she made air quotes there – 'to the murder and arson. Explain what led him to do it, the blow-by-blow of what happened inside the house, and his efforts to cover it up afterwards. Written as if he had done what everyone suspected he had, as if they'd been right about him all along. And then the start of the next chapter would be, *not*! As if. Ha, ha, joke's on you, none of that was true and you're an idiot for even thinking it was. He'd say he made it all up, because he had to, because he wasn't there, and the book would end with him reasserting his innocence.' She paused for another eye-roll. 'The way he justified it was that it would be the book he wanted to write, with the exception of that one chapter, and that one chapter was the only way he was going to get the book he wanted to write. And he'd make it clear that that part was fiction.'

'But—' Emily started, before faltering, because she didn't even know where to begin. But *everything*. Everything about this was insane. And stupid. Dangerously so, for Jack. 'But something is either true or it isn't. You can't make something up in the middle of a book you're otherwise selling as being the whole truth. And this is his memoir. It's in the first person. So, what? He's going to say "And that's when *I* killed Kate"? "When *I* hit her"? "When *I* set a fire to cover up what *I'd* done"? He's going to put that in *print*?'

Ruth threw up her hands as if to say, *What can you do?* 'Maybe you can talk some sense into him,' she said. 'Although I suppose then you'd also be talking yourself out of a job . . .'

Emily couldn't believe it. What Jack was planning was a monumentally stupid idea. Only a guilty man would confess, in any capacity, and no reader would care about what came after the bit where he said he *did* kill Kate, actually. They'd pay no attention to the denial. They probably wouldn't even bother to read it.

Not to mention the headlines its publication would generate, and far more people would read *them*.

'And Morningstar knew all this? They knew he was planning to confess?'

'They were counting on it,' Ruth said. 'That's the only reason he got the book deal. You know, I can't think of another time in his life when my brother made a genuinely bad decision. But there was just no talking him out of it. Maybe it's the grief, I don't know. I mean, Kate isn't even dead a year. Should he even be making big decisions now?' She exhaled. 'I don't want my brother to get arrested for something he didn't do, but maybe, in this instance, it's a good thing. It might shock some bloody sense into him.'

'I think I need to call Morningstar,' Emily said.

'I think you probably do.'

They both went back downstairs. There was a low murmur of voices coming from behind the closed living-room door. Ruth stopped in the courtyard to light another cigarette. Emily headed up to Bookmark and found Grace, hopping from foot to foot outside its open door, gesturing furiously for her to hurry up.

'I have Beth and Carolyn for you,' she whispered. 'They've been waiting for you for the last five minutes.'

'Waiting for me? But I didn't even know—'

'Just *go in*,' Grace hissed.

There was no time to ask why Grace hadn't come to get her, or tried her phone, or what the hell she thought she was doing letting herself into Bookmark *yet again*. Before Emily was even all the way inside, she saw that Beth and Carolyn were already on screen, specifically the one on the pink laptop set up on the breakfast bar that must belong to Grace.

The two women were sitting side by side at the same desk with a wall of framed book covers behind them.

Beth waved at her.

'Hi Emily,' she said, her smile and her tone both artificially bright. 'How have you been? How has it been going over there?'

'Not great,' she answered. 'To be honest.'

Behind her, Emily heard Bookmark's front door close.

A half-second later, Grace passed by the front windows, crossing the deck to descend the stairs back to the courtyard.

'Obviously,' Carolyn said. 'The arrest changes things.'

'But maybe not as much as you'd think,' Beth added.

'I know about the confession,' Emily said.

The two women exchanged glances.

'How?' Beth asked. 'Did Jack—?'

'His sister just told me.'

'Well, needless to say, we would've preferred if you hadn't found out that way.'

'Why didn't you tell me?'

Carolyn leaned forward, closer to the camera. 'That was the most top-secret element of an already top-secret project. Information was shared on a strictly need-to-know basis.'

'I'm his ghostwriter. Didn't *I* need to know?'

'Look,' Beth said. 'Jack was going to tell you his story and that was what his story was going to be. You've already spent hours with him. Did you know everything that was going to come out of his mouth in advance? Of course not. So whether or not you knew going in about this particular element . . .' She pressed her lips together. 'What difference, really, would it have made?'

Emily opened her mouth to say, *All the difference! I wouldn't have done it!*

But was that really true? With or without this crazy

204

confession chapter, it would still have been the only way out of her Morningstar debt. She might have been more reluctant to say yes, but she probably still would've said it.

As much as she didn't want to admit it, she doubted knowing about this from the get-go would have changed anything much at all.

Except everything would have made a bit more sense.

Emily had bought Jack's motivation. Back in the Fitzwilliam, when Carolyn and Beth had talked about his being trapped in a hellish limbo and not being able to prove his innocence and wanting the speculation and suspicion to end, she'd accepted the logic. Sure, she thought it was risky and foolish and she very much doubted Jack was going to get the result he wanted, but she could see why he was doing it.

Why were *Morningstar* buying it, though?

Yes, there was a ravenous public appetite for details of this case, but how interested were the reading public going to be in a suspected wife-killer's protestations of innocence? Enough for a publisher to risk this much? To wade into a murky sea not only of moral ramifications, but legal ones too, if the case ever went to court? That, for Emily, had been harder to reconcile, but she'd assumed Carolyn and Beth knew what they were doing.

And now she knew they did.

With a confession inside, even one signposted as hypothetical, this book's flight off the shelves would've been guaranteed to go supersonic. Observers could purse their lips, critics could stand on their morals and readers could pretend to be disgusted, but if everyone was so above it, if no one was interested in true crime, who was it all for? The podcasts. The long reads. The eight-part limited series based on a long read, streaming now along with its after-show podcast companion. If they weren't being listened to, read and watched, they wouldn't be getting made.

Now this one couldn't be.

'Is, ah, Grace there?' Beth asked lightly.

'No, I'm alone, but . . .'

Emily looked up, at the connecting doors. Was there someone standing on the other side of them, listening in?

'This is very sensitive,' Carolyn said.

'Hang on one second . . .' Emily picked up the laptop and relocated it to the countertop next to the kitchen sink, the furthest point she could get from the connecting doors while still being inside. She turned down the laptop's volume a little. 'Go ahead.'

'We always knew there was a risk of an arrest,' Carolyn said. 'Or, let's say, a change in Jack's legal status. And he knew it too. So there had to be a contingency plan. We didn't want to end up in a situation like HarperCollins did with OJ Simpson. So we only agreed to go ahead with this book if we could add a clause to the contract that would, in such an event, protect us. Offset our risk.'

'What does that mean?' Emily asked.

Carolyn looked at Beth and nodded encouragingly.

'Until such time as Jack is charged,' Beth began, '*if* that ever happens, we can proceed as planned. So long as Jack agrees. In the absence of a charge or a conviction, it's ultimately up to him whether or not he wants to publish this book. But if there *is* one, putting us in a situation where we can't legally go ahead, then we go to Plan B, which is to take all the materials collected and use them as the basis of a non-fiction account of the crime, which we are free to write and publish without his cooperation, using the writer of our choosing, without any editorial input from any other parties and without having to compensate him, which sidesteps any legal issues on his profiting from it.' She paused to take a breath. 'But we can only publish such a book *after* there's a verdict.'

Emily frowned, confused.

'We either publish Jack's story in his own words,' Carolyn clarified, 'or the definitive book on the case, using his own account, that we'll have ready to go to print the day the verdict comes in.'

His hypothetical *account*, Emily corrected silently. *Allegedly.*

'And Jack agreed to that?' she said.

'He had to. The deal was contingent on it.'

'And he maintains his innocence,' Beth said. 'So . . .'

So he was agreeing to something he never thought would actually come to pass.

Emily had to admit, it was clever. Either Morningstar got to publish Innocent Jack's yes-but-no confession now, or they got hours and hours of Guilty Jack talking in detail about the crime which they could use exclusively as the basis for a book about the case at a later date. A book that could say anything, because Jack would have no editorial control over it. A far more attractive publishing prospect, really, than *this* book—

It was then that it hit her.

This really *was* just a transcription job.

'I was never actually writing this book,' Emily said. 'Was I?'

That was why her lack of experience didn't matter. She hadn't been hired to ghostwrite Jack's story. She was here to get the raw material out of him for the book Morningstar actually wanted to publish, the one about a convicted killer.

The two women on screen shifted in their seats.

'You have a very important job,' Carolyn said. 'And it's even more important now that it looks increasingly likely we'll be going with Plan B.' She pressed her lips together again. 'Emily, it's absolutely crucial that we get the confession. You understand why, right?'

'Get the *confession*?' Emily spluttered. 'You want to keep *going*?'

'Jack wants to,' Beth corrected. 'And we have time. Grace tells us he can't go anywhere until first thing Saturday anyway. That's the earliest flight he could get on, unless he drives for seven hours, which he really doesn't want to do, she said, and the guards are OK with him arriving back in Dublin Sunday morning once he actually does that. What's it there now? Thursday lunchtime? You have the rest of today and all day tomorrow. All you have to do is keep going. Carry on as you were.'

'But due to recent events,' Carolyn said, 'this might be the only time we get with Jack, so . . . We need to prioritize.' She paused. 'Delicately.'

'Jack is hardly going to supply a confession now,' Emily said.

'He came to *us*, remember. He *wants* to do this book. I think there's a part of him that needs to. I suspect he'll be prepared to proceed as is until the situation changes – especially because he himself doesn't anticipate that it will.'

'But the situation *has* changed. He's getting arrested.'

'Listen,' Beth said, gently, in a more appeasing tone. 'If you're not comfortable with this, we understand.' Emily actually didn't think Carolyn did, but sure. 'When you signed up for this, there was no arrest on the horizon. We get it. So you have a choice. You can transfer what you've collected so far, wait to go home and forget all about this. You are free to make that decision. But we had an agreement, and if you choose not to fulfil your part in it, well . . .' She looked directly into the camera, meeting Emily's eye. 'Then we won't have an agreement.'

Translation: Emily would have had a brief, free trip to Florida, but she'd be back to owing Morningstar about as much money as she made in a year.

'From what we hear,' Beth continued, 'you and him are getting on like a house – are, ah, getting on well. So why not just talk to him for another few hours? All you're doing is listening to him say what he wants to say.'

'And steering him towards the confession,' Carolyn added, as if that weren't already crystal clear.

'OK,' Emily said. 'I mean, I'll try.'

She didn't know what other choice she had, at this point. And mainly, she just wanted to get off this call.

The two heads on screen tried not to look overly pleased with themselves, but failed miserably.

'We'll talk tomorrow,' Carolyn promised.

'Good luck,' Beth said, just as the screen went black.

Emily closed the laptop lid and put her head in her hands. What kind of mess had she got herself into? And Beth and Carolyn didn't even know about the threatening emails.

She dug out her phone, wanting to call Alice and unload the whole horrific story, and saw that Mark had sent yet another message about his stupid voice-recorder. He was looking for a file on it. Something about a spoken-word event he'd been at. Could she check if it was there? And if it was, could she download it and send it to him?

Emily rolled her eyes, annoyed.

But her backpack was sitting directly in front of her, in a corner of the couch. She might as well cross one thing off her list of problems.

She unzipped the main compartment, certain that that was where she'd put everything yesterday, when she'd been getting herself organized for Jack Smyth Interviews: Day One and didn't yet know that she wasn't supposed to bring her own electronic devices. She went from there to the internal zipped pocket. Then the side pockets. The front pocket, even though it was too small. She went back to the start and revisited each site, digging her hands right down inside them, spreading her fingers into the seams, checking and double-checking. Finally, she went to the window and held the mouth of the backpack open in a yawn, tilting it to every angle so she had enough light to do a visual search too, but Mark's Olympus wasn't there.

Someone had taken it.

Two days before the fire

'Hello? Anyone back here?'

Kate pushes her sunglasses up her nose just as her sister-in-law appears around the side of the house.

She doesn't immediately make her presence known so Ruth, dressed in a full-length, white wool coat and black leather boots with kitten heels, doesn't realize she's being watched as she stops at the edge of the back garden's muddy grass, looks down at it and wrinkles her nose in disgust.

Kate catches her breath, steels herself and says, 'Well, hello,' trying to sound the kind of surprised that's happy.

Ruth looks up. '*There* you are.'

'Were you ringing the bell? Sorry, I didn't hear.'

'Because you're sitting *outside*, in *November*, which is fully deranged.' Ruth starts picking her way across the grass on the balls of her feet, attempting to avoid the baldest, muddiest spots. 'What's wrong with you? It's fucking freezing.'

'I love this weather. Blazing sunshine, cold, crisp air—'

'Raging pneumonia, stubborn kidney infection—'

'I assure you, I'm quite toasty.'

Ruth reaches the patio. She lifts one boot and then the other

211

to survey the damage. Both heels are caked in mud. She exhales hard, annoyed, lifting a strand of hair clear off her face.

Kate stands up, holding her cocoon of a blanket to her shoulders, and lets Ruth give her a one-armed hug.

'I come out here to drink my coffee,' she says. 'It's bad for you to be cooped up inside all day with the heating on.'

'Yeah,' Ruth says. 'Sounds *awful.*'

'Do you want a coffee?'

'Would you make me drink it out here?'

'I'd get you a blanket.'

'Nah, you're grand.' Ruth sits down on one of the other chairs and winces. The cushions have been stored away in the garage for the winter; the bare cast-iron is probably penetratingly cold. 'I just had one. And I'm not stopping.'

Kate is relieved to hear this.

She and Ruth have always got on fine. As sisters-in-law. But she's also Jack's only sibling, his baby sister, and in that capacity there's been, at times, some friction. It seems like Jack had always looked after her and looked out for her, and everyone had to learn a new way to be when Kate became the woman he had to be looking after and looking out for *more.*

Ruth, twenty-seven now, wasn't always happy about the new family arrangements – but at least she took her complaints to her brother and never to Kate.

'So,' Kate says. 'Have I completely blanked or is this a surprise visit?'

'You haven't blanked.'

'What's the occasion?'

'I was passing so I said I'd drop in.'

'Passing?'

Their house isn't on the way to anywhere.

212

'I'm en route to Eyre Square,' Ruth says.

She means the store that Exis is about to open in Galway city, but she can't possibly mean to imply that the village of Adoran was on any route between where she lives in Dublin and there, because that would be a laughably obvious lie.

Kate decides to play along for now, knowing the real reason for this visit will show itself soon enough.

'How's that going?'

'The fit-out's done and the stock arrives today,' Ruth says. 'They should be open for the weekend. Emphasis on *should* be. Is it OK if I . . . ?' She's taken a packet of cigarettes out of her coat pocket and now she shakes them a little.

'Work away.'

'Want one?'

'No.' Kate does, actually, but it wouldn't be worth the hassle of Jack smelling it on her and the lecturing that would ensue. 'Thanks.'

Ruth lights up and takes a long, deep drag.

For a surprisingly long time, both of them sit in silence.

'So what's up?' Kate asks then, feeling like the pressure was building on her to break it.

'My blood pressure.'

'Besides that. Why are you really here?'

Ruth takes another drag and looks out into the garden. 'Bit of a mess, isn't it?'

'Well, it *is* November. And it's been exceptionally wet.'

'You should get that fake grass. Much easier.'

'That stuff is hideous. No, we're going to reseed it, in the spring. It'll look great by the summer.'

'In the summer,' Ruth repeats.

'Yeah.'

'So you're planning on still being here then?'

'Where else would we be?'

But even as she says this, she thinks of her conversation with Jack – about selling up, about running away – and it dawns on her that he might have told Ruth that.

That Kate had said they should cut their losses and close the business Ruth is currently managing director of.

'I found a house,' Ruth says then. 'I made an offer and it's been accepted.'

'Wait, what? You *bought* a house?'

Ruth nods, grinning a little. 'Yeah.'

'That's great. Wow. Congratulations.'

The saga of Ruth trying to buy her first house has been dragging on for, by Kate's count, at least eighteen months. She had felt a little that Ruth was being unnecessarily picky and looking for the perfect place rather than one that was good enough and could be made, over time, into something perfect but, even so, it had been an ordeal which anyone who read articles about the housing crisis would already be familiar with. Almost no homes for sale. Queues of hundreds for every viewing. Competing with cash bids that were way over the asking price. And that was all after trying to get a mortgage as a single woman, which had taken about as long.

'So where is it?' Kate asks. '*What* is it? Tell me everything.'

'A new-build in Maynooth. A three-bed semi, but it's really nice. Estate is nice too. And I'm the corner house, so I get an extra-large garden.'

Kate thinks of Ruth's earlier comment and really hopes she isn't planning on putting fake grass in it.

'Well, that all sounds great. You must be so happy – and relieved.'

'I am.' Another deep drag. 'I talked to Jack this morning.'

This in itself isn't news and when there isn't any more, Kate prompts, 'And?'

'Did something happen?'

'Well, the meeting didn't—'

'I don't mean with Exis.'

'Oh,' Kate says. 'Then . . . No?'

'He said something about a car.'

'A car?'

'That was outside, last night, sitting in the lane with its engine running and its lights pointed at the house.'

Ruth has so much detail about the incident that Kate is embarrassed now to change her tune and say, 'Oh, yeah. *That* car.'

Now it's Ruth's turn to say, 'And?'

'And what?'

'How did Jack react?'

'Oh . . .' Kate waves a hand. 'He's wound tight as a drum at the moment, so he *over*reacted. Did he tell you about the photographer we had here on Monday morning, for that thing in the magazine?'

'He didn't have to tell me, because it came back to the press office.'

'Did it? Shit. What did they say?'

'That Jack had been rude to their photographer . . . Who was in the car?'

Back to the bloody car. Why? 'I don't know.'

Which is the truth.

'Does Jack?' Ruth asks.

'Does Jack what? Know who was in the car? No.' Kate frowns. 'Why? Did he say something to you?'

215

'No,' Ruth says after a beat. She shifts her weight, straightens up in her seat. 'Look, Kate. I've just drawn down a mortgage that it was almost impossible to get, to purchase a house it was practically impossible to find. I can't lose my job now.'

So Jack *did* tell her.

'Ruth,' Kate says gently, 'if the business fails, you'll lose it anyway.'

'It won't fail.'

'It is failing, now. Present tense. It's already happening. If he doesn't manage to bring a partner on board, or get a bigger brand to buy him out—'

'Kate, look. You know I love you and I actually like you too. But – no offence – you don't know my brother like I do. You can't, because you weren't there for all the years he was fighting. National champion and Rio and a pro contract and the Tour – when they were all things he was still trying to get. You met him afterwards, when he'd been there, done that. So I'm sure he's talked about it and you've heard about it and you probably believe it, but you haven't seen what I mean when I say that Jack doesn't fail. He can't, because he's physically allergic to it. Honestly. It makes him ill. So he does whatever it takes to avoid it.'

'I know, but Ruth—'

'See, you *don't* know, though. Not really. Not the extent of it. Not the drive he has when things are going wrong and he needs to turn them around. So, look. I get it. If I were you, and I were looking at the numbers, I'd be like, yep, Exis is dying, let's get out. But you haven't seen what it's like when Jack's back's against the wall. If you had, you'd know he *will* turn

216

this around. He will. Because he has to. He always does. My brother *doesn't fail.*'

'Right,' Kate says.

Because what else *can* she say?

'Please stop talking about quitting and escaping,' Ruth says. 'Just for six months, OK? Give him six months.'

On *six*, Ruth's phone beeps with a new message.

She reads it and curses and says she has to go. The service elevator at Eyre Square is down and they have six pallets going nowhere in the loading dock.

Kate says, 'OK. And I mean, OK to what you said. I won't.'

'He'll find a way to turn it around, I know he will.'

'Will you be having a party? A house-warming?'

Ruth smiles a little. 'We'll see.'

As she gets up, the swing of her coat catches the thermal mug on the arm of Kate's chair, sending it flying, and on impact with the ground it loses its lid. If she notices that it's empty, or that both parts appear to be bone dry, she doesn't let on.

18

Emily had her neck thrown back to facilitate the swallowing of two chalky white headache pills when she heard a knock on Bookmark's front door. She turned expecting to see Grace, back to collect her laptop and demand a debrief on the meeting with Morningstar, but it was Jack, bent at the waist a little so he could make eye contact with her through the glass.

Can we talk? he mouthed.

This day last week, Emily had been sat in a featureless, claustrophobic cubicle, listening to a woman complain for half an hour about how the discounted prices available to loyalty card holders were displayed within the supermarket. She had one point, which was that they should be made clearer, and Emily had accepted that and promised to *escalate the issue* within the first minute of the call. And yet the woman kept talking, making the same point over and over, with no deviation, repeating herself ad nauseam. In return for patiently listening, or trying to, Emily was paid a little more than the minimum hourly wage. Now, walking towards the door that would let in a man who had maybe murdered his wife and was definitely writing a book in which he confessed to it, she longed for the simple, inconsequential boredom of that cubicle and that call.

Jack moved to come in but she stepped outside, pulling the door closed behind her, and motioned to the two chairs on the deck.

'I have a headache,' she said. 'I could do with some air.'

And she didn't really want to be alone with him inside. She had no idea how this conversation was going to go. Better to have it in the open.

'I'm really sorry about all this,' he said once they were both seated.

'Which part?'

Jack exhaled. 'I suppose that's fair.'

'Ruth told me that you promised Morningstar a confession, and Beth and Carolyn just confirmed that that was true. You say you're innocent, that you didn't do this, but in this book you were planning on saying that you *did*. And nobody bothered to tell me, including you.'

'I *am* planning to say it,' Jack corrected. 'I still want to. And I'm sorry you weren't told, but we were having enough trouble as it was getting someone to do this without throwing that into the mix as well. And then I didn't tell you because . . .' He looked away, his jaw working. 'I thought if you got to know me a little first, you'd understand why I have to do this.'

'But I don't. At all. Confessing to something you say you didn't do? In *print*? Jack, it's madness. And now, with the arrest—'

'Look, I know how it sounds, OK? I'm not stupid.'

Emily bit down on the *and yet all the evidence suggests otherwise* sitting on her tongue.

'Try and consider this situation from my point of view,' Jack went on. 'Everyone thinks I did it. But you know what? I don't really care. Why would I care what strangers think of me? They don't know me. They don't know what's in my heart or in my head. And I know the truth. In time, they'll move on. They'll forget about me. And if they don't, I could always move away. The suspicion, yeah, it doesn't make life very nice, but I can live with it.'

'So this is about what? Money? Confess so you can sell more books?'

'No,' Jack said firmly. He seemed offended at the suggestion. 'That side of things isn't exactly great for me right now, but when Kate died, finances became the least of my worries. I don't *want* Exis to fail, but I'm happy to let it. And, look, it's not like we're out there making a cancer vaccine. We sell clothes to people who want other people to think they're on their way to or coming from the gym. Yes, there'll be job losses, but it's mostly going to be people who are either related to me or twenty-somethings working in retail for almost no money and a staff discount.'

'Then *why*, Jack?'

'It's the price I have to pay to get this book published. It was the only way I could get anyone interested and it was the only reason Morningstar offered me the deal.' He paused. 'It's just one chapter.'

'In which you plan on saying you killed your wife.'

'I'll make it clear that part is fiction.'

No one will believe you, Emily thought. She said, 'You could've self-published it.'

'What difference would that make? I'd still have to give people a reason to read it. And I needed a big publisher to help shoulder any legal risk. Besides, I suspect it's going to be an uphill battle to get people to take this book seriously. Self-publishing it wasn't going to help.'

'But why do this in the first place? You said you were doing this book because you wanted everyone to know that you had nothing to do with Kate's death. How exactly does *confessing to her murder* help achieve that?'

Silence.

Then Jack said, very quietly, 'Have you considered that maybe this isn't about me?'

'Who else would it be about?'

But the answer came to Emily as soon as she'd said it: Kate.

'I knew before the arrest,' Jack said, 'that the Gardaí were totally convinced that I'd done it. They have been, right from the start. This arrest doesn't surprise me, really – I mean, it's a shock, of course, to hear you're being *arrested* – but it was only a matter of time. But I know I didn't do this. I know I came home and the house was on fire and Kate was lying at the bottom of the stairs. But I *also* know that the coroner says it couldn't have happened the way I thought, that she wasn't injured in a fall, and that she died before the fire really started. So someone *did* do this. There's someone out there who is responsible for the death of my wife and not only have they not been found or identified, but the guards don't even believe they exist.'

Please God, no, Emily prayed silently. *Don't start talking about the real killer or killers.*

She'd been a toddler during the OJ Simpson trial, but she'd sat through all seven hours of the ESPN documentary, completely captivated – and alone, because the only thing Mark hated more than true crime was organized sports.

'I want to know what really happened that night,' Jack said. 'I *need* to know.'

'I don't see how this book could possibly achieve that.'

'But it happens all the time.'

'What does?'

'There's a crime that hasn't been solved,' Jack said, 'sometimes for years, sometimes with the wrong guy rotting in prison for it, and then someone makes a podcast or a TV show or writes an article about it, and the people listening start digging and investigating and uncovering stuff – because no, they're not the authorities, but they only have one case, this one, and they're trying to get to the truth for no reason other than they want to, so they're happy to give it their time. And the general public aren't tied to the methods and the' – he waved his hands on either side of his head – '*mindset* of an official investigation. They think outside the box. And they find things.'

'But you said you didn't want to do a podcast or an article—'

'And I don't,' he said, cutting her off. 'Because that would be ignoring the most important reason people do that kind of armchair investigating: because they *care*. I have to get them to care. About Kate, yes – well, they already do that, I think. But about me too. About a man who didn't do this, despite what everyone thinks. A man who lost everything, and a future miscarriage of justice.'

'So this *is* about you.'

'That's not what I—' He stopped to exhale, frustrated. 'Look, if everyone believes I did it, they'll think, well, case closed. I need some public pressure, which means I have to raise doubt in people's minds. If you have a better idea, I'd love to hear it, but I've thought about this long and hard and I'm convinced a book is the best way. The only way, really. To get all the information out there.'

Emily had a *much* better idea: do nothing at all. Go home, talk to the Gardaí, plead your case, then disappear. Find somewhere you can live out the rest of your life. Stop talking about this. Forget about doing this crazy book.

'What information?' she asked.

'Well, that's just it. I don't know what's pertinent. But there were things that week, things that didn't quite add up. I thought nothing about them at the time, but afterwards . . . Maybe they were important.'

'Like what?'

'Like on the night of the fire,' Jack said, 'I was going to meet a friend. I was tired and didn't feel like it, so I said that maybe I'd skip it and stay at home. And Kate had a really weird reaction to that. She was . . . I wouldn't say *panicked*, that's too strong, but she was definitely anxious. She wanted me to go. She wanted me out of the house.'

'Why?'

'I don't know, but if I found out that someone had come over that night, someone she was expecting, I wouldn't be surprised. It would fit.'

'Are you saying you think Kate was having an affair?'

Jack's eyes widened. 'What? No. Absolutely not.' He seemed genuinely taken aback at the suggestion. 'I meant, like, a friend coming over or something. Although I don't know who that could've been. Everyone we knew was back in Dublin. Or maybe she was planning to do something she needed me out of the house for. I don't know. And that's my

223

point: *I don't know*. But these are things that I think need to be investigated.'

'But surely they have been. You must have told the guards all this.'

'I told them everything, but if it wasn't something that pointed the finger at me, they didn't seem to care. For instance, that week, one evening, a car drove down our lane. Our house is at the end of a lane, out in the middle of the countryside – there's no reason for you to be on it unless you're coming to us or our neighbours, and this car was right outside our gate. At night, just sitting there with the engine running and the headlights pointed at the house. Kate saw it and called me to the window, and when I looked out, the car sped off. Who was that?' Jack threw up his hands. 'I don't know. The guards said it wasn't important, that it was probably just someone who'd got lost. But it had never happened before, whoever it was drove off when they saw that I was home, and forty-eight hours later Kate was attacked in the same house when I wasn't there. How can that not be important?'

Emily could see how, in the situation Jack was in, something innocuous could transform itself into a tantalizing mystery, a clue to something as yet uncovered, a discovery that would change everything. But a car in a country lane that had reversed back out? He was clutching at straws – and, if he were to put that straw-clutching in a book, potentially harming his own case.

'My solicitor flew all the way out here to tell me in person that I need to reassess my priorities,' Jack said, 'but I only have one and it's Kate. Just imagine, for one second, I can beam my thoughts into your brain and you can *see* that I'm innocent, that you can know for absolute certain that I didn't

224

do this, that what's happening here is that the wrong person is about to be charged with his wife's murder, which means that his wife's actual murderer is out there getting away with it. And maybe he's done it before or will again. Would you still walk away?'

Emily sighed heavily. 'I never said I was walking away. I was just trying to understand why you want to confess to something you didn't do.'

'Do you? Now?'

'No, not really.'

'Do you need to?'

'I suppose . . .' If Jack wanted to do this, who was she to stop him? And why would she *try* to stop him, when it was a solution to her own financial problems? 'No, I suppose I don't.'

'Look, I appreciate your concern,' Jack said. 'I do. But I know what I'm doing. And whatever happens, you were hired to do a job, Emily. That's all. Nothing will be your fault or your responsibility. The only person who has to worry about the consequences of my actions is me. How about . . .' Jack checked his watch, 'we meet upstairs in thirty minutes? Pick up where we left off? Joe and Ruth have gone to check in to their hotel. We should have an hour or two before they come back.'

'If that's what you want. But, ah . . .' She hesitated. 'If we only have the rest of today and tomorrow here, we should probably skip ahead. To the night of. If that's all right with you?'

A shadow of something crossed Jack's face but he said, 'Yeah. OK.'

They both stood up.

225

'Oh, Jack – this is a weird question, but did you by any chance see a digital voice-recorder around the place? It's about this big' – she demonstrated its size with a gap between her hands – 'and silver.'

'You mean the one up in the room? It's still there. On the desk.'

'No, it's like that but I mean my personal one.'

'Did you lose it?'

'I think so. But don't worry about it. I'll ask Grace.'

'OK. I'll see you up there?'

'See you up there.'

Emily watched Jack go, then went back into Bookmark, feeling deflated.

She wasn't a ghostwriter anymore – if she ever really had been. She was a double agent. She had to transcribe Jack's fake confession, but she also had to help him protest his innocence and redirect the Gardaí's attention to other, hitherto ignored, aspects of the investigation. And all this while everyone else, including his own publishers, appeared to think his guilt was a foregone conclusion and was plotting the publication of a book that would do the exact opposite of everything Jack hoped.

I know what I'm doing, he'd said.

But he didn't.

He may have thought about this, and planned everything, and considered all angles, but he was missing a crucial piece of information.

Tell him or I will.

He didn't really know who he'd hired to help him do it, or about the terrible thing she'd done.

But someone wanted to make sure he found out.

19

'OK.' Emily pressed RECORD on the voice-recorder. 'So. The night of the fire.'

Jack was in his usual spot on the couch, directly opposite her.

'I don't know where to start,' he said, shifting in his seat.

'Why don't you tell me what that day was like?' she said. 'What were you doing in the hours leading up to . . . Up to when you left?'

'OK.' He took a deep breath, exhaled slowly. 'Well . . . Kate hadn't slept very well. She'd been awake all night the night before, tossing and turning. That never happened. *I* was always the one who had trouble sleeping. I'd even say to her, I'm so jealous of how deeply you sleep. But that night, she didn't seem to get a wink. And I wasn't imagining it – she said as much when she got up. And she was up really early too, well before me. Which was also unusual. I was nearly always the first one out of bed.'

'Why couldn't she sleep? Did she say?'

'She said she'd just had too much coffee, but there was no way it was that. Something . . . I don't know, but I felt like something was eating at her. Worrying her. And she'd been awake all night thinking about it. And, also, there'd been the thing the day before.' He bit his lip. 'This feels bad, talking about her like this. You know, insinuating things.'

'You can take anything out afterwards,' Emily reminded him – although after her Zoom with Beth and Carolyn, she wasn't certain she was in a position to make guarantees. 'There's plenty of time to decide on the wording. Let's just focus on getting the facts out for now, OK?'

'OK.'

'So what thing the day before?' Emily checked for the re-assurance of the flashing red light. 'What had happened?'

'I have no proof of this,' Jack said, 'and I absolutely accept that it could just be a case of me starting to think about things differently after the fire. Interpreting things differently. Giving them too much significance or whatever. So I have to be honest here: I don't know if I actually had these thoughts at the time, or if I've mixed up my memories with things that have occurred to me since.'

Emily thought of the police interview that was ahead of him, and how well a line like that would go down in front of Garda detectives.

'Just tell me what you think you remember. Where your memories stand as of the here and now.'

'OK, well . . .' He took a deep breath, let it out. 'The day before the fire, in the morning, Kate went out. She was gone a while. A few hours. I don't remember talking to her before she left. I think maybe I'd been out for a run and when I got back she'd already gone, but I'm not sure. But when she did come

228

back, she told me she'd driven to this beach – one a good, like, hour's drive away – to go for a walk. For the second time that week, in freezing cold weather. And I don't know why, but I just got this vibe off her that maybe that wasn't the whole truth. She said she'd driven there, walked for an hour, then driven back, but she was gone way longer than that. And she put up a photo of the beach, on Instagram, before she even came home, which was also a bit odd. It was like . . . It was almost like she was trying to prove to me that she'd been there.'

'Did you question her?' Emily asked. 'Tell her that you didn't believe her?'

'No.'

'Where do you think she was?'

'Don't get me wrong: I think she *was* at that beach. There was sand in the car, in the driver's footwell.' That struck Emily as a weird thing to know. Had he gone checking for that, specifically, or just happened to notice? 'But I think maybe she went somewhere else too, that morning, that she didn't tell me about. Or maybe she was . . . She could've been meeting someone there.'

'Who?'

Jack shook his head. 'I've absolutely no clue.'

'For what purpose?'

Another shake. 'No idea.'

'Are you *sure* she wasn't having an affair?'

'No,' he said firmly. 'Absolutely not.'

Emily tried to figure out how best to word the extremely awkward question she wanted to ask, but before she could, Jack offered an answer.

'Our relationship was better than ever,' he said. 'Stronger

229

than ever. We were good. We weren't even married two years, we still felt like newlyweds. And leaving Dublin meant that most of the time it was just us two, on our own. It felt like we were in a bubble. In a good way. A great way. And honestly, I know this sounds a bit stupid, but we spent so much time together, she just wouldn't have been able to start seeing someone else. Logistically, I mean. I know that sounds daft, but it's true. It just . . . No, I really don't think that was it.'

But twice now, Jack had alluded to Kate meeting someone he didn't know about while he himself wasn't there.

If he wasn't hinting at an affair, what *was* he hinting at?

'Did you check her phone?' Emily asked. 'Emails? Try to find out what was going on?'

Was his extreme confidence coming from the fact that he *had* done that, and found nothing?

'No,' Jack said, glancing at the flashing red light on the voice-recorder. 'It crossed my mind, I'll admit it. But I didn't check. And then I couldn't, because her phone was destroyed in the fire . . . Look, I really don't think Kate was having an affair. I know how that sounds, but I really, objectively don't. I think a much more likely scenario is that something bad was happening and she was either trying to keep it from me, or sort it out herself before she told me about it. I was under a lot of stress at the time, with Exis. Things were about as dire as they'd ever been. We were trying to get someone to buy us out, or partner up. And, actually, earlier in the week, Kate had suggested we sell up everything and move to, like, France or Spain or somewhere and live on the cheap. Like we used to, back when we first met.'

'Was she serious?'

A shrug. 'I don't know. But I think so.'

'What did you say?'

'I told her I'd think about it,' Jack said.

'When you say something bad was happening . . . ?'

'I don't know. But things had happened before. Things she'd kept from me, so as not to worry me, that I only found out about later.'

'Like what?'

'Well . . . There was the thing with the messages. I told you that when she was on *Sunrise*, she used to get all these horrible comments and stuff, right? For a while there, things went a bit further. Someone was sending her anonymous messages – through email, through DMs – and making it sound like he was possibly following her around. He'd have known where she'd been and make comments about specific things she'd been wearing. That sort of thing.'

Emily raised her eyebrows. 'Are you telling me Kate had a *stalker*?'

'I don't know if I'd go that far. She didn't. But she didn't tell me about it until after the messages had stopped.'

'Did you ever find out who sent them?'

Jack shook his head. 'They stopped, suddenly, and Kate just wanted to forget about them. And really, they weren't that much worse than the things people were leaving online, in public, with their names and photos attached.'

'How much of this did you tell the guards?'

'I told them the truth about her movements,' he said. 'And about the messages and comments she'd had in the past. But I didn't say anything about her having trouble sleeping the night before, or suggesting we move, or my suspecting she didn't go to the beach for a walk.'

'Or that she might have been meeting with someone?'

231

'No.'

'Why not?'

'Because I know how it sounds,' Jack said, his voice rising. 'It sounds like I think she was cheating on me. And if I thought that, that gives me a reason to . . . To *do* something.'

Motive, Emily thought.

'Or at least,' Jack continued, 'for us to have a big fight that evening. The night she died. Which we didn't, for the record. And I knew – I knew from the *start* – that the guards were focused on me. Solely focused. Blinkers, they had on. It was as if it couldn't possibly have been anyone else. Always the husband, good enough for us. And *I* knew I didn't do it, so I knew there was someone out there who needed to be identified and caught, and time was ticking on. I didn't want to give them even more reason to waste their time with me.'

'Are you going to tell them now? When they interview you?'

'I think I'll have to. Joe says I should. Show willing, and all that.'

She let a beat pass.

'So. You said you felt like Kate was anxious to get you out of the house that night. Tell me more about that.'

'There's not much more to it,' Jack said. 'I was tired. It'd been a long week. I was looking forward to staying in, watching some TV, getting a takeaway. But then Ben rings me up out of the blue, says he happens to be around and could we meet for a pint and some dinner? I said yes because I hadn't seen him in ages, and he's so rarely in our part of the world, but then as the day wore on and it got closer to me actually having to leave . . . Well, I said to Kate, you know, I really don't feel like going. And she was adamant that I should. It was like she was worried I *wouldn't* go meet him for some reason.'

'And Ben is . . .?'

'Oh, sorry – one of my best mates. We came up together, through the amateur ranks. And then he ended up being one of my teammates at Sync. When I had my accident, he was the guy who went down too but managed to stay on the road. This is his place.'

'What – here? He owns *this* house?'

Jack nodded.

'So this is the guy who lives in France?'

'Yeah.'

'Why didn't you want to see him that night?'

'I did,' Jack said. 'I was just tired.'

'Why didn't you just ask him to come to the house instead?'

He hesitated. 'Because it sounded like Ben wanted to chat about something. Something serious. If he came to the house, Kate would be there, obviously, and . . . Look, I'm not proud of this, but Ben is loaded. He's a multi-millionaire. This is just one of the houses he owns. He knew Exis was in trouble, and although I'd never, *ever* ask him, I thought maybe there was a chance he was going to offer to step in and help dig us out.'

'Did he?'

'I never saw him,' Jack said. 'He thought we were meeting at eight, but I'd said seven. Definitely. I know because I'd told Kate I'd probably be home and all by nine. It was only going to be one pint and a burger – I was driving, after all. We both were. When I tried to call him, I couldn't get through, so I assumed he was on his way. I was still waiting for him in the pub when my neighbour ran in to tell me about the fire. By then, he was nearly an hour late.' He bit his lip. 'I know he feels terrible, but I try not to play that game. You'd drive yourself mad, thinking about all the what-ifs. What if he'd double-checked the time with me, and I'd said, actually, eight is fine, and I'd been at home for that extra hour . . . But what happened is what happened. Nothing will ever change that, so there's no point thinking about what might have been. Ben is like a brother to me. And the only person whose fault this is is whoever did it, you know? You have to keep bringing yourself back to that.'

Jack dug in his pocket for his phone, then tapped the screen. He stood up to show Emily what was on it: a photo of two tanned men in liveried Lycra, posing with their bikes outside a bus branded with Sync-AIC's logo.

'That's us,' he said, 'on the morning of the first stage of the Tour in 2019.'

As Emily's eyes focused on the faces, her blood ran cold.

Standing on the right of the picture was a much younger, skinnier Jack.

Standing on the left was *him*.

The man who'd followed her around Sanctuary, who looked like the man she'd seen staring up at the house from the beach, who sounded like the same man Grace had seen in the court-yard, having broken in, except he didn't have to break in, because he owned it.

Jack's best friend and former teammate, Ben.

20

'I*know*,' Jack said.

Emily looked up at him in alarm. Her heart was pounding so hard, she was afraid he'd heard it.

'But that *is* me,' he added. 'I swear.'

It took her a beat to understand that he was attributing her shock to his changing appearance.

'No,' she said. 'That's not what ...' But she trailed off, whatever words she'd been about to say lost in her own racing thoughts.

On the night Jack's wife died, he wasn't at home because he was meeting Ben, who'd never showed.

Ben, who owned this house they were currently holed up in.

Ben, who'd followed Emily around town and let himself in here last night, while his best friend – his *brother* – was under the impression he was at home in France, thousands of miles away.

Was Ben all over this story because he was Jack's best friend or because he had something to do with this?

235

Could *Ben* be responsible for Kate's death?

Emily felt like she was manoeuvring around a pitch-black room with only a candlestick for light; she could see some things pretty clearly, but most things not at all. She had the sense that she was surrounded by hidden objects, cloaked in shadow, almost within reach but still invisible for now.

She needed to find the light switch, to see the whole room at once.

Meanwhile, Jack's expression had morphed into one of confused concern. He retracted the phone, pulling it to his stomach.

'What?' he said. 'What is it?'

The problem was that she had no idea how Jack felt, or what he could or couldn't see, or even in what direction he was looking.

And Ben was his best friend. Former teammate. *Brother.*

She had to tread carefully here.

'Emily?'

She needed more. To *find out* more, first.

'Ah ... Sorry.' She straightened up, cleared her throat. 'God, I just totally blanked there. I was going to ask you something but the question fell right out of my head ...' She frowned for effect, as if she were putting physical effort into trying to remember. 'What were we talking about? Oh – I know what it was. The house. How you ended up doing this here. How did that happen?'

Jack gave her an odd look, one that made her hold her breath.

But then he moved to return to the couch, and while his back was turned she quickly exhaled in relief.

'Doing it back home was ruled out right from the

236

beginning,' he said as he sat down. 'And the UK wasn't far enough away, not when the vultures can get a flight there for less than a taxi to the airport. I was thinking France, and so I asked Ben for ideas, and that's when he suggested here. Offered it. It wasn't even furnished yet, but he got it all sorted out for us.'

'I take it this is an investment property?'

Jack nodded. 'He has a few.'

'Cycling must be more lucrative than I thought.'

'It's not at all. Most professional cyclists are working for the average industrial wage. Even the top guys only make a fraction of what, like, footballers and Formula 1 drivers and golfers make. And we were never the top guys. We might've been, if we'd had more time, but after the crash . . .' He seemed to follow that sentence off the side of the mountain for a second; he looked lost in thought. But then, 'No. Ben grew his own fortune. He owns a company that leases private jets.'

'Nice.'

'It must be,' Jack said with a wry smile.

None of this was helping Emily figure out what the hell was going on.

'Let's get back to that evening,' she said. 'You're supposed to be meeting Ben, even though you don't feel like it because you're tired, but Kate, for some reason, seems adamant that you go. What time did you leave the house?'

'Around six-thirty. The pub where we were meeting was a half-hour's drive away. The River Inn.'

'Where was Ben staying?'

'I don't know. I probably did at some point, but I've forgotten. It might have been near Shannon Airport. He'd occasionally have meetings there, or near there.'

'Why not meet him somewhere closer?'

'When you live out in the middle of nowhere,' Jack said, 'a half-hour's drive away *is* close.'

'And you were going to drive home?'

'After just one pint, with food.'

'Did you drink that pint?'

'I was about halfway down it when Jim came in.'

'The neighbour who alerted you?'

Jack nodded. 'Our house is at the very end of a lane. There's only one other property on it, halfway along, and that's where Jim lives. Jim Mullin. He has his own car dealership. Very nice guy.' His face changed. 'His wife was at home, saw the flames, called 999. Then she called him, and he was on his way home, which took him past the River Inn, and he happened to see my car parked outside. So he came in and, ah . . .' He swallowed. 'He came in and said I had to come now, that there was a fire. I remember asking him questions, because I didn't really under-stand, but he was physically manoeuvring me out of the pub, into the car park, into his car . . . I don't remember much about the drive, but I remember coming up the lane and seeing flames.'

He stopped and looked at Emily expectantly, as if seeking direction.

'It must have been dark,' she said.

'It was. And there were no flashing blue lights yet, they hadn't arrived. Just a couple of neighbours who'd parked up and put their headlights on. Because of course, out in the country, it's actually dark. You couldn't see your hand in front of your face on that lane, at night.'

'What did you do?'

Jack chewed his lip. 'This sounds awful now, I know, but you see, the fire started in the master bedroom. Upstairs and at the back. So while I could see there was a fire, it seemed contained there. So I was thinking, oh my God, our house. We could lose it. We could lose everything inside it, everything we own. *That* was my panic. Because it was, like, half-eight on a Saturday night. Kate would've been downstairs watching TV. She would've smelled the smoke and run outside. When I got out of the car, there were a few people standing around, and I presumed Kate was one of them. There were people who said I ran straight into the house screaming her name, but they're remembering it wrong. I was *calling* her name, yeah, but because I thought she was standing outside the house with the rest of them and I just couldn't see her in the dark. I didn't think for one second that—' He stopped, abruptly. 'When I couldn't find her, that's when I realized.'

Jack took a deep breath.

Emily held hers.

'I only really have flashes,' he said. 'I wasn't thinking, only doing. The front door was locked. I had my key in my pocket. I opened it. I went in. All the lights were off. Or the electricity was gone, I'm not sure. The fire alarms were blaring. I never realized before how loud they are ... But actually, in my memory, the fire was louder. I couldn't see much of it – just a glow, upstairs, on the landing – but I could hear it crackling and ... And sort of roaring? And the heat was ... The heat was something else. Outside, I'd been able to see my breath. Inside, sweat was pouring off me. It was in my eyes, making them sting, and the smoke was making them sting more ... And it was so thick. The smoke, I mean. Solid, almost. Like looking into a wall. I couldn't see anything around me. I called out her name. I took out my phone and turned on the flashlight, but that didn't help that much. It just showed me the smoke.'

He stopped here and Emily prompted softly, 'What did you do?'

'I pointed it at the ground and I saw the stairs. The end of the banister. I thought Kate would've been in the kitchen, because that's where we usually hung out. So now I knew where I was and I was going to head that way when . . . When I stepped on something.'

Jack's voice was growing thick with emotion.

'What I remember is her hand,' he said. 'Her left hand, with her rings. It was perfect. It looked like it always did. And I thought, she's unconscious. She's passed out. Get her outside, get some air, get in the ambulance that must be on the way, and she'll be fine. We'll be fine. And then . . . Then I moved the beam of the flashlight up, to her face. And I saw that she wasn't OK at all.'

His voice cracked, letting something like a sob escape, and even though she wanted him to continue, Emily couldn't help but suggest they take a break.

'No,' he said immediately, forcefully. 'No, I want to get it over with. And there's not much more to say, anyway. I'm not going to go into the details of her . . . Of what I saw. If people who buy this book end up being disappointed about the fact that I didn't describe exactly how my wife's face was . . . was *gone*, then tough shit. Fuck you. And maybe, you know, see someone about that, because you're a sick individual.'

'I'm sorry, Jack,' Emily said. 'If this is too upsetting, we can move on. But I'm just thinking about this from the reader's point of view. I'm hearing this story for the first time, so if I'm wondering something – if I have a question – there's every chance the reader will have it too.'

Jack looked at her coldly, accusingly. 'What are you wondering?'

'Well, ah . . .' Emily felt her face flush. 'When did you realize that she was . . . ?'

'Dead?' he said flatly. 'I picked her up. I brought her out and someone took her away from me. I was put in an ambulance, and they were treating my hands, and I remember someone coming to tell me, "She's gone." I thought they meant to the hospital, but then I understood.'

'So when you carried her outside . . . ?'

'I didn't know then,' Jack said, his jaw set tight. 'No.' He paused. 'She was still warm.'

Noise then. Voices, from downstairs. Doors opening and closing. The smooth tones of what might be a cable news channel. It sounded like the others had arrived back at the house far sooner than Jack had anticipated.

'Look, I'm sorry,' Jack said. 'I know I'm the one who's put me in this situation. I don't want to take it out on you. But this is . . . This is awful.'

'It's OK. I know it is.'

'What else do you think the reader would want to know?'

'Um, well . . .' She stroked the trackpad of the laptop and squinted at the screen as if scanning her notes, but the truth was she hadn't typed a word and all she was looking at was a virtual blank page. 'You can put as much or as little detail as you like into this book – and specifically into this chapter. It's entirely up to you. But if I'm playing the reader here, there's one very important question that you haven't really answered. Or explained, let's say. *Explained* is a better word.'

'And what's that?'

'Your hands.'

Jack looked down at them, turning them over, as if seeing them for the first time.

'I read somewhere,' Emily pushed on – with a lie – 'that Kate didn't suffer any burns. That she was downstairs and the fire broke out upstairs, and was extinguished before it could travel to the hallway area. And you said you only went in as far as the stairs, in the hall, so . . . If you weren't in the parts of the house that were on fire, how did you burn your hands?'

Jack stared at her for what felt like an excruciatingly long time.

'Debris,' he said then. 'The fire was upstairs, yeah, but the roof was burning. The hall is double-height. Crap was falling down and it was on fire. I was batting it away, and pushing it away, and lifting it out of my way to get to Kate. Where Kate was, she would've been sheltered. She was under a ceiling. And it wasn't just my hands either.'

He stood up and, without warning, turned around and lifted his T-shirt, revealing a horrific slash of deep, red welt branded diagonally across his back.

'They think I got that from a falling joist that had been in the attic,' he said.

Emily stared at it, her mouth slack with shock.

Someone had once told her that burning alive only hurts at the start, that once the fire burns through the top layer of skin, your nerve-endings have burned away with it. But that person hadn't had any first-hand experience. How could this not have caused Jack excruciating, unimaginable pain? It wasn't just the act of the burning itself, although that must have been horrific – it looked like something hot had pressed itself against Jack's skin until it melted away, until the thing had melted *into* his skin and the soft tissue underneath, like the wax around the wick of a candle. But then there'd been the wound. Followed by treatment, surgeries, skin grafts. Bandages, dressings and creams.

All while his grief was fresh and raw.

And then, on top of all that, suspicion.

Jack let the shirt drop, turned back around and sat down again.

Emily took a shallow breath, tried to gather herself. 'I'm sorry. That that happened to you.' She meant it.

A shrug. 'That was the least of it, wasn't it?'

'Jack, I need to tell you something.' The red light on the voice-recorder flashed in her peripheral vision. 'But maybe we shouldn't record it.' She reached over, picked the device up and powered it down.

Then she held it up so that he could see that it was no longer recording.

'What's going on?' he asked, frowning. 'What is it?'

There was more noise from downstairs. Someone heading out into the courtyard while having a somewhat shouted conversation with someone else who was still inside. Ruth, probably. Going out for a smoke. They were lucky they hadn't been interrupted yet.

'Did Kate know Ben well?'

She watched Jack's reaction carefully, but saw only confusion, not suspicion.

'Why?'

'Just – did she?'

'Of course she did. He's my best friend. Best man at our wedding. And she knew him from before too. He was the guy she was seeing when I first met her.'

'Wait – Kate *left Ben* for you?'

'You make it sound like they were married. We were in our twenties and they'd been having a casual thing. And this was years ago. Before we got together, and fell in love, and actually got married. It was ancient history.'

He waved a hand dismissively to reiterate his point.

She wanted to go back to the transcript of their earlier conversation and check exactly what Jack had said about that, because in her memory he hadn't at all made it sound like the guy she'd been with was his good friend, his teammate, *a brother*, according to him.

'I think he's here, Jack. He's the guy I saw. The one that was following me around town. Who I think was also the guy Grace says she saw in the courtyard last night.'

He scoffed. 'That's ridiculous. Ben is in *France*.'

'Are you sure?'

'Why would he lie?'

'What's he like?' she asked. 'Ben. As a person?'

A shadow crossed Jack's face. 'What the . . . ? Wait a second.' He stood up. 'What are you doing? What is this? I didn't hire you so you could go around making up paranoid conspiracy theories and implicating my friends.'

'But I—' Emily started just as the door opened and Ruth walked in, bringing the smell of a recently smoked menthol cigarette with her.

They both turned to look at her and she looked from Jack to Emily and back to Jack again, concerned and questioning.

Emily wondered if she'd been outside, listening, and timed her entry to stop things escalating.

'You need to come downstairs,' she told Jack. She looked directly at Emily as she added, 'Ben is here.'

'Cycling brought something into my life that I'd never really had before: close friends.

I know that sounds a bit dramatic, but the only friends I'd ever had were the other boys at school, and that hadn't been a happy place for me. If I was part of a group at all I was on its edges, listening, reacting when expected to, but otherwise not saying anything and certainly not sharing any feelings or even details of my life. By the time I left school, I felt like a bit of a ghost.

A friend of mine has a teenage stepson, and she says the best place to talk to him about anything is when they're in the car, driving somewhere. There's something about being next to each other but not having to look at one another, and there being a reason for you being there that has nothing to do with talking something out. There's no pressure and, often, there's nothing else to do.

It's like that on the bike.

Racing is only a fraction of the hours you spend in the saddle. The rest of the time you're training, either because you have to or because you want to. And even for long parts of a stage-race, you're not pushing. There's plenty of time to chat. The guys get into all sorts of stuff out there. I've said things on the bike that I've never repeated and probably never will. It's not just exercise, it's therapy. Add in the fact that you're sharing hotel rooms, living out of each other's bags, fighting together, winning together, losing together . . .

Before you know it, these guys aren't just your teammates, they're your friends.

And then they're not your friends, they're your brothers.

And it can get confusing, because you're also their domestique.

I suppose it's a bit like being a ghostwriter, isn't it? I mean, I don't know that much about it, you'd know better than me, but a domestique can't have any ego and – I imagine? – for a ghostwriter, it's the same. Your name isn't on the cover of the book. You don't get to pose at the launch party holding it. If you're mentioned at all, it's in the thank-yous, briefly, and no one cares about them. So you have to be content with knowing that you did your job, and them knowing that you did a good job *for* them, and everybody . . .

I don't know, I'm losing this analogy here, I don't know enough about books. But I guess everybody's happy that you're on the bestseller list? My point is, you have to put your individual self aside for the team – but there's an undercurrent to it, and it's another individual's glory. The one the team has chosen, the leader they've anointed that we've then pinned all our hopes to.

I remember signing my very first professional contract. At the time, I believed two things: that cycling was a sport of gentlemen, and that the domestique's duties to his team leader did not extend beyond the peloton.

But I'd come to learn that neither of those things are true.'

V

THE DOMESTIQUE

21

Ben is here.

Emily looked at Jack, who glared at her wordlessly.

Then he turned on his heel and left the room.

Ruth moved to close the door behind him, then turned back to Emily. 'Are you all right? It sounded like things were getting a bit dramatic in here.'

'How much did you hear?'

Emily asked this in the same annoyed tone she'd have used for *How long were you snooping outside the door, eavesdropping on us?*, which was what she was really asking.

'Not a lot,' Ruth said. 'More than enough.' She crossed the room, cracked open one of the windows and took out her cigarettes. 'You want one?'

'Are you allowed to smoke in here?'

She lit up. 'Probably not.'

Emily went and joined her. She looked out over the beach. The heavy clouds had started to thin and break, revealing promising patches of bright blue and letting sunshine light spots on the sand and create patches of shimmer on the water.

Ruth waved the box at her and, relenting, Emily slid one out. She lit it, inhaled and immediately regretted her decision. *This is the thing with smoking*, she thought. *It's fucking horrible but you just have to power through.*

Kind of like this godforsaken ghostwriting gig.

Although each drag of an occasional, illicit cigarette would be slightly less awful than the one before. This job only ever got worse.

'He just showed up,' Ruth said. 'Which I suppose he's entitled to do, seeing as this is his house. But he knows what Jack is doing here, so why interrupt?' She exhaled, half-heartedly aiming her plume of smoke to the open part of the window. Most of it got trapped by the glass and billowed back into the room. 'He said something about meeting a buyer at Fort Walton Beach. That's the airport near here, right?'

'Meeting a buyer?' Emily repeated.

'That's what he said.'

But that was the airport at which private jets weren't allowed to land, so even *that* smelled a bit like bullshit.

And of course it was, because Ben had already been here since yesterday.

At least.

'You think he followed you?' When Emily gave her a reproachful look, Ruth said, 'OK, yeah, I heard that part.'

'I don't know,' she lied.

She was sure it had been him, but she was cautious around Ruth. There was something about her, a sharpness to her edges that only caught in certain lights, that made her wary of sharing too much.

And no doubt anything she said would get reported back to Jack.

They smoked in silence for a few moments, while watching the waves crash up against the shore.

'Ben is a touchy subject for Jack,' Ruth said then.

'Why?'

'You can't put anything in the book Jack doesn't say, right?' Ruth gave her a sidelong glance. 'That's how it works?'

'It's his story. His memoir. So if he doesn't say it to me, it doesn't go in.'

'My brother keeps himself to himself, so I don't have all the details. None of us do. But when they were racing, things happened. From what I was able to put together from comments here and there – and from some things Kate told me – Ben was a badly behaved boy, if you know what I mean. He liked women and he liked bringing them home with him, and he couldn't hear the word *no*. But he was getting results for the team, so it was all kept hush-hush. They cleaned up his problems for him. Swept it all under the proverbial rug. And sometimes, I think, Jack had to help with the brushing. I think he had no choice but to help.'

'Meaning what, exactly?'

'Ben threatened him,' Ruth said. 'Apparently, in that last season, when they were both with Sync, he started spreading rumours. Whispering that it was actually *Jack* who had a reputation for doing those things. And because they were always sharing rooms, and they were so close, and they were the only two Irish guys on the team . . . Jack must have felt like it was an alternative history that would make sense to people.'

'But couldn't he have just said it wasn't him? Proved it wasn't?'

Ruth barked a laugh. 'How? And who would've cared? Who would he have told?' She waved her cigarette so wildly as she said this that some burning ash fell off and onto the wooden floor. Emily moved to stub it out with her foot while Ruth continued on, not even noticing. 'It was the team that was imposing the omerta. His employers. The ones with the keys to his biggest professional dreams. And Jack thought if he tried to move, if he looked for another spot, the whispering campaign would nix his chances. So the sport he loved, the thing he'd wanted to be a part of his entire life, turned into this toxic sludge that infected everything. And then there was the crash.' She paused for a drag. 'Ben went down too, did you know that?'

'But stayed on the road,' Emily said.

'And yet quit cycling at the end of that year. Why? He could've stayed on. He only had cuts and bruises. He was able to finish the Tour *and* the season.' Ruth put her cigarette out on the white windowsill, leaving a burnt black mark. 'I know he said in interviews it was because he felt he'd lost his nerve, but . . .'

Emily was trying to put all the pieces together in her head – and fit them into the puzzle she'd already been building before this conversation started. She felt like she had whiplash from everything she was finding out, and longed to sit in a dark room with her notebook and pen and disentangle her thoughts, to make some kind of sense of them.

'But, Ruth,' she said, 'what I don't get about all this is that Jack describes Ben as his best friend. He said they were like brothers.'

She nodded. 'He is. They are.'

'But how, after all this?'

'*Because* they're brothers. They've been cycling together since they were kids. Been teammates at every level. Stuff happens, out there on the bike. Bonds are forged. They're your family. If your sibling does something terrible, you love them anyway, don't you? You kind of have to. And what if your employer insisted that you did? And then, with these two, you have to add in all that weird domestique stuff—'

'*What* stuff?'

Ruth raised an eyebrow. 'Didn't you have to do, like, research for this?'

'No, not really. And there wasn't time.'

'Well, look, you're probably better off with the internet than me,' she said, 'because the whole thing bores me to tears. But basically, in a cycling team, not everyone is trying to win. They've decided in advance who will be the star, or the guy who has the best chance of it – usually that's the same guy – and the rest of the team race to help him. They ride in front of him to protect him from the wind, they try to defend him from attacks, they bring him food and water, that kind of thing. They basically sacrifice their own chances for the team leader and the team. They call them domestiques. Literally, servants. Jack always explained it like a football team, which to be honest didn't help me much, but it was something about how the other guys are all working to get the ball up the pitch to the striker, the guy with the best chance of getting a goal.'

'So Jack was Ben's domestique?'

'They were both domestiques at Sync,' Ruth said, 'because it was a top team and there were about ten guys ahead of them in the queue for glory. But in the past, yeah. On their previous team, Jack's first professional contract. And that must be a hard thing to shake off, you know? You're sacrificing yourself

253

to serve some leader, who also happens to be a master manipulator. I mean, Ben must be one to get away with all this shit for so long, right? He sorta has Jack brainwashed, if you ask me. Jack doesn't even realize it. If you're being manipulated, how do you know what thoughts are your own? How do you know why you're really doing anything? I bet Jack thinks he's keeping Ben's secrets out of some kind of loyalty, that he owes him that. And in return, Ben doesn't pin all that shit on his friend.' She rolled her eyes. 'And people think *women* have toxic friend groups. Jesus Christ.'

Emily's cigarette was only two-thirds gone and she felt a little sick. She offered the remainder to Ruth, who shrugged and took it.

'What about Kate?' Emily asked. 'Where's she in all this? Jack said she was with Ben when he first met her.'

'Oh, yeah. But, like, not at all serious. They'd been on a few dates. I don't think that means anything. Later on, when she was with Jack, she didn't like Ben, but that was because of how he treated Jack. But she played along, like Jack did, because that's what he wanted. I honestly don't know if Jack is really friends with Ben or if he's pretended he is for so long – out of fear or loyalty or whatever – that he's just come to believe he is.'

She finished Emily's cigarette with a deep drag that made the end of it glow bright and put it out on the windowsill too, but in a different spot, making *two* very noticeable black marks.

'Ruth, can I ask you a difficult question?'

'Let me guess: what do *I* think happened?'

A knock on the door then, gentle but firm.

They looked at each other, then turned around to see Jack enter the room, wrinkling his nose.

254

'Are you *smoking* in here?' he said.

Behind him, another voice said, 'It's OK, I don't mind,' and then a second man followed him in.

Ben.

Emily recognized him from the photo Jack had shown her, and now that he was standing in front of her, she knew that he was definitely the man who'd followed her through the town and the man she'd seen from a distance on the beach.

She had absolutely no doubt.

'Hey,' Ben said to Ruth, raising a hand in a small wave. 'How are things?'

'Same old. Nice house.'

'Thanks, yeah.' He turned to Emily, locked eyes with her. 'Hello.'

'This is Emily,' Jack said before she could respond.

He sounded annoyed, but with who, she couldn't tell. She was definitely a candidate, though; he'd completely avoided eye contact with her since he'd re-entered the room and it was quite obvious that he was avoiding looking at her now.

Ben reached out a hand. 'Ben.'

On autopilot, she shook it. 'Emily.'

He gripped it firmly, pumped twice, squeezed once. She felt the bones of her fingers move inside the vice his had created.

And all this while maintaining intense, unbroken eye contact.

She felt like he was seeing inside her, that he'd turned her eyes into windows, that he could read the thoughts racing through her head.

And see all her suspicions.

'I think I've seen you,' she said. 'Around town.'

Finally, he released her.

'I don't think so,' he said lightly. 'I just got here.'

Now, she felt like she could read a message in *his* eyes: *shut the fuck up*. The air in the room crackled with tension and absolutely stank of synthetic menthol. Emily wasn't just feeling sick anymore, she was going to *be* sick.

'It's lovely, isn't it?' he said. 'The town. If you've time, I could show you around a bit.'

'I don't think I will, unfortunately. We're on a tight schedule here.' She looked to Jack. 'Are we carrying on or . . . ?'

He looked away. 'I think we're calling it a day, actually.'

She hated him in that moment for his cowardice, for not only ending their conversation but effectively telling Ben that she had some free time right now.

And then she wondered who he was doing it for. What had he and Ben discussed, before they'd come upstairs? Why had he brought Ben upstairs? Had Ben insisted on meeting her so he could treat her to his threatening death stare?

'In that case, we could—' Ben started.

'I have some calls I need to return,' Emily said, talking over him until he stopped trying to talk to her. 'Excuse me.'

She pushed through them to the door, and fled.

22

The only place she had to go was Bookmark, but now that Ben had appeared, it didn't feel safe or secure. Emily locked the front door behind her and went to check that her connecting door was locked too. She used the bathroom, then checked the connecting door a second time. Then she went outside, onto the balcony, took a few deep breaths and tried to calm down.

She wanted to leave, but she had to complete the job. Beth had made it clear: if she didn't, she'd be back in debt. But did Jack even *want* to do this now? She'd clearly upset him with her questions about Ben. But then this was what he'd wanted; to get all the information out there. Who, realistically, did he think the murderer of his wife was going to turn out to be? Some passing stranger, who'd found a house at the end of a lane and broken into it to kill the woman who happened to be home, start a fire and flee? In all likelihood, whoever the killer was, it was someone they knew. Someone in their circle.

Someone with a reason.

Like Ben.

Two sharp raps on Bookmark's front door startled Emily, then froze her with fear.

She couldn't pretend she wasn't here. The caller would be able to see the open balcony door through the glass of the front door. She could do what she'd done earlier, maybe – step outside, force the conversation to happen on the deck in full view of the house and within earshot of the courtyard.

But what if she didn't get a chance to do that? What if whoever it was forced their way in?

'Emily? You in there?'

Grace's voice. It was Grace.

Emily's muscles slackened with relief. When she went inside, she saw Grace on the other side of the glass, looking impatient.

As she started towards the door, she saw something else, sitting on the mat on the floor just inside: Mark's Olympus voice-recorder.

She bent to pick it up and then let Grace in.

'You found it,' she said, assuming she'd just posted it through the letterbox.

'Found what?' When Grace saw what Emily was holding, her face changed. 'What the hell is that? *Please* tell me you weren't recording on a personal device. *Please* tell me you didn't completely ignore everything I said.'

She grabbed the recorder out of Emily's hand and pressed one of its buttons, bringing Mark's faux-serious, sing-song poetry voice into their conversation.

'—*sorrow is the* only *thing, the* only *thing, the* only—'

Emily grabbed it back and hurried to silence it, fumbling.

'—*thing that I rest with as you* alone *see*—'

Grace was smirking.

'*—me as a—*'

Finally, mercifully, Emily hit something that silenced it.

'Who's that?' Grace asked.

'My boyfriend.' Colour was blooming on Emily's cheeks. 'I brought it with me but obviously, after what you said, I didn't use it. It's been in my bag since I arrived. Or I thought it was. I discovered earlier that it was missing. I thought it had fallen out somewhere, and you'd found it and returned it to me.'

'Nope.' Grace lifted a white paper bag onto the breakfast bar. 'I'm just delivering your dinner. And grabbing my laptop.'

'So we're done for the day?'

She nodded. 'But Jack suggested you start at nine tomorrow, to make up for it.'

So, for now at least, he still wanted to talk.

'There's a bottle of wine in there,' Grace added.

'For what?'

'*Drinking*,' she said, managing to fit an eye-roll in between the syllables. 'It's been a long day. Do you want it or not?'

'No, no. I do. Thank you.'

But now, in the natural moment for Grace to turn on her heel and leave, she didn't. She was hovering, shifting her weight from foot to foot, and looking at Emily as if she were expecting, no, *hoping* that—

'Do you . . . ?' Emily hesitated. 'Would you like to have a glass?'

'Sure,' Grace said immediately.

Emily tried not to look too surprised. They hadn't got off on the right foot – or any foot, full stop – but it wasn't incomprehensible that Grace might want someone to talk to. They were isolated here, in a crazy situation, and it had been a particularly crazy day. And from what Ruth had said, Grace truly cared about Jack. She might be genuinely upset about the arrest news and not feel like she could express that to the rest of them.

'By the way,' Emily said as she went looking for clean glasses, 'I think I need to apologize to you. I got my wires crossed, when I first got here. I thought you worked for Morningstar, that they had sent you. I didn't realize until last night that you actually work for Jack.'

'You thought I was here to do your bidding, and that you were in charge of me, and you resented the fact that I wasn't acting subordinately. I see.'

Emily found two glasses, unscrewed the cap on the wine and poured it quickly.

'Like I said,' she said, 'I'm sorry.'

She was already regretting extending this invite.

'Apology accepted.' Grace took a glass, then a generous sip of her wine. 'And *by the way*, I have a master's degree. And I'm twenty-six.'

Even though Emily didn't verbally react to this, her face must have betrayed her surprise.

'And you might think I'm sure, but I'm not,' Grace added. 'About Jack, I mean.' She took another, longer sip. 'I shouldn't be drinking. Technically, I'm on the clock. I still have those transcripts to do.'

'I didn't realize you were doing that. You type up everything, every day?'

She nodded. 'I have to. The recordings are destroyed.'

'*What?*'

'That's part of the deal,' Grace said. 'You do a day, I type up the transcripts, the recording is deleted.'

260

This was news to Emily, and also nonsensical.

'But the transcripts say the same thing,' she said. 'So what does the deleting achieve?'

Grace shrugged. 'It's just a way of making sure that those audio recordings never get out. Transcripts aren't as sexy, I guess, to the *Daily Fail* and their friends.' She drank some more. There was now barely a mouthful left in her glass but when Emily lifted the bottle, she shook her head and pulled her glass away. 'I'll only have one.'

'It's OK not to be sure, you know. About Jack.'

'I *know*,' Grace snapped. 'I can't see into his mind, can I? I'm not psychic. And I listen to enough podcasts to know that people can hide their true natures. So who would be sure? Only an idiot. And I'm not an idiot. But if you put a gun to my head and told me I had to go one way or the other, I'd say he didn't do it. Because all I can do is come back to the *logic* of it all. Which is, why would a guilty man do this?'

'What?'

'*This!*' Grace waved the hand that wasn't holding the wine glass. 'This book. Any book. Why bring this circus into town when things had just quietened down? Because it's not money. He doesn't seem to care about that anymore. And it can't be attention, because he hates that. One of the last things we had in the diary before the fire was opening a bricks-and-mortar store in Galway, and trying to get Jack to do PR for it was like pulling teeth. He agreed to one feature for a broadsheet and ended up yelling at the photographer.'

'But if he hates attention,' Emily said, 'then why write a memoir?'

'*Exactly.*' Grace snapped her fingers. 'That's exactly my point. If it's not for the money and it's not for the attention, doesn't that only leave the reason he says? That he's innocent and wants to prove it so the person who *did* do this can be found and punished? Isn't that the only thing that makes any sense?'

Grace's eyes seemed to be pleading with Emily to say yes, but the most she could muster was a neutral *mmm* noise.

'Did you know Kate well?' she asked, to change the subject.

'I mean, we weren't *friends*,' Grace said, 'but yeah. A little. I met her a few times.'

'What was she like?'

'She was great.'

'What were they like together?'

'Different,' Grace said. 'To other couples. At least, the ones I know. It felt like they were really a team. And she was so protective of him, always. Looking after him when he didn't always look after himself. Trying to minimize his stress, keep things off his plate, make sure he slept and ate. I suppose, now, I feel like . . .' She stopped, swallowed. 'I try to do that now, because I don't think anyone else is looking out for him or his interests. And I don't think he's quite realized that yet.'

'That's why you called Ruth?'

Grace nodded silently.

'What did he say about that?'

'Nothing, yet.'

'Grace, was it Ben? In the courtyard last night? The man you saw?'

'It couldn't have been, he only arrived yesterday.'

But she looked down into her almost empty wine glass as she said it. Emily had the distinct impression that Grace was lying. Or that she didn't want to contradict whatever lies Ben was telling.

Grace asked if she could use the bathroom then, and disappeared into it.

Emily was picking up her wine glass to take another sip when she saw something small and white lying on the floor in the nook.

For a second she thought it was something Grace had dropped and started towards it, intending to pick it up for her. But as she got closer, she saw that it was a piece of paper, folded multiple times until it was about the size of a credit card, and that it was just a couple of inches from the connecting door. Too far from the bathroom for Grace to have accidentally dropped it.

It had been slipped beneath the connecting door, from the other side.

Emily's insides filled with dread.

She picked it up and started back towards the kitchen, unfolding the paper close to her chest, so she'd easily be able to disappear it if Grace abruptly re-emerged. It was a sheet of A4 with only one sentence on it, written in block capitals.

TELL JACK NOW OR I WILL TELL EVERYONE.

The day before the fire

This morning, White Point Strand is getting whipped by the wind and the sea is especially ferocious. When Kate gets out of the car, she can feel grit sandblasting her cheeks and making her eyes water. She has to hold her hair back from her face while she scans the car park – and sees that the other woman is already there, sitting in the same car she was in earlier in the week, a red hatchback that's been splattered up to its door handles with mud and dirt.

She wants to get back into her own car, drive away and forget all about this. But knowledge is power and so what she wants *more* is to find out what the hell Jean Whelan is up to.

Jack thinks she's gone for a walk on the beach. She snaps some pictures of it now, in case she needs proof later.

Jean sees her, waves and reaches across to push open the passenger door.

Kate sits in and says, 'Good morning,' because she doesn't know what else to say or how to act. It's uncomfortably warm in the car, a dry heat that immediately starts to push its way down her throat, and in it is the sickly-sweet smell of a newly unwrapped vanilla air-freshener that she can taste on her tongue.

'Thanks so much for coming,' Jean says.

Kate nods. 'Sure.'

'I got us coffees. Cappuccino OK?'

The cups are in the drinks holder in the central console. Jean lifts one out and hands it to Kate, who takes a sip because if she's doing that, she doesn't have to say anything yet. It tastes like nothing and burns her tongue.

'What made you change your mind?'

Kate keeps looking forward, at the beach. 'Honestly, I don't know that I have.'

'They paid me off, you know. A year's salary if I went quietly.'

Finally, Kate turns to look at the other woman. 'What happened to you?'

Jean raises her eyebrows. 'What do you want, like, details?'

'Of course not. It's just . . . I really don't know what went on.'

'You do. Because all the stories are the same, aren't they? And we've all heard them before.'

They sit in silence for a few moments.

'So, what is this?' Kate asks. 'You're going to expose him? Punish him? Stop him from ever doing it again?'

'*Has* he done it again?'

'How the hell would I know?'

After a beat, Jean sighs. She says, 'All of those things, ideally. But I'd settle for exposing him. That should take care of the rest.'

'Why now?'

'Why not now?'

'I mean—' Kate starts.

'Why not *before* now?' Jean nods, as if this is a question she's been anticipating. 'At first, I wasn't ready. I couldn't face it. In order to survive I told myself, it's just one night. Not even that. It was, at the most, fifteen minutes. Obviously it felt longer – it felt like forever. But in reality it was just fifteen minutes. Why let it define you?' She smiled sadly. 'You know what I used to do? I'd walk around the shops, or go for a walk, or throw on some comedy show on Netflix, and I'd let fifteen minutes pass and then I'd say to myself, "See? That's all it is! That's how long it is. It means nothing." I could just forget it, I thought. Slice it out of my life like a ruined picture on a strip of negatives. I'd tape the two ends together and pretend it was never there. I actually had myself convinced for a while that I could do that, but even if you can train your mind to forget, your body always remembers.'

'What was . . . ?' But Kate stops, because she doesn't know how to ask it. She doesn't know how to have this conversation at all.

'Panic attacks,' Jean says. 'Insomnia. There was a while there I'd find it impossible to leave the house for days, even weeks at a time. At one point' – she reaches up to touch the back of her neck – 'my hair started falling out. And I was like, why? What's wrong with me? Why is this happening? Like it was a big mystery. I refused to make the connection.' She shakes her head. 'It's amazing what the mind does to protect itself. What it can do.'

'But you got help?' Kate asks hopefully.

'I drank and broke down and lost my mind and *then* I got

help,' Jean says. 'And once I was feeling better, steadier, stronger – that's when I started thinking about telling someone. But I wasn't sure I'd be believed. Scratch that. I *knew* I wouldn't be. Time had passed and the first question is always "Why did you wait so long?" As if, you know, reporting the fact that you'd been raped, making it as good as public and entering into a justice system that is totally, as far as I'm concerned, on the other guy's side, isn't anything. As if it doesn't sometimes take years just to accept that the thing happened in the first place.' She sighs. 'And look, I knew what I was up against. I had no actual evidence, aside from the go-away money, which had come with a gag order. So if I tell, they can sue me. And if I tell, I have to tell it all, including the bit where I took money to go away and be quiet, so of course the assumption will be that I'm just out to get more.'

'But you had your story,' Kate says. 'Your account.'

Jean laughs at this, a short, sharp bark. 'That doesn't mean anything. Literally nothing. When it comes to sexual assault, how many times have we seen that a first-hand account isn't treated as evidence? It's not taken as the truth. It's just a story that *you* have to prove. Someone says, "I saw that guy run a red light and cause that accident," people listen. They rely on that statement. They take it as fact. A woman says, "A man violently raped me, here's exactly how it happened, I remember everything," and people go, "Really? Are you *sure*? Because, you know, you went into that room with him. What did you *think* was going to happen?" You notice how no one ever says, "Well, you got into your car and you drove it on the road so you must have known getting hit by another car was a possibility."'

Kate nods while the word *violently* rings in her ears.

'But even if I can't prove my story,' Jean continues, 'I can maybe do something about the others. And if you take it on the totality of—'

'Wait,' Kate says, interrupting her. '*Others?*'

Jean nods slowly. 'I think I have maybe five or six, so far.'

'Five or *six*?'

'So far.'

Kate realizes on a delay that she's gripping the coffee cup so tightly, the heat of it is starting to burn her hand. She winces, drops the cup back into the holder and rubs away the pain, feeling the other woman watching her.

'These guys,' Jean says, 'it's never just a one-off. It's a pattern of behaviour. An attitude. A problem.' She pauses, then says very gently, 'You know that, right?'

The car slowly fills up with a suffocating expectation.

'Look,' Jean says. 'I know how difficult this is. You know I know. I'm not going to put you under any pressure, and you don't have to answer this if you don't want to. But the other day . . . Kate, I may have given the impression I came to you for help, that I thought you could, I don't know, corroborate dates and times and things like that. But you weren't there when it happened. Not yet. There was the possibility he'd mentioned something afterwards, of course, but I thought that was a long shot. The real reason I wanted to talk to you was because, woman to woman, I wanted to tell you about what I was doing. I wanted you to hear this from me, and not from some guard in a uniform who arrives on your doorstep someday or, God forbid, a journalist who's picked up the story. I didn't want you to find out that way. I don't want any other women to be collateral damage here. But . . .' She pauses.

'Kate, you seemed afraid. The other day. You seem it now. And so, like I said, you don't have to tell me, but—'

Kate closes her eyes and imagines the wheels of the car turning, sending them both over the edge and crashing down onto the beach below.

'—did something happen to you, too?'

23

Emily stared at the note, transfixed by it, as it shook in her unsteady hand.

TELL JACK NOW OR I WILL TELL EVERYONE.

This time, there was no ambiguity. There was a name and a deadline. And proof the sender was here.

Not just in Sanctuary, but in this house.

Behind her, the lock in the bathroom clicked open. Grace reappeared, saying, 'This place is cute, isn't it? If it weren't for, you know, the creepy town and construction site.'

The breakfast bar was a barrier between them, blocking Grace's view of Emily from the waist down. She slipped the note down by her side and then did the only thing she could think of: she bent to open the dishwasher – never used, its stainless steel insides gleaming, an instruction booklet and a free sample of dishwasher tablets still in a plastic packet in the cutlery rack – and threw the note in there. She hoped Grace wouldn't notice that the only soiled item in the entire kitchen, the wine glass she herself had just drained, remained on the counter.

'I'd better get back,' Grace said, taking her laptop from the counter and tucking it under her arm. 'I have the transcribing to do.'

'We talked about the fire today.'

'Thanks for the wine. And the heads-up.' Grace moved to leave.

'Oh – just before you go, do you know if we can get onto the beach?' Emily asked. 'There's a gate with a keypad on it. It was locked and my fob to get in here didn't open it, so . . .'

She needed to call Alice to have a conversation that she couldn't risk being overheard. That bang against the connecting door this morning; she was convinced that had been someone who'd been listening to her, accidentally revealing themselves.

*Him*self, she suspected.

And while she didn't want to go full tinfoil-hat, Ben could have let himself in here at any time and left a listening device behind him. He could be a pervert and have left a camera too, for all she knew. No room in the main house was safe either, and anybody with good hearing and an open window could catch your conversation in the courtyard.

The last thing Emily wanted to do was leave here and go walk the streets of Sanctuary, so the only option was the beach. Wide open, in full view of everyone, with no place to hide. No one would be able to sneak up on her. She'd be safe and she could be sure her conversation would be private.

If she could just get onto it.

'Yeah,' Grace said, taking out her phone. 'There's a code, I have it somewhere ...' She tapped the screen a couple of times, then said, 'Oh, for God's sake. It's two-oh-two-four.'

'As in 2024? The current year?'

'It's the year the town was *founded*,' she said with an eye-roll. 'And also a security risk, but I guess they didn't think about that. They might as well have made it one-two-three-four.' She turned to go. 'I'll see you tomorrow. Remember, starting at nine.'

'Yeah. See ya.'

Emily waited at the door until she saw the top of Grace's head appear from beneath the pergola as she started to cross the courtyard towards the main house.

Only then did she go and retrieve the note from the dishwasher.

TELL JACK NOW OR I WILL TELL EVERYONE.

The words blurred as the page shook.

The content was bad, but what was worse was the note itself. The physical presence of it. The method of delivery.

The emails could've been sent from anyone, anywhere. They could be the work of some teenage idiot halfway around the world, or sent by someone who wouldn't even beep their car horn at you in the real world. A keyboard warrior. But now, there was no denying that they'd come from someone serious – and someone *who was here*.

The note had been slipped under the connecting doors.

By Ben, surely.

Emily got her phone and her keys, tucked the note into her jeans pocket, and stationed herself by the door of Bookmark, scanning the scene below. She moved to the front windows, checking one at a time, to make doubly sure.

Then she left, hurrying down the stairs and across to the

archway and into the garage, keeping her head down and her pace fast.

She braced herself as she exited onto the street, but there was no one there.

She made it around the corner, then down the path to the gate. She punched in the code, got a whiney buzzing sound that told her she'd entered it wrong, and forced herself to calm down, take a deep breath and try again.

This time, it worked.

There was a different buzzing noise and a *click* as the gate swung open. She pushed through, ran up the marble steps and down the other side of them.

She rang Alice.

'Hey! I was just about to call you.'

'I'm in trouble here,' Emily said.

'What? What's happening?'

'Hang on, I just . . . Hang on one second.'

'What's going on?' Alice asked. 'Are you OK?'

She reached down to pull off her shoes, left them on the last step and then walked, barefoot, to the water's edge. The sand was deep and soft. It was difficult to make your way across it quickly, with every step getting swallowed up by its shifting depth. When it became firm and moist beneath her bare feet, she stopped and turned and started walking parallel to the water, scanning for other people as she did.

As far as she could see, she was the only person on the beach.

'Em? Are you there?'

'He *knows*.'

'Who does? Knows what?'

Quickly, she caught Alice up. On the third email and the

273

hand-delivered note. Jack's promising Morningstar a confession. On her suspicions that Ben had had something to do with the death of Kate Smyth. That Ben was here, watching her, following her around town and, she believed, slipping that note under the connecting doors.

'You need to leave,' Alice said. 'Call a cab, take it to the airport. Right now. Which one is the nearest to you? I'll book you the next flight out.'

'Leaving isn't really an option,' Emily said.

'Leaving is the *only* option.'

'I can't, Alice.'

A hard exhale. 'OK, fine. I'll indulge this absolutely insanity for thirty seconds. Why the fuck not?'

'Because if I quit this job, then I'll owe them the money.'

'But you'll be *alive*.'

'I only have to get through one more day before it's over anyway – wait, *alive*? Alice, this is real life.'

'That's exactly my point.'

'I'm not leaving. And if Ben didn't kill Kate, that means Jack did, and you were perfectly fine with me being out here with *him*.'

'That was before I knew about you getting followed and notes under connecting doors. You're out in the middle of nowhere with what sounds to me like a bunch of lunatics. And you're staying in one of their houses. Can't you at least, I don't know, move to a hotel? Won't you just do that until we can figure this out?'

'Jack and Grace and Ruth – that's his sister – they're OK, and they're here too.'

'To be clear,' Alice said. 'Your counter-argument is that

everything's fine because the guy who might have murdered his wife is there with his sister and a woman who works for him?'

'Well, if Ben did it, *he* didn't.'

'Silver linings,' Alice muttered. 'Look, will I open this or not?'

'What?'

'The solicitor's letter. That's why I was going to ring you.'

With everything else that'd been going on, Emily had forgotten about it.

The crash of the waves faded away, replaced by a ringing in her ears as her entire body began to thrum with anxiety.

'Open it,' she said.

Her heart started beating so fast it made her dizzy, unsteady in her position on the sinking sand. Her skin broke out in a cold sweat and her mouth filled with the metallic taste of fear. She pushed the phone against her ear and heard a rustling, a ripping of paper, and then Alice saying—

'It's not her.'

—just as the crescendo of adrenaline peaked, almost drowning out Alice's voice, and Emily had to ask her to repeat it.

'It's not her,' Alice said again. 'It's nothing to do with that. It looks like . . .' The whip of pages being flicked through at speed. 'It's a non-disclosure agreement – that you already signed? I think it's . . . Yeah, it's for this, Em. For Jack's book. They've sent you a copy for your records.'

Emily briefly closed her eyes, awash with relief.

'I don't want to say I told you so,' Alice added. 'But I told you so.'

And then it hit her.

'Oh God. I'm an idiot.'

'Why? I mean, yeah, I know, but why specifically in this instance?'

'The name of the firm,' Emily said. 'Roche and Reilly.'

'Roche and O'Reilly.'

'Joe Roche is Jack's solicitor. He's *that* Roche. I should've known it was something to do with that.'

'Well, you do now. One less problem to worry about.'

'What do I do about the note?'

'Leaving is still my advice and should be your preference.'

'But if it isn't?'

'For fuck's sake, Em.' Alice exhaled hard, frustrated. 'OK. Look. Assuming that this is about *The Witness*—'

'It has to be.'

'—why does this person want you to tell Jack?'

'I suppose so he fires me,' Emily said.

'Because they don't want this book to happen?'

'Or maybe because they *do*. Maybe they think I'm not the kind of writer you want helping you tell a truth that's already a struggle for people to believe. Maybe this is someone protecting him.'

'But why don't they just tell him themselves?'

'Maybe for some reason they can't reveal that they know. About the book. Or that they want me out.'

Alice was quiet.

Emily waited, knowing she was thinking things through.

'You should tell him,' Alice said then. 'And I'm not saying that because then this insanity might be over and I think it already should be. I'm assuming you won't listen and won't leave. So, neutralize the threat. Take away this anonymous person's leverage.'

'Tell *Jack*?' Emily said. 'Are you mad?'

'It's the easier option. And it's sort of the only one, isn't it? At this point? Look, if Jack were a journalist, I wouldn't be suggesting this. Obviously. But he's not going to have any interest in exposing you. I *think* he might have enough of his own problems? So tell him. If you trust him, you can trust him to keep this to himself. And while you're at it, I think maybe you should consider telling Mark too.'

'*Mark?* Alice, what is this? Bad Advice Day?'

'I think he suspects, Em. When I was over there he was asking me loads of questions about what you were like when you were writing the book. Not as dumb as he looks, that one. Despite the awful poetry, I think he's a keeper. And saying this will bring me out in hives because, ugh, *feelings*, but I think he really loves you and is genuinely worried that you're keeping something from him, and that's only going to make a gulf.'

'No,' Emily said. 'No way.'

'What's the downside of telling him?'

'He'd *know*. That's the downside. He'd know what I did, who I really am.'

'He already knows who you really are, you idiot. You're the woman he loves. Do you seriously think this would change that for him? That it would matter?'

'It matters to me.'

'You could tell him a half-truth.'

'Which would be what?'

'About the book,' Alice said, 'but not the rest.'

'I think, with him, the book stuff would be worse.'

'It was just a book, Em. It's not your identity. It's not your worth. It's not your heart. You know that, right? It's a thing you made.'

'But I *didn't* make it.'

'Yes, you did. It didn't exist and then it did, because of you.'

'Can this be a when-I-get-home problem? Could we focus on the murderer for now?'

'At least you haven't lost your sense of humour.'

'But I might be losing my fucking mind.'

Movement then, further down the beach.

A shimmer of a person.

Someone was coming towards her. A man.

Ben.

'Hey,' Emily said, turning to start walking back up the beach to the marble steps. 'No matter what, stay on the line, OK?'

'What's happening?'

'Just stay on the line.'

'Emily?' Ben called out.

She ignored him and quickened her pace on the sand, which was difficult now that she had crossed onto the soft, sinking part of it.

And saw that, directly ahead of her, someone else was coming down the steps.

Tall Blonde Woman.

What the hell was *she* doing here? Both flights, Seaside and now here, on the beach in front of Beach Read?

'Shit,' Emily muttered.

Ben called her name again, from much closer.

'Em?' Alice's voice said in her ear. 'What the hell is going on?'

'No, I agree,' Emily said, loudly. 'That's exactly what I was thinking.'

'Is that supposed to be some kind of code? Because it's terrible.'

'Yes, I know. Hopefully we can get to the bottom of it.'

'Emily,' Ben said from behind her.

Right behind her. So close she felt his breath on the back of her neck.

And this time her name was a command, not a question.

'I'm sorry.' She threw the words at him carelessly, over her shoulder, without turning around. 'I'm on a call—'

'It will have to wait,' he said.

Tall Blonde Woman waved. At first Emily was confused, because why would that woman be waving at her? And then – No, of course. She wasn't waving at Emily. She was waving at Ben.

She thought, *They're in this together, whatever the hell this is.*

And then Ben grabbed her arm.

Emily was so intent on getting away that the sudden force acted as a kind of slingshot, spinning her around with the surprise of it and then, rendered unsteady on her feet by the change in direction, closer to him.

It was disconcerting to see him this close, uncanny, like when you've come to know someone entirely through a thumbnail picture online and then meet them in 3-D, at all angles, in real life. He looked just like he had in the picture Jack had shown her, except red in the face, eyes wide, teeth clenched.

Furious.

'Didn't you get my message?' His words threw spittle into her face.

'*Emily!*'

It was Alice's voice, muffled but audible, because she'd shouted at the top of her lungs into her phone, loud enough to be heard in the vicinity of this one, to make her disembodied presence known.

279

It seemed to break a spell in Ben, who let go of her and stepped back.

His gaze rose over her shoulder, to where Tall Blonde Woman was standing, waiting. She'd stopped a few feet up the beach, apparently waiting for his direction.

'Just one second,' Emily said, as calmly as she could, into the phone. And then, in Ben's direction, 'I'm sorry, I have to go.'

And with that Emily took off up the beach, brushing past Tall Blonde Woman.

She dug her heels into the sand, going as fast as she could, not looking back. Her chest grew tight and her calves burned, but she pushed on.

She picked her shoes up at the bottom of the beach side of the marble steps but didn't stop to put them on, running up the steps to the gate, scanning for a release button so she wouldn't be delayed looking for it when she actually got there.

And saw Jack.

He was on the other side of the gate, punching in the code, opening it from the other side.

'What's going on?' he asked, his face full of concern. He looked behind her. 'Is that Ben?'

Emily came barrelling through the gate, pushing him out of the way, and then turned back around to push it shut. She gulped down a few breaths, trying to catch her own after the exertion.

Down by the water, Ben and Tall Blonde Woman were deep in what looked like an agitated conversation, hands flying.

'Who's that woman with him?' Jack asked, squinting.

'*Emily, for fuck's sake!*'

Alice. She'd forgotten she was still on the line.

280

She put the phone to her ear. 'I'll call you in a little while, all right? Everything's fine now.'

'What the actual f—?'

'I'm fine now. I'm with Jack.'

'Hang on. Are you—?'

'I'll call you later, I promise. OK? I promise.'

She hung up the call and turned to Jack, who was looking completely bewildered.

'What's going on?' he asked. 'I came out here because I saw you and Ben on the beach and I was going to ask you what you were saying to him. But it looks like maybe I should be asking what he said to *you*?'

'I need to talk to you,' Emily said.

'What's going on?'

'Not here. Not in the house. Not in Sanctuary.'

'All right.' Jack pulled a set of car keys out of his pocket. 'Then let's go.'

24

This time, Jack drove them out of Sanctuary in the opposite direction, making a left turn east on 30A. Within five minutes, he was parking in what a pleasantly weathered sign said was called ROSEMARY BEACH.

Emily couldn't see any beach. They were in what appeared to be the main square of a small, quaint town that couldn't have had less in common with the sterile white masonry, emptiness and straight lines they'd left back in Sanctuary. Here, there were mature weeping willows, trickling fountains and rows of crowded, colourful buildings that made her think of New Orleans a lot and Amsterdam a little bit. A towering flagpole stood in its centre; stars and stripes billowed gently in the breeze. There were people, too, and plenty of them – relaxing on park benches, dining al fresco outside cafés, lazily cycling around the square – but not enough to make a crowd, and no one seemed to be in a rush to get anywhere. The skies had cleared but the sun was already sinking, painting the whole scene with a warm, golden glow.

'This is lovely,' she said.

'This was also master-planned and built from scratch, just like Sanctuary. By the same people who designed and built Seaside, actually. I think they broke ground in 1995.' When she looked at Jack questioningly, he added, 'Wikipedia. Again.'

'Really? But it feels so *real*.'

'It *is* real.'

'You know what I mean. Organic. Haphazard. Messy.'

'Like urban sprawl?'

'I'd love a bit of urban sprawl right now,' Emily said. 'I think I might even miss it.'

Jack pointed to the café he'd parked right outside a place called Amavida Coffee Roasters.

'Do you want to go inside or . . . ?'

Emily shook her head. There was absolutely no way she was going to have this conversation in a public place. 'Can we just stay here?'

'Sure.'

A rhythmic buzzing sound: his phone, which he fished out of the pocket in the driver's door and then frowned at the screen. 'Ben is ringing me.' He tapped the device a few times before putting the phone away again, back in the door. 'Look, I think I know what you're going to say and it's not a big deal, all right? You don't have to justify anything to me. I get it.' He released his seatbelt and twisted around to face her. 'I heard you. Yesterday morning, when I first came into the room and you were already there with Grace. You said something about owing Morningstar money and a second book? Or, I guess, owing them money *because* you owed them a second book? I'm presuming that's how they convinced you to do this. And that's fine. It's not like I thought this was your dream gig or

283

anything. I just hope you felt like you had options, that's all. That you didn't come here because you thought you had no other choice.'

Emily didn't know what to say, in part because she was undone by the revelation that the moment he was referring to wasn't even thirty-six hours ago.

She felt like she'd been here for weeks.

'No,' she said. 'I mean, yes, that's true. I do owe them a book, and money because of that.' *And that's exactly why I came here.* 'But that's not what I need to tell you.'

'Then what it is? What's wrong?'

But now, Emily hesitated.

The idea of saying it out loud felt like tearing through the fabric of her life and letting something dangerous seep out, to break through. And it seemed almost silly to have kept this secret for so long, only to reveal it in this car in this picture-perfect town, to a man who, as soon as he set foot on Irish soil, would be arrested as part of a murder investigation.

But what other choice did she have?

'We spoke a little about my book,' she said. 'My novel? *The Witness*?'

'Yeah?'

'The thing is . . . I didn't make it up. I didn't have to. Because the story is true.'

'I'm not sure I understand,' Jack said slowly.

'*The Witness* is about a girl,' Emily explained. 'Roxie, she's called in the book. The night before her twelfth birthday, two teenage girls, fifteen and sixteen, go missing in her town. A few weeks later, their bodies are found weighed down in the local lake. It's all over the news. It's all anyone can talk about. The guards are crawling all over the place, going door to door.

And Roxie remembers that, that night, she woke up at three, maybe four in the morning and went downstairs – and saw her dad coming in, soaking wet.'

Jack didn't react, waiting for more.

'Her father is a violent man,' she continued. 'She's seen it, with her mother, but neither of them know that she has. They think they've been hiding it. And *she* was hiding, that night, when he came in, so he doesn't know that she saw him either. She'd crept downstairs to see if she'd got what she'd asked for for her birthday. A keyboard. And she had. It was there. But before she could slip back upstairs, she heard a key in the front door. She was crouched behind an armchair when he came in. She doesn't tell anyone what she saw. Not until she's much older. Then, she only ever tells her best friend.'

'You said that in the book,' Jack started, 'she's standing outside a Garda station, at the end.'

'She never went in. Not that time, or any of the others.'

'What happened to him? The father?'

'He died suddenly, five years after the murders.'

'He was never, like, charged or anything?'

'He was never even suspected.'

'So you were, what? Seventeen when your dad died?'

His framing of this question took her by surprise, enough for her to catch her breath in her throat.

'I was seventeen when he died, yes,' she said. 'But he wasn't my dad. The real Roxie was – is – my best friend. I'm the only person she's ever told. She let me write her story.'

He stared at her for a long moment, unblinking.

Since Jack had killed the engine and with it the air-conditioning, the car had been slowly warming up, the air collecting a solidity that was beginning to get uncomfortable.

When Emily shifted her weight now, she felt a dampness under her arms and behind her knees and in the small of her back.

She longed to roll down a window, to hold her face against a breeze.

'Let you,' Jack repeated. 'Not asked you to?'

'Encouraged me to. All I ever wanted was to write a novel. But I could never finish one. I was forever starting something, getting three or four chapters into it and then abandoning it because it ran out of story. I decided it was because I only had bad ideas – ideas too weak or flimsy to last for ninety thousand words. And then, one day, A— Roxie and I are talking, and she says, "Why don't you write about the one story only you can tell?"'

'Why only you?'

She smiled a little. 'Because she's a dentist, and no one else knows.'

Jack put an arm onto the steering wheel, letting his wrist lean on it while he stared at something in the middle distance, lost in thought. Doing this put his injuries on display and, when he seemingly realized this a few seconds later, he dropped his arm back down into his lap.

He looked back at her. 'And then?'

'I write it,' Emily said. 'And I actually finish it. I change – or I think I change – all identifying characteristics. I make up names for places and people. I set it in a different part of the country, at the opposite end of the year, in the present day. But the thing is, I'm thinking that, if I'm lucky, a couple of thousand people will read this, max. And pretty quickly, I start to lose track. When I get an agent, she wants me to do another draft. I get a book deal and do two more drafts before it's published. You start to forget what you changed and what you didn't. You start to forget, honestly, what's real and what's not. And there's one thing you didn't even know you needed to change.'

'What?'

'The shirt he was wearing that night. It had a distinctive pattern. What my friend didn't remember was that it was ripped, but it was. The, ah . . .' She took a breath. 'The missing piece was clutched in the hand of his victim.'

'Shit.'

'Yeah.'

'So what happened?'

'I got a letter. Addressed to Roxie's real name. Just before the paperback came out, so maybe nine months after the book was first published? It had been sent to my publisher's Dublin office.'

'By who?'

'The mother,' Emily said. 'Of the murdered girl.'

'Girl, singular? I thought there were two?'

'That was a detail I changed,' Emily said. 'There was one. The case is still unsolved. That girl's mother – she's in her seventies now – never stopped searching for answers. At some point, she happened upon *The Witness*, and felt like she'd found some. You see, the piece of the shirt was never made public, but the guards had told her about it. And, of course, she *had* found some answers. But we couldn't tell her that.'

'Why not?'

'It would expose us. I didn't do anything wrong, legally, I don't think, although I doubt Morningstar would be too happy with me. But that's nothing compared to what might happen to my friend. I don't have to tell you, Jack, what people are like these days. All those so-called citizen sleuths, the things they do to people – and it's not just online anymore. They're in the real world now. Doorstepping people and harassing them and shoving phones in their faces while they shout demands for answers. It could completely upend her life. No, it *would*. And for what? Who can even prove at this point whether or not he did have something to do with it? And even if they could and he did, so what? He's dead. He can't be punished for it now. The only person who would suffer for it is my friend.'

'What did you tell her? The mother of the murdered girl?'

His eyes were asking his real question: *What did you tell the* other *person desperate for answers after their loved one was murdered who came to you for help?*

Emily had to look away, down, at her hands.

'Nothing,' she said, her face burning with shame, her voice barely a whisper. 'We ignored her. We didn't know what else to do.'

Jack shook his head, either in disgust or disbelief or a combination of the two.

'I know,' she said. 'I *know*. It's awful.'

'Did she contact you again?'

'No, but ever since, I've been waiting for the other shoe to drop. I thought she might get a solicitor and force me to respond, or give up my notes or earlier drafts or something like that. I don't know what's permissible, legally, but I'm sure she could do something. She could tell Morningstar, try to get them on my case. Or worse: she could go to the guards and convince them to do something about it. I think that'd be a tall order, but you never know. My friend's mother could get a knock on the door. That's why I couldn't deliver the second book. I was falling apart over the fear of it all coming out – and absolutely destroying my friend's life – and because I hadn't really written the first one. I hadn't made it up. I took a real story and changed it. Garnished it with some fiction. That's all.' The car was getting unbearably warm. Emily looked at the controls on the door: electric windows. 'Jack, do you think you could put d—?'

'Why are you telling me all this?' he asked, cutting her off.

'Because ever since I've been here, someone else has been threatening to.'

'What? Who?'

'I don't know,' she said. 'They sent emails, to start with. An anonymous Hotmail account with "Emily Joyce" as the sender's name. The address was mostly what looked like random numbers until I realized that they're my ISBN. That's the number that appears with the barcode on a book. Each message was just one sentence, typed in all caps. The first one said, *I know who you are.* The second one said, *I know what you did.* And the third said, *Tell him or I will.* And then today, a fourth was hand-delivered.'

Jack's facial expression suggested he was curious but not concerned about the emails, but the news of the hand-delivered note seemed to genuinely shock him.

'It was slipped under the connecting doors.' Emily dug it out of her pocket, unfolded it and handed it to him. 'Do you recognize the writing?'

He frowned. 'Should I?'

'You tell me.'

They locked eyes, then Jack rolled his.

'Not this again,' he said.

'On the beach. Just now. Ben asked me if I got his message.'

'You think this is from *him*?'

'Who else would send it?'

289

'But how would he know?' Jack's voice was rising. 'And why would he care? What's this got to do with *anything*?'

'Maybe he's trying to stop this book.'

'That's ridiculous. He's helping me. He gave us the house.'

'Maybe because that way, it'd be easier for him to interfere.'

'*Interfere?*' Jack said incredulously. 'Look. On the beach, just now, and earlier, up in the room. Those are the only two times in your life you've met Ben, right?'

Emily nodded reluctantly, suspecting what was coming.

'So you've spent, what? Five? Ten minutes with him? Let's be generous. Let's say it was a full fifteen. And yet you think you know him. Well, *I've* known the guy since I was a teenager. And there's no way . . .' He shook his head. 'No. No way. It's just not even possible. No. Not Ben.'

Emily was thinking of what Ruth had said, about how she didn't know if Jack was really friends with Ben or if he had pretended to be for so long, out of fear or loyalty or both, that he'd just come to believe that he was.

Ruth had also said that Kate didn't like him.

'The woman on the beach,' Jack said then. 'Was he with her?'

'They seem to know each other, yeah.'

'Who is she?'

'I don't know. But I saw her before today. She was on both my flights here, which was some doing considering my route. And she was in Seaside, last night. At Bud and Alley's, but downstairs on the lower deck.'

'When *we* were there?'

'Yeah.'

'Is she Irish?'

'I don't know. I haven't heard her speak.'

'What the fuck is going on?' Jack muttered to himself.

It sounded rhetorical, so Emily didn't respond.

And she couldn't answer him. She had no idea what was going on. All she knew was that *something* was.

'Ben denied being here,' Jack said then. 'I mean, before today. He told me he only arrived in Sanctuary this morning. I didn't say anything about you being followed around town, but I did tell him about Grace seeing a man in the courtyard last night. He said it wasn't him. That it couldn't have been, because he was in Atlanta on a layover.'

'Did he say why he came here?' Emily asked.

'He heard about the arrest.'

'And so he flew here from France without even *calling you* first? And on what? Concorde?'

Jack's jaw worked. 'He was going to Miami, he said. For a trade show. He was already in Atlanta. He made a detour.'

But Ben had told Ruth he'd come here to meet a client at Fort Walton Beach Airport.

'Where's he staying?' Emily asked.

'In the same hotel as Joe and my sister, and Grace. In a place called Sandestiny? Sandustin? Sandestin? Something like that.'

Through the windscreen, Emily saw what was presumably a mother and her two young kids exit the store next to the café, clutching tote bags. Only now did she notice its colourful window displays and the sign hanging near its door: THE HIDDEN LANTERN. A bookshop.

'You know what's weird?' Jack said. 'Remember I told you that Kate was getting messages? Anonymous messages?'

Emily turned towards him. 'Yeah?'

'Some of them were emails. With her own name as the sender. And *they* were always in all caps, too.'

291

25

By the time they returned to Sanctuary, the sky was as dark as their mood.

They'd driven back in silence, each lost in their own thoughts. Emily's were mostly a mental list of all the things she felt she knew.

Kate had been sent anonymous emails. The night she died, Jack had been lured out of his home by Ben, who then hadn't shown up to their meeting. The same Ben that Ruth said Kate didn't like, who had a history of abusing women and getting away with it. Now here they were, almost a year on, in a house owned by Ben, writing a book about that night, and Jack's ghostwriter was getting anonymous emails not unlike the ones Kate had received, plus one note slipped under an internal door. Soon after, Ben, having already followed Emily, accosted her on the beach and demanded to know if she'd got his message.

As far as she was concerned, there was only one way to connect the dots.

It seemed overwhelmingly obvious that the common denominator in all this was Ben, that he must have had something to do with Kate's death. That he was behind whatever was happening here, now, presumably in a bid to stop anyone from revealing that.

To make sure that it was Jack who took the fall.

But Jack was in denial.

Despite everything, he seemed to still feel there could be a logical explanation for all this that didn't involve his best friend.

'What happens now?' she asked him as he turned the car onto Beach Read's street. 'What are we going to do?'

He didn't answer until he'd pulled up outside the house, at the kerb. He kept the engine running.

'I'm going to drop Grace back to the hotel,' he said, 'and then, while I'm there, I'll go talk to Ben.'

She raised her eyebrows in surprise. 'But I thought you didn't—'

'I don't. But you do, and this is a house he has access to, and I want you to feel safe. I'll tell him I really need a drink and ask if it's OK for me to crash there. That way you'll know he won't be anywhere near here tonight. I'll make sure of it.'

It also meant she'd be completely alone in the house.

But out of two bad options . . .

'In the morning,' Jack went on, 'I'll tell him he can go, that I'm fine, that I'll be leaving soon anyway, and see him off to Miami or wherever. Then I'll come back here so you and I can continue as planned. We have to. Because if Joe gets wind of any of this – the emails and the note and that blonde woman and Ben supposedly following you—'

Emily resented that *supposedly*.

'—then this will be over. Completely. There'll be no book. Ever. Not the one I wanted to write, anyway. Same if Ruth finds out, because she'll tell Joe. Or Grace, because she'll tell Ruth. So, please, Emily. Can we just . . . ? Can we just set all this aside for now? It's just for one more day. I need to finish telling my story and that might be the last chance I have.' He had said all this to her face but now he turned away, to stare straight ahead into the darkness. 'I don't know what's going to happen when I go back home.' The lights on the dash gave his face a bluish glow and revealed that his eyes were glistening.

Jack looked exhausted, deflated – a man made of only broken pieces. Emily wanted to reach out to him, to put a hand on his and tell him that it was all going to be OK, that they were going to make sure Kate's death was where the terrible things stopped happening to him.

But enough people in his life were already lying to him.

Including her.

It wasn't Alice's dad who'd come home that night so long ago, soaking wet, on the same night a girl was murdered and thrown in a local lake.

Alice was the best friend, the only person Emily had ever told about it.

She'd made a horrible mistake. Not that night, not back then. She'd somehow found enough grace not to blame a girl who'd been twelve years old for only a matter of hours for what she had or hadn't done. She didn't even know what she'd seen, really. It wasn't like her father had come home covered in blood, or drunkenly confessed on one of the nights when he went too far down a bottle of Powers. But later, when she was older and he was still alive, she did put the pieces together – and did nothing with the picture that emerged. Later again,

294

she did something to compound this failure to act: she wrote *The Witness*. Centred herself in someone else's tragedy, someone else's nightmare. And when its rightful owner came to claim her pain, to beg for answers, Emily had, once again, done nothing.

That letter had contaminated everything with shame, stopped her from writing another word and ever since hummed like a constant, anxious anticipation running beneath the floors of her life.

But didn't she deserve it? Didn't she deserve so much *worse*?

Emily thought so.

And now, here she was, with another desperate person trapped in a waking nightmare, looking for answers and coming to her for help with the search.

But this time, she could get them.

And *in* time.

She could help Jack and maybe, in doing so, redeem a little of herself. Start to fill the yawning hollow at her core, to lower the temperature at which her shame burned.

To try to make things right.

'You're right,' she said now. 'It's just one more day and it might be all the time we have, so . . . Yeah.'

She hadn't told him that Morningstar had explicitly instructed her to use the remaining time to force the confession, but it had been a bad enough day as it was.

They could broach *that* subject in the morning.

Jack held up a plastic fob and Beach Read's garage door began to retract. He asked her if she had his phone number. She didn't. He called it out while she tapped it into her phone, then rang him so he'd have hers. His device was still in the car door; it glowed and buzzed angrily at the incoming call.

'Keep your phone on,' he said, 'and call me if you need to. Any time, it doesn't matter how late. OK?'

She nodded. 'OK.'

'I'll see you in the morning.'

Emily climbed out of the car and went into the open garage, through the archway and out into the courtyard.

Grace was sitting by the pool with a tote bag slung over a shoulder and her phone in her hand, ready to leave.

'Jack is outside, Grace. He's going to drive you back to your hotel.'

'Where were you two *this* time?' she snapped as she stood up. But then she seemed to register Emily's demeanour, and her expression softened. 'What happened?'

'Nothing. Everything's fine. I'm just exhausted.'

Grace looked at her doubtfully.

'Really,' Emily said. 'I'm fine. I'll see you in the morning.' She pointed behind her, towards the street where Jack was waiting with the engine running. 'You should go.'

'Your dinner arrived,' Grace said. 'I had to put it in your refrigerator. I didn't know when you'd be back, so . . .'

'That's fine. Thank you.'

The last thing Emily wanted now was food. All she wanted to do was crawl into bed, close her eyes and forget about everything for the next eight hours. She waved Grace off and started up to the stairs, to Bookmark.

She was halfway up when she felt her phone buzz with a call from Mark.

'Hey,' he said when she picked up.

And that was all it took: one word. And that word was *hey*. But something about hearing Mark's voice, after everything that had happened today, so far this week, since that night all those years ago . . .

Whatever had been holding her together – just about – crumbled in an instant, and Emily burst into tears.

'Em?' Mark said in her ear. 'Em? Are you all right?'

'I'm sorry.' A sob broke in between the two words.

'What's going on? What's wrong?'

Everything, and she missed him.

'Nothing, I'm fine,' she said, wiping at her eyes.

'Sounds like it.'

Down below, the courtyard was empty. No audience for her emotional unravelling, thank God. She hurried to let herself into Bookmark, flipping on all the lights and closing the front door firmly behind her.

'Em, can we switch to FaceTime? I want to see you.'

She saw her reflection in the glass and said, sniffling, 'No. No, you really don't.'

'Then talk to me. What's happened?'

'Nothing. I'm OK. It's just . . .' She sat down on the couch. 'This is a lot more stressful than I thought it was going to be. And I'm absolutely exhausted. Today felt like a month long.'

'Why?'

'Mark, I can't really talk about it.'

'Of course you can.'

'No, I mean I physically can't. Not right now. I don't have the energy. I'll tell you everything when I'm back, I promise.'

'Are you OK, though? I mean, are you safe? Because that file I asked you to send me. Off the Olympus—'

'I sent it.'

Last night, just before she'd gone to bed, she'd remembered

to do what Mark had asked her to do in his last message: download the most recent recording from his voice-recorder and email it to him.

'You sent something,' Mark said, 'but it wasn't that. I think you accidentally sent me a recording of Jack.'

Emily frowned. 'What?'

'Yeah.'

'But that's not possible. I didn't use that device at all, to record anything, and there's nothing of him on my computer I could've accidentally sent instead.'

'What's going on over there, Em?' Mark asked. 'Are you sure you're OK? You'd tell me if you weren't, right?'

Why did he keep asking her that?

'There's some weird stuff on there,' he said. 'Nearly three hours of it. I only listened to the first couple of minutes – don't freak out, I've already deleted it from my laptop and the email you attached it to – but that was enough.'

'Enough for what?' Emily rubbed at her eyes. 'Maybe I, I don't know, sat on my backpack and accidentally recorded some audio off the TV. Don't worry about it.'

'He uses your name.'

'Who does?'

'Jack.'

'But it can't be Jack. I didn't use that recorder. They gave me one here and insisted I use it. That I only use it. I haven't even taken yours out, it's been in my bag the whole—'

But the rest of that sentence died in her throat, because it hadn't been in her bag the whole time, had it?

It had, temporarily, disappeared. Had someone transferred one of Jack's interview sessions onto it while it was gone? But how?

And *why*?

'Hang on,' she said, before putting the phone down on the coffee table and tapping to switch the call to speaker. 'I'll go get it.'

Emily stood up and scanned the room, looking for her backpack. It was on the floor, under one of the stools.

And the Olympus was on the breakfast bar.

She stopped short at the sight of it. What was it doing there? She'd put it back into the backpack, hadn't she? She remembered slipping it into the interior pocket, zipping the compartment closed. Or was she remembering what she'd done after it reappeared? Had she actually done that last night, after sending Mark the file?

'*Emily?*' Mark's voice, tinny from the phone's speaker.

'Yeah,' she said absently.

She reached to pick it up. It was an older model, chunky and cumbersome, its LCD screen giving her flashbacks to her first mobile phone, which had been a hand-me-down from her mother. She pressed buttons to navigate her way to the file menu, making at least three wrong turns, until finally she managed to bring up a list of all the recordings that were currently on the device. There were a dozen or so, named for dates.

They'd all been made weeks ago, except for one.

'*Hello?*' said disembodied Mark.

She turned back to pick up the phone and said, 'I'm really sorry, I'll have to call you back,' just as Mark said, '*Emily, what the—?*'

She ended the call.

She went back to the Olympus, leaned against the breakfast bar's edge, and held it with two hands as she played the file recorded yesterday, the one that was two hours and fifty-six minutes long.

A rustling noise, a gentle *thump*, and then a woman's voice, far away from the microphone, saying what sounded like, *'It's on now.'*

Then another voice, male and clear and much closer.

'Emily, hi. I know this is weird but please just listen. We don't know how else to do this. I've tried to approach you, but I think I scared you. Or maybe he's got to you. He does that. Don't blame yourself. But whatever he said about me, it's not true. Most of what he says in general isn't true. But anyway. We're trying this. We figure it'll be easier to tell you to listen to the message than find an opportunity to tell you all this without him knowing. So, yeah. This feels strange, talking to you like this. But it's time. I want to tell my story. You'll be the first person in the world to hear it in full. Here goes.'

She stared at the device in confusion.

'Most guys say they were born to be cyclists, that it was in their blood. I became one by chance. I was thirteen when I got my first serious bike, for my birthday. The first birthday without my dad in the house.'

She jabbed at the fast-forward button, holding it down for a few seconds.

'—spend their entire careers chasing this one thing – a win at Wimbledon, an F1 world championship, an Olympic gold medal – and I wonder, what happens when it doesn't happen? How can you point everything in your life towards one goal, only to never make it? How can a person recover from that level of disappointment?'

She skipped forward some more.

'—they're not your friends, they're your brothers. And it

can get confusing, because you're also their *domestique. I suppose it's a bit like being a ghostwriter, isn't it? I mean, I don't know that much about it, you'd know better than me, but a domestique can't have any ego and – I imagine? – for a ghostwriter, it's the same.'*

And some more.

'—when the door opened and a woman I had never seen before came running out. I say woman, but she was probably sixteen or seventeen. Let's say eighteen, at most, for the benefit of the doubt. I remember her dress was ripped at one shoulder and she was running with her hand up against her heart, holding it up. She had no shoes on. She didn't look at me. To be honest, I'm not even sure she saw me. She just pushed past and took off down the corridor.'

She skipped almost to the end of the recording, pressing PLAY when there was less than a minute left to go.

'—is here, by the way. Here in Florida. She's staying nearby, hiding away so he doesn't see her. But she wants to talk to you. She wants to tell you everything she knows. About her conversations with Kate, especially. And . . . And what happened that night. Because she was there. I don't know how all this is going to work out, but we'll find a way.'

But it wasn't Jack's voice telling her all this.

It was Ben's.

Movement, across the room, caught her attention.

Emily looked up and watched in pure, paralysing horror as the connecting door – *her* connecting door, on this side – began to slowly open.

301

'The first time it happened, we were in Girona for a pre-season training camp.

One evening, I was standing outside my hotel-room door, lifting my key card to hold it to the lock, when the door opened and a woman I had never seen before came running out. I say woman, but she was probably sixteen or seventeen. Let's say eighteen, at most, for the benefit of the doubt. I remember her dress was ripped at one shoulder and she was running with her hand up against her heart, holding it up. She had no shoes on. She didn't look at me. To be honest, I'm not even sure she saw me. She just pushed past and took off down the corridor.

When I went in, Jack was getting up from the edge of his bed, the one furthest from the door. He looked a bit dishevelled, like he'd woken up from a nap. I asked him who the girl was and he said, "Someone who couldn't make up her mind." I said she looked upset and he shook his head, sort of mockingly, as if the girl was being overly dramatic. I asked him what had happened and he said, "Not enough to make it worth the hassle."

Maybe now that I'm older and away from it all, I should know what I was supposed to do. But to be perfectly honest, I'm *still* not sure. If I found myself reliving that moment, what would I do? What could I do? Run after the girl and ask her if she was OK, check that she was? But she obviously wasn't, so what was my next step? Confront him? This was a guy I'd known since we were Juniors. He was one of my best friends, both on and off the bike.

Although, at that point in our lives, there really wasn't any "off".

And by then it was very obvious to all of us that Jack was being groomed by the team to be a future team leader. He was the chosen one. He was already the existing team leader's favoured domestique.

One day, I might be his.

A first lieutenant to a man I loved like a brother. We would win together; his victories would feel like mine.

It was a goal I desperately wanted to reach and I knew that doing anything about what I'd seen would throw a brick wall between me and it.

And I told myself, nothing like it had ever happened before. I had no reason to believe that he'd "done" anything based on everything I knew about him up until that point, and while I know this sounds naive, it never even occurred to me that I had "witnessed" anything.

So in my mind, I wasn't staying quiet. There was nothing to choose to stay quiet about. No one made a complaint. No police arrived the next morning asking questions.

He never mentioned it again, and I wouldn't have dared.

I actively forgot about it.

Later, when we were in the Basque Country, I opened the door of the team bus just in time to hear someone say *Jack and Ben*. They were talking about us, about me, and I stopped on the steps, unsure of what to do. It was the directeur, a coach and the Comms guy inside. The directeur waved me in and asked me if there was anything I wanted to talk to them about, anything at all that might be playing on my mind. I said no, which – I know how this makes it look – was the truth. He said something about the good of the team and not gossiping, and I said I understood.

You tell yourself it was an isolated incident, or that you can't possibly know what happened or who's at fault, and that it's not your business.

But every time you look the other way, you're helping to build a monster.'

VI

BURN AFTER READING

26

Time seemed to slow to a crawl as the door continued to swing open, until it was meeting its own hinges at a right angle.

A hand came into view then, pressed against its other side, pushing it. A woman's hand. Deliberate but tentative. Attached to an arm, the sleeve of a striped shirt. A familiar face. Short blonde hair. Eyes wide, searching, landing on Emily.

Tall Blonde Woman was *here*, inside, standing just feet away.

Emily blinked and time seemed to *whoosh* forward at hyper-speed, moments passing like missed opportunities while she stayed stock-still but her mind raced. She should turn and run out the front door, she thought. Or run towards her with her arms out, to push her back through the door and onto the ground so Emily could get the connecting door closed before she got to her feet again. Why wasn't it locked already? What should she say? *What are you doing here? Get the fuck out?* Should she say anything? This woman was with Ben. She had broken in. Maybe Emily should just scream, but who would hear her? What she actually did was nothing, paralysed by inaction.

The woman raised both hands, fingers splayed, as if to say, *Please, don't shoot.*

'It's OK,' she said. 'It's OK. I'm Jean.'

The name didn't mean anything to Emily.

The other woman's focus moved to the Olympus. 'Did you listen to it yet?' Back up to meet Emily's eye. 'Do you know who I am?'

Listen to what? Emily asked in her mind before remembering what she'd been doing before the door began to open.

She'd been listening to the recording Ben had made on Mark's Olympus.

Didn't you get my message? That was what he'd spat at her, down on the beach. It had sounded like a threat and it had made her feel afraid. But what if he'd been asking about the recording? What if she'd mistaken desperation for intimidation?

And if she had and that was what it was, then what was *this*?

'I knew Kate,' Jean said. 'I was trying to help her. And before that, get her to help me. I was there that night. The night of the fire. I need to tell you what I know. I've been trying to, but—'

'What are you doing here?' Emily said, finally finding her voice. '*How* are you here? That door was locked. I locked it. I know I did.'

'I came in here earlier,' Jean said, keeping her voice infuriatingly even, gentle, calm. As if she feared she was dealing with a wild animal, when *she* was the threat. 'After we tried to talk to you on the beach. Ben gave me his keys and I snuck in while he tried to keep Grace distracted. After your reaction, we

308

figured you hadn't found the Olympus. I came in here to look for it, to check. It *was* here, in your bag. I'm sorry for going into your things, but—'

'That doesn't explain what you're doing here,' Emily shouted, louder than she'd been expecting herself.

When Jean continued, she spoke faster.

'I put it out on the counter so you'd see it when you came in. But then I saw Grace coming up the steps. Delivering something. I had only seconds. I opened this door' – she jerked a thumb behind her – 'and found the one on the other side already unlocked.'

When Emily looked over Jean's shoulder now, she saw a dark room beyond. A bedroom, it looked like. Its other door, the one that presumably led to a hallway, was closed.

'I've been hiding in the main house,' Jean said, 'in that guest room, all evening. I didn't know what else to do. I couldn't risk leaving via the main house. If Jack sees me—'

'Jack isn't here,' Emily said. 'He's gone.'

'Where?'

'To the hotel. To talk to Ben.'

Jean dropped her hands to her sides. 'Then we mightn't have much time.'

'You were on my flight,' Emily said. 'Flights.'

'Was I?' She looked surprised.

Emily nodded. 'I saw you.'

'That must have just been the best route anyone got when they booked last minute. I only booked my flights Monday evening, after I found out that this was happening. That you were coming here. But I didn't know it was *you*. I had no name or anything. I only knew that they'd hired someone and that the interviews were going to start.'

'How did you know that?'

'Well . . . from Ben.' Jean said this as if it were obvious.

'Are you and he . . . ?'

She shook her head. 'No. We're just helping each other out. Joining forces against a common enemy, you could say. Making up for mistakes we made in the past. If I'd tried to expose Jack earlier, Kate might still be alive. She might have got away. And look, I know how Ben can come across, especially when he's worked up. He said he tried to talk to you when you were walking around the town, but that you ran off? He didn't mean to scare you. He was actually trying *not* to do that. He was waiting for the right moment, making sure that you two were really alone, that Jack wasn't around, and . . . Well, I guess it didn't go to plan. And then you clearly didn't want to talk to us on the beach, and we didn't want to make a scene – we knew that if Jack was looking out a window up at the house, he might see us. And then when he did appear, I couldn't risk getting any closer to him. He doesn't know I'm here. But you should know: you don't need to be afraid of us. We're the good guys.'

Emily didn't know if she believed this.

'Ruth, Jack's sister, told me Ben was . . . That *he* had done things. To women. And that he was forcing Jack to keep his secrets.'

'And who told her that?' Jean shook her head. 'Everyone thinks Jack is a great cyclist and a great speaker and a great businessman, but you know what he's *really* good at? What his actual talent is? *Storytelling*. He doesn't just lie. He builds worlds. He makes you doubt reality. He's doing it right now, I bet. With you. Which is why I need to tell you what I know. And then you'll have that, and you have Ben's story' – Jean nodded at the Olympus – 'and hopefully that'll be enough to counter Jack's lies.'

'Counter them how?' Emily asked. 'And where? I don't understand.'

'Can we sit down?'

Jean took a seat on the couch. Emily pulled out one of the stools at the breakfast bar, but remained standing.

'A few weeks before Kate died,' Jean began, 'I sent Ben a message. I'd been approached by an Italian sports journalist who was doing a piece about sexism in cycling. She didn't know anything about Jack, but I thought, you know what? I'm going to tell her. Everything. What happened to me, what I saw, what I know was covered up. Fuck the shit they made me sign and fuck their hush money. I was ready and I was prepared. But what I didn't want was for Kate to read about it in a paper or see it online.'

'You were friends?'

'She didn't know me at all. We met once, at some event, for a second. But I knew this was her husband. And I knew Jack, so I thought, *She has absolutely no clue.* This will come as a complete shock. I wanted to warn her, somehow. So I got on to Ben to see if he could connect us. We met up for a drink – this isn't the kind of thing you say over the phone – and we had a few, and we got talking about back then, and eventually it came out: Ben has his own stories about Jack. And he decided that *he* was done keeping quiet, too.'

'So you both went to Kate?'

Jean shook her head. 'Kate didn't like Ben. They had some – brief – history, and they were friends for a while, but since she and Jack had got together, she'd avoided him like the plague. We figured Jack was feeding her lies – and, based on what his

311

sister said to you, we were absolutely right. So it had to be me. I tried to approach her, a couple of times, but it went about as well as our attempts here, to approach you.'

Emily had a flash of Ben's reflection in the window of the café on the square, the blur of his figure standing with his back to the shore on the beach. Him grabbing her arm, on the sand. Looking furious, she'd thought at the time.

But in hindsight, it could have been panicked desperation.

'She didn't want to listen, naturally,' Jean said. 'And she had a bruise above her eye. I know it sounds fucking idiotic now, but it didn't occur to me that Jack might be that man at *home*, too.'

Emily tried to imagine Jack – Jack who'd cried in front of her, who'd talked to her about sunsets in Seaside, who less than an hour ago had told her that what mattered to him was her feeling safe – hurting the woman she'd watched smiling and laughing in the *Sunrise* clips she'd found online, the woman who'd loved him, who'd married him. She was about as successful as she'd been on the first day, when she'd tried to imagine him killing her.

'And then,' Jean said, 'we fucked up. When I'd approached Kate, she could always walk away – and she did. I thought, how do I force her to listen to me? I can't send her something, Jack could see it. She's not going to stay on the line if I call. But what if I went to her home? Their place was out in the middle of nowhere, so it'd be private, too. All we needed to do was get rid of Jack. So Ben arranged to meet him for a pint and I went to the house after he was supposed to have left.'

'Is this . . . Are you talking about the night of the fire now?'

Jean nodded grimly. 'I parked my car about ten minutes' walk away, just in case any of their neighbours saw me and made a comment to Jack later on. I rang the doorbell, but no one answered. I rang it again. I had Kate's number so I – I know I shouldn't have, I know, but – I sent her a text, asking if Jack was home. And literally, as I pressed send, I saw a glint of something, just at the corner of the house. Another car. Jack's. He hadn't left yet.'

'What did you do?'

'Nothing. I didn't do anything, except leave.'

They fell into a long silence, Emily thinking about how things might have been different if Jean had done something and sure that Jean was, in that moment, wondering the same thing.

'I think she told him,' Jean said. 'Confronted him. That night, before he left to go meet Ben. And I think he knew his time was up. He knew it was all about to come crashing down, and there was no way he would let that happen. He'd lived a life where every bad thing he'd done had just gone away. Why wouldn't this too? He probably felt confident he could spin another story. And he *did*, didn't he? Within a few days, they knew Kate hadn't died in the fire, that she'd been beaten to death. And yet, what happened? Nothing fucking much. Yeah, OK, *now* he's getting arrested. But it's been almost a year. And how much do you want to bet he'll be released without charge?'

'When you say every bad thing?'

'Ben thinks he had something to do with Charlie Heeney's suicide too,' Jean said. 'Their friend who took his own life just before the Olympics? He and Jack were really close, and the only sport Jack truly loved was tormenting people. Ben told me that just before Kate quit her job on TV, she was getting messages. Stalker-y stuff. Really nasty. He thought Jack was sending them to her, and I'd tend to agree. Because that's what he does. He chips away at you, little by little. You don't notice until it's too late, by which time the chips have turned into cracks, and then all it takes is one more blow from him and you've broken down completely.'

Emily thought of her own messages, the note under the door. Even the casual mention of Neil when she'd arrived, which had shaken her confidence from the get-go. Had Jack been chipping away at her, undermining her all this time? Was that why she'd come to feel sorry for him? To want to help him? Why she'd *believed* him? Enough to tell him her secrets?

But then how did she know that *Jean* was telling the truth now?

'Why did Ben offer him the use of this house?' she asked.

'He didn't. Jack asked him for it.'

'Why didn't he say no?'

'Because with Jack, it's always easier to go along. And this way, Ben knew what was happening. He was in the loop.'

'Why do *you* think he's doing this book?'

'I think it's about sympathy,' Jean said. 'That was always the ink he wrote his lies with. Because what are you going to say about a guy who saw his dad die in the car next to him when he was thirteen? Or whose friend took his own life right before he went to the Olympics? Who Jack dedicated his silver medal to? Or whose beautiful wife died in a fire while he was out having a pint? But when the facts about Kate's death came out, and people's opinions of him changed, well . . . It was only a matter of time before the allegations followed. So he knew that he needed that sympathy back, or he was going to be in real trouble.' She paused. 'And he needs money. Exis is crumbling – not that that would really matter to Jack, but

314

people *knowing about it* would. He can't be seen to fail. He can't stand it. But he doesn't get paid for this, does he? So I'm not sure where that fits in. I'm sure he has some kind of angle.'

'He does get paid for this,' Emily said, frowning. *Of course he does – it's his book.* 'Although the publisher said something about the proceeds going to his charitable foundation.'

'Really? I didn't think sources did.'

'*Sources?*' Emily repeated, confused.

'Yeah,' Jean said. 'Isn't that what he is here, technically? A source on a story?'

Emily had no idea what Jean meant. But the bigger, more pressing issue was that she had no idea what Jean expected her to do.

'Jean, look. When I said to you that I didn't understand, I meant I don't understand why you're here, telling me this. Why it's so important that you do. I don't know what I'm supposed to do with this information. What you expect me to do with it.'

'Use it,' Jean said, frowning. 'Put it in the book.'

'But I can't.'

'Not right now, I know that. You have to investigate. Get evidence. Back it up. And there'll be legal challenges. I'm sure that's why we've had no luck so far in getting anyone in the media to care about this. They're too afraid to print anything about him that might prejudice a future trial. But this book *is* happening, right? I mean, you're still here, so . . .'

Emily let a beat pass.

'Jean, I'm sorry, but I think you've misunderstood. I'm not writing about Jack, or this case. It's not that kind of book. I'm helping him write *his* story. In the first person. A memoir. I'm not an investigative journalist. Really, I'm just a typist.'

Now it was Jean who said she didn't understand.

'Whatever Jack says goes in this book,' Emily clarified. 'And that's *all* that does. He says it, I write it down and then he gets to approve every last word before it goes to print. This is about him telling his side of the story. Unless he's charged, that is. If that happens, then there might be the kind of book I think you're hoping for. But it will be a long ways away. They'll have to wait for a verdict. And it wouldn't be me who'd be writing it.'

Emily saw the facts of the situation dawn on Jean's face, flashing up one after the other like the stages of grief. Denial. *No, it can't be.* Anger. *So Jack wins yet again?* Bargaining. *There must be something we can do.*

'What made you think I was writing *about* him?' Emily asked.

'Because that's what he told Ben. He told him it was a top-secret project so he couldn't say much, but he said that. Or at least gave Ben that impression.'

'What about the guards? What if you went to them?'

'I did go to them. Maybe not soon enough, but I did. And I told them I'd sent Kate a message that night, that they should be able to find a record of it even if her phone did go missing. And about the bruise. But so what? What does any of that prove? Do you know how much it takes to build a case? To even get it brought to court?'

'He's being arrested, Jean.'

'That's no guarantee of anything, especially with him.' The look on Jean's face was now one of acceptance. 'I'm sure Jack Smyth will find a way to get away with *this*, too.'

The morning of the fire

Kate slips out of bed before Jack stirs and tiptoes into the bathroom. The light switch is outside the door and she doesn't want to risk waking him, so she goes into the black, closes the door fully behind her and finds her way by touch to the bathroom sink. Then she pats the wall in front of her until she feels the button that illuminates a ring of light around the mirror hanging there.

The woman she sees in it looks exactly how she feels. Exhausted. Hollowed-out. Dying inside.

She hasn't slept at all. Last night, she poured herself a glass of wine as usual, but the first sip had tasted like battery acid and then sloshed around her otherwise empty stomach until she got up and went to the bathroom, thinking she was about to be sick. Everything is different now. What she knows changes everything. Nothing is right. It's all upside-down, tilted, wrong. She's spent the night staring at their bedroom ceiling, turning everything over in her mind, spinning the various jigsaw pieces around and around, trying to make them fit, trying to make it make sense.

But she failed.

She still can't see the full picture.

She's afraid that that's because she doesn't *want* to see.

She does what she can with the contents of her make-up bag, if only to stop Jack asking questions. He seemed to sleep soundly last night, which made her, by turns, angry and jealous. She starts with a layer of brightening moisturizer. Three drops of pearlescent liquid gold. A CC cream that goes some way to banishing the dullness, the redness and the shadows, but isn't thick enough to alert Jack to the fact that she's gone to the trouble of putting on a face before he opens his eyes. Finally, she dots some rose-coloured blush on the apples of her cheeks, meets her own eye in the mirror and whispers, 'You can do this. You can. Come *on*.'

But neither Kate is convinced.

She turns off the light and feels her way back to the door, then slips out of their bedroom and down the stairs. The house is cold, even with the heating on a timer – it hasn't been on for very long. She takes a pair of socks from the laundry basket and slips on a cardigan of hers that's hanging on the back of a kitchen chair. She starts a pot of coffee, cuts fruit into pieces and turns on the oven to bake some frozen pastries.

She has no appetite and Jack never eats breakfast these days, but if she doesn't have something to do, a task to focus on, she feels like she will disassemble right here, right now, in the kitchen. Like those superhero movies where someone gets frozen in nitrogen, she fears one knock will break her, reducing her to a pile of shattered glass.

She thinks, *How did I get here? How did it come to this?*

Jack appears just as she's laying the table. He's already dressed, shoes and all.

'What's all this?' he asks, looking bemused.

'I was up early,' she says.

'More like awake all night.' He moves to kiss her on the cheek and she proffers it for him. She smells mint on his breath. 'Everything all right?'

'Yeah, I just . . . I don't know. Too much caffeine yesterday, probably.'

'I don't think I even saw you drinking coffee yesterday.'

'I had a couple, when I was out.'

'Anywhere nice?'

She shakes her head. 'Circle K's finest.' And then, even though this is the kind of unnecessary detail that risks exposing it as a lie, she adds, 'I got one on the way there and another on the way back. And I'd had a cup for breakfast. Two seems to be my limit, these days.'

She pours two cups of coffee and takes them to the table. She sits in the chair next to the one at the head of the table, which is where Jack always sits and will when he finishes doing whatever it is he's doing now, moving around in the kitchen behind her. She looks out at the garden. She yawns.

She questions every single thing she's doing.

Is this what I'd do if I hadn't met Jean? Is this how I'd be acting if I didn't know what she told me? If I were still the person I was yesterday?

'How did *you* sleep?' she asks. She can hear him opening a cupboard, flicking the switch on the kettle, the tinkling of a teaspoon. What's he doing? 'I didn't keep you awake, did I?'

'A little bit,' he says. 'But it's OK.'

A hand appears in front of her then, holding a steaming cup of herbal tea.

When she doesn't take it, he sets it down in front of her and takes away the cup of coffee.

When she looks up at him questioningly, he grins and says, 'Probably best to avoid it today, don't you think?' He takes his seat, stirs milk into his own coffee, takes a slurpy, noisy sip.

'Oh,' he says then. 'I'll be out tonight. Ben called. He'll be around.'

Kate feels her heartbeat ramping up to a speed that seems to risk breaking out of her chest.

'What?' she manages to say.

Jack says, 'I know. You wanted to watch that thing. I'm sorry. But I shouldn't be too long. I'm just meeting him for a pint. I'll be back by nine, ten at the extreme latest.'

But she's still stuck on the first revelation. 'Ben is *here*? Since when?'

'He got here yesterday. But that wasn't his car, if that's what you're thinking. In the lane.'

He meets her eye and she feels like he's warning her off the subject.

Then, to remove all doubt, he actually does that.

'Don't start, Kate. With him, it's always easier – and safer – to play along. Act like I don't know. If it seems like I'm trying to avoid him, he'll start asking questions, and that'll only make things worse. And I do *not* want him coming here. I won't let that happen.'

He reaches across the table to squeeze her hand. She pulls it out of his grasp, puts both palms flat on the table and steadies herself to take a deep breath.

And then, quickly, she drops her hands into her lap because she thinks, *No, if I hadn't met Jean yesterday, I wouldn't do that.*

Jack frowns at her, concerned.

'Is everything OK?' he asks.

'Well, no. Obviously not. You're meeting him.'

'I meet him all the time.'

'Even though you don't want to. Even though you know who he is, who he really is. What kind of man. What he did.'

'Kate, don't.'

'You've been keeping his secrets, all this time—'

'I've been protecting us. Protecting *you*.'

'I know, but—'

He puts up a hand. '*Stop*,' he says. 'Don't.' He breathes in deep, exhales slowly. 'There's no way out, if that's what you're thinking. Believe me, I've thought about it. But this – keeping him on-side, not rocking the boat, him pretending I don't know, me pretending there's nothing *to* know – it's the best way. Honestly, Kate. It is.'

'What did he say to you? "You haven't seen me in months and I live in Nice, but I'm here, let's meet for a pint?"'

Jack looks away. 'Pretty much.'

'What did he *say*, Jack?'

'That he needs to talk to me about something,' he admitted. 'And he said that it has to be tonight.'

27

Friday's construction-site cacophony woke Emily up at 7:30a.m. sharp.

She felt like shit, as if she hadn't slept at all – and she hadn't, really. She made two coffees in one cup and took it outside, onto the balcony. The sun was still low behind the house, but there were no clouds. A blue-sky day for Jack's fake confession.

She showered and dressed. She found a safe place for the Olympus – she ripped a small hole in the lining of her suitcase and slipped it in there – and she did that after emailing another copy of Ben's recording to Mark, this time with instructions not to delete. She silenced her phone and put it on Airplane mode too, for good measure, then slipped it into her jeans pocket before she went outside, down the steps and across the courtyard. It was deserted and in a chilly shadow.

When she entered the main house, it felt empty.

She thought of her first morning here, which was only seventy-two hours ago but felt like a scene from another life.

Following Grace into the main house, down a long corridor and through the barn-style doors. Being surprised by the view out of the window: cloudless sky, shimmering water. Grace's stern instructions, security precautions, rules.

Where *was* Grace?

She ducked into the kitchen, but there was no one there and no evidence that anyone had been so far this morning. It occurred to Emily that something seismic could've happened overnight or early this morning, and she wouldn't know. Jean had left quickly after their conversation the evening before, scurrying away into Sanctuary's empty night. She hadn't heard anything from Jack since, although she hadn't expected to. There'd been no more emails, no other notes.

As she climbed the back stairs, Emily wondered how the hell she was supposed to do this.

What *this* even was now.

She hadn't decided who to believe. On one hand, what Jean had said about Jack had made sense. She had no reason to lie and seemed genuinely devastated when she'd learned that Emily wasn't the help she'd hoped for. After Jean left, Emily had put her headphones in and listened to Ben's recording in its entirety. It made sense, too, and slotted pieces into the puzzle.

But she kept seeing Ben's face, inches from hers, red and angry, on the beach yesterday. Recalling the tension when they'd first met, up in the room she was heading to now. The fact that he'd followed her. Stared at her, from the beach.

Yesterday evening, she'd been sure that he was the villain here.

How did she know that everything that had happened since wasn't all some elaborate scheme to throw her off the scent?

323

What Emily really wanted was to not have to decide who to believe at all. She wanted to check out, to quit. And she was going to. She'd already made that decision. But she'd go through with this last session just so no one – not Jack, Ben or Jean – would be alerted to her plan. It seemed like the safest option. Then she'd fly home, tell Morningstar and go back to being thousands of euro in debt. After her time here – after everything she'd seen and heard – it was starting to look like the best-case scenario.

Jack was already in the room.

He was standing by the window, looking out over the beach, hands dug deep in his pockets.

'Morning,' she said.

'Morning.' He turned around to face her. 'How are you feeling? Did you sleep?'

He looked pale and a little dishevelled, as if he hadn't.

'I'm fine,' she said. 'You?'

'Fine.'

'Did you talk to Ben last night?'

Jack nodded but said no more; she wasn't going to get any details.

'How was your night?' he asked. 'Was everything OK?'

'Yeah.'

'What did you do?'

He'd never asked her how she'd spent her other evenings. She froze, searching for clues in his expression. Did he know? Had he somehow found out about Jean coming to Bookmark last night?

Or had he forced Ben to confess all back at the hotel?

'My boyfriend rang,' she said. 'I spoke to him for a while. After that I was so tired, I just went straight to bed.'

324

He nodded, seemingly accepting this.

'Um, Jack. Listen. I didn't want to tell you this yesterday – there was so much else going on – but Morningstar—'

'—want the confession,' Jack finished. 'I know.' He crossed the room to take up his usual spot on the couch. 'Let's just get it over with, then.'

She tried to cover her surprise. 'You still want to do that?'

'Nothing's changed, Emily. I want to do this book for the same reason I always did: Kate. I know it won't happen unless I give them the confession chapter. I'm getting arrested as soon as I get home, so I'm betting they told you to make sure that's what we use our last day here to do.'

If she hadn't heard Ben's message on the Olympus or spoken to Jean, this would make sense. Jack had a plan and he wanted to proceed with it. Getting the book out there was the most important thing to him, because he saw it as a way to prove his own innocence and, in doing so, force the authorities to look for Kate's real killer.

But she *had* heard the message and spoken to Jean, so she couldn't begin to understand any of this.

Unless Ben and Jean weren't telling the truth.

She didn't know what to do, so she decided to do what she'd been hired to do: be Jack Smyth's ghostwriter. Get his fake confession. Finish this job.

'OK,' she said. 'Then let's begin.'

Emily may not have seen Grace, but there was evidence that she'd already been here, in the room. The laptop and voice-recorder were neatly lined up on the desk as before, along with the legal pads and pens. She took her seat and pulled the laptop closer, opened its lid, booted it up. There were now two files on the desktop: TRANSCRIPTS and TRANSCRIPTS2. She powered up the voice-recorder, checked its memory: no files. It was just as Grace had promised. The audio recordings were being deleted at the end of each day, once she'd finished transcribing them.

She slipped her phone out of her pocket and put it in one of the desk drawers. If Jack saw her do this, he said nothing.

At the same moment, he was doing something on his own phone. Probably silencing it.

'The thing is,' Jack said, 'I don't know if I can do this.' He met her eye. 'Will you help me? With the confession? I don't know if I can, you know, make something up. I've never written fiction before.'

That makes two of us, she said silently.

And then she wondered if he knew she'd think that, if he was needling her, reminding her of the huge secret she'd revealed.

Emily pressed RECORD, checked for the blinking light, and swivelled the device around until its microphone was facing Jack.

'How about we take it one step at a time, OK? Think about what Carolyn and Beth want.' She started typing some nonsense onto a virtual blank page just so she wouldn't have to look directly at Jack as she spoke to him. 'What they know the reader will be expecting. They're going to want questions answered, right? Like I said yesterday.'

'But that's just it. I can't answer their questions because I wasn't there.'

'Neither were they. So they won't know what's true and what's not. They'll just want you to say that you did it, and offer a satisfying explanation. All you have to do is provide one that fits for long enough to keep them reading this chapter, and then afterwards, you can do your denial.' She checked the blinking red light one more time. 'Why don't we start with reality? That will make it easier. That night. When you were at home and you were getting ready to leave to go meet Ben, Kate was where? What was she doing?'

Jack raised a single eyebrow. 'This is the real bit, now?'

'Yes.'

'She was upstairs, in our room.'

'Doing what?'

A shrug. 'I don't know. Organizing her wardrobe or something.'

'She was planning to stay in, right? She wasn't going anywhere.'

'We were both supposed to be staying in, until Ben called. We were going to get a takeaway and watch a few episodes of something—'

'Do you remember what, specifically?'

'Some murder show on Amazon,' Jack said. 'I don't remember the name. More her thing than mine.'

'Do you remember talking to her before you left?'

'Not specifically. But it was probably the usual. You know, what time I'd be back. Say hi to Ben for me.'

'She said that?'

A shadow of something crossed Jack's face. 'Yeah.'

'But I thought she didn't like him?'

'Who told you that?'

Shit. Emily was just about to enter a full-blown panic when she remembered that she could blame it on—

'Ruth,' she said. 'Ruth told me.'

Jack rolled his eyes. 'My sister doesn't know what she's talking about almost all of the time.'

There was no way Emily was going to invite him to say more on that subject. She needed to keep this on track, and they were coming to their first crucial juncture.

'Then what?' she asked.

'Then I kissed her goodbye, left her upstairs, went to go meet Ben.'

'But you didn't.'

Jack looked annoyed for a beat, then something like uncertain.

'Not for the purposes of this,' Emily clarified. 'If you're guilty – which you're saying you are here, in this chapter – you would've had to have done it before you left the house, because by the time you got back, the fire had taken hold and Kate was already gone. Right?'

Jack looked down at his hands, which made Emily look at them, which made her think again about the pain of his injuries.

'I can't, Emily,' he said softly.

'It's just a few lines.'

'You're asking me to say I did something I didn't.'

'*I'm* not asking anything. This is what you agreed.' This was probably a dangerous game but . . . 'Do you want to stop? Forget about all this? We can, you know. *You* can. You could just go back to Morningstar and tell them it's off. That you've changed your mind. That Joe changed your mind, after the arrest.'

'That wouldn't be a lie,' Jack said. 'He's been trying to.'

'But if you do that, then this might be the end. You said yourself, if we don't get this done before you go back home, it might never happen. So if you don't do the confession today, and then, I don't know, a few days or weeks from now you

328

change your mind and decide that, actually, it's worth it to get the book published, Morningstar mightn't be interested anymore. They might decide to move on. To go to Plan B.'

What followed was an awkwardly long, excruciating silence.

'Could *you* write it?' Jack asked then. 'The confession?'

'What do you mean?'

'Just, you know, make something up and then I'll say, yeah, that's how it happened. I know you said you haven't technically written fiction before, but—'

He stopped when he saw her grab the voice-recorder and hit it to turn it off.

'Jack!' she said, partly in reprimand, partly in disbelief.

'What? What's wrong?'

'Please don't do that. Don't say anything about what I told you while we're recording. I can't have it on the record here. All the material we generate belongs to Morningstar. *Morningstar*. Who published me, too.'

'Oh, shit,' Jack said, either realizing what he'd done or putting on a good show of pretending to. She couldn't tell. 'Sorry, I wasn't even thinking. Can you delete that bit?'

'I don't know.' She picked up the device, studied the options on its digital display. 'I don't think I can do it without deleting the whole file.'

'Maybe you should. We can start again.'

But he'd already spoken about being with Kate that evening, and she didn't want to have to get him to repeat it.

'No,' she said. 'It's all right. We can worry about that later. Just, please, don't do it again.'

'I think the recorder is the problem, actually,' Jack said. 'It's too much pressure. Could we leave it off?'

'But we *have* to record it. That's sort of the whole point.'

'I know, but what if we do a dry run first, to, like, figure out what I'm going to say, and then we do it properly, for the record? I think that might be easier for me.'

She searched his face, trying to figure out if this was a scheme or what he genuinely needed to make this happen.

The look he returned was one of hopeful pleading, and it felt real.

But she didn't love the idea of an unrecorded dry run, and she didn't like his use of the word *we* at all.

But she wanted this to be over already, and if that was what it was going to take . . .

'OK,' she said. 'Let's try that.'

Jack pointed at the legal pad. 'You could take notes, so we know what we said. The main points, I mean. So we can come back to them when we're recording.'

'I might do that on the laptop, actually. I'm quicker at typing than writing.'

'No laptop,' he said. 'Please.'

Why? Was he worried she might use it to secretly record him?

If he was worried about that, then maybe she should. And what if Jean and Ben were telling the truth, and Jack was about to reveal, inadvertently or otherwise, his guilt beyond any doubt?

She thought of her phone, sitting in the drawer of the desk.

'I'm going to grab a water.' Jack stood up. 'You want one?'

'No, thanks.'

As he crossed the room to the snack table, she opened the desk drawer and put the laptop in there, letting it fall into place with a loud, careless *thump* that caught Jack's attention. Once his back was turned again – he was opening the silver ice-bucket, transferring cubes to a glass – she quickly woke her phone, tapped in her passcode and set a voice-memo recording.

Then she closed the drawer again, but not all the way.

Emily had no idea if it would even be able to pick up the voices in the room, but it was all she could do. She pushed the voice-recorder away, to the far side of the desk; she wanted Jack to be able to see that it was indeed off. When he turned back around, glass of iced water in hand, she had only a legal pad directly in front of her.

'Right,' she said as Jack resumed his seat. 'You were saying that you said goodbye to Kate and left the house, but you can't have done that, so . . .'

Jack opened his mouth, closed it again.

He was still struggling.

'OK, look,' Emily said. 'How about this? How about you say it in the third person? *He* was there, *he* did that, then *he* did this. Pretend you're talking about some other guy. Tell it that way. It might be easier for you.'

'I *am* talking about some other guy.'

'Right. Yes.'

He took a long drink of his water, then held it with two hands and stared into it.

'Where do I begin?' he asked then.

'Well, he didn't leave the house, did he? And we know that, before the fire, Kate was attacked. So something must have set him off, right? Unless he was planning it in advance, but it doesn't really seem like that kind of crime, does it? I don't think the reader would buy that it was premeditated. It seems more like a spur-of-the-moment, crime-of-passion thing. An argument that got out of hand.'

331

'Yeah,' Jack said and she wondered if that was *Yes, that's where I should start* or *Yes, that's exactly what happened.*

Emily picked up her pen. 'Ready when you are.'

'This is horrible.'

'It's a means to an end, Jack. Like you said yourself, let's just get it over with.'

He took a deep breath. 'So, ah, *he* was on his way out,' he started. He looked to Emily as if to check he was doing it right; she nodded encouragingly. 'He went to their bedroom, to say goodbye to Kate. And to get his phone. He'd left it there, on the dressing table. And what was weird – what he thought was weird – was that when he first walked into the room, she was putting a suitcase back in the wardrobe. And he said, what are you doing with that? And she said, *Nothing, I was just moving stuff around in here, it's a mess. I think when you're away next week I'm going to pull everything out and go through it.'*

During this, Emily had written *bedroom, phone, film/take-away, suitcase.*

'He kisses her goodbye,' Jack continued, 'takes the phone and goes downstairs. But when he gets to the bottom, when he's almost at the door, his phone goes, in his pocket. He thinks maybe it's his friend, checking the time they agreed or asking for directions or something. But when he takes it out and looks at it, he sees it's a text. A new message, from someone called Jean.'

Eight days before the fire

Kate knows why she's not sleeping. It's because she also knows that what she's been experiencing isn't burnout. Or social anxiety or agoraphobia or sensory processing disorder or any of the other diagnoses the internet has offered up.

It's because she's afraid.

The latest reason is in her pocket, on her phone. The messages have started up again, and Kate can't tell anyone.

Especially not Jack.

Because even though he doesn't sign them, even though they come from some anonymous, untraceable email address, she knows exactly who they're from.

Ben.

Five days before the fire

'We should've said no.'

'I did.'

'To the feature, I mean. To the whole thing. From the start.'

'It was *supposed* to be about Exis,' Jack says. 'And I was

333

clear: I didn't want to talk about cycling.' He shakes his head. 'I'm never going to get away from it, am I?'

Kate goes to join him at the window. She stands behind him, wraps her arms around his waist and rests her cheek against his back. She stays like that until she feels his body relax, the tension slowly leaving it.

He can stop having to hold himself together for these few moments.

She'll take over, do it for him.

'People don't understand,' she whispers. 'But they can't unless you tell them. If you told the truth about it all, you wouldn't have to go through things like this. You wouldn't have to pretend.'

She feels his body tense up again, pull away from her.

'Kate, don't,' he says.

'I just think if—'

'No.' It isn't angry, but it is firm and final. 'You know as well as I do that I can never say a word.'

'But why not?'

'You *know* why not.' He pushes her arms open, slips her embrace and walks into the middle of the room.

She turns to face him.

'Jack, this can't go on forever. It's like' – and then the words are out before she can think about whether or not to say them – 'you're letting him win. Helping him to. Sacrificing yourself, and us, and everything, to keep Ben's dirty secret.'

Silence.

Not just a silence, but *the* silence. The kind that is heavy and pregnant and thrumming with an undercurrent of what will soon be a boiling rage.

The one that signals that she's made a terrible mistake.

'But I understand,' she says quickly, trying to backtrack. 'I get it, I—'

'Oh yeah?' Jack says mockingly, walking to her. 'What, exactly, do you get? What do you understand about this situation that you know nothing about? What is it you think you know about what I've been through, about what I'm dealing with, about what I'm doing for *your* fucking benefit?'

'Nothing,' she says. 'I'm sorry.'

'Why are we even talking about him?'

'We don't need to. Never mind. Let's just—'

'You brought him up,' Jack says, wagging a finger right in front of her face, *in* her face. 'You always bring him up. Is there something you're trying to tell me? Is this how you let me know that you wish you'd chosen him over me? Are you regretting your choice?'

'Of course not.'

'That's what it sounds like.'

'It's not.'

'You're trying to hurt me,' he says.

'No, I—'

'I've disappointed you.'

'Jack—'

He steps forward and grabs her.

His fingers dig into the flesh of her upper arms – the prequel, she knows from experience, to a pattern of fingertip bruises. His eyes are wide, his jaw tight. His face is not even an inch from hers; his breath is hot on her skin.

She braces herself, turns her face away, closes her eyes.

The blow doesn't come.

Not this time, not now. Instead, he releases her and she

stumbles backwards and he storms out of the room. But she's not relieved. Far from it.

The waiting for it, she knows from experience, will be much, much worse.

Four days before the fire

Kate opens the door, gets inside, reaches to pull the door closed – but Jean is holding it open.

They both freeze in motion and hold their positions for a beat, each woman looking pleadingly into the eyes of the other, but desperately wanting different things.

'I don't know anything,' Kate repeats. 'I can't help you. I'm sorry.'

'He still sends me messages, you know. He doesn't sign them but I know they're from him.'

Kate freezes.

'*How* do you know, then?' she asks. 'How do you know it's him?'

'Because of what else I know,' Jean says. 'He knows I have enough to destroy him. The messages are threats.' She pauses. 'And sometimes, Kate, they mention you.'

'What?'

'I think it's to dissuade me from ever saying anything. To remind me that if I did expose him, I'd be hurting you too. Which is why I wanted to talk to you.'

'I don't understand,' she says.

And she doesn't, at all. Ben is sending her messages and also sending messages *about* her to this woman?

Or is he? She only has this woman's word for that. And this

woman has followed her here and pretended to have found her purse.

She could be crazy. She could be completely unhinged.

Or Ben might have even sent her, to test Kate's loyalty, to see if she's planning to say anything.

'I'm sorry,' Kate says. 'No.'

'*No?* You can't just opt out of this.'

'Look, I'm sorry if something bad happened to you—'

'Something bad?' Jean repeats. '*Something bad?* Is that what you call it?' But then the anger seems to flare out and she says, in a less confrontational tone, 'I know this is hard. It's worse than that. It's horrific. And I don't want to blow up your life, believe me. I just want to talk. That's all, for now.'

'For now? Is that supposed to be a threat?'

'What? No. God, of course not.'

Jean finally lets go of the door, steps clear of its arc.

'I don't know anything,' Kate repeats. 'I can't help you. I'm sorry. And please, I'm asking you – begging you – leave us out of this. We can't . . .' She bites her lip. '*Please.*'

She wants to say more, wants this woman to understand what talk of Ben does to their lives, the disaster it brings, the rage it sets off.

But she can't.

28

'Jean?' Emily said in surprise.

The name had come out of her mouth spontaneously, before she'd had a chance to remember that she wasn't supposed to know it. The name should be meaningless to her. She shouldn't have reacted at all.

'Yeah, why?' He frowned. 'Is that all right? I just picked that name at random. This part is made up, remember?'

If this was made up, why choose the name of the woman who said that she was really at the house that night?

But then, he didn't know that Emily knew there was a Jean in real life.

Or did he? Had he forced Ben to reveal all last night and now he was toying with Emily, trying to scare her, or were they somehow in this together? Was Jean in on it too?

'Right.' Emily added *bottom of stairs*, *new message* and *Jean* to her notes. 'So why is Jean texting him?'

'She's not. It's not his phone. He realizes he's picked up Kate's by mistake, when he was up in the bedroom. So he turns and starts back up the stairs, but then he stops and thinks, *Jean?* Kate doesn't know any Jean, does she? But you see, *he* knows a Jean. From when he was cycling. And that Jean' – he met Emily's eye and glared at her with a new, unprecedented coldness – 'was a lying little *bitch*.'

Emily wanted to look away. She wanted to *run* away. But she didn't want to do anything that would make Jack stop, because she was recording this.

Which, now, was starting to feel like a dangerous act.

She scribbled something else on the pad, something illegible, a faint tremor in her hand.

'So,' Jack said, 'if it's the same one, the same Jean, contacting his wife . . . Well, he wants to know what's going on. And he can read the start of the message, you see. The preview or whatever they call it. The first few words. And it says, *Is Jack gone? Ben said they* . . . Ben, his friend. Who he's heading out the door to meet. He knows her passcode, so he opens up the rest. And that's when he gets *really* mad.'

Ben.

Not a name chosen at random for this made-up story, but Ben – who Jack knew Emily knew he was meeting in the real story of this night.

When she said, 'We're, ah—' the words came out sounding like the croak of a dying man burning alive in the desert. Emily cleared her throat, moistened her lips, tried again. 'We're going to need some more text there, Jack. The full message. What might it have said?'

He chewed on his lip, making a show of thinking. 'Actually, you know what? Let's just go with him not having her passcode. That way we don't have to come up with the whole thing.'

We, again. But she wanted no part in this.

'All right,' she said. 'So what's next?'

'He goes back upstairs and confronts her with it.'

He stopped there, offering no more, and she realized that he was toying with her. Forcing her to ask questions, to draw the horror out of him, agonizingly slowly, bit by terrible bit.

To him, this was all a game.

What was it Jean had said? Something about how the only sport that Jack had ever truly loved was torment?

But she was recording, so she had to play too.

'How does he do that?' she asked. 'Does he show it to her? Read it out to her?'

'He throws the phone at her head.'

'Which phone?'

Something like a smirk flitted briefly across Jack's face.

'Her phone,' he said.

'Does it hit her?'

'It caught her a little' – he pointed at his right temple – 'on the side of her head.'

Caught.

In the pause that followed, Emily strained to listen for evidence that there were other beating hearts in this house.

Because now she was sure she was in a room with a murderer.

Alone in a room with him, secretly recording him.

And now she began to doubt herself. Had she actually silenced her phone? Was it really on Airplane mode? Could it still buzz? Any vibration at all would be amplified by the drawer. Jack would definitely hear it.

'And then what?' she asked. 'Why don't you just try to keep going, for as long as you can, without me prompting you?'

This won her what she could only describe as a look of pure hatred.

'Fine,' he said. 'Whatever you want. Well ... I think he probably says to her, *What the fuck is going on?* and they start arguing. They've argued before, it's nothing new. But the arguments always end very quickly, because she's afraid of him. Because he doesn't put up with it, normally. But there's something different about this one. She's not cowering, or shouting. She's very calm. She doesn't raise her voice. She tells him that she's been talking to Jean. That Jean approached her in a car park, at the beach. And that at first she was confused, because she thought the things Jean were saying were about Ben, because they were the same things that *he's* always been saying about him. But she's realized that it was her husband this woman was talking about. At first, she thought it couldn't possibly be true, the things this woman was saying he did, the things she was accusing him of, but when she started to actually think about it . . .' He paused here. 'Kate said there was a wall, and Jean had made a crack, and that that was all Kate needed to see through to what was on the other side. To open her eyes and really look.' His own eyes were unfocused now, staring at something that wasn't there. This memory, perhaps. 'She says she's going to leave him. That she doesn't want to be with a man like him. She was planning on doing it when he was away – he's due to go away for a few days, a work thing, the following week. She was planning on being gone when he got back. Because she believes the lying little bitch.'

He didn't immediately carry on, and Emily didn't want to encourage him. Recording or no, she wasn't sure she could listen to any more.

'It's not really him,' Jack said then. 'It's like the thing that

341

lives inside of him. In the core. He tries to control it, tries to keep it there, but sometimes there's nothing he can do. It gets out. He grabs her by the hair. He's holding her with one hand.' Jack mimes holding Kate's imaginary hair with his left hand, curls his right into a fist. 'And he just starts, you know . . .' The fist starts pummelling an invisible object, over and over and over again, harder and harder, as grunts of exertion escape Jack's mouth. *He's not just acting this out*, Emily thinks. *He's reliving it. He wants to.* 'And then he lets go and she falls and he leans over and he . . . He keeps going.'

Emily couldn't speak. All her words were trapped in her throat, held down there by the horror of this.

'And her arms stop,' Jack went on. 'At first they were coming up, trying to defend herself.' He raised his arms, miming this too. 'But now they're just lying out beside her on the floor – and that's when he wakes up. The outside man, the one the rest of the world sees. The man he is most of the time, or tries to be. He comes back and he sees what he's done. And he just can't . . .' Jack shook his head a little. 'He can't believe it. He doesn't understand. He wants to go back, to when he found his own phone on the table in the hall. He wants to put Kate's down and walk out, leave, to not even look at it. But he can't. This has happened. There's no going back. So now, he has to take steps to hide what he's done.'

Emily remembered then that she was supposed to be taking notes, even though surely this charade was over. For the sake of appearances, she scribbled a few more nonsensical words on the legal pad.

'She's lying on a rug,' Jack said, 'so he rolls it up, rolls her up into it. Carries her out into the hall and to the top of the stairs, and then he releases her. He does it sort of over the banister and onto the stairs, so the fall doesn't look how he's expecting. It doesn't look the way you'd imagine someone falling down the stairs. She goes down more like a pinball. It's like *bang*' – he shifted his body weight to the left – '*bang*' – and then back to the right – '*bang*' – and then slammed it back to the left. 'There are smears on the wall afterwards. Blood, all over the place. And he thinks, no one is going to believe this. I'm good, but I'm not this good. No matter how convincing I can be, this isn't going to work. Not like this. So, he has to destroy as much evidence as he can. And then he thinks, *fire*.'

With a shaking hand, Emily wrote what she intended to be the word *rug*.

'He calls Ben,' Jack went on, 'and says he's going to be an hour late. Ben says that's fine. Later, he'll deny this – he'll say he actually called Ben to say he was going to be early and that Ben picked him up wrong. But it'll be fine. Ben will fall in line. He always does. Always has. Then he wonders, how can he start a fire? And he remembers something that happened once, at a race in Barcelona, when he was away with his cycling club, when he was just fifteen or sixteen.'

Emily wrote *Barcelona*, drew a line under it.

'One of the older guys in another room – I think it was an older brother, actually, who'd come along as a chaperone – had lit a candle to try and mask the smell of whatever substance he was smoking. But he'd put it on a window sill, left the room, and it had set the curtains on fire. On a delay, though. So I thought, I can do that. I can light a candle under the blind in our bedroom, put it halfway up, set the candle underneath it, light it and walk away. So I did.'

If Jack had noticed that he'd slipped into the first person, he didn't let on.

343

She suspected it wasn't a slip.

'You know what's weird?' Jack asked her then. 'The door-bell rang while I was looking for a lighter. Twice. I went to the window in my office to have a look outside, but I couldn't see any car.'

The doorbell. Not just ringing, but ringing twice – and with no stranger's car parked outside. That had been Jean, hoping to find Kate home alone.

If Emily had had any lingering doubt by this point, that would've finally disappeared it.

'But the biggest problem,' Jack said, 'was my hands.'

She knew what was coming, what he was going to say.

He'd already said it. She just hadn't understood what he'd been telling her at the time. All that talk about pain and how much he'd always been able to take, how good he was at suffering . . .

He'd been telling her what he'd done. How he'd *really* got his burns. He'd needed them to hide his injuries, the bruising and the cuts and the scratches and whatever else he'd sustained when he was ferociously pummelling his wife to death.

'I'd managed to hide them,' he said. 'At the River Inn. Kept them in my pockets, sat at a table by the window with my back to everyone else. There'd be no one to say, "Oh, I saw his hands and they looked like he'd been bare-knuckle fighting."'
I kept an eye on the time, to make sure I left before Ben arrived – he'd be an hour late, of course, at least. My plan was to ring Kate's phone, supposedly to tell her Ben hadn't showed, and when she didn't answer, head on home out of concern. I wanted to get there before anyone else arrived. I needed to, so I could get inside. I wasn't counting on Jim Mullins, but luckily it all

344

worked out in the end. Trickier to hide my hands from him in the car, but it was dark outside, and he was panicked.'

Emily stayed statue-still.

She felt as if she wasn't even breathing anymore.

'When we got to the house, there were a few neighbours there,' Jack said. 'They all tried to stop me going in, but I wouldn't be held back. I had to get in. I knew I only had a couple of minutes before the cavalry arrived. I had my key. I opened the front door. I walked over Kate – maybe on her, a little – and ran up the stairs and along the hall until I got to our bedroom. The flames were coming out the door, like a solid wall of fire. I'd never seen anything like it. Fire, when it's like that, it's *alive*, you know? It moves and it roars and it feels like it's coming for you. Like it's conscious. I held my hands out and I pushed them into it.'

Emily closed her eyes.

'I can't describe the pain. Whatever I'd felt on the bike, even with the accident, this was . . . This was something else. Like someone was ripping me apart. But I did it. I held them in the fire. I watched it burning away my skin. I waited while it did, because that meant it was also burning away the evidence.' Jack exhaled. 'What I didn't plan on was that, on the way back downstairs, a beam or a joist or something came down from the ceiling and almost knocked me out. I didn't even realize it had burned me until later. I picked Kate up, held her to me, making sure to get her blood all over me, and I carried her outside.' Jack raised his eyes, met Emily's. 'I mean . . . That's what I *would've* done.'

Silence.

Neither of them moved. Neither of them looked away.

Every cell in Emily's body was screaming at her to run, but she had to pretend. Even though she knew, and *he* knew that she knew, she couldn't show it.

She still had to get out of this room, and with her phone.

'Right,' she said, swallowing. 'Well, I think that's more than enough.' She reached for the voice-recorder. 'Are you ready to do it for real?'

In a flash, Jack had jumped up and reached for it too, trapping her hand under his. His fingers grabbed at her flesh, his weight pressed down.

'I don't think so,' he said.

She hadn't seen his injuries this close before. She stared at the melted skin, the angry redness, the bloody scabs on his thumb, the missing nails.

He did that to himself, she thought. *He did that to himself.*

Sympathy was the ink Jack wrote his lies with, Jean had said.

Suddenly he released her, straightened up, stepped back. When Emily dared look up at him, she saw that the man who'd just told her that horrific story had disappeared and Other Jack was back, looking fragile, spent, diminished.

'Maybe later,' he said. 'But I need a break.'

And then he turned his back to her and walked out of the room.

Emily held her breath, tracking his footsteps down the stairs, into the hall, across what might have been the tiles in the kitchen. Only then did she open the drawer and with shaking, fumbling hands, stop the recording.

She let out the sob in her throat, put her head in her hands and cried.

Three days before the fire

Outside, the view is of a thick, solid dark, except for two headlights glowing bright and steady, and pointing directly at the house. Their house is the only thing at the end of a narrow country lane. No one has any business being parked halfway down it.

The lights make it impossible to see if anyone is behind the wheel but the engine is running; Kate can see a mist of warm air illuminated by the rear lamps.

'Jack?'

'Yeah?'

'Come here a sec.'

He reappears, shirtless now, and obeys her silent instruction to look out the window. But just as he steps up to the glass beside her, they both hear the sudden roar of an engine and the car starts reversing at high speed, away.

'What am I looking at?' he asks.

'That car,' she says. 'It was just sitting there, idling.'

She feels him turn and look at her in a way that charges the air between them. Reluctantly, she turns and looks at him.

'What?'

'What?' he repeats, mocking her. 'There was a car. Why did I need to see it?'

'I don't know, I thought . . . Maybe you'd recognize it.'

'What difference would it have made?'

'Maybe you'd want to go down and confront them, I don't know.'

'"Them"?'

'Whoever was inside.' And then, because she can sense what's coming, she says, 'Jack, don't. Don't get upset. There's no need,' even though she knows – she absolutely *knows* – that once the switch is flipped, that's it.

'But that's what you want, isn't it?' he says. 'You *want* to drive me mad. You love it when I get angry, don't you?'

She shakes her head. 'There's no point talking to you when you're like this.'

'Like what?'

'Like *this*. Totally unreasonable. Paranoid.'

She leaves the window and goes to the nearest wardrobe, opens it, starts looking for an extra sweater to put on.

More layers, fewer bruises.

'You *wanted* me to see that car,' Jack says.

'Yes, obviously I did.' She finds a thick sweatshirt, the kind that comes from an expensive yoga brand, and goes to pull it on. He's moving towards her. 'That's why I called you. But not in the way that you—'

In the split second her vision is filled with the sweater's insides, his arm connects with the back of her head.

She can't see, can't put her hands where they need to be to protect herself, and white spots burst in her vision as her right eye makes contact with the hard wardrobe door.

Two days before the fire

Kate knows the sound of Jack's car, and this isn't it. Which means that whoever is coming up the drive is someone who absolutely *cannot* see her like this.

She goes to the window and, holding her body back, tries to get a look.

A forest-green Ford Focus parks right next to her own car – the signal, when you live all the way out here, that you are absolutely, positively, definitely at home.

Shit.

Blind panic sets in, scrambling her thoughts. The bruise is blooming on her right temple, next to the eye, which is a little swollen. She thinks *make-up*, but there isn't enough time. Or enough make-up. Then she thinks *sunglasses*. She runs into the kitchen and plucks them out of a drawer. She checks her reflection in the glass of the cupboards: perfect. They exactly cover the area that's blooming with blues and yellows and starting to show a little purple.

Only problem is, why the hell would she be wearing sunglasses?

The doorbell rings.

Why would anyone be wearing sunglasses? She could pretend to have a migraine, but she doubts Ruth would fall for that.

And then she thinks *sunshine*.

There's a glare of it today. But it's freezing. It's November. Could she pretend to be on her way out? No. She would never run off like that, and they both know Kate doesn't have the kinds of appointments these days that you can't cancel. If she's going somewhere, she can delay it. They'd inevitably come

349

back inside and have a coffee, and then she'd be forced to take them off.

The doorbell rings again.

Kate sees the blanket hanging over the back of a chair. The thermal mug by the sink. The door leading to the garden just feet away.

It's so stupid, so desperate, so silly.

But it's also her only option.

She runs out the door to the rear garden, wrapping the blanket around her as she moves, dropping the mug on the table for show. She double-checks the sunglasses are high enough up, wincing as she accidentally pushes the frame into her sensitive flesh. She tries to look like she's relaxed, settled, that she's been sitting out here like this for more than a few seconds.

The glasses slip down.

'Hello? Anyone back here?'

Kate pushes her sunglasses up her nose just as her sister-in-law appears around the side of the house.

She doesn't immediately make her presence known so Ruth, dressed in a full-length, white wool coat and black leather boots with kitten heels, doesn't realize she's being watched as she stops at the edge of the back garden's muddy grass, looks down at it and wrinkles her nose in disgust.

Kate catches her breath, steels herself and says, 'Well, hello,' trying to sound the kind of surprised that's happy.

The day before the fire

Kate closes her eyes and imagines the wheels of the car turning, sending both her and Jean over the edge and crashing

350

down onto the beach below, just as the other woman asks, 'Did something happen to you, too?'

'*What?* No!'

Jean looks relieved, then confused. 'But you're – you're afraid of him?'

'*Jack* is afraid of him,' Kate corrects. She immediately colours. She shouldn't have said that. 'No, afraid isn't the right word. He's ... He's wary of him, I'd say. He tries to keep things between them on an even keel. Jack knows what happened when they were competing. What Ben did. What he was like. We've never really discussed it – Jack gets too upset, too wound up – but over the years, I've pieced things together myself. Jack helped keep Ben's secret. He had to. The team made it crystal clear that that was what was expected of him if he wanted to stay, and Ben ... Well, I don't know if Ben threatened him outright, if it was that explicit, but Jack knew what would happen if he didn't play along. And you know, sometimes I think ...' Kate can't believe she's saying this out loud, and to a stranger, but it feels so good to get to say things that have lived inside her head for so long. For *years*. 'Jack has never said anything about it – ever – but sometimes I wonder what happened on the Col that day. Ben went down too, but he stayed on the road. Jack can't remember what happened exactly, and the only footage is from a distance because of the weather conditions, so—'

She turns to Jean and stops when she sees the other woman staring at her, wide-eyed and pale.

She has shocked her, Kate realizes.

'Maybe not,' she says quickly. 'Maybe that *was* just an accident.'

Silence.

351

'Kate, I honestly can't tell if you're . . .' But Jean trails off.
'What?'
'Do you really not know?'
'Not know what?'
'It wasn't Ben who attacked me.'
'Then who are you—'
'It was Jack.'

In one heartbeat, Kate's entire world screeches to a stop.

But then, in the next, she hears herself laugh.

'No,' she says. She scoffs, shakes her head, laughs some more. 'No.'

It's so absolutely, ridiculously, preposterously insane. This woman is insane. Deranged, clearly. Kate shouldn't be here with her. She should've ignored the message she found in her Instagram DMs after their last meeting. She shouldn't have even entertained her.

It's all lies. Unhinged lies. She's probably just trying to extort money out of Jack. Well, the joke's on her, because he doesn't have any.

'I'm not sure what's gone on here,' Jean says gently, 'but it sounds like Jack has told you a version of the truth, but with his and Ben's roles swapped. Ben did say something like—'

'You talked to *Ben*?'

'I talk to Ben all the time. He's helping me.'

And now, the pieces fall into place.

'I see,' Kate says.

'You should talk to him too. He tried to talk to you the night before last. The day after we met. He came to your house and was going to try and knock on your door, but he was trying to figure out if you were home alone, and then he saw Jack in the window – Wait!'

Kate has thrown open the car door and is climbing out. She only makes it a few steps before Jean, having got out the other side, is standing in front of her, blocking her path.

'Please,' she says, holding up her hands. 'You need to hear this.'

But Kate has had enough.

'Are you really that fucking *stupid*, Jean?' she says, screaming her words into the wind. 'Seriously? Don't you see what's happening here? This is all Ben's doing. He's masterminding this and you're falling for it hook, line and sinker. You think Jack is lying to me about what Ben did. That *my husband* is lying to me. That he has been lying to me since we met. But it's *Ben* who's lying to *you*! If you can't see that, then I can't help you.'

'I know who raped me, Kate.'

'Oh my God. You're delusional.'

'Then what happened to your face? The make-up probably looked pretty good at home, but out here, in the daylight—'

'Leave me alone.'

'If you need help, I can—'

'Fuck off.'

Kate pushes the other woman out of her way and runs to her car, making it to the driver's door. But she's delayed getting in, fumbling with the handle.

'He hurts you, doesn't he?'

Jean is standing right behind her.

'That would be convenient for you, wouldn't it?' she spits over her shoulder. 'That would fit perfectly with your little narrative.'

'Trust me when I say none of this is convenient for me. Look, Kate, I know we're as good as strangers but if you need help, if you need to leave—'

'Oh *God.*' Finally – *finally* – the door opens for Kate. 'Stop with the fucking drama.'

'Do you seriously think I'm lying? After everything I've said?'

'I don't know what the fuck you're doing, but I'm done. Don't contact me again.'

Kate gets into her car and, for the second time in four days, drives away from Jean Whelan as fast as she possibly can.

29

It took Emily a while before she felt confident that, when she stood up, her legs would cooperate. She waited another few minutes until the selfie camera on her phone stopped showing her a woman with puffy eyes and blotchy red skin; she couldn't let anyone see that she'd been crying. This was a game of pretend now, and the only way out – the only *safe* way – was to play along.

Jack Smyth had just confessed to murdering his wife. What he didn't know was that he really *had*. He'd accidentally corroborated Jean's story. He'd heard the doorbell go twice after he'd killed Kate, but before he'd started the fire. That felt like something tangible, something they could maybe even give to the guards.

And unbeknownst to him, he'd said it all on tape.

Down in the courtyard, Grace was anxiously pacing back and forth by the pool, obviously waiting for her.

'What happened?' she asked the moment she saw Emily.

'Jack said that was the last session, that you're not doing any more?'

'Did he?'

What else had he said, Emily wondered? She was running on fumes and didn't have the energy or the headspace to come up with any lies of her own. The best she could hope for here was that Jack had come up with something she could go along with.

Luckily—

'He's too upset.' Grace's expression was a mix of pity and apology. 'He said that talking about Kate so much over the last few days took more out of him than he'd expected. And I guess the business at home isn't helping now either.' *The business at home.* Had that been Jack's horrifically minimizing phrase, or was it a Grace original? 'And he said you have enough to get going? That you could write up what you talked about this morning? I'll go on up and transcribe it now.'

'We didn't record anything this morning, Grace.'

She frowned. 'What? Why not?'

'It was at Jack's request. I think he wanted to figure out what he was going to say before he said it. I wrote some notes, but there's no audio.'

At *audio*, the phone in Emily's pocket suddenly seemed to develop its own pulse. She was hyper-aware of its presence, a burn against the denim of her jeans that was threatening to break through to her skin. She was certain that any second now Grace would look down and see its outline – and then into her mind, and know exactly what she'd just done.

'I guess that means I have the afternoon off,' Grace said, brightening a little. 'We both do. Although I should tell you: you might want to pack. Tony is picking you up at five a.m. – sorry about that. But I got you a flight home that'll have you back in Dublin by Sunday morning. You have a five-hour lay-over in Charlotte – sorry about that too.'

'No, that's great.' Emily meant it. She couldn't care less about the details. Any route out of here was a welcome one. Then it occurred to her that maybe she shouldn't sound so ecstatic about it, so she said, 'Is Jack sure about this, though? When is he leaving? What if he decides he wants to do another session first?'

'He's out of here a couple of hours after you. He has to fly with Joe and Ruth, so they're going to Panama City and connecting in New York. Oh, and just FYI: Ben is staying here tonight.'

'Why?'

Grace shrugged. 'Don't know. Maybe they want to catch up. The book stuff is technically finished now, so . . .'

On one hand, Emily was relieved to hear that Ben would be staying in Beach Read this evening, because the alternative was that it would just be her and Jack here, alone. But she doubted it was because Jack and Ben wanted a catch-up, which made her wonder if this was happening because Ben and Jean had thought he needed to stay here *so that* Emily wouldn't be alone with him.

Which made her feel afraid.

But should she be? She never wanted to see Jack Smyth ever again, let alone talk to him, but was there a reason to be physically afraid of him? He was going home to be arrested; she doubted he'd be stupid enough to do anything to make that situation worse. And she didn't pose a threat to him – he'd made that clear, in the session they'd just had – so as long as she played the game, she should be OK.

Which meant staying here until Tony arrived at 5:00a.m.

She could tell Grace she wanted to leave right now, or that

she wanted to spend tonight in a hotel. Or say nothing, call an Uber and just go. Alice would help with sorting flights. But Jack could return at any moment, or Grace could call him to tell him his ghostwriter was escaping, and then there'd be no way to keep playing pretend. Then she would become a threat. And she was getting out of here at 5:00a.m. tomorrow anyway.

'Jack has the car,' Grace said, 'so I can't leave. I might go for a walk on the beach.' She raised her eyebrows at Emily. 'Wanna come?'

'Ah, no. Sorry. I think I'm going to have a lie-down, actually. My head is starting to throb.'

'I have some Tylenol, if you want it?'

'Thanks, but I have something.'

'Do you need anything else? Did you get some lunch? It's in the kitchen. I could bring you up a plate?'

'No, no. I'm fine.' She had no appetite and was desperate to bring this exchange to a close, to get away, to be alone. 'Thank you, though.'

'Dinner will be here at six.'

'Great.' Emily turned to go. 'I'll see you later.' She didn't know if she would, actually, but she didn't want to prolong this with a goodbye. 'Enjoy your walk on the beach.'

'Wait – is that your phone?'

Shit.

Emily said a few more, far worse swear words in her head, then turned back around.

Grace's eyes had narrowed. 'Did you have that with you upstairs?'

'By accident. I totally forgot it was in my pocket. Jack said it was fine, to just stick it in the desk drawer while we talked. So I did.'

358

He'd actually said that yesterday when she'd genuinely forgotten she'd had her phone with her, but a half-truth was less risky than an all-out lie.

'You didn't use it for anything, did you?' Grace asked.

'No, no. Of course not.'

Not only was an audio of Jack's confession on it, but before she'd left the interview room, she'd used her phone to connect the laptop to a personal hotspot and emailed herself the previous days' transcripts.

'Because even a note on there—'

'I didn't, Grace. It was off the whole time. Don't worry.'

A beat passed.

'OK,' Grace said then, although her face didn't match the sentiment.

'Well, anyway . . .' Emily just wanted out of here. She turned and started towards the stairs, calling a casual 'See you later' over her shoulder as she went.

The first breath she took inside Bookmark with its door closed behind her felt like the first one she'd taken all day.

She started a circuit around the space then, pulling down blinds, securing doors and windows, and checking for any signs that someone had been in here while she was out. There was none. She checked twice that the connecting door on her side was locked, then checked it once more just to be sure.

She pulled out her suitcase, put it on the floor and flipped it open. The Olympus was still hidden in its lining; it had made a reassuring *thud* as it landed against the edge of the case. She packed up as much as she could for now. She emailed herself a copy of the confession recording.

For one brief, dangerous moment, Emily wondered what would happen if she emailed a copy to the other Emily.

I know who you are. I know what you did. Tell him or I will.
Tell Jack now or I will tell everyone.

And, like a fool, she had.

The anonymous messages had to have come from Jack. Just as Jean had described, that's what he did. He needled. He undermined. He chipped away until the chips made cracks and he did this until you were *all* cracks and then, with one last blow, he broke you.

With Emily, his plan must have worked better than he ever could've hoped. Maybe he'd always known, somehow, about the true nature of *The Witness*, or maybe all he'd actually known about was the failure to deliver another book and the twenty-five-grand debt that had forced her to take this job. She could envisage a scenario where he pretended to be hurt by that, to be upset by the fact that his ghostwriter didn't want to help him tell his truth but had been forced into doing it by her financial situation, and how she'd naturally have moved to reassure him, to overcompensate, to go to great lengths to show she was on his side. Instead, she'd offered up what he thought was her deepest, darkest secret and, in doing so, enough ammunition for Jack to blow up her entire life.

And then a new horror presented itself.

Emily had just secretly recorded Jack as good as confessing to murder. But what if *he'd* secretly recorded *her* confessing that Roxie was real? She had a flash of them sitting in the car last night, in Rosemary Beach, Jack slipping his phone down beside him, into the pocket in the driver's door. Out of her line of sight, but in a position to pick up anything that was said. Had that been his plan all along, to get her admitting everything on tape? To have something to lord over her if she didn't cooperate? If she threatened to quit?

360

Or was she underestimating him? Was it all much more sophisticated than that?

With a sudden, sickening clarity, she saw his plan.

He didn't care that Emily had a secret, or what it was. What mattered to him was what she'd done with it. What mattered to him was *The Witness*. What was it she'd told him, in the car last night?

I took a real story and changed it. Garnished it with some fiction.

That was going to be his way out.

She was it.

Jack wanted to publish this book, his side of the story. He had to publish it if he was ever going to get the public back on-side. As a bonus, it would give just enough detail to raise questions about Ben as a suspect but not actually ask them, staying on the right side of libel. But the only way that book was going to happen was if Jack did what he'd promised and confessed. How to do that while still maintaining your innocence?

Blame the ghostwriter.

Say she made that bit up. Took his truth and embellished it. It wouldn't even be the first time. Look, here. She's done it before.

Her phone buzzed.

A new message.

It's a feature of 17th-century Bermudian design. Like an outhouse for storing food that needed to be kept cool – an outdoor fridge, basically. The pointed roof is on purpose, something about convection that I don't understand, but it keeps the warm air off the food.

Mark.

He'd sent an accompanying picture, showing a smaller version of one of Sanctuary's butteries in situ, in a garden in Bermuda.

And earned her only real smile of the day.

She called him.

'I have to tell you something,' she said before he could say anything.

He sighed. 'You don't have to tell me anything, Em.'

'It's about *The Witness*.'

'I already know.'

'What do you know?'

He hesitated. 'That you're Roxie. That what happens in it happened to you.' He paused. 'Right?'

Emily felt her world tilt. 'How long have you known?'

'Since I read it.'

'*How* did you know?'

'Because I know *you*,' he said.

The fact that Mark already knew the thing she'd been terrified of telling him – he'd known for nearly as long as they'd been together, and they were still together – was too much to take in. All the guilt, the pain, the anxiety she'd felt about keeping secrets from him dissipated in an instant. He'd discovered them by himself and he was still here. So much weight had just lifted off Emily's shoulders, she felt light-headed, as if she might float away.

But not all of it.

In that moment, she made a decision: when she got home, she was going to tell him the rest, and then she was going to tell the person who needed to be told, the devastated woman who'd lost her daughter and was desperate to know why.

She was, finally, going to respond to that letter.

The morning of the fire

It's only when Jack starts snoring rhythmically beside her that Kate even allows herself to think about her conversation with Jean. She's kept it to the back of her mind all day, afraid that her face would betray her, or her actions would, or that Jack would somehow be able to sense what was behind her eyes.

Now, in the pitch-black of their bedroom, she imagines a box. She opens the lid, chooses one thought, lifts it out. Tries it on for size.

Does Jack hurt me?

No. No, definitely not. Not in that way. Not in the way that people mean when they say things like *domestic violence* and *abusive husband* and *battered women*. God, *no*. That's actually really insulting to the women – and men – who genuinely suffer, who are trapped in real abusive relationships, who desperately need help. To compare *their* fights to that . . .

That's offensive.

Jack gets upset, yes. His emotions are always just beneath the surface. He's had a hard life. Who *wouldn't* struggle in the face of all that he's had to deal with it?

So sometimes he lashes out, big deal. Doesn't everyone?

That happens to be how he does it, what his venting looks like. It's not about her, it's just that she's usually the nearest person. It's happenstance. It's in the heat of the moment. It's not premeditated or planned, and it's not a pattern. He's not that kind of man. He's a *good* man with a kind soul who loves her, and he's trying his best.

Nobody's perfect. All couples fight. Marriage is hard. Everyone has a breaking point. She would never stay with a man who hurts her. There were only a few bruises, only accidents. Moments an inch or two beyond the edge of his control. But he always comes straight back inside the line, immediately. It's over in seconds. He's tormented by what he's done. Genuinely remorseful.

Because that's not who he is, not what they are, not what this is.

Kate puts that thought back in the box, takes out another one. *Who is Ben, really?*

She's known him longer than she's known Jack. She was with him first. Well, they'd been flirting for a while and had gone on a few dates. They weren't *together* together, but if she hadn't met Jack, that's where things would've ended up. He was nice to her, seemed nice. They'd had fun together. He was gentle. He never got mad, never even raised his voice. But then, they didn't know each other that well.

And why would Jack lie? Why would he have performed this thing with Ben, this dread of him, this ever-present threat, the stress of this secret-keeping, all this time? For *years*? And why on earth would he have done it in the first place?

She places that thought back in the box but doesn't lift out the last one.

She can't. Not yet.

364

Jack as a liar. An abuser. A serial rapist. Jack in the role she has always thought Ben played.

(*It makes sense.*) It makes no sense at all. What kind of man would do those things? (*The kind who hits his wife.*) She can't imagine her life without him but, if it were true, she couldn't stay. (*She already has. Is. Continues to.*)

She shuts the lid of the box and rolls onto her side, to face him in the dark.

And sees, in a glint of moonlight, that his eyes are wide open.

She startles and jerks with fright, but only *then* does he stir; she was imagining it. It's too dark to see anyway.

She rolls onto her back and opens the box again, takes out the first thought, examines it.

The entire night passes in this way.

When the sky is finally grey, Kate slips out of bed before Jack stirs and tiptoes into the bathroom. The woman she sees in the mirror above the sink looks exactly how she feels.

Exhausted. Hollowed-out. Dying inside.

The jigsaw pieces still don't fit, but their edges feel sharper, spikier. Dangerous. And while she still can't see the full picture, she knows this much: she was wrong about what she thought it was.

She doesn't want to look, but she has to see.

Jack is due to go to London next week. Some trade-show thing. He'll be away for three, maybe four days and nights. She'll use them. She wants to talk to Ben. Sit down and have a conversation with him. And she wants to talk to Jean again, too – if Jean will talk to *her* after how awful she was at the beach.

But for now, she must be normal.

She does what she can with the contents of her make-up bag, if only to stop Jack asking questions. He seemed to sleep soundly last night, which made her, by turns, angry and jealous. She starts with a layer of brightening moisturizer. Three drops of pearlescent liquid gold. A CC cream that goes some way to banishing the dullness, the redness and the shadows, but isn't thick enough to alert Jack to the fact that she's gone to the trouble of putting on a face before he opens his eyes.

Finally, she dots some rose-coloured blush on the apples of her cheeks, meets her own eye in the mirror and whispers, 'You can do this. You can. Come *on*.'

30

Footsteps. Floorboards creaking. Tinkling of metal on metal—

Emily opened her eyes.

—and the unmistakable *clink* of a key in a lock.

It took her brain a beat to slip the bonds of sleep and piece together where she was and what was happening. Lying fully dressed, on the couch in Bookmark, in the dark. She didn't remember deciding to lie down, or even feeling sleepy. In fact, when she searched for the last few hours of her day, the results came back empty.

Why couldn't she remember?

Flashes, from her afternoon. She'd come back here. She'd pulled down the blinds, checked the doors, packed her suit-case. She'd talked to Mark. She'd watched a few hours of mindless TV. She'd waited to hear voices in the courtyard, but it got to be four, five and then six in the evening and there was still no sign of Jack or Ben, and no Grace either. She'd started to wonder if Grace had already left. Around seven, she'd risked opening Bookmark's front door. That was when she'd discovered a white paper bag outside: takeaway in cardboard cartons, and a bottle of wine. She'd figured Grace had left it for her. She'd felt anxious and wired and uneasy. She'd picked at the food, if only to silence her gurgling stomach. She'd thought a glass of wine was a good idea. She was right about the first one, so she'd had another.

And then . . .

Nothing else.

Drinking the wine was the last thing she remembered, until she'd heard noises.

Emily jerked upright, into a sitting position. What little light there was had an odd quality to it, like a sunrise over snow.

She thought, *Jack. Jack has got in.*

But then she saw a shadow move on the other side of the glass in the front door: a tall figure, bent at the waist, their head level with the lock, and she thought, *He's trying to get in, right now.*

Her heart began to hammer beneath her breastbone. She should've left. It had been stupid to stay. Too late. What she needed now was to banish the dark. She jumped up and smacked the light switch on the wall behind her, but nothing happened. She flicked it again, and again, and tried the lamp and the bathroom, but the power was out.

Then she smelled the smoke.

And she *saw* the smoke now, too: a thin, lazy haze, hanging in the air. It was what had made the light look odd to her, she realized in hindsight. She found her phone in the gloom, activated its flashlight and saw that the smoke was coming in from underneath the connecting doors.

Beach Read was on fire.

*

The front door was jammed. The hurricane shutters were down. Emily was trapped in here.

The shadow hadn't been trying to get inside, she realized. It was Jack, locking the door behind him as he left.

Locking *her* in.

This time, he *was* going to kill someone in a fire.

He'd put something in the wine that *he'd* left for her, not Grace. To knock her out long enough for him to lock her in. Maybe Grace had innocently mentioned to him about Emily having her phone on her today and he realized that she'd recorded him. Or maybe he didn't want to go home and face the consequences of his actions, so this was his out and he was taking her with him.

Well, Emily thought, *at least the book will have an ending.*

As she closed her eyes, she wondered who they'd get to write it now.

She heard a *crack*, a heavy object against something that wouldn't give.

It felt distant and far away, like the sound of a television in another room. She wondered if she'd already fallen asleep and was dreaming it.

But then, no—

Crack.

She opened her eyes. All she could see was black. The smoke stung her eyes, making them water, making the blackness ripple.

Crack.

And now someone was calling her name as well.

'Emily? Emily!'

A man's voice.

She wanted to answer. In her head, she already had. In her

369

head, she was screaming, loud and clear and desperately, but in reality, nothing was coming out. The distress signals her brain was sending couldn't seem to connect with her voice, her throat, her breath, her mouth.

But then she thought, *What if it's Jack?* Come to make sure the deed is done? What would he do if he found her alive? Resume pretending? Put his Good Guy act back on? Try to convince her that this was all Ben's doing too?

He'd got away with it for so long, she wouldn't put it past him.

'Emily! Emily, if you can hear me, shout out. I can't see . . .'

It wasn't Jack's voice.

It was Ben's.

There was a heavy, suffocating weight on Emily's chest, making it nearly impossible to breathe. When she inhaled, nothing happened. There was no relief, only pain and tightness. She felt like she might vomit. She didn't think she could stay awake for much longer.

She wished Ben would just leave her be.

'Emily?' His voice was louder now, nearer. '*Emily!*'

No, she couldn't think like that. She had to try. She had to survive. To get out, and to tell the truth about Jack.

To tell the truth about that night all those years ago to the one person to whose life it might make a difference.

To tell the truth about *The Witness*.

'I'm here,' she said – or thought she said. She didn't even hear it herself. The fire was roaring like thunder, crackling and sizzling and popping, and the smoke had reached into her throat and stolen her voice.

And there was heat now, more than before. She could feel it singeing the skin on her face. And, at the edges of her vision, a bright ball of glow in the black that she didn't even want to think about.

She couldn't help but remember Jack's hands. The melted skin. The deep welt on his back, like a thumb pushed into soft candle wax.

If Ben was here, trying to save her, where was Jack?

'Here,' she said.

But it wasn't even a whisper.

She tried again, one last time, taking in a breath that was hot and burned and didn't feel like air, pushing it back out with as much volume as she could manage.

'Here, I'm here.'

And then hands were grabbing her. Hands were grabbing her hands.

She couldn't see who they belonged to, but she presumed it was Ben. He was somewhere behind her. He'd pulled her hands over her head and now he was dragging her along the floor. She winced in pain as her hip met a corner, and something sharp dug momentarily into her thigh, and her T-shirt rode up her back and the bare skin there burned as it crossed the rattan rug.

She pushed her heels against the ground, trying to help, to make this evacuation go quicker.

And then, the strangest thing: she was rising up. Being lifted up.

And being burned – no, that was a jagged piece of glass slicing open the skin on the small of her back.

The sting of it, the pain, jumpstarted her senses and she looked up and saw Ben's upside-down face leaning over hers.

And behind him, the night sky.

She was outside.

He'd got her outside, onto the deck.

'We have to get down the stairs,' he said now. He'd righted her into a standing position but she was entirely leaning on him, her own legs like jelly. 'Can you walk?'

The answer was no and the staircase was too narrow for Ben to carry her down, so they improvised. He sat her down on the top step and walked down backwards, ahead of her, helping her scoot down, step-to-step, until they reached the end.

The swimming pool was a glowing blue gem, lit from underneath, its surface like glass – but a heavy haze of smoke hung in the air above it. When Emily looked up, she saw more billowing out from broken windows.

'Come on,' Ben said, pulling her towards the archway, into the garage, out onto the street.

He forced her across it, then lowered her into a sitting position on the kerb.

'I'm sorry,' he said. 'It was the only way.'

She nodded, thinking he was talking about manhandling her out of there.

'I knew what I was doing,' he went on. 'I left the fire extinguisher by the door so I could break the glass and get in to you. But I had to put the shutters down and I couldn't use the key. I had to make it look real. It all had to look real.'

'*Real?*' she repeated.

'I thought there'd be more time. I should've put something down by the connecting door. A towel or something. I didn't realize how quickly the smoke would start to get through.'

Just as she put together what Ben was telling her, she heard sirens, in the distance.

'Jean,' she said.

'She's fine. She's nowhere near here.'

'Grace?'

'She's been back at the hotel since this afternoon.'

'Jack?'

Ben looked away.

'He was never going to stop,' he said. 'So someone had to stop him.'

Headlights, screeching around the corner, and then a car jerking violently to a stop just a few feet away.

Grace, Ruth and Joe got out of it, leaving doors open behind them.

Grace's mouth fell open and when Emily turned to follow her gaze, she saw Beach Read's gleaming white walls pumping out thick, black smoke.

Joe was looking around, scanning, as if trying to evaluate the situation before he made any moves.

Ruth was already panicking, her face distorted with shock and confusion and abject fear.

She ran straight to Emily, grabbed her by the shoulders.

'Where's Jack?' she demanded, her eyes wide. 'Where's my brother? Where is he? *Where's Jack?*'

'When I got picked for the 2019 Tour team, I should've been happy. I should've been delirious. This was the peak of my professional career. But I was consumed with dreams of quitting. I lay awake at night, trying to come up with ways to get out that wouldn't turn Jack against me. During the day, I was crumbling from the exhaustion on top of the exertion. Pain on the bike, my old reliable friend, deserted me. It didn't keep the bad thoughts out anymore. It *was* the bad thought. It was just pain.

That was the season things came to a head.

The scales fell from my eyes, and I saw everything as it really was. Years of friendship, of training, of competing, of dedicating our entire lives to this one, shared thing. Of helping each other. Of being teammates. Of sharing the highs and lows, the wins and the losses. I finally saw him for what he was: a manipulative narcissist. A man performing his personality. There was no empathy in there, no real love, no real compassion. He didn't care about me. He only cared about winning, whether that was on the bike, or later with Kate, or in general, at life.

Sometimes I even wondered about the car accident that had

killed his dad, or why a former teammate had become so disillusioned and depressed that he had taken his own life.

I wondered if the same would happen to me. It didn't seem impossible.

And then, in a moment, I let it all get the better of me.

To be fair, it felt like the universe was on my side, that it knew what needed to happen and offered me an opportunity on a platter. How else do you explain hail and ice, on the Col de l'Iseran, in July, the week after a heatwave?

I was already too close to Jack, and he was looking back at me, over his right shoulder, as if to say so. I watched the road behind us, checking for the team cars and the motorbikes on which riders sat with cameras on their shoulders, pointed at us. But because of the conditions, they'd already dropped back, keeping a careful distance from us riders. The helicopter had already pulled up and away.

And I thought, *do it now*.

But by "it" I mean something that would be the end of *me*. Of my race. Of my season. Of my career. I thought Jack would react; he always had an incredible reaction-time when it came to crashes. Those ones that cause the peloton to go down like folding dominos? Jack could be right in the middle of one and still manage to stay upright. He had incredible instincts. And it had to involve someone else. I couldn't just lose control, that wouldn't be believable – especially since we were all riding like timid children, heeding the warnings about the slippery roads being constantly fed to us via our earpieces.

As we rounded that corner, the slightest pull in the wrong direction sent my front wheel into his rear and he was gone.

Just . . . Gone.

Like I'd magicked him away.

Jack had just gone straight over the edge.

And then, for me, the absolute horror of clarity. What the fuck had I done? I pulled on my brake and shifted my weight to the right, letting my body hit the ground. Scrapes and stings and blood and the hot pain of soft, bare limbs twisted in sharp metal. But I was OK. I was moving. I was able to extricate myself from the bike.

I looked around, but Jack was still gone.

I couldn't believe what I'd done, what I'd risked, who I might have just become. I screamed and shouted, and help sped through the hail. Sirens and shouts and the whine of engines as tyres skidded on the ice. I could barely breathe, but it wasn't because of my injuries. I was terrified everyone had seen what I'd done, that everyone knew.

But Jack didn't remember – or claimed not to – and because of the conditions, no lens had filmed it up close. In the footage that does exist, it's too difficult to make out. None of the other riders would ever say I'd pushed my teammate off the road on purpose.

Teammate, friend, brother.

They wouldn't believe it even if their eyes had seen it. It was just a racing incident. I won sympathy. I couldn't take it. I hated who Jack had made me. I hated that I had let him change me.

At the end of the season, I quit anyway.

Jack and I remained friends. I called him regularly while he recovered. I heard all about his budding relationship with Kate. He never acknowledged that I had been with her first, that there had been an overlap, that he'd asked me for her phone number and like the fool I was, like the good little domestique I was destined to be, I'd given it to him. I kept up appearances, played along.

I waited for the day he'd tell me he remembered what happened on the Col that day, but he never did.

And then, one day, a woman named Jean Whelan got in touch.'

VII

ALL NAMES HAVE
BEEN CHANGED

31

The room is twenty storeys above London, in the north-west corner of a giant glass castle. Two walls of windows look down over a carpet of mostly dull, grey concrete running all the way to the horizon. A third offers a view into open-plan workspaces at the building's core, a puzzle of interconnecting desks and Kallax bookcases stocked with Morningstar's own titles. The only solid wall is the one directly behind Carolyn Heatherington's desk, on which she's hung a bookshelf and several classic book covers, blown up to poster size and framed. Francis Cugat's *The Great Gatsby*. David Pelham's *A Clockwork Orange*. Wendell Minor's *Jaws*.

A driver had met Emily at Heathrow and brought her straight here. It's so early, and on a Sunday the city below looks deserted, missing its swarming ant-people and silent matchbox cars. There isn't any white-noise office thrum; there is no one here, bar the cleaners and security, and the nervous assistant who met Emily downstairs, brought her zooming skywards in a lift that needed a code, and deposited her here, in this office with CAROLYN HEATHERINGTON printed on the nameplate by the door. The light outside is weak and watery, the autumn sun struggling to rise above the horizon, still trapped beneath the smog for now.

But it's not Carolyn who eventually appears. It's not Beth either. It's an older woman Emily has never met before, with a pixie-cut of silver hair and a roll-neck cashmere sweater. She introduces herself as Diane Woods, Morningstar's managing director, offers coffee and water, and asks Emily how she's been.

She got back from Florida four days ago and has spent most of her time since talking to some very nice Garda detectives who make her tell them everything three, four, five times. The repetition isn't helping anything that happened in Florida feel real. More and more, with each passing day, it's like a movie she watched, not an event she was a part of. Surely Sanctuary was a set, Jack an actor, his death just a climactic scene from a script.

But the evidence that it wasn't, that it *did* happen, is all around her. Mark, treating her like she's made of crackle glass. Her croaky voice, what feels like desert sands lining her throat. The emails from 'Emily Joyce' she's moved back into her inbox. Ben's recorded message. The voice-memo of Jack's confession from that last day, named automatically for the place it was recorded, *Sanctuary*.

'I'm fine,' she tells Diane.

When she'd told Alice that she was struggling to take it in, Alice had said, 'But what would it look like if you had taken it in? What are you even aiming for here?'

Emily didn't know.

'Sorry to force you onto a plane again, and at such an early

382

hour,' Diane says, 'but I wanted to have this conversation in person and at a time when no one else was here. I'm afraid my schedule didn't permit me to come to you, so . . .'

'I understand. It's fine.'

'You're probably wondering why you're having this conversation with me.'

Emily had assumed it was because things had been, to use a term she deployed daily in her normal job, *escalated*.

'Carolyn has left the company,' Diane announces, 'and Beth has moved on to another department.' She gives Emily a meaningful look that suggests both the leaving and the moving weren't by choice. 'I can't go into too much detail, but I want you to know that when this project was presented in-house, it was very different. If we had known the reality of the situation, we would never have proceeded with it. Morningstar is *not* that kind of publisher.'

Emily didn't know if she believed this. She wondered whether, if everything had gone as planned and Jack were still alive, they'd still be having this conversation.

And how contracts could've been drawn up, flights paid for and Emily herself hired without the approval of everyone in the chain of command.

This Carolyn-went-rogue storyline was, she suspected, damage control.

'The other thing I want you to know,' Diane continues, placing both beautifully manicured hands flat on the desk in front of her, 'is that we were not, and are not, pursuing you for any part of your advance. This is a creative endeavour, our authors are not machines, and we know that sometimes unforeseen situations occur. So please rest assured, you are not – and never were – in debt to us.' The full stop at the end of that sentence came with another of Diane's meaningful looks.

So, Carolyn and Beth had lied to her.

Or, Diane was lying to her now.

'In fact, I checked on our system, and *The Witness* has almost earned out. The paperback is still in print, and ebook sales have been very consistent. I suspect that, soon, we'll owe *you* money.'

Emily knows this means that, twice a year, Morningstar will pay her, maybe, if she's lucky, a grand or two – she can't quit the day-job or anything – but still, it'll be *something*.

'You should also know that, last Friday, Carolyn received an email from Jack Smyth making accusations about *The Witness*. About the basis for it. He wanted us to know that it wasn't strictly fiction and that he wasn't going to continue with you as a ghost for that reason. But I want you to know that we are not concerned. All good fiction comes from something real. It might be a single moment in the author's life that sparks an idea, something they see or hear someone say, or it might be a real-life event or crime or conflict that inspires a story, or they might take something that happened to them and fictionalize it. I know when I think of my favourite novels, they all feel like the author was making something up to work out something real.' Diane pauses. 'How did he find out, do you think? About *The Witness*?'

'I'm not sure yet,' Emily says. 'But if you look hard enough online, you'll find people posting theories. I presume that, either before I was hired or after, Jack found that stuff. If it was before, it might explain why Beth and Carolyn lied about the money, about me owing it. Because Jack might have said it had to be me.'

'I have a theory myself,' Diane says. 'Jack's email included a prompt for us to contact a Deirdre Lyons, whose daughter was murdered in Tipperary in 2004. He said we could contact her through her solicitor, David O'Reilly, of Roche and O'Reilly Associates, and that she would confirm that details in *The Witness* weren't fictitious. In our negotiations with Jack Smyth, he was represented by the same firm.'

Emily raises her eyebrows. 'You think he found out through his *solicitor?*'

'We don't want to accuse Roche and O'Reilly of anything, but it's an amazing coincidence, don't you think?' Diane pauses. 'Anyway, from a legal standpoint, we don't have to worry for *The Witness*. The disclaimer is more than sufficient protection.'

'The disclaimer?'

There is a short stack of books to the side of the desk: three hardbacks, two paperbacks and one with a strange blank, blue cover that Emily thinks must be a very early bound proof. Diane picks up the top one – a hardcover, looks like something bloody and dark – and flips past a couple of pages, before handing it to Emily.

It's open to the copyright page.

This book is a work of fiction and, except in the case of historical fact, any resemblance to actual persons, living or dead, is purely coincidental.

'Even when, strictly speaking, it's not,' Diane says. 'What was Jack's plan, do you think? I'm still not clear.'

'Neither am I.' Emily closes the book and puts it down on the desk. 'But I think it was to pin everything on Ben. Or to get me to do it for him. Kate and Ruth, his sister, seem to be the only ones he ever said all that stuff about Ben to, presumably

385

as a strategy for keeping Kate away from him and maybe so Ruth would help with that. Everyone else saw Ben and Jack as friends, which meant he could be thoroughly shocked and upset when I put Ben to him as a suspect. The arrest threw a spanner in the works, along with Jean having contacted Kate and visited the house that evening. And he didn't know that Ben wasn't still under his control.'

'What about the confession?'

'I think Jack was telling the truth about that – that it *was* a means to an end. He'd do it to get the book published, and then claim that I, the fiction-writer, had made that bit up. He always had his phone with him in the room, and once when we were talking in his car . . . I think it's possible he recorded me saying things that I think, out of context, could've corroborated that somewhat. And you would only have had the transcripts, which he could deny too – and maybe even edit, since his own PA typed them up.'

'But if the book had come out, and he'd been able to distance himself from the confession chapter, then what?' Diane asks.

'Then it would set public suspicion onto Ben,' Emily says. 'Jack gets the public's sympathy back – and well paid, since I don't believe for a second that that "charitable foundation" thing wasn't just a well-covered path to his own coffers. But I think he ended up confessing to me just to get off on frightening me. To let me know that he was guilty. To scare me. And just because he could.'

Diane shakes her head. 'The whole thing sounds like pure insanity. How could he possibly have thought it was going to work the way he hoped?'

'Everyone who has ever committed a crime,' Emily says,

'and didn't immediately surrender themselves to the authorities, thinks they're going to get away with it. I'm no expert, but I suspect that Jack Smyth was a narcissist, and they don't walk around thinking, *I hope it all works out OK for me.* They never doubt it will. And it *did* work out for him, for many years, in his cycling days. He got away with doing terrible things. When he signed this book deal, it looked like he was going to get away with murder. And this is a man, let's not forget, who not only killed his wife, but who then set a fire to hide the evidence. Are we really expecting good life decisions from someone like that?'

'I take your point,' Diane says. 'And the fire?'

Emily tells her the same thing she told the first responders on the scene, Ruth and Joe, the Walton County Sheriff's Office, and the Gardaí.

'Why Jack did that, I don't know. My guess is he planned to escape, but only after ensuring that all my evidence was destroyed. He didn't know I had the recording or that I'd managed to get the transcripts onto my device. Or maybe he'd decided the jig was finally up and he couldn't face the music, and I was going to be collateral damage. Maybe he was punishing me.'

So far, she hasn't told anyone what Ben had said to her outside on the street.

'What's next?' Diane asks. 'Do you have any plans?'

'No.'

Emily's gaze moves to the windows, to the deserted, foreign city below, lit by a ghostly grey light.

And, quite unexpectedly, feels the tendrils of disparate ideas reaching to entwine themselves with one another from the edges of her conscious mind.

The week in Florida that doesn't feel real. Jack Smyth confessing to murder, to her. Transcripts and recordings and memories and feelings, all of which have nowhere to go because this book isn't happening, can't happen now.

This book is a work of fiction and, except in the case of historical fact, any resemblance to actual persons, living or dead, is purely coincidental.

She could write it as a novel.

Everything that happened. All of it. Not just what happened to her in Florida, but what happened to Jean and Ben and Kate. *The Witness.* What she saw on that fateful night all those years ago.

She'd have to change all the names, including her own, and all identifying characteristics, but she could do it.

The point wouldn't be to write the story, but to tell the truth.

When I think of my favourite novels, they all feel like the author was making something up to work out something real.

'But,' she says to Diane, 'I might have an idea.'

Acknowledgements

The author wishes to thank everyone who helped her write and publish this book.

And you, for reading it.

Dear Reader,

The sparks that set me on the path to new book ideas often come from real life. It might be a single line in a magazine article (*The Liar's Girl*), or an Instagram post (*Rewind*), or the fact that a bestselling book about a serial killer who'd gone unidentified for decades was published just weeks before he finally was (*The Nothing Man*). But sometimes, the truth is far stranger than any fiction I could make up.

In 1982, Lyn Dawson disappeared from her home in Sydney. It took her husband, Chris Dawson, a PE teacher at the local high school, six weeks to report her missing but only two days to move a sixteen-year-old student of his into the marital bed. In their last phone call, a groggy-sounding Lyn told her mother, 'Chris has made me a lovely drink.' She was never seen or heard from again. Yet everyone, including the police, accepted Chris's story, which was that Lyn had left him and their two daughters by choice. You may recognize this as the focus of the podcast *The Teacher's Pet*. If I ever attempted to put that scenario in a book, my editor would find a nice way to break it to me that it was completely implausible.

I wrote my last novel, *The Trap*, while thinking about the

eight women who vanished over a five-year period here in Ireland in the 1990s. Thirty years on, not one trace of any of them has been found, and no one has been charged in connection with their disappearances. It seems impossible in a country this size, but it happened.

In 2006, OJ Simpson, who had always maintained his innocence in the brutal murders of Nicole Brown and Ron Goldman, and who had been famously acquitted of them in what was dubbed 'the trial of the century' in 1995, signed a deal with HarperCollins to publish his confession. *If I Did It* would be the story of how Simpson committed the murders – *if* he had, because he was still saying that he hadn't, even though thanks to a truly staggering amount of physical evidence, everyone knew that he definitely *did* and now, as if to confirm it, he was going to confess, in print. But only hypothetically.

If you find that hard to believe, buckle up.

Pablo F. Fenjves, the man hired to be Simpson's ghostwriter, *had testified at Simpson's trial*. Crazier still, he had done so for the prosecution. He lived one street over from Brown and had heard the 'plaintive wail' of her dog on the night of the murders; his testimony helped establish prosecutor Marcia Clark's timeline. But he'd also worked with Judith Regan, the publisher of *If I Did It*, years before, which is how he came to be offered the job. No crime or thriller writer I know would get a coincidence like *that* past their editor.

When word of the project leaked, outrage ensued and HarperCollins eventually cancelled it. Rupert Murdoch ordered 400,000 copies pulped. Regan was fired. The Goldman family, who'd won a civil judgement against Simpson and were owed tens of millions in damages, fought for the rights, won them, and then published the book themselves. *This just proves what we know to be true*, their reasoning went. *Let Simpson tell the world he's guilty.* Proceeds would go to the Ron Goldman Foundation for Justice and the Nicole Brown Charitable Foundation. On the cover of my copy, the 'if' is barely visible and a subtitle has been added, so the name of the book appears to be *I Did It: Confessions of the Killer*.

A fascinating prologue by Fenjves reveals what it was like to be a murderer's ghostwriter. He describes how Simpson almost reneged on the deal at the eleventh hour, claiming that he'd been told the book would be billed as a novel. How Simpson minimized the violence he'd inflicted on Brown during their marriage and, sickeningly, blamed her for provoking him. How, in this supposedly hypothetical confession, he included what Fenjves called 'telling details', such as noting that Brown's security gate was broken and that Goldman was, in Simpson's words, into 'karate shit'. (The horror of the latter, I think, takes a moment to fully land.) Fenjves recalled how Simpson, outlining his route home from the crime scene, accidentally slipped out of the conditional tense. It had been all *I might have* and *maybe I would've*, but now he said, 'I took a left at the end of the alley and went up Gretna Green to San Vicente, and from there to Sunset.' There was a pregnant pause. 'Or that's the way I *woulda* gone,' he added.

Fenjves kept asking himself why on earth Simpson had agreed to do the book. 'I could only come up with three reasons,' he wrote. 'One, he needed the money.' (Simpson was reportedly paid an advance upwards of $1 million.) 'Two, he missed the attention. And three, he genuinely wanted to confess. I was hoping for number three, of course, but there was one other nagging possibility: the whole thing was a con.'

I, too, was fascinated by Simpson's staggeringly bad decision.

What the hell was he thinking? That he'd make money, sure, but weren't there easier ways? Was there a reason no one had thought of? What if this book was by someone whose guilt *wasn't* so cut and dried? What could possibly drive an innocent man to do such a thing? Could anything? I was also intrigued by the dynamic between a man suspected of murder and the ghostwriter hired to help him tell his side of the story. What if that ghostwriter were a woman, I wondered, inexperienced and potentially hiding a secret of her own?

Soon after I first read *(If) I Did It*, I visited a place called Seaside for the first time. Most people know it as the place where *The Truman Show* was filmed, but it's one of three master-planned, New Urbanist communities on Florida's panhandle designed by architects Andrés Duany and Elizabeth Plater-Zyberk (DPZ). Read: picture-perfect, walkable towns, built entirely from scratch. I adored Seaside and appreciated the warm, European feel of Rosemary Beach, but was unsettled by the odd, white-walled emptiness of neighbouring Alys Beach which I found eerily deserted early on a November morning. My fictional ghostwriter, I decided, would meet her fictional subject in a fictional place much like there.

I really hope you enjoyed *Burn After Reading*. Remember: none of this actually happened, and all of it really did. Truth is far stranger than fiction. There are some things that you really can't make up.

Catherine Ryan Howard

Don't miss Catherine Ryan Howard's number one bestseller, *The Trap*

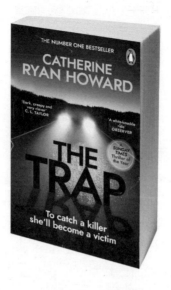

Stranded on a dark road in the middle of the night, a young woman accepts a lift from a passing stranger. It's the nightmare scenario that every girl is warned about, and she knows the dangers all too well – but what other choice does she have?

As they drive, she alternates between fear and relief – one moment thinking he is just a good man doing a good thing, the next convinced he's a monster. But when he delivers her safely to her destination, she realizes her fears were unfounded.

And her heart sinks. Because a monster is what she's looking for.

She'll try again tomorrow night. But will the man who took her sister take the bait?

Inspired by a series of still-unsolved disappearances, The Trap is the startlingly original new thriller from internationally bestselling author Catherine Ryan Howard.

Read on for an extract . . .

She'd been *out*-out, and town had been busy. Stumbled out of the club to discover that there wasn't a taxi to be had. Spent an hour trying to flag one down with one hand while trying to hail one via an app with the other until, resigned, she'd pushed her way on to a packed night bus headed not far enough in sort of the right direction. Her plan was to call someone at its terminus, apologize for waking them and ask them to come get her, but by the time she got there – to a tiny country village that was sleepy by day and empty by night – her phone had died. She'd been the last passenger and the bus had driven off before she could think to ask the driver if she could perhaps borrow *his* phone. It was four in the morning and beginning to drizzle, so she'd started walking. Because, really, what other choice did she have?

This is the story she tells herself as she leaves the village and crosses into the dark its streetlights had been holding back.

All around her, the night seems to thrum with disapproval.

Silly girl. This is exactly the kind of thing your mother told you not to do. There has to be some kind of personal responsibility, doesn't there?

An ex-boyfriend had once told her that his favourite part of a night out was the walk home. Just him and his thoughts on deserted streets, the evening's fun still warm in his chest. He had no tense wait for a taxi. He didn't need to walk to the front door with his keys squeezed between his fingers, ready to scratch, to disable. He had never texted a thumbs-up emoji to anyone before he went to sleep so that they could go to sleep as well.

The part of the night he loved was the part *she* had to survive.

When she'd told him this, he'd pulled her close and kissed her face and whispered, 'I'm so sorry that you think that's the world you live in,' in so patronizing a tone that, for a brief moment, she'd considered using her keys on his scrotum.

The drizzle gives way to a driving rain. When the footpath runs out, her high heels make her stumble on the crumbling surface of the road. The balls of her feet burn and the ankle strap on the right one is rubbing her skin away.

For a while, there's a watery moonlight inviting forms to take on a shape and step out of the night – a telephone pole, a hedgerow, a pothole – but then the road twists into a tunnel of overhanging trees and the dark solidifies. She can't see her own legs below the hem of her dress now. Her body is literally disappearing into the night.

And then, through the roar of the rain—

A mechanical whine.

Getting louder.

She thinks *engine* and turns just in time to be blinded by a pair of sweeping high-beams. Twin orbs are still floating in her vision when the car jerks to a stop alongside her. Silver, some make of saloon. She stops too. The passenger window descends in a smooth, electronic motion and a voice says, 'You all right there?'

She dips her head so she can see inside.

There's a pair of legs in the driver's seat, lit by the blue glow of the dashboard display, wearing jeans.

'Ah . . . Yeah.' She bends lower again to align her face with the open window just as the driver switches on the ceiling light. He is a man in his thirties, with short red hair and a splotchy pink face of irritated skin. His T-shirt is on inside out; she can see the seams and, at the back of his neck, the tag. There are various discarded items in the passenger-side footwell: fast-food wrappers, a tabloid newspaper, a single muddy hiking boot. In the back, there's a baby seat with a little stuffed green thing belted into it. 'I got off the night bus back in the village, and I was going to ring for a lift but—'

'Sorry.' The man taps a forefinger to a spot just behind his left ear, a move which makes her think of her late mother applying a perfume she seemed to fear was too expensive to ever actually spritz. 'My hearing isn't great.'

'I got off the night bus,' she says, louder this time.

He leans towards her, frowning. 'Say again?'

The passenger-side window isn't all the way down. An inch or so of glass digs into the palm of her hand when she puts it on the door and leans her head and shoulders into the opening, far enough for the roar of the rain to fall away into the background, for the sickly-sweet smell of a pine air-freshener to reach her nostrils and – it occurs to her – for the balance of her body weight to be inside the car.

If he suddenly drove off, he'd take her with him.

'I got off the night bus in the village,' she says. 'I was going to ring home for a lift, but my phone died.'

She pulls the device from her pocket, a dead black mirror, and shows it to him.

'Ah, feck,' he says. 'And I came out without mine. Although maybe . . .' He starts rooting around, checking the cubbyholes in the driver's door, the cup holders between the front seats, inside the glovebox. There seems to be a lot of stuff in the car, but not whatever he's looking for. 'I thought I might have a charger, but no. Sorry.'

'It's OK,' she says automatically.

'Look, I'm only going as far as the Circle K, but they're open twenty-four hours and they have that little seating area at the back. Maybe you could borrow a charger off someone there. Or they might even let you use their phone. It'd be a better place to wait, at least?'

'Yeah.' She pulls back, out of the window, and looks down the road into the empty black. 'Is it far?'

'Five-minute drive.' He's already reaching to push open the passenger door and she steps back to make room for the swing of its arc. 'Hop in.'

Somehow, the last moment in which she could've decided not to do this has passed her by. Because if she steps back now, pushes the passenger door closed and says, 'Thanks, but I think I'll walk,' she may as well say, 'Thanks for your kindness, but I think you might be a monster so please leave me alone.'

And if he *is* a monster, then he won't have to pretend not to be any more, and she won't be able to outrun him, not out here, not in these shoes – and where is there to run to?

And if he *isn't* a monster, well, then . . .

It's perfectly safe to get in the car.

She gets in the car.

She pulls the passenger door closed. *Clunk*. The ceiling light switches off, leaving only the dashboard's eerie glow and whatever's managed to reach them from this wrong end of the headlights. Her window is ascending. Then, as the engine revs and he pulls off, she hears another sound.

Click.

The central locking system.

'So,' he starts. 'Was it a good night, at least?'

Now the seatbelt sensor sounds and she fumbles in the shadows, first for the belt itself and then for its buckle, both of which feel vaguely sticky.

'It was all right,' she says. 'If I'd known how much trouble I'd have getting home, I might have just stayed there. How about you?'

Why are you out driving around at four in the morning?

'I was fast asleep,' he says, 'when I got an elbow to the ribs. I'm on a Rennies run. My wife is expecting our first, and she can't eat a thing now without getting heartburn. You got kids?'

She says, '*God* no,' before she can think to be a bit less aghast at the idea of doing the thing this man and his wife have already done.

He laughs. 'There's plenty of time for all that.'

In front of them, the surface of the road is dashing beneath the wheels. The wipers slash furiously across the windscreen, back and forth, back and forth. There are no lights visible in the distance.

They don't pass any other cars.

He asks her where she's living and she provides the name of the townland, purposefully avoiding specifics.

A sideways glance. 'You there by yourself, or . . . ?'

She wants to say no and leave it at that, but saying that risks coming across as unfriendly, mistrustful, suspicious. But telling him she lives with her boyfriend is telling him that she *has* a boyfriend, and that could sound pointed, like she's trying to stop him from getting any ideas, which would also be accusing him of *having* ideas, and offending him might anger him, this man she doesn't know who's driving the locked car she's in. But then, saying yes would be telling him that the young woman with the dead phone he just plucked off a country road has no one waiting up for her, no one wondering where she is, and if she doesn't come home tonight it could be hours or even days before anyone realizes—

'I live with my sister,' she lies.

'That's who'll come and get you?'

'If I can find a way to call her, yeah.'

'They're a curse, those bloody phones. Always dead when you need them.'

And yet, he's come out without his.

Would you, with a pregnant wife at home?

Maybe you would, she concedes, *if you're only on a quick run to the shop.*

'You know, you look really familiar to me,' he says, and then he turns his head to look at her some more, for a fraction longer than she'd like on this road at this speed and in these conditions. 'Have we met before?'

'Don't think so.' She's sure she's never seen this man before in her life.

'Where do you work?'

She tells him that she works for a foreign bank, in an office block near the airport, and he makes a *hmm* noise.

Twenty, thirty seconds go by in silence. She breaks it by asking, 'Is it much further?' Because all that is out there in the night ahead of them is more night.

Still no cars. Still no lights.

No sign of anything except more road and dark and rain.

'No.' He jerks the gearstick with more force than he has before and, as he does, she feels his warm fingers graze the cold, damp skin of her bare knee. The touch is right on the line between an accidental graze and an intentional stroke. His eyes don't leave the road. 'Nearly there.'

'Great,' she says absently.

She doesn't know what to do. If it *was* an accident, wouldn't he apologize? Or is he not apologizing because there's nothing to apologize for, because he hasn't even realized he did it, because he didn't *do* anything at all?

The rain is heavier now, a steady roar on the roof.

'Awful night,' he says. 'And you're not exactly dressed for it, are you?'

Then he turns and openly appraises her, and there can be absolutely no mistake about this. His gaze crawls across her lap, combing over the thin cotton of her dress which, wet, is clinging to the outline of her thighs.

It feels like some slinking predator, cold and oily, slithering across her skin.

She moves her hands to her knees in an attempt to cover up and waits for his eyes to return to the road while a cold dread swirls in the pit of her stomach.

But then, she *isn't* dressed for this weather. That's a statement of fact.

Jesus Christ, you really can't say anything *these days, can you?*

'Yeah, well,' she says, with a brief smile she hopes won't encourage him *or* antagonize him. 'I thought I'd be able to hop in a cab.'

'They really need to do something about the taxi shortage.'

'Yeah, the—'

'Especially considering the missing women.' He glances at her. 'How many is it now? Three? Four?'

The temperature of her cold dread has dropped a few degrees to an icy, nauseating fear.

But then, what if it were a woman behind the wheel? She wouldn't think anything of this. They'd just be making conversation. They'd just be talking about what everyone was talking about, discussing what was in the news.

Now he's pointing towards the mess at her feet.

'Did you see the latest?' he says. 'It's on the front of the paper, there.'

The safest option feels like reaching for the folded tabloid. As she picks it up, it obligingly unfurls to reveal its front-page headline, screaming at her in all caps. MISSING WOMEN: SEARCH CONTINUES IN WICKLOW MOUNTAINS. There are two pictures underneath it: a large one showing people in white coveralls picking through a wild landscape, and a smaller one of a young, smiling brunette holding a dog in her arms.

She is familiar to anyone who follows the news. Not just the woman herself, but this specific picture of her.

'That's not that far away from here, you know,' he says. He jerks his chin to indicate the road ahead. 'If you drove for fifteen minutes up into the hills, you'd probably be able to see the floodlights.' A pause. 'They're always at that, though, aren't they? Conducting searches. Everyone gets all excited, but they never find anything. Thing is, people just don't understand how much space we got up here, you know? My old fella was always giving out about that, back when the first lot went missing. The ones from the nineties. There was always some reporter or relative or whatever saying, "Oh, she's up in the Wicklow Mountains, we just need to search." They'd think if you just looked everywhere, you'd find them. But you *can't* look everywhere, you see. Not around here. There's just too much ground to cover.' Another pause, this one a shade longer. 'So they probably *are* out here somewhere, but no one's ever going to fucking find them.'

THE TRAP IS OUT NOW

Catherine Ryan Howard is the author of eight novels, including the No. 1 bestsellers *The Nothing Man*, *56 Days* and *The Trap*. Her work has been shortlisted for the Mystery Writers of America Edgar Award for Best Novel, the Crime Writers, Association New Blood and Steel Daggers, and Irish Crime Fiction Book of the Year multiple times. The screen adaptation of her lockdown thriller, *56 Days*, is currently in production and will debut on Amazon Prime Video this year. She lives in Dublin.